"I hate to a[...]
long time."

"You should do it more often," Aaliyah said, sitting up straighter in the boat as they approached the other side of the grassy island.

"Let's get out here," Bryant suggested as he hopped out of the boat and pulled it up onto the sand. He stuck out his hand to assist Aaliyah, but quickly decided to help her by her waist instead.

She went along with it and Bryant couldn't help but hold on to her a little longer than he should have.

"Thank you," she said, clearing her throat. Her cheeks were flushed and it felt good to know that he was the cause.

"Sorry, I didn't bring a blanket," Bryant said.

"I think I saw one in the back of the boat." Aaliyah ran to the rowboat and returned with a beige blanket that was large enough for them to lie on. "Is this a good spot?" she asked, getting comfortable on the blanket.

"It's perfect," he said, lying down next to her. "Thanks for agreeing to join me."

"I'm just happy you asked." She turned her head to him. "I always thought you didn't like me."

Bryant frowned. "What would make you think that?"

Sherelle Green is a Chicago native with a dynamic imagination and a passion for reading and writing. She enjoys composing emotionally driven stories that are steamy, edgy and touch on real-life issues. Her overall goal is to create relatable and fierce heroines who are flawed, just like the strong and sexy heroes who fight so hard to win their hearts. There's no such thing as a perfect person…but when you find that person who is perfect for you, the possibilities are endless. Nothing satisfies her more than writing stories filled with compelling love affairs, multifaceted characters and intriguing relationships.

Books by Sherelle Green

Harlequin Kimani Romance

Visit the Author Profile Page
at Harlequin.com for more titles.

SHERELLE GREEN
and
SHERYL LISTER

Road to Forever &
A Love of My Own

HARLEQUIN® KIMANI™ ROMANCE

If you purchased this book without a cover you should be aware that this book is stolen property. It was reported as "unsold and destroyed" to the publisher, and neither the author nor the publisher has received any payment for this "stripped book."

ISBN-13: 978-1-335-00587-8

Road to Forever & A Love of My Own

Copyright © 2019 by Harlequin Books S.A.

The publisher acknowledges the copyright holders of the individual works as follows:

Road to Forever
Copyright © 2019 by Sherelle Green

A Love of My Own
Copyright © 2019 by Sheryl Lister

PLEASE RECYCLE

THIS PRODUCT IS RECYCLABLE

Recycling programs for this product may not exist in your area.

All rights reserved. Except for use in any review, the reproduction or utilization of this work in whole or in part in any form by any electronic, mechanical or other means, now known or hereafter invented, including xerography, photocopying and recording, or in any information storage or retrieval system, is forbidden without the written permission of the publisher, Harlequin Enterprises Limited, 22 Adelaide St. West, 40th Floor, Toronto, Ontario M5H 4E3, Canada.

This is a work of fiction. Names, characters, places and incidents are either the product of the author's imagination or are used fictitiously, and any resemblance to actual persons, living or dead, business establishments, events or locales is entirely coincidental.

This edition published by arrangement with Harlequin Books S.A.

For questions and comments about the quality of this book, please contact us at CustomerService@Harlequin.com.

® and TM are trademarks of Harlequin Enterprises Limited or its corporate affiliates. Trademarks indicated with ® are registered in the United States Patent and Trademark Office, the Canadian Intellectual Property Office and in other countries.

HARLEQUIN
www.Harlequin.com

Printed in U.S.A.

CONTENTS

To my grandfather, John, the loving and faithful man who taught me that there is no wrong way to pray because God hears all. To the reason I love extra crispy—almost burned—bacon. To the man who understood my love for coffee better than most because we shared that love. To the man who gave me quarters for every A I earned in school; to this day, I love collecting quarters. To the deacon who made sure his children and grandchildren volunteered and understood the impact that a dollar could make in someone's life. To the reason I have received hundreds of rosaries in my lifetime. It was so unique to your character to give a rosary to every person who crossed your path. To the one who may have been a man of a few words, but your words held power, wisdom and lessons that I will pass on to my children. You may be gone, but you will forever be in my heart. I love you, Papa! Enjoy Paradise and kiss Grandma for me.

Acknowledgments

To my cousin Harrison "Alex" for being the inspiration behind Bryant. Growing up, you were such a good sport, especially since you were one of the only male cousins around. One of the things we all love about you the most are your random messages or calls that remind us about a funny or exciting part of our childhood that we may have forgotten. Just like Grandpa, you are strong in your convictions and you only speak when you have something important to say. You may hate us teasing you about your dimples, but your smile is one that makes us all smile when we're having a bad day. You've matured into an amazing man and you've continued to be there for your family despite how busy life gets. Can't wait to see what the future has in store for you!

ROAD TO FOREVER

Sherelle Green

Dear Reader,

When Bryant and Kendrick initially came into the scene in *Her Unexpected Valentine*, I was anxious to write their stories because it gave me a chance to revisit the Burrstone family. The Burrstones were originally introduced in my An Elite Event series, and Bryant is the cousin of Imani, Cyd and Lex.

Some may not know that the Burrstones were inspired by my family, so these characters are near and dear to my heart. I hope you enjoy catching up with the Elite Events crew in *Road to Forever*. Unlike his cousins, Bryant is definitely not the charmer in the family, but he has a valid reason for being his stoic, grumpy self. However, it takes a woman like Aaliyah to peel back those layers to discover the man he keeps hidden.

Kyra Reed is up next, and her story will be the last installment in the Bare Sophistication series. Hope you're ready for Kyra's wild self!

Much love,

Sherelle

Chapter 1

"Honey, if you can make a ripe peach look this sexy, your competition better watch out."

Aaliyah Bai laughed as her friends gushed over her latest portfolio. She could always count on Danni Allison-Walker and Summer Dupree-Chase, co-owners of Bare Sophistication Lingerie Boutique and Boudoir Studio, to be supportive.

Aaliyah had been the boudoir photographer at Bare Sophistication Miami for five years now, and popping up to assist the Bare Sophistication location in LA for two. The opportunity to work with Bare Sophistication had been exactly what she'd needed a few years ago, and although she loved showing a woman's true beauty through the lens of her camera, she was ready to spread her wings. She'd still do boudoir sessions for Bare Sophistication, but she wanted a chance to shine in other areas of photography.

"Thanks, ladies," she said, looking over their shoulders as they flipped through a few more photos. "When Aiden told me about the competition to work with Jacques Simian, I knew I had to enter." Simian was an extraordinarily talented—and successful—food and product photographer, and Aaliyah knew she'd benefit from his tutelage.

Aiden Chase, Summer's husband, was also a well-known photographer, so he knew the struggle of trying to make your own path in the industry. Aaliyah needed to find what made her different. She needed to stand out and discover her niche, and she had a feeling that winning an opportunity to work with Jacques Simian was just what she needed.

"When will you learn if you won the competition?" Summer asked.

"Soon, but not soon enough," Aaliyah said. "All ten finalists have to submit a final portfolio within the next three and a half weeks, but the topic can be of our choosing as long as it's in the food or product genre. The winner will be announced at Jacques's LA event."

"I'm so excited for you," Danni said. "And I'm glad that Nicole and Kyra will be able to attend the event with you to show you some love."

Aaliyah smiled. "Me too." Nicole LeBlanc and Kyra Reed were two of Aaliyah's close friends who also co-managed Bare Sophistication LA. Although Aaliyah rarely got a chance to go to the flagship store in Chicago, she was glad she had the opportunity to bounce between working in LA and Miami. Her family already called her a wandering soul, and she embraced that title to the fullest.

"Mama. Mama."

They turned to the tiny voice that was toddling through the front door of the boutique.

"How's my sweet boy?" Summer said as she leaned down to pick up her twenty-one-month-old son, Anthony, before kissing her husband, Aiden.

"I's fine, Mama. Daddy taked me to da parr."

"Did you have fun at the park?" Summer asked, kissing Anthony's forehead.

"Yep, but I wented to see Auntbe Yani and Lea."

Aaliyah laughed at the broken language of the toddler. He had such a hard time pronouncing Danni and Aaliyah's names, but both women thought it was adorable.

"We missed you too, munchkin," Aaliyah said, showering him with playful kisses while a very pregnant Danni waddled to the other side of the counter to give him a hug.

"We should lock up and head to our place," Summer said. "Aiden and I prepared a feast last night for Aunt Sarah's arrival today, so all we have to do is warm up the food."

"Is Jaleen meeting us there?" Aiden asked.

"He sure is," Danni said, referring to her husband. "He can't wait to see Aunt Sarah again."

Aaliyah smiled as she gathered her portfolio and placed it in her messenger bag. Even though Aunt Sarah was technically only Aaliyah's aunt, all her friends loved the woman as if she were theirs too.

"I can't wait to see her either," Aaliyah said. "I'm picking her up from the airport in an hour, and we'll head right over."

"Did someone place an order for one crazy auntie?"

Aaliyah's head turned to the voice of the person who busted through the front door of the boutique. Her eyes widened as she beheld her aunt who was one of her favorite people. But she also wondered if she'd messed up—had she gotten the airport pickup time wrong? "Aunt Sarah, what are you doing here? I was supposed to get you from the airport."

Aaliyah walked to the front of the boutique and pulled Aunt Sarah in for a hug.

"I got an earlier flight, so I rented an SUV," she said with a shrug. "Couldn't have my niece picking us all up in her tiny two-door Coupe Pure. We wouldn't fit."

"Nothing's wrong with my little car," Aaliyah said, squinting her eyes together. "And who is 'us'?"

On cue, Aunt Sarah's boyfriend, Benjamin Burrstone, and his son, Bryant Burrstone, walked into Bare Sophistication.

"Nice to see you again, Aaliyah," Ben said, pulling her in for a hug.

"Uh, hi, Ben." Over the man's shoulder, Aaliyah eyed her aunt suspiciously. During all the phone calls they'd exchanged regarding this visit, Aunt Sarah never mentioned that she'd be bringing her boyfriend to Miami. *And that's not the only person he brought.*

There weren't too many people who Aaliyah didn't like, but Bryant was probably at the top of her list. She had known the man for a couple years now because her friend Nicole was married to Bryant's cousin and Ben's nephew, Kendrick Burrstone.

Bryant and his father lived in LA and, as of last year, Aunt Sarah had moved in with Ben. Between her aunt and her friend's connections to the Burrstone family, Aaliyah had to see much more of Bryant than she wanted to. She always found him cold and distant, and she'd given up on trying to be nice to him.

"Aaliyah," Bryant said. No "Hey, how are you" or

"Nice to see you again." Or even a simple "Hello." He just stated her name like he always did, so she felt the only appropriate response was to reply to him the same way.

"Bryant."

He looks different today. Aaliyah was used to seeing Bryant in some suit or slacks and a polo. She rarely saw him in jeans and a basic gray tee like he was wearing now. He looked good in casual clothes. *If he wasn't so annoying, I'd probably give him a compliment. He is a fine male specimen, after all...* She was busy observing the change in his normal attire when she felt as if someone was watching her. Her gaze made its way to his, and just as she'd caught him so many times before, his dark brown eyes were scrutinizing her. Observing her. His look never changing from its usual resting grumpy face as Aunt Sarah introduced Ben and Bryant to the group.

Aaliyah tried her best not to roll her eyes at the cold way Bryant addressed her friends. *I doubt he has a friendly bone in his body.* Kendrick swore that his cousin was a good man and friendly to those who knew him, but Aaliyah had known him for two years and she'd yet to see him even break a smile.

"Summer mentioned that she and Aiden cooked for us," Aunt Sarah said, interrupting her thoughts. "But would you mind if I steal you to take a walk with us so we can talk before we head over to their place?"

"Sure," Aaliyah said. "What do we need to talk about?"

Aunt Sarah smiled. "You'll find out soon enough."

They said goodbye to the others, and Aaliyah led them to a nearby park. Once they'd arrived at the green space, Ben excused himself and Bryant, leaving her alone with Aunt Sarah.

"Let's sit here, sweetie," Aunt Sarah suggested, pointing to a nearby bench. She followed her aunt and sat down, growing a little apprehensive at the mystery of this talk.

"What's on your mind?" Aaliyah asked.

"Well, first, I wanted to ask you if you'd heard from your dad and sister. I haven't spoken to them since before they left."

"They're good," Aaliyah said. "Everyone sounds really excited, and they told me that they would FaceTime with you soon."

Aaliyah's sister, Monique, brother-in-law, Terrance, nieces Mia and Shay and her father, Jim, had just left for France last week. Her brother-in-law had gotten the opportunity to work in France for two months for business, and he'd invited them all along. There was no way Aaliyah was going to leave with the competition approaching, and work at both Bare Sophistication locations was busier than it had ever been. But she was glad her sister and dad had gotten off work to go. And it promised to be a great summer trip for her nieces.

"That's good to hear," Aunt Sarah said. "Do you remember what I told you about the two of us taking a vacation together while they were out of the country?"

"Of course." Aaliyah's family wasn't big, and since her mom had passed away years ago, Aunt Sarah was like a second mother to her. It wasn't unusual for the two of them to take a trip together since they were extremely close.

"Well, what if I told you that I already spoke with Summer and Danni at the shop and asked if it was okay for you to take a two-week road trip starting tomorrow from Miami to California, getting you to LA just in time for Jacques to announce the winner of his photography competition?"

Aaliyah's eyes lit up. Her aunt knew she'd always wanted to travel cross-country, capturing fantastic images on her camera. Her fingers itched to get started, to plan the route, to think through what equipment to bring. What pictures she'd be able to take! "That sounds amazing! Are you sure Summer and Danni said they don't mind? It's sort of short notice."

Aunt Sarah shook her head. "I called the girls weeks ago and asked them not to say anything, so it's fine. You can talk to them about it more tonight, though, if you're worried."

"Then I'm in," Aaliyah said with a smile. "I can't wait to set an itinerary. I'm so glad you came up with this idea!" Movement nearby got her attention. She glanced to her left to find Ben and Bryant seated on a bench not too far away, and a shadow crept over her joy. "Did Ben and Bryant just come down for the day?"

"Um, not exactly," Aunt Sarah said, pretending to find interest in the chipped wood on their bench. "The itinerary is kind of already set for us. We'll be visiting different wineries and going to industry events in several states along the way from Miami to Cali. Ben and Bryant are going with us."

Aaliyah frowned and sighed. *So this is the catch?* "What do you mean Ben and Bryant are going with us? I thought this trip was for you and me only."

"Sweet cheeks, you and I will have our time together on this road trip. I promise. But Ben is retiring soon and Bryant is taking over Burrstone Winery and Distillery, so they both need to visit some of their partners and friends to ensure an easy transition."

"That makes sense. I understand," Aaliyah said. "What I don't understand is why you and I have to go with them and not on our own vacation."

Aunt Sarah pushed her long brown hair over her shoulders and looked up to the trees, her flowing yellow sundress blowing in the summer wind even though she remained seated. Aaliyah had always loved Aunt Sarah's luscious locks, and growing up, people often thought that Aunt Sarah was her mom and not her aunt since they looked so much alike. Aaliyah's sister, Monique, looked like Aunt Sarah too, but didn't have her bohemian style like Aaliyah did.

"What else are you not telling me, Aunt Sarah?" All the signs that she was holding something in were there. Aunt Sarah often glanced away and focused on a distraction when she didn't like the direction a conversation was going.

"I may or may not have suggested to Ben that you could help out Bryant," Aunt Sarah said after a few seconds of silence.

Aaliyah squinted her eyes. *This just keeps getting better and better.* "And what exactly would I be helping Bryant with?"

Aunt Sarah sighed and spoke quickly, as if she'd rehearsed her statement. "I told Ben that you're a qualified corporate trainer and team builder, and would join us on the trip to help improve Bryant's interpersonal and social skills, while also forging the broken bond between Ben and Bryant by making their relationship stronger than it's ever been."

"What!" Aaliyah exclaimed. "Please tell you're joking! I did corporate team building for six months about five years ago. Hardly long enough to call me qualified. And I hated that job."

"I know you did," Aunt Sarah said.

"Then why did you let them believe I was perfect for this?"

"Because I think you are." Aunt Sarah grabbed Aaliyah's hand and placed it in hers. "You're too hard on yourself, and even though you didn't enjoy that job, you excelled at it. I remember the glowing reviews you received from companies you helped."

Aaliyah's stomach growled, partially because she was hungry, but more likely because it was voicing her inner frustration. What had started out as a dream vacation idea was turning into a nightmare scenario. *Accompany them on a road trip and train Bryant Burrstone? No way.*

"Aunt Sarah, I'm not sure I can do this," Aaliyah said. "Bryant isn't a normal human being, and we don't even get along. As a matter of fact, I haven't seen him get along with anyone except for Kendrick. I couldn't possibly improve his social skills in less than a month. Ben should hire someone for that."

"We both prefer if you would help Bryant out," Aunt Sarah said. "And whether you see it or not, you and Bryant have more in common than you think. He lost his mom a few years ago, and he's never been the same since then. Bryant is a troubled soul, and I think you could help him realize that he doesn't have to let tragedy define his life."

Aaliyah glanced in the direction of Bryant and his father, her eyes paying close attention to things she hadn't noticed before. *Strained smile on Ben's face.*

More closed-off than usual physical contact from Bryant. Disappointment and guilt in Ben's face. Sadness and regret in Bryant's. To the outside eye, one wouldn't think there was anything wrong. But even from a distance, Aaliyah could pick up on the signs. She'd been great at deciphering body language since she was a child.

"You see it too, don't you?" Aunt Sarah whispered as Aaliyah continued to look Ben and Bryant's way. "You always were a sharp girl, and I'm sure now you see why I need your help?"

Aaliyah sighed. She had a hard time saying no to Aunt Sarah. They were both intuitive women, connected in that way. When her Aunt Sarah battled cancer, the woman never bothered masking how she felt in front of Aaliyah—she knew her niece would be able to see through her. Even when she got better three years ago, Aunt Sarah knew that Aaliyah had realized she was in remission before she'd even told the family what the doctors had said to her.

"I'll go on the road trip and try to help Bryant," Aaliyah said, finally turning from the man and his son who had quickly warmed their way into her aunt's heart. "But I want to be clear that I can't work magic. If Bryant doesn't listen to what I must say, then I walk and you three can enjoy the rest of the road trip without me."

"Um—" Aunt Sarah glanced over at Ben and Bryant, a worried look on her face "—is now a good time to tell you that Bryant doesn't know about this plan yet?"

"Seriously," Aaliyah said a little louder than she'd planned. "Aunt Sarah, please tell me you're joking."

Her aunt shrugged. "Ben and I thought there wasn't any reason to tell him before we came out here. Otherwise, he wouldn't have agreed to this road trip. He knows he's going to chat with the friends and associates of his father to ensure a smooth transition when Ben retires."

Aaliyah dropped her head into her hands. "Precisely why does Bryant think I'm tagging along on this trip?"

"He thinks I'm asking you to go along so that you can take photos of the wineries and to build a portfolio to land additional photography jobs," Aunt Sarah said. "And I mentioned the rest of the family is out of the country and you needed a vacation."

Aaliyah leaned back on the bench and stared up into the clear blue sky. She almost felt like giggling. This plan was getting crazier by the second. "When are you telling him the truth?"

"Funny you should ask," Aunt Sarah said with a laugh. "The only thing Ben has told him is that he needs to prove that he can be personable enough to succeed in this industry. Business-wise, he's amazing. We figured it was best if you work your Aaliyah magic without him knowing. I've seen you do it before, so I know you can. I think if Bryant can see how you interact with others in the wine and liquor industry, he'll follow suit."

"So basically, you don't plan on telling him." Aaliyah closed her eyes to let the idea take shape in her mind. She wasn't going to back out of the favor her aunt had asked her to do, but spiritually, Aaliyah needed to summon any ounce of faith and hope she had if her aunt and Ben thought she could turn Mr. McGrumpy into the world's most charming business owner. *Lord, give me strength.*

Chapter 2

Bryant took a swig of his beer and tried his best not to get too fidgety. He remembered Summer, Aiden, Danni and Jaleen from Kendrick and Nicole's wedding, but he hadn't spoken to them much. Now that he was dining in Summer and Jaleen's gorgeous backyard, he understood why his cousin enjoyed coming to Miami to visit his wife's friends so much.

A massive wooden table in the backyard that was great for entertaining was positioned to the left of an outdoor sitting area and small lap pool. Twinkly lights hung from the tree to the white fence, but his favorite part about their yard was the sleek metal bar with matching stools.

"Where did you get this bar from?" he asked Aiden. When his dad had originally asked him to mingle with Aiden and Jaleen while he and Sarah took Aiden's son to the beach, Bryant hadn't wanted to. He was tired from traveling, especially with his father and Sarah, since being with them triggered dark memories. However, he hadn't been able to come up with an excuse not to socialize, and he knew his dad was watching his every move. That was two hours ago. He'd been talking to Aiden and Jaleen all that time, and he had to admit that he was enjoying the conversation.

"Jaleen made it for us," Aiden said. "We love this bar."

"This is really nicely done," Bryant said, rubbing his hands along the cool metal top. "Do you have more? I'd love to purchase a few for our winery and distillery back in Cali." This retro industrial look was trending now, and it would be a good addition to their decor.

"Seriously?" Jaleen asked in surprise. "You'd buy a few?"

Bryant nodded his head. "Yeah. It's what I've been looking for to add some freshness to the place."

"See, I told you, man," Aiden said, hitting Jaleen on the shoulder. Aiden glanced at Bryant as he continued to make the ladies' drinks. "I've been telling this fool that his stuff is too nice to only sell to friends. He claims he has too much going on with flipping resorts, but I think he needs to add this to his list of things he's good at."

"I agree," Bryant said. "How did you make it?"

As he listened to Jaleen talk about the different scrap yards he'd visited to find metal pieces for the bar, he couldn't help but want to smile…but he didn't. As crazy as it sounded, he was a bit out of practice.

It seemed like ages since Bryant had hung out with guys who didn't really know him without having his cousin as a buffer. Bryant used to be a guy's guy, having more friends than he knew what to do with. But that wasn't him anymore. He'd changed and in doing so, he'd lost a lot of friends. He still had some close guy friends, but still, things were different.

"The drinks are ready," Aiden said to Aaliyah as she approached to get hers and Summer's drinks.

"Thanks," she said, quickly glancing in Bryant's direction before grabbing the cups. She was wearing a pink summer dress that flowed around her knees every time the wind caught the hem.

Her hair was in a bun on top of her head, but it didn't matter that she wasn't letting her hair hang down because Bryant still remembered how bouncy her light-brown-highlighted curls were when she walked. He'd been watching them bounce for two years. Two long years. Two sexually frustrating years.

When she'd almost reached her friends again, she looked over her shoulder and glanced right at him. He stared right back as he had been doing for the past couple years. Eventually, she returned to her conversation with her friends, so Bryant shifted his attention back to the men.

"What?" Bryant asked when Aiden and Jaleen were looking at him curiously.

"What's going on between you and Aaliyah?" Jaleen asked.

Bryant shrugged. "Nothing. We can barely stand each other." It had been bad enough when he was best man and she was maid of honor for Kendrick and Nicole's wedding, let alone any other time they were near each other.

"Judging by those looks you both keep giving one another, it doesn't seem like nothing," Aiden said. "And since Jaleen and I think it's something, we only think it's fair that we tell you that Aaliyah is like a sister to us."

"Right," Jaleen said, taking a sip of his drink. "She hasn't had the easiest life, so don't hurt her."

Bryant wasn't one to randomly bust out in laughter, but that almost got him. "Fellas, you don't have anything to worry about. Aaliyah and I can barely stand to be in the same room as one another."

Jaleen glanced around the backyard. "Well, this isn't a room, but ya'll are in the same space and seem to be doing just fine."

Bryant shook his head again. "Trust me, you should see us when she's in LA. If we're at something that Kendrick and Nicole are throwing, Aaliyah and I are on completely opposite sides of the room. I would be surprised if we didn't kill each other on this road trip."

"The road trip sounds fun," Aiden said. "Next time I'm in LA, I'll have to visit your winery."

"That would be cool," Bryant said. "The Northern Cali wineries get more recognition than us Southern Cali wineries, but Southern Cali wine country is pretty amazing."

Bryant spent the next few minutes talking to Aiden and Jaleen about the winery before Jaleen went to check on his wife, who was yelling for some pickles and ice cream.

"Those pregnancy cravings are no joke," Aiden said with a laugh as they watched Danni give Jaleen specific instructions on what brand of ice cream and pickles that she needed him to go to the store to get.

As if they had a mind of their own, his eyes found their way back to Aaliyah, soaking in her carefree laugh and the way she used her napkin to dab the corners of her eyes to catch the happy tears seeping past her eyelids.

Just like she usually did when he was nearby, her face grew more serious as she glanced around the backyard until her eyes landed on him again. Bryant took a swig of his beer, looking at her over the bottle. *I love when she does that.* He secretly enjoyed the fact that she always met his gaze whenever he looked her way.

Bryant broke eye contact and turned back to Aiden when he heard him clear his throat.

"Just remember what I said while you're on this road trip." Aiden pinned him with a serious stare.

"I will," Bryant said with a nod. He really wanted to continue telling him that it was an unnecessary threat because he'd bet money that Aaliyah was going to avoid him the entire time. And he wouldn't blame her. He wasn't the friendliest person; especially when it came to her. Sometimes, being around Aaliyah made him so agitated he couldn't help but piss her off, just to see those beautiful eyes blaze. *And damned if I don't like seeing her all hot and bothered.*

Bryant shook the thought from his mind. *Okay, so you're attracted to her. Big deal. You've dealt with it for the past couple years, so another two weeks won't be so hard.* Even as the thought left his mind, he knew he was underestimating how hard it would be.

He thought he was a pretty decent guy when you got to know him, but Aaliyah hadn't gotten to know him. She hadn't seen the okay parts. Hell, it had taken forever for him to convince her friend Nicole that he was a decent guy after the way he'd behaved when they first met. Kendrick had basically told Bryant that he had to work on his relationship with Nicole, or else.

They weren't just cousins. They were best friends. Bryant knew that Kendrick would never really end their close relationship, but Kendrick had issued that warning so Bryant knew that no matter how close they were, Nicole came first. Folks may not think that Bryant understood certain aspects of a relationship, but he'd understood Kendrick loud and clear, and he'd agreed with him. Had the roles been reversed, Bryant would have felt the same way.

Commotion at the side gate got all their attention. Bryant turned in time to see his dad and Sarah return with Anthony, Aiden and Summer's son. *He looks so happy*, Bryant thought, observing his father. The sight tugged at his heartstrings. He recalled a time when he hadn't looked so happy.

Bryant watched Sarah give Aaliyah a hug, and he immediately felt guilty about the fact that he didn't care for Sarah the way everyone else did. Whether in LA or Miami, everyone loved Sarah…except him. It really wasn't fair to her since she seemed like a nice woman, and it wasn't one of those situations where he was upset that his dad had found love again after his mom had passed. Bryant was a grown-ass man so none of those were the reasons, but the truth was much harder to accept than he was willing to admit. The only person who knew why he really couldn't give Sarah the chance she deserved was his dad.

His father was great at pretending not to know the reason Bryant had changed all those years ago, but deep down, Ben had to know the truth. Bryant figured he just didn't want to admit that reason to himself.

Bryant's sister, Kylie, often asked why things seemed so strained between them whenever she returned home from Europe where she'd worked for the past three years; Bryant had decided that the less she knew, the better. So he'd made up some lame excuse that he couldn't even remember anymore, but it was enough to get his sister off his back whenever she visited.

Bryant frowned before he took another swig of his beer. There was no part of him that wanted to go on this road trip, but he had to do it. As upset as he was that his father felt a need to make him prove himself at a company he'd been VP of for six years, he needed to get it over with so his dad could retire and leave him in charge. He may not like this situation, but Bryant had gone through much worse with his dad over the years. This should be a piece of cake.

Chapter 3

"Thanks for pulling over," Aaliyah said as she got back in the SUV.

"You're welcome," Ben said as he restarted the engine.

"I shouldn't have to go again for another couple hours."

"Let's hope not," Bryant muffled under his breath.

"What was that?" Aaliyah asked.

Bryant looked her way. "Nothing."

"Are you sure?" Aaliyah asked. "Because it sounded like you were talking about the fact that we had to stop again."

"So you do realize that you're holding us up?" he asked. "Before we left this morning, you said you wanted to get to Charleston, South Carolina, before nightfall. But then you have us stop three times within five hours." Bryant knew he shouldn't be battling Aaliyah, but he couldn't help it. He waited for that flash in her eyes that signaled she was annoyed with him.

"What is your problem?" she asked.

"No problem," he said with a shrug. "I just like to be punctual and stick to the plan. If we said we would get there before nightfall, I want to stick to that goal." In his peripheral vision, Bryant caught his dad glance to Sarah, but he kept his gaze on Aaliyah.

"I'm not going to let you get to me," Aaliyah said, scooting closer to her side of the car. "So maybe we just shouldn't say anything to one another until we get to South Carolina."

"Fine by me," he said. "As long as we don't have to stop four more times before we arrive."

"I'm sorry, but you aren't even driving," Aaliyah said, her voice higher than he'd heard before. "And not that it's any of your business, but I have a tiny bladder!"

Bryant managed to suppress a smirk. He didn't really mind making extra stops because, like she said, he wasn't driving. But it was much more fun to tease Aaliyah than listen to his dad and Sarah whisper sweet nothings to one another the entire ride.

"Now, now kids," Sarah said. "Play nice."

"He started it," Aaliyah said.

"I have an idea," Ben said after they'd gone a mile or two. He took a quick right to get off at the upcoming exit. Bryant wasn't sure what his dad's idea was as they traveled farther, until they arrived at a small strawberry farm.

"Is this Mark's place?" Bryant asked. He'd only met his dad's friend Mark when he'd paid them a visit in California, but he remembered Mark had a Georgia strawberry farm not far from the Florida border.

"It is," Ben said, getting out the car. "When we talked the other day, he mentioned the season was almost over, so he and his brother Tom may not be home."

As if on cue, a six-foot-five man Bryant guessed was Tom opened the door to the small home, followed by Mark.

"Well, if it isn't my West Coast friend in my beautiful southern state," Mark said, walking up to Ben to give him a hug.

"It's good to see you too, Mark." Ben turned to Mark's brother. "Tom, it's good to see you too." Tom returned his hug, as well.

"You remember my son, Bryant," Ben said, waving a hand in his direction. "And these beautiful ladies are my girlfriend, Sarah, and her niece Aaliyah."

While they all exchanged pleasantries, Ben informed Mark that they had been passing through on their way to Charleston, and Mark told them that they were in luck. There were still a couple weeks before strawberry season was over.

"Did you want to go picking?" he asked the group. Everyone nodded their heads except Bryant. "Great."

After they were given baskets and directions, they headed into the fragrant fields. At least it felt good to get out of the cramped car and stretch his legs.

Bryant had to admit that picking strawberries ended up being a lot more fun than he'd thought it would be. He and Aaliyah had ventured off to the same section of the farm where Mark said the berries were the juiciest, and he enjoyed finding the ripest, fattest fruits for his basket.

"There is something very therapeutic about picking strawberries," Bryant said aloud. He glanced up at Aaliyah, who was eyeing him suspiciously.

"Are you talking to me?"

"Yes," he said with a nod. "You're the only other person here."

She frowned. "Why do you always sound rude every time you say something?"

Bryant shrugged. "I think people just take what I say the wrong way." He bent to get one of the biggest strawberries he'd seen yet. "As I recall, the first time I met you, you were talking about me behind my back to your friends."

"Do you remember the day you came into the Bare Sophistication shop in LA?" she asked.

"Of course," he said. "You, Nicole and Kyra were preparing for a party or something and needed my dad, myself and Kendrick to do some heavy lifting. I remember that you and I had been introduced, and within seconds into our conversation, you walked away and went straight to your friends to talk shit."

"No, no, no, no, no." Aaliyah placed her strawberry basket on the ground. "You're leaving out the part where I was being beyond friendly to you and asking you questions about LA, since I hadn't been coming to LA long at the time, and you basically told me that I needed to go to a bookstore and pick up a tourist book or Google activities, but not to ask you."

"That's because I'm terrible at finding things to do in LA," Bryant said. "I didn't want to recommend the wrong thing, so I made two suggestions that I thought were better."

"Then why didn't you say it like that instead?" Aaliyah stepped closer to him, his senses temporarily consumed by her floral scent, which mingled with the fruitiness of the strawberries. *She's right, dude. Why were you so rude back then?*

"I'm not sure why," he said sheepishly, rubbing his chin, "but I often offend people first and think about what I said after. I know it's messed up. I've been doing it for so long that I don't even realize it."

Aaliyah's eyes widened in surprise. "That's the most honest thing I've ever heard you say."

"You should pick strawberries over there," Tom said, pointing to another patch as he approached them.

"Thanks, Tom," Bryant said, happy for the distraction from Aaliyah. "I overheard Mark telling my dad one time that you make amazing strawberry jam. Maybe one day we can watch you whip something up."

"I can show you now if you want."

Bryant looked to Aaliyah, who nodded her head. "Sure, we'd love to see that." They followed Tom back toward the main barn, and along the way, he and Bryant engaged in small talk about strawberries. Tom wasn't really a talker, and Bryant remembered Mark saying that his brother had autism. Conversing about strawberries seemed to liven Tom up, though, and Bryant enjoyed seeing him speak so enthusiastically about something he loved.

"He's a gentle giant," Aaliyah whispered halfway through the walk back.

"Often misunderstood, but always meaning well," Bryant said, referring to Tom, but realizing that he was also referring to himself. It was only the first day of the road trip, and already Aaliyah's presence was doing crazy things to him. Whether he was annoying her or making her smile, he was enjoying every minute.

Chapter 4

Aaliyah was glad when they finally made it to Historic Charleston in South Carolina because she'd needed a break from Bryant. A break from her aunt and Ben wasn't going to hurt either. They'd decided to get hotel rooms in the downtown area, one for Ben and Sarah, and one each for her and Bryant.

She'd always been the type to love road trips, yet, after the strawberry farm, the large SUV had seemed extremely small and Aaliyah had no idea what had happened to make it feel that way. Mark and Tom had been amazing, and Aaliyah had been impressed by how great Bryant had been with Tom, who hadn't seemed comfortable around the group at first.

One of Aaliyah's nieces had autism, so she'd picked up on the signs from Tom immediately. Although she was still young, her niece had a hard time communicating, while, if one hadn't been paying close attention to Tom, they wouldn't notice he was autistic. She'd loved seeing him work around the strawberry farm, and it was even more touching to see how great Bryant had been with him.

Overall, Aaliyah had thought the stop was a much-needed break, but the tension between Ben and Bryant in the car when they'd returned to the journey was at an all-time high.

"This place is so beautiful," Aaliyah said aloud to herself as she walked in the direction of the lights and music outside the hotel doors. She wasn't much of a night owl, but there was no way she was staying in her room tonight when Historic Charleston promised to be much more fun.

"You shouldn't be out this late by yourself," a deep voice rang out from behind her. She gasped as she clutched her chest, caught off guard by Bryant's baritone.

"You scared the bejesus out of me!" Aaliyah smoothed out her dress. "And I'm a thirty-two-year-old woman, so I can go out late if I want to."

"Bejesus," he repeated as he shook his head. "I didn't mean to scare you. And what I meant was that it was late to be out by yourself in a different state. How about I walk with you?"

Aaliyah quirked an eyebrow. "You're asking to spend time with me? On purpose? Are you sure you didn't hit your head getting out of the car?"

"Ha-ha." He looked down at her, his intense eyes making her swallow a gasp. "Can I take that as a yes?"

"Sure," Aaliyah said. After a few minutes of comfortable silence, she asked the question she'd been wanting to pose for hours.

"Why was the car ride from the strawberry farm in Georgia to Charleston so tense? Did I miss an argument between you and your dad or something?"

"Or something," Bryant said. "You didn't miss anything. Benjamin Burrstone was just being his usual self when it came to me."

"But I thought strawberry picking went well."

"It did." Bryant looked out toward the street as if he were reflecting on the strawberry farm. "My father's attitude toward me had to do with my interaction with Tom."

"What!" Aaliyah exclaimed. "He didn't want you talking to Tom? Is it because he's autistic? I thought the way you interacted with Tom was wonderful."

Bryant glanced back at Aaliyah. "Thank you. One of my cousins in Chicago is autistic, so that wasn't the reason he was frustrated with me. My dad likes Tom. Maybe I misspoke. It wasn't my interaction with Tom that bothered my dad. It was the conversation I was having with Tom about his strawberry jam."

Aaliyah racked her brain to try to recall the conversation. "Are you referring to when you told Tom that his strawberry extract would go great in a dessert beer? It couldn't have been that, right?"

"Bingo," he said. "If you recall, then Mark jumped in and began talking about beers too. For years, I've tried to get my father to expand the business by letting us test our brewery skills, but he's old school and he doesn't want to change too much."

Aaliyah frowned. "But your company is already a winery and distillery. Would opening up a brewery be that much of a stretch?"

"Not to me," Bryant said. "Back in the day, my dad

tried to open a brewery first and it didn't do well. So whenever I bring up the subject, he gets annoyed. It seems to make him question leaving the business in my hands because he knows once he officially retires, I'll get to make the call."

"That's unfortunate," Aaliyah said. "I'd think your father would want you to do whatever you could to grow the business." With a pang, Aaliyah realized she'd missed an opportunity to "coach" Bryant, as her aunt wanted her to do. Maybe the majority of her mentoring, such as it was, should focus on Bryant's interactions with his father instead of clients. From Bryant's conversations with Tom, it was clear the man had some skills in that area, even if they weren't always apparent.

Bryant nodded his head. "Me too, but he's a proud man. I'm stubborn as hell too, so I can't even fault the old man for that. It just seems like the closer we get to his retirement, the more strained our relationship gets."

Not knowing what else to do, Aaliyah gently touched Bryant's arm, the warmth from his skin almost making her stop dead in her steps. *Get a grip, girl. Has it been that long since you've touched a man?* Aaliyah didn't even have to think about that long before a blinding *yes* flashed across her face.

"I was just headed to get some food from this taco stand that I heard was good," she said, changing the topic. "Are you hungry?"

"I've got a better idea," Bryant said. "How about we head to that lounge that the receptionist mentioned when we checked in since they are playing reggae music tonight. That way, we can get some of that jerk chicken too."

"I'm so in," Aaliyah said, her mouth already salivating. To prove how good that sounded, she did a goofy dance that she often did when she was about to get some good food.

Bryant froze. "What in the world are you doing?"

Aaliyah kept dancing. "It's my 'going to get some good food' dance. If you think it looks ridiculous, that's because it's supposed to."

She swung her arms and hips a little more to the faint beat they heard from the lounge.

"Dance with me," she said.

"I'll pass," Bryant said, shaking his head. "I don't dance, and there are too many streetlights shining down on us. I can't have people seeing me do that."

"Oh really?" Aaliyah said, her voice getting louder to try to embarrass him. "I thought Bryant Burrstone didn't care what anybody thought of him."

"I don't," he said. "But you look ridiculous." His serious face hadn't moved an inch.

Forty-eight hours ago, Aaliyah would have been offended by Bryant's comment. Even ten hours ago she would have been offended. However, strangely enough, Bryant was starting to grow on her, especially after she'd witnessed his kind interaction with Tom. Maybe he just needed to loosen up.

"Oh come on, Bryant," she said. "Dance with me." She was prepared for him to turn her down again, but instead, he started mimicking her movements to the beat of the music. He wasn't as into it as she was, but it was enough for her to be impressed that she'd even convinced him to try.

"Yeah, yeah. Get it. Get it."

Aaliyah turned toward the voice that was yelling

across the street, and noticed a group of people had stopped to watch them.

"What's that dance called?" a person yelled from a different group.

"You've got to be shitting me," Bryant said, shaking his head. They had gotten the attention of a couple more groups, and although Aaliyah was prepared for Bryant to stop doing her crazy dance, he surprised her by getting even more into it and doing the beats at the same time she was so that it really looked like a dance they often did.

"It's called The Hangry Dance," Aaliyah yelled to the crowd. "When people are between hungry and angry or angry because they are hungry, they do The Hangry Dance. It's all the rage in Miami."

"Oh, nice!" someone said, right before they started doing the dance. The song finally changed, and Aaliyah slightly increased her movements to go with the faster beat. Before long, they had fifteen other people along the Charleston sidewalk doing the dance.

Once more people began joining, Aaliyah stepped aside and took off her backpack so that she could take out her camera. She'd gotten a few shots at the strawberry farm, but having people do the crazy dance she'd made up was too funny. She had to capture the moments.

Although she was observing the entire group of dancers, Bryant still held most of her attention. The guy wasn't breaking a sweat or a smile, which made his stoic concentration face even more hilarious. He must have heard her laugh because he finally walked over to where she was standing.

"I can't believe all these people stopped to do The Hangry Dance."

"I know," Aaliyah said with a laugh. "And I totally made up that name. I usually do the dance when I'm starving, and I taught my nieces and Summer's son, Anthony, how to do it too. But I've never gotten adults to do it."

Bryant stretched out his arms. "You mean to tell me I'm the first adult to ever agree to do that dance with you? Why would you do that to me?"

Aaliyah smiled. "Honestly?"

"Honestly."

Aaliyah studied his eyes. "Because I was dying to see you crack a smile or laugh, and I figured if I got you to loosen up and do a crazy dance, you'd show me those pearly whites."

Bryant blinked a couple times, his eyes briefly dropping to her lips. *He's thinking about kissing me.* She could feel it. She could see it in his eyes. Even more crazy, she wanted it. He'd demonstrated a glimmer of kindness today. He'd gone from being a robot to…something human. Vulnerable. And attractive. Even sexy.

To break up the sudden sexual tension, Aaliyah started doing the dance again, which was now getting even more attention. She wasn't sure what did it. She wasn't even sure when it had happened. However, the next time she glanced over at Bryant, he was wearing one of the sexiest smirks she'd ever seen. So sexy, that she bumped into the woman dancing next to her. *Holy mother of pearl.* It wasn't a full smile, but it was the most she'd ever seen from him.

Somehow, she'd known he would have a great smirk, but she hadn't been prepared for how delicious his smirk would be. *And he has the nerve to have dimples!* At least one dimple that she could currently see, but she bet both would be on full display when she finally got him to smile.

Aaliyah had always been a sucker for dimples, and she stifled a moan at the deep indentations of his cheeks on his beautiful brown skin. "I wish a man looked at me like that," the woman she'd run into said to her. Aaliyah didn't have to turn around to know she was referring to Bryant. Instead of facing his way again, she continued dancing with the crowd, hoping to regain control of her body in time for them to eat.

The next day, Bryant was still thinking about the surprisingly pleasant dinner he'd had with Aaliyah the night before, as he and his father visited Turner Winery and Distillery right outside Charleston. They'd talked easily, shared stories, mostly tales of their work, but it had felt good, comfortable. She'd seemed to enjoy his company. Maybe Aaliyah didn't think he was such a cold monster after all.

"It's great to see you again, Jeff." Bryant extended his hand to the owner of the business. Turner's was a smaller operation that specialized in five original wines and six different flavors of vodka.

Turner's was also one of the places that carried three of Burrstone's white wines and three of their gins.

"Good to see you too, Bryant. Your father tells me that you'll be taking over the family business soon."

"I will," he said. "Which is why we wanted to pay you a visit and answer any questions you may have regarding the transition."

He heard his father clear his throat from the corner of

the room, but chose to ignore him. At thirty-four-years-old, with six years as vice president under his belt and over a decade and a half worth of experience working in the industry, Bryant never could have guessed that his dad would be sitting in on his work meetings as if this were a parent-teacher conference.

"I appreciate the visit," Jeff said. "I don't have many concerns, but I did want to talk to you about the situation we're dealing with in Charleston right now. A lot of wineries have been hurting financially, and I'm afraid that Turner's is included in that scenario."

"I'm sorry to hear that," Bryant said. "Please know that you have our support during this time."

Jeff nodded his head. "Thank you. I was hoping you felt that way because I'm afraid we can only afford to carry one of your white wines and one gin next year."

Bryant frowned as he glanced through the paperwork sitting in front of him. "Based on the contract you signed with us last year, you agreed to carry our product in your winery and distillery for three years, and you've only fulfilled one year of your contract."

"I understand that," Jeff said. "But we couldn't have predicted that we would be in a financial bind this year."

"Jeff, I'm sorry to hear about your situation, but we cannot allow you to breach your contract. We do business with three other wineries in the area and if we give you a break, we'll have to give the same offer to others."

Jeff ran his fingers across his forehead. "Bryant, I know you don't know me as well as your father does. My winery may not survive the next few years if we sell other product that's not unique to our brands. You have to understand that continuing with the contract means signing my company's death sentence."

"I think you're being a bit dramatic," Bryant said. "Letting you out of the remaining two years of your contract is not an option, but I want to work with you and see what's best for both of us. Maybe we can discuss this further over dinner tonight? That would give me time to create a new plan of action."

"There's no need," Ben said from the corner of the room. "I let Turner out of their contract last week."

Bryant turned to face his father. "You let them out of their contract without consulting me?"

"I still run this company, son." Ben walked over to the table and took a seat in between Bryant and a guilty-looking Jeff.

"I spoke to your father last month," Jeff said. "Sorry, but he asked me to have the same conversation with you that I'd had with him."

Bryant clenched his jaw. "Dad, can I speak with you outside?"

"Sure."

I can't believe this. It was typical Ben Burrstone behavior, but Bryant hadn't seen it coming.

Once they were outside, Bryant let loose his frustration. "Why would you let me hold this meeting if you'd already decided what to do without me?"

"To prove that you don't listen to what our clients say," Ben said. "Did you know that Jeff Turner lost his dad last year and was left with a mountain of debt? Or that his twins just went to college and he can barely afford to pay for it? Or that his wife's mother needs 24/7 care because her dementia is getting worse?"

"Of course I didn't know those things," Bryant said. "But that's called life, Dad. Everyone has issues, and not all our clients' companies are doing well. We can't let everyone out of a contract just because times are hard."

Ben frowned. "We also have to be sympathetic to people's situations. No one client is the same, so we can't treat them the same."

"How much did you make Jeff pay to get out of his contract?" Bryant asked.

"Nothing," Ben said. "Didn't you hear what I said? Jeff has a lot of financial worries right now."

"I heard you," Bryant said, pacing outside in the gravel. "Last year, the Wilsons in Tennessee called and told you that their barn had burned down and they needed to breach their contract with us. In the end, you made them pay us a percentage of fees they still had due and they only had a year left in their contract."

"So," Ben said with a shrug. "The Wilsons are different. Their barn burned down, but I knew they have always been a little shady."

"That's because you don't care for Mr. Wilson," Bryant said. "When it comes to how you run the business, you take things too personally and you think too much with your heart. If the Wilsons weren't given a break, Jeff shouldn't be given one either. I agree that we have to approach our clients differently, but you play favoritism and instead of running the business dispassionately, your heart is too involved." It angered him that his father was intent on proving he was the bigger man. Bryant had said he'd make a plan for Jeff. That plan would have been fair, even if it involved some compensation for the broken contract.

"And your heart isn't involved enough," Ben said, slightly raising his voice. "You walk around like a robot

and you expect for everyone to be emotionally disconnected like you. You can't run a business that way, son."

Instead of responding, Bryant walked away before
he said anything he'd regret. He shouldn't have even
been surprised that his dad had pulled a move like this.
At least now, he knew what to expect from him for the
rest of the road trip.

Chapter 5

Bryant glanced around the hotel lobby, hoping he would spot Aaliyah. He hadn't seen her much yesterday, and after the argument he'd had with his dad, he wouldn't have been good company anyway.

Man, who are you kidding? You're rarely good company. It was true that most people wouldn't consider him a joy to be around, but Bryant was working on it despite what his father thought about him.

"There she is," he said to himself when he spotted her in the corner of the lobby, curled in a chair reading a book. She looked so content, he almost didn't want to bother her. When he was a couple feet away, he stood still and observed her. A couple nights ago, he'd had a great time with Aaliyah; even doing her crazy dance had been fun. It hadn't surprised him that they'd been able to get a lot of others to dance along with them. Aaliyah's spirit, her joy, was infectious.

Today, she was wearing blue jean shorts and a yellow tee, the color making her honey complexion seem even brighter. Her hair was pulled up into a high ponytail, giving her this playful look that he'd seen before, but had never taken the time to truly appreciate like he was now.

As if she felt his eyes on her, she lifted her head from her book. "Hey, Bryant."

"Hey," he said, walking closer to her. "I was hoping to find you down here."

"You were?" she asked in surprise. "I know we leave tomorrow morning, so I was trying to think of something to do, but this book was calling my name."

"What type of book is it?"

"A mystery," she said. "I love mysteries."

"Me too," Bryant said. "I'm not much of a reader, but when I do read, it's usually a mystery."

She smiled. "What are you up to?"

"I was going to rent a small rowboat and check out one of the lakes nearby. Would you like to go with me?" He'd been thinking about Aaliyah all morning. He knew she would brighten his mood, and he needed some of her infectious joy after the argument with his father.

"Sure, sounds like fun," she said, closing her book. "Let me head up to my room and grab my purse first."

Forty minutes later, they were stepping into the boat, an hour before the sun was due to set. Aaliyah had offered to help Bryant row, but he told her not to worry about it. He wanted her to enjoy the experience without any distractions.

"It's beautiful out here," he said, rowing in between a section of tall grass in the water. The area was surrounded by beautiful homes, and in the middle of the lake sat a raised sandbar where people were already gathered with beach towels to await the sunset.

Bryant chose to row to a section that wasn't so crowded.

"Do you want to talk about it?" Aaliyah asked.

"Talk about what?"

He didn't look away when Aaliyah studied his eyes. "About the disagreement you had with your dad yesterday. Aunt Sarah and I were outside when you both stepped out."

"Nothing out of the norm," Bryant said, continuing to row. "I'd much rather talk about the fact that your dance went viral the other night."

"Not exactly viral," Aaliyah said with a laugh. "But I did notice some folks recording the dance, so I should probably check to see if we made YouTube." Her laugh turned to a smile. "It was nice seeing you actually smile that night. It was more of a smirk, but still. I probably liked that more than seeing people do my crazy dance."

"I hate to admit it, but I haven't smiled in a long time." Bryant studied her eyes.

"You should do it more often," Aaliyah said, sitting up straighter in the boat as they approached the other side of the grassy island.

"Let's get out here," Bryant suggested as he hopped out of the boat and pulled it up onto the sand. He stuck out his hand to assist Aaliyah, but quickly decided to help her by her waist instead.

She went along with it, and Bryant couldn't help but hold on to her a little longer than he should have.

"Thank you," she said, clearing her throat. Her cheeks were flushed, and it felt good to know that he was the cause.

"Sorry, I didn't bring a blanket," Bryant said.

"I think I saw one in the back of the boat." Aaliyah ran to the rowboat and returned with a beige blanket that was large enough for them to lie on. "Is this a good spot?" she asked, getting comfortable on the blanket.

"It's perfect," he said, lying down next to her. "Thanks for agreeing to join me."

"I'm just happy you asked." She turned her head to him. "I always thought you didn't like me."

Bryant frowned. "What would make you think that?"

Aaliyah leaned up on her elbows. "Call me crazy, but the fact that we never got along whenever we were in the same room together was part of the reason."

"Excuse me for not understanding how you can always be all butterflies and roses," Bryant said. "Took some getting used to."

"I took some getting used to," she said, placing her hand over her chest. "What about you, Grumpy Mc-Grumperson? Better to emulate sunshine than a dark cloud."

Grumpy McGrumperson? Bryant had been called a lot of things before, but that was a first. Despite himself, he let out a loud, robust laugh, his shoulders shaking in a way that they hadn't in years. "That's your nickname for me?"

"Among other things," she said with a smile. "And I can't believe that's what made you finally laugh. I can fully see your dimples now."

Bryant rubbed his hands against his cheeks, surprised she could see them through his five-o'clock shadow. "Care to share some of those other nicknames?"

She shook her head. "Not a chance."

They fell into a comfortable silence and awaited the

sunset until Aaliyah broke the silence. "We've known each other for years, but we don't know much about each other."

Bryant nodded his head in agreement.

"Let's play the questions game," she suggested. "What's your favorite color?"

"It's going to sound crazy," Bryant said.

"No, it won't," she said. "What is it?"

"Well, I wear a lot of blue, so most people think it's blue. But it's actually midnight gray."

"Midnight gray?" she asked. "Is that a gray so dark that it's almost black?"

"Yes," he said. "But it's not to be confused with dark gray."

Aaliyah laughed. "Gotcha. Midnight gray, not to be confused with dark gray. And not blue because everyone thinks it's blue."

"Right. What's yours?"

Aaliyah picked up a wildflower a few inches away from their blanket. "I love the color yellow."

"Somehow, I knew that," Bryant said.

Aaliyah squinted. "How's so?"

Bryant observed her more closely. "Over the past couple years, you've worn yellow more than any other color. At least when I see you, you're wearing yellow. And over the past three days, you had some form of yellow on whether it be in your jewelry or outfit."

She smiled. "That's quite an observation."

Bryant shrugged. "I notice a lot about you." He glanced back up to the sky when he couldn't handle her searching eyes anymore. If she kept digging, she was going to remember why she didn't like him. "Favorite ice cream flavor?" he asked.

"That's easy," she said. "Chocolate chip mint."

"Nah, butter pecan all the way," Bryant said.

They were still having the ice cream debate when the sky began to turn a brilliant orange and red. This time, instead of Aaliyah initiating another question, it was Bryant.

"What's your biggest fear?" he asked. He assumed the question caught her off guard, because when he looked her way, her face was turned to his and her mouth was slightly ajar.

"That's a tough one," she said. "I hate to admit this, but I have a lot of fears, and although I've overcome a few, I still battle with a couple big ones."

"Like what?" Bryant asked, studying her eyes.

"You go first," she said."

Bryant looked back to the sky, nervous that he'd never get it out if he kept looking at Aaliyah. "One of my biggest fears is that I'll never be able to open my heart up to a woman for fear of losing her." *And fear of her not liking what she sees when she gets to know the real me.* Bryant didn't say the last part aloud. It made him too vulnerable, and he didn't want to reveal that much to Aaliyah.

Aaliyah didn't say anything for a while, and Bryant kicked himself for being so honest with her. He should have kept to himself and observed her from afar like he always did. It was safer that way.

"One of my fears is giving my heart to a man, only to find out that he doesn't love the person I am once he begins to peel back the layers," Aaliyah said. Bryant let out a breath he hadn't known he'd been holding after she responded. *We have the same fear.* It was almost as if she'd gone into his mind and hand-plucked that exact insecurity, the one he'd left unsaid.

Bryant looked back to the sunset. "When we lived in Chicago, I would visit my grandparents all the time, and my grandmother used to always tell me that she didn't want my life to be rooted in fear and limitations, but rather, she wanted me to face my fears and decide my own fate."

"Sounds like an amazing woman," Aaliyah said, scooting closer to Bryant.

"She was."

Before the sun was almost completely gone, Bryant and Aaliyah returned to the rowboat so their trip back wouldn't be in the dark. They were silent on the journey to shore, but it wasn't an awkward silence like Bryant had experienced many times with others. It was a comfortable silence. One that was filled with a newfound understanding and awareness that Bryant hadn't expected.

Aaliyah stuck her right foot outside the car window, enjoying the feel of the wind racing through her toes. Today, Bryant was doing the driving, so Aaliyah had gotten in the passenger seat to make sure he stayed awake.

Just admit it. You enjoy his company. She smiled to herself at the thought. It was true, she enjoyed talking to Bryant much more than she had ever thought she would. She was even more surprised that talking to him was so easy. Even though he was still blunt and didn't always think about what he said, she was getting used to him.

"If we got into an accident that was outside of my

control to stop, you do realize that the airbag would probably break your leg or foot, right?"

Okay, so I'm still trying to get used to the brutally honest part. "Or worse," Aaliyah said, pulling her foot back into the car. "My foot could get caught between the car door and the airbag."

"Exactly," he said in his usual, serious voice.

Aaliyah laughed and directed her attention to her aunt and Ben. "They've been sleeping for two hours already. Sort of makes you wonder why they were up so late."

"I've been trying not to think about what they may or may not have been doing all night," Bryant said, his eyes briefly leaving the road to glance at her.

Aaliyah's eyes widened. "Eww, I didn't mean it like that. I just meant that I haven't seen them so tired before. My aunt mentioned that they went on a hike."

"A hike?" Bryant asked. "Are you sure you're talking about Benjamin Burrstone? My dad can play basketball with the best of them, but he hates hikes."

"Aunt Sarah loves them," Aaliyah said with a smile. "When I was little, she used to take my sister and me on hikes all the time. I fell in love with hiking because of Aunt Sarah. There's something so relaxing about breathing in the fresh air and reaching a high peak that overlooks a beautiful city or landscape."

"My dad used to take my sister and me camping when we were younger," Bryant said. "But instead of going someplace far, we would camp out in the backyard or vineyard."

"That sounds wonderful." Aaliyah tucked one of her legs under the other, careful not to get caught up in her seat belt. "I haven't camped in forever. It's funny how your dad loves camping, but hates hiking."

Bryant's jaw clenched. "I'm not sure he ever really liked camping. It was more of a way for him to distract my sister and me by getting us out of the house when my mom got sick. Kylie was only seven at the time, so she didn't notice what dad was doing, but I was twelve when mom first got sick, so I knew his antics."

"I'm sure he did it to protect you and your sister from the pain going on inside your house," Aaliyah said. "Pretty honorable of him."

Bryant shrugged. *Okay, so the tension between him and his dad may go deeper than what Aunt Sarah told me.* "If you don't mind me asking, how long was your mom sick?"

"My mom, Sherry, initially got breast cancer when I was twelve, but by the time I was sixteen, she was in remission. The cancer returned when I was in college and that fight was a rougher one, but she made it through that too. We had eight years of her being cancer-free. Eight years getting to know our mom without the lingering thought that she could pass away any day. Eight years of being like other normal families."

Aaliyah hadn't even realized she was crying, until Bryant reached over and wiped a fallen tear from her eye.

"I didn't mean to make you cry," he said.

"It's okay. I want to hear the story. I guess I just didn't know how it would remind me of my mother. She suffered for a while too."

The car grew silent, and it took a few minutes before Aaliyah realized that Bryant was rubbing her knee for comfort.

"Whenever you want to talk about it, I'm all ears," he said.

Aaliyah gave him a small smile. "Thank you." Adjusting herself in her seat, she decided to brush off her sadness and change the direction of the conversation.

"So, can you give me a little insight into our next stop?"

"Sure," Bryant said. "It's a wine and cheese festival in Virginia that our winery and distillery is a sponsor for. We've been a sponsor for over a decade, but I haven't made it to the festival in a few years. For this stop, we purchased a booth and will be passing out samples of our signature wines."

"Sounds exciting," Aaliyah said. "I love festivals!"

"I'm not surprised," Bryant said with a smile. *Wow, another smile! I wonder if he even notices!* "I'm sure you'll get some good photos too."

Aaliyah studied his profile as he continued to drive to their next destination. His strong jawline was more defined than she'd previously noticed. His fade and five-o'clock shadow adding a sexiness to him that caused her to hold back a moan.

She didn't want to distract him by taking his photo in the car, but there was no way she wasn't snapping his profile the moment he was too preoccupied to catch her.

Chapter 6

"We're almost there," Bryant said to Aaliyah as they walked past people setting up for the festival. They were nearing the Burrstone Winery and Distillery booth.

The small Virginia town had shut down six blocks in their downtown area for the festival.

"Hey, Bryant," a man called from behind them. Bryant stopped walking and turned.

"Seth, it's good to see you, man." The two men dabbed fists. Bryant and Seth were around the same age, and had been introduced through their fathers who were both in the industry when they were kids. Seth's father passed away a decade ago and since then, Seth had turned his father's winery into a profitable restaurant and had opened three more dining locations in Virginia.

"I'm glad I spotted you," Seth said. "Is your dad here, as well?"

"Yes. He and his girlfriend went to get us something to eat, but they will be here shortly."

"Great. The booth space right across from you canceled today, so I was wondering if you wanted to set up in their place, free of charge. I had another sign printed earlier this morning just in case."

"Of course, man. We'd love to take the extra space. But I'm not sure we shipped enough wine here for that."

"I didn't think so," Seth said. "But I was wondering if maybe you wanted to do a tasting of something else?" He lifted his eyebrows to imply this something else was a secret. After a few seconds of waiting to see if he would say what it was, he gave up.

"I'm lost, man. What would we sell instead?"

Seth looked to Aaliyah.

"It's fine," Bryant said. "You can talk in front of her."

Seth smiled. "Well, I was referring to the beer that you sent me for a test run in a couple of our restaurants. I tried it and I was really impressed, man. I think you have some winning concoctions on your hands. I have some stock left, so I was thinking if you were interested, I would give you the rest of my stock for the second booth and you could send me more cases for my restaurants when you return home."

"Right," Bryant said. Things had been so busy in California lately, he'd forgotten that he'd sent cases of beer to Seth.

He glanced at Aaliyah. "I created three different flavors of beer in hopes that my father would let us test them at our winery, but he wasn't going for that. Seth was kind enough to let me place the beers in his restaurants so that I could test them that way instead."

"And so far, they've done amazing," Seth said. "Bryant, I was going to talk to you more about it while you're in town for the festival, but if you want to take that extra booth space, you have to let me know now."

Crap. It wasn't that he didn't want the chance to sell his beer. However, he also wasn't trying to cause any more unnecessary drama between him and his dad.

"You should do it," Aaliyah said, breaking his thoughts. "My aunt can help your dad with the other booth, and I can help you with the beer booth."

Bryant didn't say anything, still uncertain if he wanted to take this chance.

"Come on," Aaliyah said, tugging on his arm. "I know you're worried about what your dad will say, but soon you'll be running the company, and even though we haven't discussed it, I'm sure you have plans to expand the business. Let me help you."

"Okay," Bryant said. "We'll take the booth."

"Great," Seth said. "In hopes that you would say yes, I took the liberty of having the rest of the cases delivered to the booth already and the sign has been put up. I figured you can use the additional chalkboard sign we supplied you with to write down any info about this side of the business."

Bryant thanked Seth and walked over to space. Both booths were in a prime location, and although Bryant knew his father was going to have a fit, he was glad that he was taking a chance, grateful that Seth had pushed him in this direction. His friend's preparations gave Bryant fresh confidence. If the restaurateur thought the beers were good, then maybe others would too. Including, at some point, Bryant's dad.

Thirty minutes later, Bryant had already set up the

winery and distillery booth, and now he and Aaliyah were setting up the beer booth.

"Did you personally create all three beer flavors?" Aaliyah asked.

"Yes, I did." Bryant opened one bottle of each and took out some small cups to pour Aaliyah samples. "I got into making my own beer back when I was in college. It seemed like every party I went to, someone was buying cheap beer, which made sense because it was all college kids could afford. But I remember getting so sick off some cheap beer that when I'd returned home for the summer, I decided to spend some time experimenting."

He passed Aaliyah one cup. "This was the first flavor I created, called Lazy Dayz."

She took a sip of the beer. "Oh my God, I don't even like beer, but this is amazing." Next, he passed her Warm Nights and Winter Chill.

"They all taste amazing," Aaliyah said. "Has your dad had any of them yet?"

"I tried to get him to taste a few samples, but he refused."

Aaliyah frowned. "Why?"

Bryant opened his mouth to answer, but the sound of Ben's voice halted their conversation.

"What is going on?" Ben looked from one sign to the other before his eyes settled on the beer bottles Bryant and Aaliyah were setting up. *Here we go.*

"Someone canceled, and Seth offered us the extra booth space for me to introduce our brewery line."

The crease in Ben's forehead deepened even more. "I thought we discussed this. Burrstone Winery and Distillery will never sell beer."

"But we could if you stopped being so stubborn," Bryant said, pulling Ben to the side so they could talk a little more privately. "Look, it's already been decided today that we will manage both booths. We don't have enough wine to go around, so let me sell the cases of beer that we have, and we can discuss this later."

Bryant could tell by the look on his dad's face that he wasn't too happy with this plan. However, he also pinpointed the exact moment when Ben decided to let the situation go and deal with it later.

Three hours into the festival, Aaliyah was secretly throwing a fist pump in the air at how busy their booth was. Ben and Aunt Sarah were doing well too, but Aaliyah couldn't believe the constant flow of people they'd had since the start of the festival.

Apparently, quite a few people were already familiar with the beer because they'd sampled it in one of Seth's restaurants. Even better than having folks come up to their booth and ask to purchase several bottles was the look of pure elation on Bryant's face as he listened to the enthusiastic beer drinkers.

"We're targeting a different crowd with this beer selection," Bryant whispered to her when they had a brief few seconds to catch their breath.

"That's amazing," Aaliyah said. She counted the full cases behind her. "We've already gone through ten cases, so we only have a few more left."

"Wow," Bryant said. "I can't believe my beers are doing so well."

Aaliyah glanced over to the other Burrstone booth and caught her aunt giving her a thumbs-up. She smiled in response, wishing she could spend some time talking to her aunt about how much fun she was having, but knowing there was no way they could each leave Ben's and Bryant's side right now.

Bryant. She'd already known that he knew the wine business because Kendrick was always boasting about his cousin's skills. However, she'd had no idea that he was so multitalented.

When they'd first met, he'd seemed so one-dimensional, yet, even after a week, she was beginning to realize how wrong she'd been about him.

"Uh, it's beer. You either like it, or you don't."

Aaliyah glanced over at Bryant in time to catch him talking to a group of women who were debating on whether they should each get a bottle. Half the group loved beer, but wasn't sure about trying something new. The other half hated it. *Okay, so maybe he still needs to work on his people skills.*

"Hey, ladies," Aaliyah said. "What he was trying to say is that beer in general is an acquired taste." Aaliyah placed samples of Lazy Dayz in front of each of them. "But Bryant here is a bit of a beer connoisseur, and he created this lovely concoction back when he was in college. Lazy Dayz is refreshing with a hint of peach and plum that stays on your taste buds way after you've taken your first sip."

Each of the women took a taste of their samples. A couple minutes later, Aaliyah was popping off the caps to their beers and waving bye to them.

"You were amazing," Bryant said. "I was sure they weren't going to get anything."

"That's because you don't know how to talk to people," Aaliyah said with a laugh."

Catching her off guard, Bryant took a step closer to

her, ignoring the fact that a group had just approached their booth. "Maybe you could help me with that."

Aaliyah studied his eyes. "Help you with what?"

Bryant went back to serving the guests and didn't respond until he'd finished with their purchase. "Maybe you can help me improve my people skills. Everyone seems to love you, and if I'm going to prove to my dad that I got this shit and he can retire without worry, then I need you on my side."

Aaliyah bit her bottom lip. *Great, now I must fess up.* "Would you be upset if I told you that my aunt invited me on this trip because your dad is under the impression that I can help you feel more comfortable talking to people?"

Bryant pinned her with an intense stare. "I guess I'd say it's probably the best idea my dad has had in years."

Aaliyah smiled. "So you're not mad?"

Bryant shrugged. "At you, no. At my dad…the jury is still out."

The next couple hours of the festival went smoothly. So smoothly that they sold out of all sixteen cases that Seth had given them. Right before the last two cases went, Aaliyah was able to grab her camera and capture a few shots of Bryant in action. Then she headed over to Ben and Aunt Sarah's booth to get some good photos of them too.

Despite the tension between Ben and Bryant, the energy between both Burrstone booths was buzzing, and it was clear that they were the favorite at the festival.

Aaliyah couldn't quite place her finger on why, but working beside Bryant had felt easy. Simple. Like something they did together all the time. She'd reluctantly taken the assignment to help him become more "social," but now she was enjoying it.

Chapter 7

"**I** should have never agreed to this shit," Bryant huffed as Aaliyah dragged him into the bar where they were meeting Seth and his wife.

"Oh come on," Aaliyah said. "We agreed to meet them here, so you can't back out now."

"I agreed before I knew the bar was doing karaoke night," Bryant said, his eyes growing wider. "Do I look like the type of guy to do karaoke night?"

Aaliyah laughed as she took note of his khaki shorts and white tee. "Actually, you look exactly how I'd expect a man to look who does karaoke."

"Bullshit."

"I'm serious," she said, putting her hands in the air. "Your outfit is fine for karaoke."

Bryant shook his head as he allowed her to pull him farther into the bar. "That's not what I meant and you know it."

They spotted Seth and his wife, Jessica, who Aaliyah had been introduced to before the festival ended.

"Glad you two made it," Jessica said.

"Me too, but I can't believe you got Bryant to walk into a bar on karaoke night." Seth placed his arm on Bryant's shoulder. "Does Aaliyah have any idea how much you hate being here right now?"

"No," Bryant said, looking to the stage as if it were some sort of plague.

"What do you have against karaoke night?" Aaliyah asked. Bryant's frown deepened until Seth was laughing so hard, Aaliyah knew something was up.

"What's the story?" she asked.

"Senior year of college," Seth said.

"In a bar like this," Jessica added. "Bryant and I had class together and a few of us went out one night."

"I was visiting Bryant at school," Seth said. "Which is how I met my beautiful wife, Jessica." Seth leaned down and placed a quick kiss on Jessica's lips. "But that's not relevant right now. So, picture this. We're all at this local college bar and it's karaoke night."

Bryant placed his hand in the middle of the table. "Guys, she doesn't want to hear this."

"Yes, I do," Aaliyah said. "Please continue."

"Well, Bryant and the rest of the group had just taken this really tough business test," Seth said.

"It really was tough," Jessica said in agreement. "So we decided to toast to the completion, and by toast, I mean take so many shots that we wouldn't be able to walk straight in the morning."

Aaliyah laughed. "I'm already loving the direction of this story."

"Back then, Bryant couldn't hold his liquor," Seth

said. "And we were all too drunk to notice that he'd gotten on stage to sing."

"Only it wasn't just his singing we were worried about," Jessica said with a laugh. "Seconds after he made his selection, the room fills with the sound of 'Pony' by Ginuwine."

Aaliyah's hand flew to her mouth. "No way." She looked to Bryant, who simply shook his head and took a sip of a drink she hadn't even heard him order.

"You see, Bryant was serious even back then," Seth said.

"So the sexy song choice was the first shock for the audience," Jessica added.

Seth nodded his head. "The really bad vocals were the second shock."

"But it was the third shock that made it one of those nights he'll never live down," Jessica said. "Bryant started stripping to the song."

Aaliyah gasped before she laughed so loud, she got attention from people sitting nearby.

"Not only did he strip on beat," Jessica continued, "but he was good at it."

"Which didn't make any sense because I'd never seen Bryant dance in all the years we'd been friends," Seth said. "So the fact that he was so good had me forgetting that he was already damn near naked in front of all those folks at the bar."

"Thank God it was before social media was a big thing," Bryant said, downing the rest of his drink.

"By the time we did take notice," Jessica said, "he'd already stripped completely down to his boxers, and it's only then that the bar manager realizes that he's going to take them off and forces him to get offstage."

Seth shook his head. "Me and another one of Bryant's classmates try to help him down, but that's when drunk Bryant won't be ignored and decides to lose the boxers before we can stop him."

"This is too good," Aaliyah said, looking toward Bryant whose face was showing no emotion.

"The next morning, we told him everything that had happened, and to my knowledge, he's never attended another karaoke night."

"And I wouldn't be here now if Aaliyah hadn't asked me to come in," Bryant said.

"So all Aaliyah has to do is ask you nicely and you do something you haven't done in years?" Jessica raised her eyebrows. "Methinks she's more than just your dad's girlfriend's niece."

Prepared for Bryant to deny the accusation, Aaliyah laughed a little louder than she'd meant to, only to find him watching her. Studying her. His eyes following her lips as she licked them out of nervousness.

"I'll take that as a yes," Jessica said. Aaliyah broke eye contact and pretended to be engrossed in a new topic Seth and Jessica were introducing…something about the area and its bars and restaurants. But honestly, her attention was still on the man sitting to her right. The man who, at times, didn't make any sense to her, while at other times, made all the sense in the world.

"Are you ready?" Aaliyah asked.

Bryant looked out at the crowd of people attending the second day of the festival. "Not really."

"It will be fine," Aaliyah said. "All you have to do is start a conversation with three strangers and engage in small talk."

Bryant frowned. Although he was glad that they'd sold out of all the beer during the first day of the festival, he would suddenly rather be helping his dad and Sarah at the other booth than participating in Aaliyah's experiment.

"Trust me," she said. "When it comes to people who know you, you're fine. A little awkward, but fine. Yet, when it comes to people who don't know you, you can come across as rude or indifferent."

"It's not my fault that most people can't handle the truth and are offended by my honesty."

Aaliyah rolled her eyes. "When the lady in the boutique we stopped in this morning asked you if the sweater she wanted to buy made her look fat, you told her yes."

Bryant shrugged. "It did. She said she wanted a male's opinion, and in my opinion the sweater made her look fat. She was an attractive woman, and that sweater didn't do her justice."

"Then you proceeded to tell her that it not only made her look fat, but that she should never wear white because it's not a flattering color."

"What's wrong with that?" he said. "Studies show that white isn't a flattering color."

"She was wearing white jeans," Aaliyah said. "You could have at least paid attention to see if she was wearing that color before you insulted her. Besides, who cares if it's not a flattering color? She was waiting for you to say she looked beautiful, and the saleswoman was waiting for the same confirmation so she could make a sale."

Bryant stared at her. "She didn't look beautiful in it, and that saleswoman knows she was wrong for trying to sell her an ugly-ass sweater. If anything, I helped that woman."

Aaliyah frowned. "The woman left the shop damn near in tears."

"Further proving my point that most people don't want the truth," Bryant said. "If you don't want the truth, don't ask."

Aaliyah squeezed the bridge of her nose. "Your father is the complete opposite. He's personable and charming. People like him and want to do business with him. Yesterday, you said you were willing for me to help you improve your social skills. Well, this exercise is part of that."

Bryant let her words sink in, hating that she was right. "Okay, let's get this over with." He glanced around to try to find the victims for his exercise, and settled on a couple checking out chocolates at one of the booths. *Great, I can knock off two of three if I charm this couple.*

Bryant walked over to where they were standing. "They all look so good, right?"

"They look delicious," the woman said.

"My wife wants me to buy them all," the man said. "But I told her that's it's too much money to get them all. She's trying to break my pockets."

"No, I'm not," the woman said. "I just have a sweet tooth, and you know I'm craving all sorts of weird desserts lately." She rubbed her protruding belly. The movement made Bryant think about how Jaleen had to run out and get Danni some strange food for her pregnancy craving.

"My friend is going through the same thing with his wife," Bryant said to the man. "She was craving some pickles and ice cream, and he had to stop everything and attend to her pregnancy cravings." Bryant looked to the woman. "How far along are you?"

The woman frowned. "I'm not pregnant." She looked to her husband. "Why did he ask if I was pregnant?"

"Your stomach," Bryant said. "You said you've been craving strange desserts and you look pregnant."

"I'm not pregnant, you idiot," the woman yelled. "If you must know, I'm bloated because I'm on my period and when I'm on my period, I crave weird things."

Shit. "Oh," Bryant said. "Well in that case, I think you should eat whatever you want."

The man shook his head, no doubt frustrated that Bryant had managed to ruin their time at the dessert booth. He tried to backpedal, but the damage had already been done. The couple walked away from the booth offended and upset.

"Thanks," the woman behind the counter said sarcastically. "They went from asking me if they could have one of everything to walking out of here with nothing. That promised to be my biggest sale of the day."

"Sorry," Bryant said.

"I don't want your sorry," the woman said. "Just leave my booth before you run off any more of my customers."

By the time Bryant had reached Aaliyah, who had been observing close by, she was rubbing her head even more.

"That was painful to watch," she said.

"It was even more painful to be a part of." He hadn't meant to ruin the couple's time, and it surprised him that he actually felt bad about it. He thought the pregnancy talk had been a good icebreaker. Until he found out that the woman wasn't pregnant.

"Maybe I should find them and apologize?"

"Oh no, you don't," Aaliyah said. "The best thing you can do for that couple is to leave them alone."

Bryant glanced around the festival. "Okay, since I bombed that last exercise, how about you pick someone for me to engage in small talk with this time?"

Aaliyah glanced to her left, then to her right. "Maybe we should continue this exercise in another city," she said. "I think you've offended enough people in Virginia for one festival."

Bryant shook his head as they started walking to another section of booths. "I know I did horrible if you're afraid to have me talk to any more people."

"You can talk to me," Aaliyah said. "I'm getting used to your bluntness. Plus, I saw a really nice bench to our right that promises to be great for people-watching."

"Let's go," Bryant said.

When they arrived at the bench, Aaliyah glanced around to make sure she didn't see that couple Bryant had offended anywhere near them.

Had she not been trying to teach him the art of small talk, she would have laughed at how horribly he'd handled it. He wouldn't be the first person to mistakenly think a woman was pregnant. He'd been so sincere, so eager to make pleasant conversation, he'd been oblivious to the minefield he'd walked into with his comments.

"I overheard you asking your dad if you could talk about what happened at this festival," Aaliyah said.

"Did you also overhear him telling me that what's done is done and he didn't want to talk about it?"

Aaliyah nodded her head. "Yeah, I heard that too."

Although Aaliyah was all for folks talking to work

things out and not letting issues fester, she was glad that Ben and Bryant had chosen to ride in the car from the festival to the hotel in silence. "Why does he hate the idea of you making your own signature beer for the company?"

Bryant sighed. "It probably has something to do with the brewery my dad tried to open when he first moved to LA, right around the time that he and my mom got engaged. She was dead set against it, but he was determined to make it work."

"Wow, so you and your dad have that in common."

"You would think so," Bryant said. "But my dad doesn't see it like that. For years, my dad tried to sell signature beers, and they did good for a little while, but eventually he listened to my mother and they opened the winery and distillery. The business took off, but my dad couldn't let the brewery go and tried to incorporate them both together."

"Kinda what you want to do," Aaliyah said.

"Exactly what I want to do." Bryant leaned back in the bench and crossed his legs at the ankles. "The brewery put a strain in my parents' relationship because she felt like they were spending unnecessary money and that my dad was wasting time trying to make a failing business work, when he could be spending more time with his family."

"But he was chasing his dreams," Aaliyah said. "You never know if you will fail at something if you don't at least try."

"I agree," Bryant said. "But my mom didn't." He looked to Aaliyah, the sadness in his eyes pulling at her heartstrings. "When he found out that my mom was sick, he finally dropped the brewery idea. At least, that's what he told me. I remember my parents fighting over it before my mom got sick and then suddenly, instead of arguments filling the house, there were tears."

Aaliyah scooted closer to him and placed her hand on his. "I guess I understand why you creating those beers was such a big deal for your dad."

"I want to see the company continue to thrive and grow," Bryant said. "But when my dad got angry at me yesterday, I wasn't the businessman who could see potential in a new venture. I reverted to the boy who had sat in his room praying that his mom would get better and wishing he could hear them argue again. Anything to replace the constant tears."

"I'm sorry if I pushed you to sell the beer yesterday," Aaliyah said. "Had I known that story, I wouldn't have."

Bryant lightly rubbed circles in her forearm with his thumb. "I'm glad you pushed me," he said. "Otherwise, I'm not sure how long it would have taken me to see firsthand how successful my beers could be."

They relaxed into a comfortable silence, lost in their own thoughts, and Aaliyah put her head on his shoulder. Suddenly, she didn't feel like talking about anything anymore. She only wanted to continue to soak in this moment with Bryant.

Chapter 8

"Are you sure you're okay with this?" Aaliyah asked.

"I'm good," Bryant said, getting in the driver's seat of the car. "Now get in so we can beat my dad and Sarah there."

Earlier this morning, his dad had told him that he and Sarah would be driving the SUV and asked that he rent a separate car for him and Aaliyah. At first, Bryant had been annoyed because traveling in two separate cars seemed a little extreme. But then he'd thought about it further and realized that he and his dad needed some space if they were ever going to be in a good place to have a conversation.

"What's our next stop?" Aaliyah asked as she got in the car.

"We're headed to Chicago," Bryant said. "We'd planned on making a stop in Michigan, but my aunt called my dad and mentioned that they were having their annual family picnic this weekend. My dad and I had completely forgotten about it, but I texted Kendrick and he said he and Nicole had originally thought they couldn't make it. But they are flying to Chicago today."

"Great," Aaliyah said. "I haven't seen Nicole in over a month, so it will be nice to catch up with her and Kendrick."

"I thought your aunt mentioned that you were heading to LA soon anyway."

Aaliyah tucked one foot under the other. "Right, I was. I'm a finalist for an extremely important competition that could change my career. Famous photographer Jacques Simian and his wife are founders of The Simian Foundation, which is dedicated to furthering photography in any way possible. Jacques's wife, Rachel, is the business side of the company and Jacques is the talent. The foundation is having all ten finalists submit a final portfolio within the next couple weeks to decide who will be able to work and train under Jacques."

"Sounds like a great opportunity," Bryant said. "What photos are you taking for your portfolio? Are you able to do that while we're on the road?"

"Oh, I had an idea for my portfolio for some time, so this trip was a nice break from obsessing over it, just going with the moment, capturing things naturally. I haven't narrowed it all down yet, but the topic can be of our choosing as long as it's in the food or product genre. I'm thinking of somehow incorporating parts of this road trip into my portfolio, but I'm not sure. The winner will be announced at Jacques's LA event, which is why ending this road trip in LA is perfect."

"I'd love to see your work sometime," he said, glancing at her before looking back at the road. "Kendrick said that your boudoir work is incredible too."

"I do okay," Aaliyah said with a shrug. "A lot of what I do is self-taught. I majored in marketing in school, but took a few photography classes on the side. But I think what I lack in schooling, I make up for in the way I capture a photo. Here, I'll show you." While traffic slowed due to construction, Aaliyah took out her camera and showed Bryant a few shots that she'd taken at the festival.

"You almost make the wine bottle look…"

"Pornographic?" Aaliyah asked.

Bryant laughed. "I was aiming more for alive, but yes, pornographic works."

Aaliyah looked up from her camera, her smile growing even wider. "You laughed again," she said. "And it wasn't a fake one or a drive-by. It was a really good-hearted laugh."

"Damn, am I really that bad?"

"Pretty much," she said with a sly smile. "But a week around me and you're already smiling and laughing more."

"So I noticed," he said, his eyes dropping to her lips. *Damn, I want to kiss her.* It wasn't the first time he'd had that thought, and he figured it would happen a few more times before they even made it to Chicago. He might have even kissed her right there in the car if he hadn't heard a loud beeping noise from the car behind them. His eyes went back to the road.

"Apparently, I can't drive slowly and watch your pornographic photos at the same time."

"Really?" Aaliyah placed her hand over her chest, mocking surprise. "You mean to tell me that you can't drive while engrossing yourself in the sexy wine bottle photos I took?"

"Imagine that," Bryant said teasingly.

"I have an idea that won't get us into an accident," Aaliyah said. "How about we continue with our questions game?"

"I'm down," Bryant said. "At first I thought you were going to make me play some obnoxious radio game that my sister always wants to play when she's home."

"You mean the game where you ask a question aloud and scan the radio, then whatever song the radio lands on is the answer to your question?"

Bryant nodded. "That's the one."

Aaliyah placed her hand on his arm. "Don't worry, buddy. That game is next." She turned in her seat so that she was facing Bryant a little more. "Okay, my first question… How old were you when you had your first kiss?"

"Real kiss?" Bryant asked. "Or playground kiss."

"Playground kiss."

He thought back to when he was little. "I think I was in kindergarten and her name was Emily."

Aaliyah clapped her hands. "Bonus points for remembering her name, but I win. My first kiss was in preschool and his name was Jimmy Valentine."

Bryant squinted his eyes together. "I thought this was the questions game. How can you win answering questions?"

"When one person's answers are better than the other's," Aaliyah said with a shrug. "And I get triple bonus points for remembering my first kiss's full name."

"Horseman," Bryant said. "Emily's name was Horseman, so I get those points because she has a funnier last name."

Aaliyah turned back to look at the farm they'd just passed. "Horseman was not Emily's name. You made that up because we just passed some horses."

"You're speculating," Bryant said. "You can't prove that."

"Anyway, next question is yours to ask me."

Bryant smirked. "What's the most embarrassing dream that you've ever had?"

Aaliyah laughed. "How did we go from our first kiss to embarrassing dream? Where are the in-between questions? The buffer questions?"

"Fine," he said. "How old were you when you had your first real kiss? No playgrounds allowed."

"When I was fifteen," Aaliyah said. "It was right after my first school dance. His name was Johnny Slate."

"Was it a good first real kiss?"

"Not really." Aaliyah's body shivered as if the memory still disgusted her. "I only went with Johnny to the dance because the week before the dance I'd overheard the boy I had a crush on telling the other kids that I was one of those hippie kids who probably didn't even shower or wear deodorant."

"Young boys are stupid," Bryant said.

"Yeah, they are. But this stupid boy had hurt my feelings, so I said I'd go to the dance with the first boy who asked me. The reason the kiss was so bad is because I'd had braces at the time and so did he, so you can imagine what it was like when we kissed."

"That's not a pretty picture," Bryant said with a laugh.

Aaliyah clapped her hands. "Wow, two laughs in less than two hours. That must be some sort of record for you."

"Ha-ha." Bryant cleared his throat. "Let's see. My first real kiss was at thirteen. Her name was Amanda Black. And yes, it was a *very* good kiss. No braces. No awkwardness. Just lips."

Aaliyah swatted him on the shoulder. "Show-off."

The questions game continued until Aaliyah said she was getting sleepy and was going to take a quick nap. A quick nap turned into a two-hour nap, but Bryant didn't mind. She'd asked him to wake her up in twenty minutes, but honestly, Bryant had needed the time to clear his head. He needed to decipher what was going on between him and Aaliyah. He needed to figure out if this feeling of wanting to be close to her was ever going away.

Think straight, Bryant. You don't get close to people so getting so close to Aaliyah is a mistake. He heard the warning in his mind, but couldn't get that warning to communicate with his heart. While he listened to her soft snores that blended with the low music coming from the radio, he concluded that he may not ever want it to go away and *that* was a scary feeling.

"I've never been to Ohio," Aaliyah said, leaning against the car while Bryant lifted the hood. Just as it had when he'd lifted the hood ten minutes prior, smoke came from the engine.

"I've never run into engine trouble in a rental," Bryant said. "Roadside assistance should be here soon."

"Are you sure you don't want to contact your dad and Aunt Sarah?"

"Not yet," Bryant said. "Let's see what the auto shop says once they take a look at it."

"Okay," Aaliyah said, not confident they would get the answer they wanted. She'd never seen a car smoke so badly.

An hour later, her suspicions were confirmed.

"Can you repeat that?" Bryant said. "Because it sounded like you said it would take you two days to fix the car."

"It will," the mechanic said. "My cousin lives a few towns over, and they have the part you need. He can't get here until tomorrow, but you should be able to leave the following morning."

"Thanks." Bryant turned to Aaliyah. "Maybe now we should call my dad and Sarah."

A few minutes later, they realized that their backup plan wasn't a plan at all.

"You both flew where?" Aaliyah asked.

"Instead of hitting the road like you and Bryant did, we decided to turn in our rental and take a short trip to Niagara Falls instead."

Aaliyah rubbed her forehead. "Aunt Sarah, why didn't you tell me?"

"I planned on calling you when we landed and we just landed," Aunt Sarah said. "Besides, you and Bryant seemed mighty cozy getting into that rental car. I didn't want to mess up the vibe by having you both worry that we'd lost our minds by going on a quick trip." *Did she forget I have her on speakerphone?* Either that, or she didn't care.

Aaliyah glanced at Bryant in time to catch the smirk on his face. *Grave improvement from his resting grumpy face.*

"We plan on making it to Chicago before Ben's family picnic in a couple days," Aunt Sarah said.

"Okay, I guess there isn't more for us to do except stay in town and wait for the car." Aaliyah glanced at the mechanic. "What town are we in exactly?"

"You're in Sandusky, Ohio, right off the shores of Lake Erie and home to Cedar Point."

"Cedar what?" Aaliyah asked.

"It's an amusement park," Bryant said. "My family had a reunion there when I was younger."

"I have a cousin who can get you a discount for one of the Cedar Point hotels," the mechanic said.

"You sure have a lot of cousins," Bryant said. "What was your name again?" Aaliyah had wondered the same thing since his name tag had been smudged off.

"I'm Andy," he said. "Of Andy's Mechanics." He pointed to a sign that was hanging overhead.

"Right." Bryant looked from her to the phone. "Aunt Sarah, we'll just stay at a hotel here, and we'll see you and Ben in a couple days."

"Okay, sweetie. You kids have fun."

Aaliyah hung up with Aunt Sarah and Ben, who she assumed was listening to the call as Bryant had been.

"Andy, before we book that hotel, I'm going to check with the car rental agency about getting us new wheels so we can be on our way."

Andy shook his head slowly. "That's likely to take just as long as the repair. Nearest rental place is one town over, and they've got a small fleet. All of them are rented out for some convention, I hear."

Bryant sighed heavily. "I think we'll take the name of that hotel," Bryant said.

Andy smiled. "I'll make a call to my cousin right away."

Once they were left alone, Bryant leaned closer to her so that Andy wouldn't overhear them. "Are you sure you're okay with staying in this town for a little bit?"

"If you're okay, I'm okay."

"I'm okay," he said. "I've been to this town before. It's just been a while."

"Great news, folks," Andy said, returning. "My cousin was able to secure the last available room in one of the property hotels that they usually keep open in case of emergencies."

Aaliyah cleared her throat. "Did you say one room? As in, we have to share a room?"

Andy looked from Aaliyah to Bryant. "Oh hell, don't tell me you're one of those couples who sleep in separate beds and shit."

"We aren't," Aaliyah said. "Because we aren't a couple." Sharing a car with Bryant was doing enough for her libido. She didn't need to be shacking up with him too.

"Well darn, pretty lady." Andy lifted his greasy hat and winked at Aaliyah. "You should have told me you were free for the taking. My cousins and I are single."

Oh hell, no. "I'm taken," Aaliyah said, pulling Bryant closer to her. "It's just, we're engaged and I told him no nookie before the wedding. So if we share a room, I may be too tempted. But since that's all you have, I'm willing to try to contain myself."

Bryant snorted, so Aaliyah squeezed his side to keep him from blowing her cover.

"Hmm." Andy looked from one to the other. "Such a shame."

"Yeah," Aaliyah said with a forced laugh. "Such a shame."

Andy waved his hands. "Well, come on and get in my truck. I'll take you both to the hotel."

"We can take an Uber," Bryant said.

"Sure, go ahead." Andy rattled off the hotel address and went back to working on whatever he'd been working on when they'd arrived.

"Okay, Uber is reserved," Bryant said.

"How long until he or she gets here?" Aaliyah asked. Instead of responding to her, Bryant's eyes widened as he reviewed his phone screen.

"Andy, really?" Bryant said. "You're our Uber driver?"

"I am," Andy said with a smile.

Bryant shook his head. "Why the hell didn't you just tell me that you'd be our Uber driver if we requested one?"

Andy shrugged. "I thought you were one of those people who insisted on paying his way for everything and didn't want any handouts. So I let you pay."

Bryant was still shaking his head as they gathered their bags and made their way to Andy's car.

It wasn't until they'd arrived at the hotel and checked in that Aaliyah realized that Bryant had successfully talked to multiple people without saying anything extremely rude or off-putting.

She was just about to tell him that she was proud of how he'd socialized in this situation, when they opened the door to their room.

"The honeymoon suite!" Aaliyah exclaimed. "You've got to be kidding me."

"Doesn't seem to be a joke," Bryant said. "This is definitely our room number."

Too tired to even think about the craziness that the day had brought, Aaliyah dropped her bags and collapsed on the bed. However, her relaxation was short-lived.

"What the hell is that?" she said as the lights dimmed and music began playing.

"I can't be sure," Bryant said, reading a white card that had been placed on the nightstand. "But I think you just figured out that our comforter activates the music and dims the lights whenever we sit or lie on it."

Aaliyah would have laughed, had she not noticed the creepy looking cupid hanging from the wall. He seemed to be mocking her, the hint of a smile teasing her for reasons she hadn't figured out yet. It may have been for only two nights, but in a room like this, she was certain it would feel much longer. *This should be interesting.*

Chapter 9

"Despite our crazy room" Bryant said, "it's pretty nice to have a hotel on the beach."

After finding a few more unwanted romantic surprises in their room, Aaliyah had suggested that they take a walk and check out the area. The beach was bustling with people playing volleyball or having fun in the sand.

Aaliyah glanced out at the people riding Jet Skis. "Lake Erie is no ocean, but I'll take it."

"Are you hungry?" Bryant asked.

"Yeah, I am. Especially since the last time we ate was this morning."

Bryant pointed to a restaurant. "Have a taste for barbecue?"

"That's fine."

When they got to the restaurant, the only available

table was one that was outside on the patio near the marina. Neither of them seemed to mind.

"I've always wanted to own a boat," Bryant said after they'd ordered.

"Me too," Aaliyah said. "I used to daydream about escaping life's difficulties by hopping in my boat and going wherever the waves took me."

"I know the feeling," he said, studying her eyes. "You don't have to talk about it if you don't want to, but how did your mom pass away?"

Aaliyah sighed. "Unlike your mom, my mom passed away unexpectedly from a brain aneurysm. I'd just gotten off the bus and was home from school when I found her. My dad hadn't gotten home yet, and my sister had gone to the mall with her friends. I remember heading straight to the kitchen to tell my mom about the A I'd gotten on my test, and I found her lying on the kitchen floor. Dinner was everywhere, proof that she'd grabbed the counter and knocked over the food when it happened."

Bryant reached over the table and held her hand. "That's terrible. How old where you when it happened?"

"I was fifteen. I was a little shocked at first, but I immediately ran to her side and shook her. She wouldn't move and I was too afraid to take her pulse. I called 9-1-1, and the operator stayed on the phone until the ambulance arrived."

Aaliyah looked out into the marina. Bryant continued to hold her hand, wanting to offer her whatever form of comfort he could. "I remember one of my neighbors coming to the house and asking if I called my dad, and I couldn't even respond to her. They let me ride in the ambulance as they tried to revitalize my mom, but I knew she was never waking up. I wasn't sure how I knew, but I did."

"You probably sensed it," he said. "A therapist I had to see after my mom passed told me that oftentimes, we can sense when a soul is no longer here."

"You're probably right," she said. "My dad had just gotten all of us cell phones, but by the time I called my dad and sister when we'd gotten to the hospital they were already walking through the door. My neighbor had called."

"That must have been hard," he said. "To go through all of that by yourself."

"Yeah." Aaliyah looked back at Bryant. "By the time we got the news, my family had already been crying and accepted that she may not make it. I remember asking my dad sometime after the funeral how did he know that she was gone. What was the moment he realized the next time we saw the doctor, it wasn't going to be good news?"

"What did he say?" Bryant asked.

"He said that I had this look on my face that he couldn't quite place when he'd first arrived at the hospital. It took him a while to figure it out because he wanted to remain hopeful, but he noticed that I had already started grieving her loss. Since I was the most positive person in my family, he said looking at my face, he just knew. He didn't think it was the scared look of a girl whose mom was just rushed to the hospital. But rather, it was the look of a girl who'd known that her mother had passed before the ambulance had arrived."

"Wow," Bryant said, wiping a few of her tears that had fallen. "That doesn't sound like an easy thing to hear."

"It wasn't. It made me feel as if I didn't do enough to try and save her, although I know based off what the doctors said, there was nothing I could have done. It took me a long time to forgive myself for not calling my dad and sister right away or not at least trying CPR on my mom."

"There wasn't anything you could do for her," Bryant said. "And it may have been best that your dad and sister didn't see your mom that way." Bryant clenched his jaw. "When my mom passed, we were all at the house with her because we knew it would be happening someday soon. She wanted to be at home for it. She wanted to be surrounded by her family."

"And it sounds like she was," Aaliyah responded.

"Yeah, she was." Bryant thought back to the day his mom had passed. "My dad had gone outside to pick some new flowers for the vase so that my mom could continue to look at fresh flowers, and my sister went to boil some water for tea. My mom chose the moment they both left to grab my hand and bring it to her chest. She passed away at that moment, and I sat there for two minutes with her after she'd passed before my sister had returned and immediately started yelling for my dad."

Aaliyah scooted her chair closer to Bryant's. "It's crazy, isn't it?" she said. "The fact that all you want to do is call your loved ones and be together for the passing of a family member, but when it happens, it's only you in that moment. It's you and them as their soul leaves their body. My mom may have already been gone, but I sat with her on that floor and I didn't want my dad and sister to see her that way. I didn't want them to see the blood on the floor from where she'd hit her head or the food all around her from where she'd clearly tried to catch herself."

"I hadn't wanted that either," Bryant said. "I knew

my mom well, so I knew she'd purposely held on until my dad and sister had both left the room. The only part of that day that truly pulls at my heart is the fact that I remember her opening her mouth to say something, but she didn't have the strength. I'm not sure I'll ever forget that moment." He'd felt so helpless then. Like his world had been ripped apart.

"You probably won't," Aaliyah said. "With time, the pain eases, but we'll never forget. And honestly, I don't want to. I remember all the amazing times I had with my mom, but I don't want to ever forget that moment either. I said my goodbyes in that moment, right there with the 9-1-1 responder on the phone, I said my goodbyes."

"All right folks," the waiter said. "Your food's here."

Bryant knew that, like him, Aaliyah didn't feel much like eating after that conversation. "Can we get to-go containers instead?"

"Sure," the waiter said. "I'll be right back with the containers and your bill."

"What's going on?" Aaliyah asked after the waiter had left.

Bryant glanced at the amusement park. "What if we drop this food off at our room, and spend a couple hours clearing our minds at the amusement park? I read somewhere that they have evening park tickets."

Aaliyah smiled. "I'd love that."

"I changed my mind," Aaliyah said. "I'm not sure this was a good idea." She glanced over the side of the largest roller coaster in the entire amusement park as it slowly ascended to the top.

"It's too late to change your mind," Bryant said. "You're already strapped in."

She looked over the edge again. "Oh my God, I'm going to throw up." She heard a gasp from the couple on the other side of her and Bryant.

"Maybe avoid any mentions of vomiting," Bryant whispered. "And I'm here with you. I'll be holding your hand the entire time."

It was then that Aaliyah noticed that Bryant *was* holding her hand. She couldn't even relish the warm feel of his hand because she was too anxious to concentrate on anything but the approaching peak of the roller coaster track.

"I can't believe I let you talk me into this," Aaliyah said. "I've never liked roller coasters." The closer to the top they got, the more she was talking. Bryant never acted like he minded. He only squeezed her hand harder.

"Whatever's on your mind in this moment," he said for the brief few seconds the coaster lingered at the top, "release them now and let them go."

Aaliyah wasn't sure if she was heeding his advice, but she definitely felt as if she were in jeopardy of letting the contents in her stomach go as she wailed at the top of her lungs at the large dip of the roller coaster.

The rest of her time on the ride flew by after she got over the initial shock of the big drop.

"That was insane," she said to Bryant, when the ride was over. "I was scared out of my mind, but after that large dip, I really started to enjoy the ride."

"I could tell," he said with a laugh. "Are you ready to get in line to ride it again?"

Aaliyah froze. "I didn't enjoy it that damn much."

His laugh got even louder, the sound just as infectious as it had been all the other times he'd let loose.

"Now, it's my turn for you to do something that I

want." She took out her map of the grounds, finally finding the perfect ride. "Got it. Come on."

During the short walk to the ride that she had chosen, Bryant didn't seem to be worried about her selection. After the ride they'd just gone on, she could tell why. It was clear that Bryant loved the thrill of roller coasters. He'd already taken her on four of them, with the last one making her squirm in her seat from nerves.

"Here we are," Aaliyah said, pointing to the ride. She grabbed his arm and led them to the entrance. Luckily, there weren't many people in line. If there had been, she was sure he would have backed out.

"You can't be serious," he said, following her onto the ride. "A carousel? You can't expect a grown man to get on a pony that goes in circles."

"You already agreed." They stepped up on the carousel, and Aaliyah looked for the girliest pony she could find, painted in pinks and purples with a glittering bow in its artificial mane, for Bryant to sit on, while she chose a nearby brown one.

"Everyone's looking at us," he said. Aaliyah glanced behind them at the little girls who were snickering.

"They're little girls. Of course they are laughing."

"Not them." Bryant nodded his head to the opposite side. "Them."

Aaliyah followed the direction of his eyes and immediately burst out in laughter. Bryant was right. All the moms were standing to the side watching them on the carousel.

"Can you blame them?" Aaliyah said. "They've probably never seen a man so sexy on the carousel before."

As soon as the words left her mouth, she realized the

weight of them. A quick glance at the smirk on Bryant's face proved it was too late for her to take it back.

The carousel ride seemed to go on forever, and Aaliyah was sure she'd turned every shade of red there was. When the ride stopped and they got off, she tried to brush off her previous words, but Bryant wasn't having it.

"You think I'm sexy?" he said as they approached a nearby fountain. The sun had finally set and people were starting to leave the amusement park, so it wasn't as crowded.

"It cleared out here fast," Aaliyah said, glancing around.

Bryant stepped closer to her. "You didn't answer my question."

Instead of responding to him, she leaned against the railing and stared at a waterfall. "It's pretty that they change the colors at nighttime to the beat of the music playing in the background."

"That is nice," Bryant said, leaning next to her. When his arm grazed hers, it took all her energy not to react to him. "Are you cold?" he asked.

So much for not reacting. "The temperature dropped a little, but I'm fine."

They were quiet for a few minutes, each looking out at the fountain. Aaliyah had always been the type of person who was perfectly content in the quiet moments of the day. Yet, it wasn't until she was leaning against the railing, watching the water change color, that she realized she'd never been with anyone who understood that part of her personality. She'd never dated a man who was content to just be in the moment, who didn't always need to be doing something or watching something.

"Despite the car breaking down, I had a great time today," Bryant said, turning his face toward her. She could feel his gaze on her left cheek.

"I did too." She took a deep breath before turning to face him eye to eye. "A lot more fun than I have in a long time."

Bryant's glance dropped to her lips, causing her to suck in her breath. If Aaliyah could have pieced together any additional words, those words died on her lips when Bryant took another step closer.

His mouth lingered over hers for a while, as if asking permission, the anticipation for what was soon to come wreaking havoc on Aaliyah's nerves. When he finally placed his mouth on hers and pulled her closer for a toe-curling kiss, Aaliyah released her nerves and turned into him so that she could take the kiss even deeper.

Aaliyah wasn't sure what she'd expected, but the way Bryant's lips felt on hers was doing crazy things to her insides. He was a good kisser. Scratch that. He was a *great* kisser.

The way his lips moved with hers was something she wasn't prepared for. She felt consumed by his kisses and her arms went around his neck, bringing him closer to her.

"Get a room," someone yelled in the distance. Aaliyah expected Bryant to pull back. After all, they were at an amusement park, and even though it was nighttime, there were still a lot of kids around.

But Bryant wasn't having it. If anything, he deepened the kiss and placed his hand at the back of her head to keep her in place. The kiss was delicious. Mouthwatering. Downright sexy.

Chapter 10

"I told you kayaking was fun," Aaliyah said from the kayak in front of him the next day. "I can't believe you've never gone before."

"I must admit. This is much better than the carousel idea," Bryant said. After that intense kiss they'd shared last night, they'd returned to the room and eaten the food they'd ordered earlier.

Bryant hadn't known what to expect after a lip-lock like that, but things hadn't been awkward at all. Aaliyah had suggested they watch whatever crazy shows they could find online, and they did just that. Bryant couldn't remember the last time he'd had such a good time.

"I've never wanted to get in this small contraption," he said. "But now that I'm in it, it's not as bad as I thought."

"I'm telling you, Burrstone. Sooner or later, you're

going to start realizing that I'm a pretty intelligent person."

"I already know that," he said. "Plus, Sarah always speaks so highly of you that even before we got to know each other, I recognized that about you."

Aaliyah grew strangely quiet, and Bryant wondered if he'd said anything wrong. He couldn't see her face from his angle in his kayak.

"I've been meaning to ask you," Aaliyah said as they approached a shallow clearing that allowed them to be side by side in their kayaks. "Sometimes, I get the feeling that you don't like my aunt. Not all the time, but sometimes."

Bryant nodded his head. "I can see how you'd think that."

"Is it true?" she asked. "Do you hate that my aunt is dating your dad?"

Bryant glanced down at his paddle, not ready for the seriousness of this conversation. For Aaliyah, she probably thought her question was harmless, but for him, it wasn't just an issue of his dad and Sarah's relationship, but much more.

"I don't hate that they're dating," he said honestly. "Let's just say that my dad and Sarah's relationship took place at a time when my dad's and my relationship was very strained. When he began dating your aunt, he used that as an excuse to ignore our issues and devote all his attention to his new relationship instead. She's a good person, I know."

There was a lot that Bryant was leaving out of the story, but he was enjoying his time with Aaliyah so much that he didn't want to weigh it down with unnecessary drama. For a few seconds, she studied his face and he wondered if she was going to push the subject or let it go.

She opened her mouth to say something else, but the sound of thunder made her look to the gray sky. Bryant glanced at the shore. "Looks like the guys we rented these kayaks from are waving for us to come back."

They weren't too far from land, but by the time they'd gotten out of the kayaks, it was pouring rain.

"My hair," Aaliyah yelled, her long locks now wet and sticking to her body. Without giving it a second thought, Bryant pulled off his black tee and gave it to Aaliyah so she could try to cover up as much of her head as possible. They dashed across the beach to their hotel, but by the time they'd made it to the room, they were soaked.

"The weather took a turn pretty fast," he said, slipping off his wet shoes and running his hands over his swimming trunks. When Aaliyah didn't say anything, he looked to her.

He wasn't sure what he expected to see, but a stare of unadulterated interest in her light brown eyes definitely wasn't it. He looked down at his damp chest, remembering that he'd removed his shirt. Her eyes didn't leave his abs, so he took the time to check her out, as well.

Aaliyah's white shorts were almost see-through right now and her pink top was clinging to her breasts, revealing a navy blue bathing suit. She walked toward him, and Bryant found himself holding his breath as she reached out and ran her hands over his chest. Her fingers dipped in and out of the crevices of his abs, and it took all his energy to stand there and let her explore.

He'd heard her say that she hadn't wanted her hair to get wet, but in his opinion, she still looked amazing, wet hair and all. Instead of the soft curls he was used to seeing her wear, her hair was curling into tighter ringlets that he itched to run his fingers through.

His eyes became fixated on the rise and fall of her chest as her hands traced circles over his lower abdomen. Unable to stand there any longer and not touch her, he pulled her toward him and placed a sweet kiss on her lips that quickly escalated.

Kissing Aaliyah was unlike anything he'd ever experienced before. Ever since he'd met her, he'd wondered what it would be like feel her lips on his. To have her grow limp in his arms after an intoxicating make-out session.

Although he'd thought about it more times than he could count, he never thought he'd actually be experiencing this moment with her. It felt so surreal, but perfect at the same time.

Aaliyah broke the kiss and took a step back, her chest rising and falling with heavy breaths. He was about to reach for her to come back into his embrace, when she grabbed the hem of her shirt and took it off over her head.

Bryant's eyes traced over the swell of her breasts, down to her stomach, stopping at her shorts, which she was currently shimmying down her hips. Considering she was wearing a bikini, the act shouldn't have been so erotic, but it was.

Aaliyah's steps toward him were purposeful, and Bryant found himself following her every move, waiting to see what was going to happen next. When she stood in front of him, he figured they'd pick up where they left off, but he should have known to always expect the unexpected where Aaliyah was concerned.

She stood there only a few seconds before she turned and headed to the bathroom, untying her swimsuit top as she did so. "You coming?" she asked, looking over her shoulder.

Damn. Even her voice sounded sexier than usual. There was no way Bryant would have ever imagined that he'd be following an almost-naked Aaliyah into the bathroom, but that's exactly what he was doing. And even though he wanted to make sure they were on the same page, mama didn't raise no fool. He was done watching life pass him by, and there was no doubt in his mind that Aaliyah was a blessing. There was no way he was passing up on a blessing.

You're good, girl, just relax. Aaliyah could be described as a lot of things. An upbeat person by some. A free spirit by most. A loyal friend to those whom she was close too. Yet, no matter who you asked out of the people who knew her best, the last word they would use to describe her was *sexy.* Clumsy maybe, but sexy? That wasn't her. Not by a long shot.

But despite how badly she was trying to tame all her awkwardness, she quickly realized that being around Bryant—or being halfway-naked around Bryant—didn't feel strange at all. In fact, it felt so right. Too right.

Just as she'd hoped, he followed her into the bathroom. Aaliyah bent down to turn on the water for the shower, loving the fact that his eyes were intently following her every move. When she turned back to face him, she heard the whistle of appreciation as he zoned in on her bare breasts.

When his eyes reached hers again, she saw concern reflected in them.

"You know," he said, stepping closer to her, "this moment doesn't have to go any further if you're not okay with it."

Not okay? Did he hear her ask him to follow her into the bathroom and did he watch her discard her bikini top? "I'm ready." She reached out her hand to run it along his chest again. "I've thought about this for a while now."

"Me too," he said, dropping his lips down to hers. It was true, even when he'd been this stoic, grumpy man who always seemed to say nothing but rude things to her, she'd still had a dream or two about getting him naked. Often, she'd told her friend Nicole that it wasn't fair that he was such a jerk, but looked so damn good.

You don't think he's a jerk anymore. Socialization-wise, Bryant still had a way to go, but Aaliyah understood what Kendrick had been trying to tell her. Once you got to know Bryant, you learned what a decent man he was. He cared about others, despite the fact that he didn't like to advertise it. And he was multitalented if those beers were any indication of how great he was at all aspects of the wine, spirits and beer industry.

Aaliyah's hands played with the top of his swimming trunks, eager to remove them, but nervous at the same time. It had been a long time since she'd been alone with a man, and had she seen this intimate moment with Bryant coming, she would have done a little more preparation to make sure her body was ready for his viewing.

"You look beautiful," he said, reading her thoughts. "I've always thought you were beautiful, even when you were driving me crazy." Bryant untied the sides of her bikini bottoms until the stringy material fell to the floor. "But seeing you like this," he said, taking a step back to view her naked body, "is much better than anything I imagined in my dreams."

She smiled. "Thank you." With a newfound strength, she slid his trunks down his thighs, each inch revealing more of him that left her salivating by the time they were completely off. Unable to help herself, she placed her hand around his shaft, lowered herself and stuck the tip in her mouth.

"Shit," he said, gripping the bathroom counter. She knew she'd taken him off guard, but it seemed only fair. She hadn't been prepared for the likes of Bryant Burrstone. Hadn't known that when her aunt had asked her to accompany them on this road trip that it would result in her learning more about the man behind the frown and liking what she was learning.

"I can't handle much more of that sexy mouth of yours," he said. She smiled as he helped her up and led them into the shower. As soon as she closed the curtain, Bryant was on his knees, lifting one of her legs over his shoulders.

"Oh my," she said when his tongue found her sweet center and began twirling in a way that was causing her to cling to the shower pole. Just like the man's kisses, his lips were lethal no matter what part of her body he touched.

Bryant didn't hold anything back, his tongue dipping in and out of her in a way she'd never experienced before. She wasn't sure when he'd lifted her other leg over his shoulder, but the only thing holding her up was him and the wall. As the passion in the shower grew one hundred degrees hotter, Aaliyah became mesmerized by the way the drops of water were hitting his smooth back.

"Bryant," she said as a warning. Or at least, it was meant to be a warning. She said his name a few more times until it sounded more like a chant instead of a warning, and her moans seemed to encourage him to quicken his pace.

A few seconds later, Aaliyah released a strong orgasm that had her convulsing all over Bryant's tongue. She felt like a limp doll as he led her back to the floor of the shower.

"I'll be right back," he said, placing a sweet kiss on her neck. Aaliyah barely heard what he'd said, but realized he'd gone to get a condom when he'd returned with one securely placed on him.

In the back of her mind, she wondered if her idea of having sex in the shower wasn't such a great one because there wasn't enough to hold on to. She was going to ask Bryant if he wanted to move to the bed instead, but moments later, the thought died on her tongue as Bryant captured her lips while lifting her onto him at the same time. He slid inside her with an ease she hadn't expected, causing them to both moan aloud at the power of their intimate connection.

Bryant began moving in slow strokes, which shocked the hell out of her because he was doing so while holding her up. Of course, she'd wrapped her legs around his waist, but he was doing all the work.

Bryant increased his movements, bracing her as if she weighed nothing at all. She had to give it to him. The man had skill. He treated her as if she was as light as a feather, while also increasing her pleasure by hitting her sweet spot in repetitive strokes.

"Bryant, I'm almost there," she whispered. Anything above a whisper would have been too much effort.

"Me too," he said. Bryant slightly adjusted their bodies so that he could provide even deeper strokes. The new motion was all Aaliyah needed to send her over the edge in an orgasm so strong, she wasn't even sure she could unlock her legs from Bryant's waist.

A few minutes later, Bryant released his orgasm, grunting her name aloud as he did so. Aaliyah tried to unlock her legs so that Bryant wouldn't have to continue to hold her up, but he asked her to remain still, so she stayed put.

"That was..." Her words trailed off when she realized she couldn't find the right ones.

"I know," he said, placing a kiss on her forehead. His lips moved to her ears. "And although I know you probably want to talk about what happened tonight, I'd much rather spend tonight cherishing your amazing body and leave the talking for the drive to Chicago."

Aaliyah swallowed, her nerves getting the best of her. It wasn't his suggestion that had her nervous, but rather, the way he made it seem like there were still more things he wanted to do to her body. And damned if she didn't want that too.

The stress lines in Bryant's forehead that she'd seen throughout most of the trip were no longer present, and it brought a smile to her lips to think that she was his stress reliever.

Like her, Bryant had experienced a major loss when his mom had passed away. Aaliyah still hadn't felt like she'd recovered from the loss of her mother, but it had been a quick one. Granted, she still worried about Aunt Sarah, who was like a second mother to her, but Aaliyah hadn't been warned about her mother, so in a way, she felt as if it worked best for her personality type that her mom had been taken quick.

Aaliyah had learned that life was short and you had to live every moment to the fullest. Her mom had lived an amazing life, and Aaliyah knew that she wouldn't want her to spend her time grieving, but rather, she'd want Aaliyah to live.

There was so much more about Bryant that she wanted to know, but she could also see the toll that losing his mother took on him. He still hadn't recovered from that loss, and because of the disconnect he had with his father, Aaliyah wondered if there was anyone in his life who Bryant felt really understood him.

I could be that person, the voice inside her head said. "Okay," she voiced breathlessly. "I'm yours."

Bryant smiled slyly in a way she hadn't seen before. "You shouldn't have said that," he said, right before he dropped his lips to one of her nipples, causing her to squeal in pleasure.

Chapter 11

I'm yours. Bryant had been thinking about Aaliyah's words all morning, and even two hours into their drive back, he still couldn't get them out his mind.

She'd managed to stay up for the first hour of the ride, but thirty minutes ago, he'd told her she could get some sleep because he noticed her eyes kept closing. He could only smile when he heard her soft snores, knowing that he was the cause of her lack of sleep.

They'd only gotten three hours of shut-eye before Andy, the mechanic, had called and said that their rental was ready for pickup. They'd both walked in wearing huge smiles that Andy had observed.

He glanced at his sleeping beauty. *His.* Damn. After ten days, he already felt like she was his girlfriend, which made no sense because Bryant didn't do relationships. Being in a relationship with someone meant there was a possibility that you could fall in love with someone. Falling in love meant that there was a chance you could lose her. And if losing his mom had taught Bryant anything, it was that going through life was harder when you had to worry about others.

A dinging noise sounded in the car, indicating that they needed to get gas. "What the hell?" When they'd left the car at Andy's the other day, it had had almost a full tank. Bryant shook his head. He didn't even want to know what Andy or his cousin had done to the car to have it almost on E after two hours.

Pulling off at the next exit and making his way to a gas station, Bryant got out the car as quietly as possible so that he didn't wake up Aaliyah. He also cracked the window just in case, so she wouldn't get too hot and wake up while he pumped gas.

Once the gas was pumping, Bryant pulled out his phone to call Kendrick.

"Hey, man. Are you and Aaliyah almost here?"

"We have about three hours left to go," he said. "So we should be there soon."

"That's good to hear."

"Yeah." Bryant grew quiet.

"Is something wrong?" Kendrick asked.

Bryant glanced back at Aaliyah still sleeping in the passenger seat. "Yes and no."

"Let me guess," Kendrick said. "You've been spending so much time with Aaliyah that you're starting to develop feelings for her, which upsets you because you made a vow never to fall in love after your mom passed away."

"Uh." Bryant rubbed his fingers across his face. *Damn, Kendrick was perceptive.* "Yeah, pretty much."

"I called it," Kendrick said. Then he heard Kendrick yell to Nicole that she owed him fifty dollars.

"You betted on us?"

"Not 'us,' little cousin. You." Kendrick laughed. "I told Nicole that Aaliyah could make you fall for her in less than two weeks, but Nicole figured if you hadn't in two years, it would take a lot longer."

Bryant laughed. "I guess I understand that twisted logic."

"Whoa, who the hell are you?" Kendrick asked. "You laughed at what I said. Actually laughed. No speaking about how wrong it is to place a bet on you without you knowing? Or no long, drawn-out talk about why you're not falling for Aaliyah and I just got it wrong."

"I'm too exhausted to play any games," Bryant said.

"Damn, Bryant. Aaliyah really has made some grave improvements in your personality so far."

"Oh, you have jokes," Bryant said. "Well, I didn't call to shoot the shit with you. I just need some advice."

"Shoot."

Bryant sighed. "Man, I don't even know where to start. I'm already letting Aaliyah into my world and the crazy thing is, I like it."

"Then roll with it. Don't fight it. Aaliyah's a good one, and for years, I've thought that the two of you would make a good team."

"I feel you," Bryant said. "And I'm sure you're going to tease my ass for saying this next part, but is there any way you think the family won't pick up on our attraction?"

"Ha!" Kendrick was laughing so hard that Bryant heard Nicole asking him what was so funny. "Man, if you think the family isn't going to eat this shit up, then you have another thing coming. A lot of our Chicago cousins are married with kids. And since Nicole and I are married and already had our adorable baby girl, the family needs to focus on someone else in our generation. Your sister, Kylie, is out of the country, so you're up, little cousin."

Bryant frowned. "Yeah, I know. Better hearing you confirm it, though. Guess I have the next three hours to figure out how I'm going to handle this."

"Like I said. Just go with it."

Bryant and Kendrick spoke for a few more minutes before they hung up with each other. When Bryant got back into the car, the start of the engine rattled Aaliyah awake.

"Hey, sleepyhead." His eyes made their way from her bare legs to her green sundress, which was gathered around her thighs.

"Sorry I slept so long," she said, rubbing her beautiful brown eyes. "I guess I was more tired than I thought I would be."

"I'll take that as a compliment," he said with a smile. "Did you sleep well?"

"I slept great." She stretched and her dress rose even higher. Bryant didn't even pretend not to look. "Like what you see?"

He smiled, loving the sexy smile she was giving him. "Very much."

"Well, stop looking." She playfully slapped him on the arm. "You're driving, so you have to keep your eyes on the road."

"You're right. If we don't make it to the family picnic in time for the games, Kendrick will probably kill us because he hates losing and we're on his team."

Aaliyah clapped her hands together. "Family games? That sounds like so much fun."

"They usually are," Bryant said. "And competitive. None of us in California could make the picnic last year, but one of my family members sent us a video of one of the competitions, and it was much more competitive than I remember."

"I'm excited," Aaliyah said. "Sounds like a huge picnic if there are enough people for competitions."

"I'm not sure why they call it a picnic since it's more like an annual family reunion with the number of people who attend."

Aaliyah sat up straighter in her seat. "My family is small, so we don't really do competitions or things like that. I mean, I guess we could, but it would be over pretty quickly."

"How many people are in your family?" Bryant asked.

"It's my dad, my sister, her husband, my two nieces and Aunt Sarah."

"Any cousins?"

Aaliyah shook her head. "No, my mom was an only child, and my dad's only sibling is Aunt Sarah who never had any kids. I didn't get a chance to meet any of my grandparents since they'd passed before I was born. What about you? How many cousins do you have?"

"On my dad's side, I have about twelve cousins," Bryant said. "On my mom's side, I have about eight. Combined on both sides, I have about eighteen aunts and uncles, but that is including the married couples."

"Wow," Aaliyah said. "That's something else. My sister and I always wondered what it would be like to be from a big family, and surprisingly, my brother-in-law comes from a large family, so she got to experience it and she loves it."

"But you know what?" Bryant said. "I always wondered what it would be like to be from a small family."

"Very nosey." Aaliyah laughed. "I love my family, but there is no such thing as keeping anything a secret when we're so small and close-knit."

Bryant smiled. "I hate to break it to you, sweetheart, but that doesn't change for big families. If anything, it's even worse. Nothing stays secret for long, and instead of your news or secret traveling between five to ten people, it's thirty to forty."

"Oh come on," Aaliyah said. "Every secret gets passed around? Even secrets between you and Kendrick?"

"Okay, so maybe I'm exaggerating a bit. Those of us in California can probably keep our secrets a little more to ourselves than the folks in Chicago, but that's only because Kendrick and I don't tell our parents everything because, trust me, if we did, Kendrick's mom, Felicia, or my dad would have called everyone in a phone tree sort of style before we even knew our secret was out there."

"Felicia and Ben don't seem that fast."

"Two hours," Bryant said. "It took Aunt Felicia two hours to inform the members of the family that Kendrick and Nicole were expecting. Hell, Kendrick had told me, but I also got a call from my cousin Imani thirty minutes after he told me he'd informed his mom."

Aaliyah was laughing so hard, tears were coming out of her eyes. "That would explain why Nicole kept receiving gifts that were mailed to Bare Sophistication in LA. Kyra and I were trying to figure out why we received so many packages from Burrstones or other people from your family. I'm sure Kendrick told Nicole why, but I'm not sure I ever heard the reason because I had to fly back to Miami."

"Can never say a Burrstone isn't giving," Bryant said with a wink. He hadn't meant for it to sound dirty, but he knew it had when Aaliyah's cheeks began to flush.

"Do you want to talk about it?" he asked. "About last night?"

"And this morning," she said, her face flushing even more. "I'm not even sure how to approach this conversation." She sighed. "I didn't expect for it to happen, but I'm glad it did."

"I'm glad it did too." He moved his hand to her knee, his thumb twirling in circles over her skin. *She feels so soft.* And now he knew firsthand that she felt soft *everywhere.*

"Question time," she said. "If given the chance, do you want to have a repeat of last night?"

"Easy answer. Yes. Shooting the question back at you."

"Yes." She scooted as close to him as the car would allow. "Another question. Are you nervous to bring me around your family?"

Bryant briefly looked at her before bringing his eyes back to the road. "Truthfully, yes, I am. But it has nothing to do with you. You're amazing, but my family can be overwhelming."

Aaliyah shrugged. "We're friends, so I'm sure it will be fine."

"They'll know we're more than friends," he said. "My family knows me, and one look at me and they'll know you have my nose wide open."

"Do I?" Aaliyah's eyes widened. "Have your nose wide open?"

Shit. He hadn't meant to say so much, but since he'd already spilled the beans, he might as well be honest. "Yeah, you do. My family will notice how much I'm laughing and smiling. And even if they didn't, I've never had much of a poker face when I'm happy. I know you and Nicole call me Grumpy McGrumperson…"

"Oh right." Aaliyah placed her hands over her eyes. "Sorry about that."

"It's fine," he said. "And it's true. I often look grumpy. I wasn't always like that, but my family has pointed it out to me on more than one occasion that I'm different from the man I used to be. But my stoic face is hard to keep in place when—" Bryant stopped midsentence, once again sharing much more than he'd planned on sharing.

"When what?" Aaliyah asked, placing her hand over the one that was rubbing her knee. He'd practically said the whole thing aloud, so he had a feeling she already knew what he was going to say, but wanted to hear it anyway.

"When you're around, it's hard for me not to smile or laugh," he said. "So, I guess I'm saying all this as a warning that my family will pick up on us being more than friends."

"And are we?" she asked hopefully. "Are we more than friends?"

Bryant brought her hand to his mouth and placed a soft kiss on her knuckles. "I think we are," Bryant said. The smile that filled Aaliyah's face was one that he was sure he'd never forget no matter how old he was. When he'd gotten up this morning, he'd originally given himself a mental pep talk to make sure he didn't move too fast. Bryant didn't do relationships, but he did realize that he was a relationship guy. He wasn't the type to date multiple women or sleep around. For him, he needed an emotional connection, and if he were being honest with himself, he'd already felt an emotional connection with Aaliyah way before she'd joined them on the road trip.

So, yes, he was 100 percent sure that his family was going to pick up on the fact that he had feelings for Aaliyah, and he was pretty sure that no matter how excited she was to meet his family and have a good time, she wasn't prepared for the Burrstone clan. She wasn't prepared at all.

Chapter 12

"I'm the worst at names," Aaliyah whispered to Bryant.

"Just breathe," he said. "My guess is that this has Kendrick written all over it. When he first brought Nicole around the family, I set him up really badly."

"But Nicole and Kendrick were dating," Aaliyah said. "So at least they knew what to refer to each other as."

Aaliyah looked out at the huge backyard of people, and tried her best not to run back to the safety of the car. At first, Aaliyah had been excited to meet the Burrstones because she loved meeting new people, but everyone was looking at her as if she and Bryant were fresh meat.

Aunt Sarah and Ben hadn't arrived yet, so there wasn't a new couple to push the clan off on, and based off the snickers she saw coming from Kendrick and Nicole, she knew they wouldn't be any help.

"We can just say we're friends," Bryant whispered

right before a group of people approached them. "This first group is a few of my cousins and their kids. You make it past them, then you meet the aunts and uncles, followed by my grandfather last."

"Okay," Aaliyah said, suddenly struck by the fact that their roles had reversed. Instead of coaching Bryant in a social situation, he was coaching her. However, when it was actually showtime, she forgot everything she was about to say when people began pulling her into hugs.

"Are you cousin Bryant's girlfriend?" a little girl with pigtails asked. "You're pretty."

Aaliyah stumbled over her words. "Uh."

"Sorry about my sister," an older boy said. "My name is DJ and this nosy girl is my sister Shay."

"Oh, nice to meet you, DJ and Shay."

"Are you his girlfriend?" Shay asked again. *A persistent little thing.*

"We're friends, sweetie."

Shay raised her eyebrows. "Like boyfriend girlfriend?"

Aaliyah sighed. Out of all the explanations she'd considered giving on the ride over, she didn't think about the fact that the first person grilling her would be a girl who looked no older than five or six."

Aaliyah bent down to the little girl's ear. "Yes. Boyfriend and girlfriend. But it's our little secret, okay?"

Shay's eyes lit up. "Okay, I won't tell anyone."

"I'm Imani, the mom of those two," a woman said as she approached. Her daughter was a spitting image of her. "And this is my husband, Daman."

"Hello," Aaliyah said.

"Hey, girl," another voice said. "I'm Cyd and that's

my husband, Shawn, making his way over with our rug rats."

"Nice to meet you." She gave Cyd a quick hug before waving to a man who had one little girl holding on to one leg as he walked and a slightly older girl on his shoulders.

"We've actually met before," a woman said as she approached. "I'm Lex. We met at Summer and Aiden's wedding."

"Oh, right," Aaliyah said, snapping her fingers. "You're married to Summer's cousin Micah."

She smiled. "Sure am. Our kids are somewhere over there with their dad and cousins. You met Mya at the wedding too. She's here with her husband, Malik, Micah's brother, and their kids. And Summer's sisters, Winter and Autumn, their husbands and kids are here too."

"Wow, this really is a celebration," Aaliyah said with a laugh. "Sounds like everyone's here."

"Chicago is a big city, but we all tend to run into each other all the time," Lex said. "Plus, we're all family one way or another, so it's easier to celebrate together than have a lot of separate parties."

Introductions continued to be made for the next hour, and Aaliyah couldn't believe that Bryant had so much family. There had to be over one hundred family members and friends at this picnic.

When Aaliyah got a moment to herself, she glanced around for Bryant.

"Looking for your lover boy?" Nicole said as she approached.

Aaliyah swatted her on the shoulder. "I could hurt you. I've been here for over an hour, and you're just now coming to save me from all the questions from the cousins and aunts."

"Oh, sweetie, you were fine," Nicole said. "Everyone loves you, and bets are already being made on if you will get married in a few months this fall, or if you'll wait to next summer."

"Get married," Aaliyah gasped. "Bryant and I aren't even dating."

"Girlfriend, I hate to break it to you, but you failed the girlfriend test."

Aaliyah froze. "Girlfriend test? How did I fail a test I didn't know I was taking?"

Nicole shook her head. "You didn't see it coming because this was your first time meeting Shay. As soon as you told her that you were dating Bryant, she told her brother and the rest of her cousins, who all told their parents."

Aaliyah slapped her forehead. "How was I supposed to know she would tell everyone? When I tell my nieces something and ask them to keep it a secret between us, they usually listen."

"Welcome to the Burrstone clan," Nicole said with a smile. "Where the little kids are better at getting information than the adults are."

Aaliyah shook her head. "Bryant tried to warn me that the family could be overwhelming, but I thought he was exaggerating. Especially since I met a few of them already."

"They're a good group of people," Nicole said. "And you love meeting new people, so my guess is that you don't know where you and Bryant stand, so it's making meeting his family a lot more difficult than it otherwise would have been."

Aaliyah nodded to a nearby bench for her and Nicole to take a seat. It was the only section of the massive backyard that wasn't filled with people. "Is it that obvious?"

"Only because you're one of my best friends." Nicole nodded in the direction where Bryant was standing talking to Kendrick and his other cousins. "I've never seen that one smile so much in one day. What did you do to grumpy pants?"

Aaliyah laughed. "You probably won't believe me, but he hasn't been that grumpy to me throughout most of the road trip."

"That's not answering my question," Nicole said with a sly smile. "Come on, friend. What did you do?"

"Ugh." Aaliyah groaned and looked up to the sky. "We had sex."

"Oh my God," Nicole yelled.

"More than once."

Nicole's hand flew to her mouth. "You're lying."

"And it was the best sex I've ever had."

Nicole pretended to faint on the bench. "This is too much. I can't believe that Kendrick was right. He really did win the bet."

"Please tell me you're kidding," Aaliyah said. "You and Kendrick made a bet on when Bryant and I would have sex."

"Girl, no." Nicole waved her hands in the air. "We placed a bet on how long it would take you and Bryant to fall for each other."

"Oh."

"I placed the sex bet with Kyra, and it seems like I lost that bet too," Nicole said with a shrug. "I thought you'd hold out for longer, but homeboy must have been laying down the pipe if you let him hit it twice."

All Aaliyah could do was sigh. "Four times, Nic. I let him hit it four times in less than twenty-four hours."

Nicole's eyes widened. "Dayum." She turned to look in Bryant's direction and yelled, "Okay, Mr. Grumpy. I see you."

"Nicole!" Aaliyah placed her hand over her friend's mouth and smiled innocently when Bryant gave her a questioning look. "There are kids at this picnic. Your kid included."

"These kids have freaks for parents, so this isn't something they haven't heard," Nicole said. "And my baby girl is too young to understand, but when she gets older, she'll realize that her parents are freaks too."

Aaliyah laughed. "I'm never letting you babysit mine and Bryant's kids." At her words, Aaliyah stopped laughing immediately. *Mine and Bryant's kids? Did I just say that out loud?*

She looked at Nicole who had one eyebrow raised. "You already know I'm telling Kyra what you said, right?"

Aaliyah dropped her head into her hands. "Oh my gosh. The man rocks my world, and I'm already talking about having his kids. I must have lost my mind."

"It's those damn Burrstones," Nicole said. "After sex, Kendrick still has me agreeing to things that I never thought I would. Word of advice, never have serious conversations after sex. Your mind is all lust-filled and ready to give him the world for laying it on you just right."

Aaliyah looked over at Bryant, worried that even if

they hadn't had sex, he'd still have a stronger hold on her than anyone she'd ever dated in the past.

Aaliyah sighed. "This was never supposed to happen."

"You're in so much trouble then."

She chanced another glance at Bryant and found his eyes still on her. "Tell me something I don't know."

Nicole cleared her throat. "Is now a good time to tell you that one of the games Kendrick and I signed you and Bryant up for is The Nearlywed Game?"

Aaliyah's head flew toward Nicole. "Nic, please tell me you're joking! That game is for engaged couples!"

Nicole lifted her shoulders in defeat. "I know! I know! But a lot of the couples here are already married, so a lot of us started signing up those who were dating instead."

"But we're not even dating," Aaliyah said a little louder than she'd planned. "Since we aren't dating, we don't know much about one another. Not only are we going to look stupid in front of everyone, but I'm sure folks are going to wonder why we're together when we don't know much."

"You don't have to win," Nicole said. "Just get enough points to come in third or fourth place. There are six teams competing in that one, and the way the competition works is that they kick things off with that game so that folks can get to know the new couples. Then, it starts a series of minute-to-win-it games."

"So the entire kickoff for the competition starts with the game you signed Bryant and me up for," Aaliyah said. "This is going to be bad."

"Or," Nicole said hopefully, "you may be surprised by how well you know one another."

Aaliyah shook her head. "I doubt it."

* * *

An hour later, Aaliyah was in complete disbelief that she and Bryant were tied for first place with only one question left. She glanced over at Nicole in time to see her mouth *I told you so.*

"And for the win," Bryant's cousin Imani said. "Ladies, what is your partner's favorite color?"

Aaliyah looked at Bryant who smiled. Thanks to the questions game that she and Bryant had been playing for the past ten days, they knew a lot more about each other than she realized.

They both wrote their answers on their dry erase boards and kept them hidden until Imani asked them to reveal their answers.

"Okay, Ashley, what is Paul's favorite color?" Ashley turned her board over to reveal the color green.

"Paul," Imani said. "Reveal your answer." Paul turned over his board and had written the color orange.

"Orange," Ashley said. "Paul, I've never seen you wear orange. You didn't even like the fact that I'd chosen orange as our primary wedding color."

"Well, now that I see the color all the time, it's my favorite." The audience laughed at Bryant's cousin Ashley and her fiancé, Paul. Out of the six couples, they were the only engaged couple who were playing, which is why the audience was so surprised that Bryant and Aaliyah were in the running.

"Okay, you're up, Aaliyah," Imani said. "Please reveal Bryant's favorite color." Aaliyah glanced at Bryant as she turned over the board, smiling when she heard some of his family members whisper that they thought she got it wrong because his favorite color was blue.

"Is midnight gray even a color?" someone said.

"Man, I thought they would win, but his favorite color is blue, so I guess the couples in the lead will have to play another round."

"Bryant, your turn," Imani said. "Please reveal your answer."

Bryant was already smiling before he even turned over his board completely.

"Midnight gray," Imani announced. "It looks like Aaliyah got the answer right and is our winner for The Nearlywed Game."

The crowd was cheering them on, including Ashley and Paul. Ashley had even whispered in her ear that the family was predicting that she and Bryant were next up to get engaged.

As much as Aaliyah hated to admit it, it felt great being a part of a family like the Burrstone clan. Even the friends of the family who were in attendance were awesome. It was hard enough coming to the realization that she was falling for Bryant, but in reality, she was falling for his family just as hard.

"They're an obnoxious bunch, right?" Bryant asked, giving her a hug as they accepted the basket of goodies they'd won.

"They're pretty amazing," Aaliyah said. "I feel like I've known them for years, much less a few hours."

"Give it another day and you'll be itching to get rid of them."

"Not likely. Plus, you probably didn't hear the news, but one of your cousin's daughters managed to get me to say I'm your girlfriend, then went around the party and told everyone."

"You must be talking about Shay," Bryant said. "You can't tell Shay another thing. That little girl may only be six, but she's the family gossip. And don't let her corner you when she's with Cyd's two daughters and Lex's daughter. Together, the four of them will talk you out of twenty dollars."

Aaliyah laughed. "That's not too bad. Little girls should be spoiled."

"Nah." Bryant shook his head. "I meant twenty dollars each! Today, they talked me out of thirty dollars each. I swear, their moms used to pick on me when we were little and dress me up in wigs when we would put on plays for our parents. Imani, Cyd and Lex didn't stop talking me into doing stuff until I started getting bigger and taller than them. And now, the three of them have the nerve to each have daughters. And Cyd has the nerve to have two mini divas!"

"The nerve." Aaliyah was laughing hard, but didn't care if others were looking at them. "I could just imagine how adorable you looked in those wigs. Especially with these dimples." She pinched his cheeks.

"Keep pinching my cheeks and my mouth will be too sore to please you tonight."

She dropped her hands immediately. "Then consider that my last pinch because your mouth is too valuable to be out of commission tonight."

Bryant's laugh was even louder than Aaliyah's had been, but it wasn't his hearty chuckle that caught her off guard. It was the quick kiss he placed on her lips that didn't do anything but leave her wanting more. He must have sensed her need because he dipped his head to kiss her again, and this time he didn't make it a quick one.

Just as it did every time he kissed her, everyone around them faded to the background until there was no one but Aaliyah and Bryant. She would have kept on kissing him, embarrassment be damned, if she hadn't felt a little hand tug on her dress.

Aaliyah glanced down at her new little friend. "Yes, sweetie?"

"We have a few questions for you," Shay said. She waved her hands over to three other little girls. "These are my cousins. This is CeCe, short for Cydney Jr. And this is her little sister Meka."

"What's up," CeCe said, giving Aaliyah a head nod. "Welcome to the family." *Did she really just give me a head nod?* Bryant was right. These little girls were something else.

Meka just smiled and stayed close by her sister CeCe. Aaliyah waved at the little girls, searching for the other one and finding her near the dessert table.

"And the tiny one over there trying to get another cupcake is Lena." The little girl turned to Aaliyah and gave her a cupcake smile.

"You're all adorable," Aaliyah said.

"Yes we are," Shay said. "And we all have questions for you."

"Lena, come on," Meka shyly yelled to her cousin. Meka rushed over with two hands full of treats.

"I know. I know," Lena said. "I needed food."

CeCe gently grabbed Aaliyah's arm once all the girls were together. "Time to step into our office before our parents come and drag you off for the next competition." She pointed to a picnic table nearby.

Aaliyah looked to Bryant for help.

"Sorry, my hands are tied." He leaned down to Aaliyah's ear. "I told you that my cousins' daughters are little divas. And keep in mind that they already weaseled me out of money and probably a lot of others. You can answer their questions, but don't give in. They're good at what they do. Trust me."

Twenty minutes later, Aaliyah had answered all their questions, and was also out two tubes of lip gloss, some bubblegum and an extra pair of stud earrings she kept in her purse. As she made her way back to the adults in time for the rest of the competition, all she could do was laugh. Aaliyah was all about women empowerment and independence, and those girls had warmed their way into her heart. Much like everyone else she'd met today.

Chapter 13

"We were close," Kendrick said.

"We were. We'll get them next time."

Although Bryant's team had ultimately come in second in the competition, he still felt like he'd won, considering that Aaliyah was a huge hit with his family.

"We have to tell Lex and Mya that they have to stop bringing their husbands to the picnic," Kendrick said. "Either that, or ask them not to compete."

Bryant knew that Kendrick was joking, but he also understood his frustration. Bryant and Kendrick had always been on the winning team when it came to the Burrstone family games. However, when Lex and Mya married two of the Madden brothers, they found themselves up against stiff competition.

"So, you and Aaliyah have been the biggest topic today," Kendrick said. "I'm glad to see that you're just letting things fall the way they were meant to fall."

"I'm not sure I could stop this relationship from happening even if I wanted to," he said. Just as they always did, his eyes made their way around the backyard until they landed on Aaliyah.

"You admit that you're in a relationship now?" Kendrick asked. "Damn, you really are maturing a lot in a week."

"We haven't officially talked about it, but I feel like it's headed in that direction." Bryant turned his attention back to Kendrick. "Can you believe that my dad had her aunt ask her to come on this trip so that she could help me work on my people skills?"

Kendrick laughed. "Sounds like something Uncle Ben would do. By the way, where is he?"

"Their flight was delayed, so they may miss the picnic altogether. If they do land, it won't be until tonight."

Talking about his father reminded Bryant that they still needed to have a conversation about the beer. There was always tension between him and his dad, but he wasn't used to it lasting this long or being this intense.

"She has, you know."

Kendrick's voice broke into his thoughts. "She has what?"

"Aaliyah." Kendrick nodded his head in her direction. "Aaliyah has already changed the way you socialize. You're smiling more than I've seen you smile in years. I've been waiting to have you back, brother, and it seems like the beautiful Ms. Aaliyah Bai has brought your grumpy ass back from the dead."

All Bryant could do was laugh because he knew Kendrick's words were true. "Being around Aaliyah is making me feel things I've never felt before. You already know that we've known each other for years, and honestly, I've always had a thing for her. But actually getting to know her on a deeper level is intoxicating, but in the best way."

He looked toward her again, only this time, his eyes caught hers and she held his gaze. If Bryant hadn't been living it, he never would have guessed that he'd be lucky enough to get the attention of a woman like Aaliyah. She was kindhearted and generous. She cared about other people, and did her best to make people feel special. Important. He wasn't surprised that her favorite color was yellow because as cheesy as it sounded, she was a bright, shining light for him, and in more ways than one, she was forcing him to live again. To feel again. To want again.

"Yeah, you're done for," Kendrick said. "Do you want me to walk over to Aaliyah right now and ask her if she plans to hyphenate her last name or take the Burrstone name completely?"

"Shut up." Bryant pushed Kendrick in the shoulder. Kendrick pushed him back.

"Seriously, though, I'm happy for you, man." Kendrick pulled him into a quick hug.

"Thanks, man."

Someone cleared his throat behind him. "If you two are done hugging one another, can we get to some flag football?" Micah asked. "I told the guys that the two of you needed to have an emotional conversation, but the rest of them are getting bored watching this lovefest."

Kendrick and Bryant laughed. "We'll be right there," Kendrick said. As soon as Micah was out of earshot, the cousins dapped fists. "Ready to smoke these dudes?"

Bryant nodded his head. "I was born ready." Last year, the family had started playing flag football, but

Kendrick and Bryant hadn't been at the picnic, so the new members to their family didn't know that the pair was on a pickup team back in Cali. Bryant had even played football in high school and college.

"Let's do it," Kendrick said, "and show these Maddens a thing or two about the Burrstones."

"The surprises just keep on coming," Aaliyah said to herself as she watched Bryant get another touchdown in flag football. He was on fire. So was Kendrick.

They hadn't gotten a chance to talk about any sports in school, but it was clear to Aaliyah that he'd definitely played some football. She'd been sitting on the bench watching him for almost an hour, and she was mesmerized by the way he moved in the backyard.

"Quite a sight to see, isn't he?"

Aaliyah glanced to her right and noticed that Bryant's grandfather, Ed Burrstone, had joined her on the bench.

"He is," she said, assuming he was talking about Bryant. Actually, she knew he had to be talking about him because he was the best one on the field.

She glanced around the backyard and noticed that Nicole and the other wives were now a few feet away playing with the kids. *Wow, I was so engrossed in Bryant that I didn't even see them leave.* It shouldn't have been all that surprising since she hadn't been able to take her eyes off him for too long the entire day.

"It's nice to see my grandson smiling again," Ed said, turning to face her. "I guess I have you to thank for that, don't I?"

Aaliyah could feel her face flush. "I didn't do much," she said. "We've gotten to know each other during this road trip my aunt and I are taking with him and his dad, so we're becoming good friends."

"Friends? Is that what kids are calling it these days?"

Aaliyah laughed. "It's true. We are friends."

"I understand," Ed said. "His grandmother, Faith, and I were best friends until the day she passed away. Even now, she's still my best friend. We were married over fifty years, and before she passed, I was still learning things about her."

Aaliyah smiled. "I love that. I never got to meet my grandparents, so I don't know anyone who's been married that long."

"It takes hard work and dedication," Ed said. "And any of my kids and grandkids will tell you that Faith was the heart of the family. Everyone loved being around my wife. She was the person who made you feel welcome and loved. I was also the quiet one or a man of a few words as they say. But when Faith passed, I saw that my family needed me to be more vocal. They needed me to be there for them in a way that I wasn't ready to be."

"That must have been hard," Aaliyah said. "Your family needing you to fill a role that you never had to before. Especially when you needed to grieve."

"I agree," Ed said. "It was hard. For a while, I was a shell of the man I was when she was alive. I was going through the motions of living, but I wasn't actually living. As hard as it is for me to admit, I wanted to die the day Faith passed away. I even wanted to die years after Faith passed away. It was a rough time for all of us."

"How did you get past it?" Aaliyah asked. "When did you decide that life was worth living again?"

Ed looked to the sky. "One night, I had a dream

about Faith and me, and in the dream we were laughing and carrying on as if nothing had ever happened. The dream was so vivid, and it felt like I'd had my Faith back again." Ed smiled. "We were having a conversation in my dream, and I told Faith that I wanted to be with her and that I was tired of living on Earth without her beside me. And true to my Faith, she told me that I needed to suck it up because it wasn't time for me to go yet."

Ed was laughing, but Aaliyah noticed the unshed tears in the corners of his eyes. She dabbed her own eyes when she felt wetness on her cheeks.

Ed turned to face her. "Faith told me that my family needed me, and it wasn't time for me to go yet. She said that because she'd left the world so unexpectedly, our family needed me to leave the world a little slower."

"That's a powerful statement," Aaliyah said.

"That was my Faith," Ed said. "And when Faith spoke, we all listened. Of course, I didn't want to hear it. I wasn't in the right place to hear it. I'm a retired deacon, so I've always been a man of faith, but I hadn't wanted to hear Faith's words that night. I hadn't wanted those words to be true. Yet, when I woke up the next morning, I knew what I had to do. I knew that I had to live."

Aaliyah wiped a few more tears from her eyes. "The day my mom passed away, I felt like I had to live my life the best way I could, not just for her, but for my dad and sister."

"I had the pleasure of meeting your aunt Sarah when my son Ben brought her down here last year, and she had nothing but remarkable things to say about you. From what Sarah told me, you lost your mom when you were a teenager, and then not soon after, Sarah was diagnosed with breast cancer and you watched her go through that battle."

"I did," Aaliyah said. "She's been in remission for a while now, and I'm so happy for her because she had a rough few years."

"You're a strong woman," Ed said. "Sarah said you're the reason your family didn't fall apart, and now that I've met you in person, I can see that you're all those great things she told us and more."

"I'm just a normal person," Aaliyah said with a shrug. "And I did what I knew I had to do for my family. Everyone was so sad, that they needed someone to be that light. I never would have predicted that my family would have had to go through what we did, but when the time came, I knew I had to be their light. I felt it in my bones."

"Bryant has gotten a piece of your light," Ed said, turning toward his grandson, who was still playing flag football. "Bryant has always been the grandchild who was most like me, so I understood him even when some of the family didn't. When we lost his mother, it hit everyone hard, but it hit him the hardest. You see, Ben and Bryant have never seen eye to eye. Ben was always like Faith. Full of life. Charming. Can walk into a room and immediately become everyone's favorite person. Bryant was a lot like me. Quiet until you got to know him. Calculated. Blunt and honest. The two of them are like night and day, but Bryant's mother, Sherry, was able to help Ben and Bryant understand each other more. My son is a great man, but Sherry was the backbone of their family, and whenever Ben didn't understand Bryant, Sherry was able to help Ben get his son. And for some reason, my son was always a lot tougher on Bryant than he was on his daughter, Kylie. Still is.

"Sherry suffered for a long time, so from age twelve until he was in his upper twenties, Bryant watched his mom suffer on and off, the sickness taking a toll on Ben and Bryant's relationship. As Bryant got older, he had his ideas on what treatments may work best for his mom and if Ben didn't agree—which he often didn't— then Bryant's voice went unheard."

"That explains a lot," Aaliyah said. "My gut is telling me that if they had a heart-to-heart, they could start repairing their damaged relationship. They are both good men, and sometimes, we get so wrapped into how we feel about a certain situation, we fail to see life through someone else's eyes."

Ed smiled. "You're a smart woman. I agree. I think if they talked, and I mean truly talked, it would save them a world of hurt and misunderstanding in the future."

Aaliyah gave Bryant a smile as he made another touchdown. He was still doing so well, she'd lost count on how many points he'd scored.

"I'm so sorry to do this to you Aaliyah," Ed said.

Aaliyah turned back to Ed. "Do what?"

Ed sighed and reached over to touch her hand. "Aaliyah, my time on Earth is coming to an end. I'm dying of stage four lung cancer."

Aaliyah's hands flew to her mouth, and she couldn't stop the tears from falling down her cheeks. "Now, I don't want you crying over this old man. I've lived a full life, and I have this amazing family to show for it." Ed glanced around the backyard before facing Aaliyah again. "I haven't gotten to tell all the family yet. I told a couple of my kids, but they understand that I want to personally talk to all my kids and grandkids before the news got out. I'm too old to go through treatment, so I only have a few months left. And I know this is a lot to lay on you, but I'm hoping that when I'm able to tell Bryant this weekend, you will be there to comfort him because he isn't going to take it well."

Aaliyah nodded her head. "I will," she said between her tears. "Is that why you're telling me? So that I can make sure Bryant doesn't revert back to how he was when his mom passed away?"

"Yes, but also because your aunt told me that you could handle the news and be there for Kendrick and Nicole as well, since I know you're all so close."

Aaliyah's eyes widened. "You told Aunt Sarah?"

Ed nodded. "I know that your aunt and Ben told you and Bryant that their flight was delayed, but truthfully, they stopped by my house early this morning, and since Felicia was here already, I told them together. Ben didn't take the news too well, so Sarah took him back to the hotel. Felicia is with my other daughter, Hope, and they'll return to the picnic a little later."

Aaliyah hadn't even noticed that she hadn't seen Kendrick's mom, Felicia, until now.

"I also told my granddaughter Imani's husband, Daman," Ed said. "Imani is my oldest grandchild and the leader of the bunch. But Daman is her strength, and she will need his strength once I tell her this news."

"That makes sense," Aaliyah said. She was still so shocked, she didn't know what to say.

"I know this isn't fair to you," Ed said. "But as my wife, Faith, and I used to always tell our kids and grand-kids… Sometimes, we're born into certain roles and placed in this world for a purpose to serve others when they aren't able to serve themselves." Ed smiled. "Faith would have loved meeting you, and I know telling you was the right decision. I'm sorry if this news is too heavy for you, but I want you to know that no matter what happens between you and Bryant, I want to thank you for putting a smile back on my grandson's face. You have made this old man very happy because I didn't think I'd live to see the day when he smiled again the way he has been today."

Aaliyah leaned over to hug Ed, unable to do anything else but grieve for the old man who'd warmed his way into her heart so quickly.

"And one last thing," Ed said. "If my grandson proposes before I kick the bucket, can you have a quick wedding so I can be there to see it? I have money in a bet that says even though he's usually stoic with his emotions, he's going to cry when you both marry."

"Another bet," Aaliyah said with a laugh. "Who comes up with these things?"

Ed nodded his head to the kids. "This one came from my great-granddaughters. Those little divas have been coming up with the best bets ever since they learned how to talk."

As Ed continued to tell Aaliyah about the different types of bets that the girls had created, Aaliyah found herself hanging on every word. It seemed the patriarch of the family was an amazing storyteller, and before long, more family members had gathered to watch him speak.

Halfway through one of his stories, Aaliyah teared up, heartbroken because she didn't know if she'd ever get to hear one of his tales after this picnic. She and

Bryant weren't really dating, so the odds of seeing his family again in this type of setting were slim.

Yet, the more she listened to his powerful voice, the more grateful she felt from even having the opportunity to get to know him at all. *She'd left the world so unexpectedly, our family needed me to leave the world a little slower.* Ed's words from his dream echoed in her mind as the men finished the flag football game and the entire group started singing along with a song that Ed had taught his kids when they were little. They'd passed the song on to their kids, and even the family friends had taught their children the song.

The words of the song really resonated with Aaliyah because Ed sang of family, faith and friendship. Three things that built character in a person. "Always know your heritage and never forget that family comes first," they sang. Aaliyah found herself swaying to the words being sung by everyone around her. Ed reminded them that you must accept people as they were and there was no such word as "can't" because, through their resilient faith, they could never forget that God would guide them to overcome any obstacle and help them face adversity.

The song wasn't filled with words that rhymed, and every note that Ed sang had a meaningful purpose. Looking out at the Burrstone family, her heart ached at the news that they would soon learn, but although all the family didn't know yet, Aaliyah was glad that Ed was choosing to tell them about the cancer over the next couple days.

She recalled Ed saying that Faith was the heart of the family, but it was clear to her that Ed was the soul. His family and close friends needed a couple months to say their goodbyes. Bryant needed this time to say his goodbye.

Bryant. Her eyes caught his from the other side of the group where he was standing near Kendrick. Even from a short distance, she could read the emotion in his eyes. They held promise and hope, but she wasn't sure what he was promising or hoping for, nor had she come to terms with how deeply she was already falling for him. *Goodness, I hope it's a promise for the future. I hope he can see us together past this moment.* The feeling crept over her faster than she'd realized, the emotion from learning about Ed's sickness mingling with the feelings she had for Bryant that were growing stronger by the second.

Regardless if Bryant wanted to enter a relationship with her or not, she was going to keep the promise she'd made to Ed and be there for Bryant any way that she could. Aaliyah never broke her promise. Especially one to a man as special as Ed.

Chapter 14

"Any idea what Grandpa wants to talk to us about?" Bryant asked the room.

"Nope," Kendrick said.

"No idea," Imani said.

"I wish I knew," Cyd said.

Lex shook her head. "Last time he wanted to meet with Micah and me, it was because Lena had eaten most of the cake he'd ordered from that bakery he loves." The room laughed at Lena's obsession with food. She'd definitely gotten that from Lex.

His grandfather had asked the five of them to gather in his study after the picnic had ended, and they'd been waiting there for a while. He'd also asked that they bring their significant others, and told Bryant to make sure he'd brought along Aaliyah.

Bryant noticed that Aaliyah and Daman shared a

knowing look. *Hmm, I wonder what that's about.* He was about to ask them if they had heard what the meeting was needed for, when his grandfather walked into the room.

"Thank you for joining me," Ed said, taking a seat at his desk. "Our family has never beat around the bush, so I'll jump right into it. You aren't going to like what I have to say, but I don't have an easy way to tell you."

"I don't like the way this is headed," Cyd said.

"Me neither," Imani said. Bryant looked her way and noticed her eyes were already tearing up. She looked to her husband, Daman, who nodded his head, but instead of her crying more, she covered her face.

"I have stage four lung cancer," Ed said. "I'm dying, and because of my age, I'm not doing treatment."

The entire room grew quiet, but it didn't take long for Bryant to begin to hear sobs. His grandfather was still talking, but the rest all sounded like things he'd heard before.

I can't believe this. They were all close to their grandfather, but it was no secret that Bryant and Ed had the tightest relationship among the grandchildren. Bryant felt a hand grasp his shoulder, and he knew it was Kendrick's. It didn't take long for him to feel several eyes on him as his cousins directed their attention to him, even through their tears.

He was glad his sister was living her life, but he could really use her here with him now. She was the only one who'd gone through what he'd gone through. She was the only grandkid in the room who'd lost a parent to cancer. Although he would never wish that type of pain on anyone, let alone another family member, they didn't know how it felt to have someone in your family who you are so close to say that they are dying from a disease that took your mom. A different type of cancer, but cancer, nonetheless.

"How long?" Bryant asked his grandfather. "How long do we have with you?"

Ed sighed. "Two months max."

Bryant cringed. His mom had been able to last longer than doctors had ever predicted, but she'd been a lot younger than his grandfather.

"All your parents and aunts and uncles know, and I'm telling the rest of the grandkids tomorrow morning," Ed said. "Some of them couldn't stay later, and I wanted to tell you all together."

They were the oldest of the grandkids, so it made sense. Bryant was still wrapped up in his feelings when Imani rose from her seat and went over to hug her grandfather.

Cyd and Lex were next, the three of them wrapping their arms around Bryant's grandfather the way they used to when they were younger. Kendrick walked over next and placed his arms around the girls before they all turned to look at Bryant.

I can't. Or rather, he didn't want to. He was angry, even though it felt wrong. He was angry that cancer was taking another person from his life, and he was even more frustrated that, once again, he had a countdown to spend time with a loved one. A loved one who lived a four-hour flight away from him.

"Go over there," Aaliyah whispered to him. He hadn't even known when she'd gotten that close. "You can't repeat moments like this, so don't waste them being mad at the circumstances. Find a way to accept it enough to enjoy this precious time."

He looked to her, her tear-filled eyes reinforcing her words. *He told her beforehand.* He didn't even have to ask her because he could tell by the look in her eyes that she'd known about this already.

His mind flashed to earlier that day when he'd been playing flag football and he'd looked over to Aaliyah talking to his grandfather, and had thought Aaliyah was getting emotional over something kind he'd said, but never anything like this.

Aaliyah was one of those people who hurt when others hurt and showed empathy when others would fail to emotionally relate.

She's right. You need to cherish this time. Bryant stood from his seat and walked over to finish the circle that his cousins had built around his grandfather.

"Life is short," Ed said. "Never forget that the people in this room will have your back no matter what. Things won't always be easy, and there will be days when you want to give up. But your grandmother Faith and I didn't raise any quitters, so I want each of you to wake up every morning and fight with everything you've got. The Burrstones are a strong and mighty bunch, and whenever you get too sad when you think about me, remember that I'm in heaven dancing with the love of my life…your grandmother Faith. I've missed her for a long time, and although I hate to leave you all, I can't wait to be with her again."

Everyone in the room was emotional, but Bryant refused to cry. Not here. Not now. He knew if he cried now, he wouldn't be able to stop. For years, he'd held back from feeling so many emotions, but ever since the start of the road trip, his feelings had slapped him across the face whether they concerned Aaliyah, his relationship with his dad, memories of his mother, or news about his grandfather.

"Embrace it."

Bryant lifted his head to see who his grandfather was speaking to and noticed he was talking to him. "When you're ready, embrace it."

Bryant wasn't sure if he meant embrace the feelings he had for Aaliyah or embrace the pain he was suffering for a loss that hadn't yet happened. Knowing his grandfather, Bryant concluded Ed Burrstone was probably talking about both.

"Call me if you need anything," Bryant said to Aaliyah as he walked to the door of their hotel room before going to see his father. As late as it was, Bryant knew he couldn't get a good night's sleep until he talked to his dad, and luckily, he'd texted that he was still up.

Bryant's sister, Kylie, had texted him an hour ago and said that Ben had told her the news and she was heartbroken by it. She planned to go to Chicago sometime this month to spend some time with Ed.

As for Bryant, he was sad about his grandfather but glad Aaliyah had been there when he'd heard the news. When they'd arrived at the hotel twenty minutes ago, Bryant had asked her if she would mind if they shared a room, and she'd agreed. He didn't want to be alone tonight, and he was grateful that he had her with him on this trip. They'd only checked in after the picnic, having gone straight to the big family celebration as soon as they'd come into town.

When Bryant reached his dad's hotel room, he knocked. His dad answered right away.

The moment Bryant saw his father, he pulled him in for a hug. "I'm so sorry to hear about Grandpa."

"Thanks, son," Ben said. "I've been a mess all day."

"I figured when Aaliyah told me Sarah had to take you back to the hotel."

"Dad hadn't gotten a chance to tell all the kids, and Felicia and I didn't take it well, so your aunt Hope took Felicia to her place and Sarah took care of me."

"I know it's late, but the hotel has a courtyard outside. Do you want to take a walk?" Bryant asked.

"That would be good."

They walked to the courtyard in silence, but Bryant could already tell that some of the tension started misting away. Instead, it was replaced by this cloud of sadness.

"I can't believe we're going through this again," Ben said.

Bryant shook his head. "Me neither. It almost feels like a nightmare that I can't wake up from."

"Your grandfather is a strong man, but you and I both know how cancer can take a toll on your body."

"All the cousins had their eyes glued to me when we were hanging out with Grandpa today," Bryant said. "It was as if they thought I may break if they took their eyes off me for one second."

"They just care about you, that's all. Your aunts and uncles who'd already spoken to Dad came by the hotel after they left the picnic to check on me. The scene was probably similar to what you experienced."

"I was angry when Grandpa first told us," Bryant said. "But Aaliyah convinced me to get over my anger and cherish the moment I had with everyone tonight."

"Aaliyah is a pretty special woman," Ben said.

"Sarah told me that Dad told Aaliyah the news earlier today so that she could be there for you."

Bryant nodded his head. "He did. And he was right to do so. Since she'd known what Grandpa was going to say, she was right by my side."

Ben smiled. "Son, I never thought I'd see the day when you openly gave your heart to a woman."

Bryant laughed. "Me neither." There was no point in denying it, especially to his dad. There hadn't been enough good news in their lives, so if talking about Bryant's feelings for Aaliyah made him smile, he'd take it.

"She's a keeper," Ben said. "And she's a strong woman. Aaliyah has experienced a lot of heartache, so she understands that part of you, yet, her character complements yours."

"She doesn't judge me either," Bryant said. "You know I'm not the easiest person to get to know, but Aaliyah doesn't make me feel strange or misunderstood. Instead, she understands me and if she doesn't, she tries to."

"I'm glad to hear that, son." Ben's face grew serious. "And I know this is a long time coming, but I want to apologize for failing you as a father."

Bryant shook his head. "Dad, you didn't fail me as a father. We just never understood each other. Mom is what connected us, but toward the end of her sickness, you weren't there. You'd checked out on her and me, but for some reason, you were there for Kylie." He knew this might be hard for his father to hear, but Bryant felt they'd never be close unless he was brutally honest.

Ben sighed. "I know I wasn't there for you, but I don't think you understood how it was for your mom and me during those final months. I have a feeling that you think certain things happened that I need to clear up."

Bryant knew exactly what his father was talking about, but the last thing he wanted to do was hash out this particular issue on the same day his grandfather gave them the terrible news.

"Not today, Dad," Bryant said. "I know we have a lot to work out, but I wanted to talk to you because getting that news about Grandpa shook me tonight, and I knew I couldn't sleep without seeing you."

Ben nodded his head. "Understood. I needed to see you too, son." He pulled Bryant in for a quick hug. "In the hotel room earlier, a bunch of us were talking about how many quarters we've gotten from Dad over the years."

Bryant laughed. "You know, Kylie keeps her quarters from Grandpa in a jar. She's been doing that ever since we were kids."

"Your grandfather was the only man I knew who gave you a quarter every time he heard good news."

"Sure did," Bryant said. "And it didn't matter who you were, if you had accomplished anything that you told him about, he gave you a quarter. I remember he gave me a quarter the first time I mowed the lawn by myself."

"When I'd introduced Dad to your mom, she'd just taken a chance on trying a new haircut, and somehow, she and Dad got on the subject and that's how she got her first quarter."

"Such an Ed Burrstone thing to do," Bryant said.

Ben smiled. "Yep. Such an Ed Burrstone thing to do."

Bryant and Ben spent the next hour exchanging stories about Ed, neither of them in a hurry to end the night but knowing that they needed to. By the time Bryant got back to the hotel room, he was still smiling after spending the type of night with his dad that he'd often hoped for, but never thought would happen.

Bryant took a quick shower and threw on his shorts before climbing into bed, careful not to wake Aaliyah.

"How did it go?" she asked, waking up anyway.

"Sorry, I wasn't trying to wake you." He scooted closer to her.

"You didn't," she said. "I kept waking up every half hour or so to see if you made it back, then I heard the shower going."

"Our talk went well," Bryant said. "We didn't talk business or anything. We just shared stories about Grandpa." He smiled. "It was the first time my dad and I have had casual conversation in years. I didn't realize how much I missed it."

"Maybe you should tell him how much you missed it," Aaliyah said, curling up underneath his arm.

"Maybe I will." Bryant bent his head down to place a kiss on her lips as he pulled her even closer to him.

"I have to tell you," Bryant said. "Today, that green dress you were wearing was doing crazy things to my body and had me thinking even crazier things."

"Like what?" Aaliyah asked, biting her bottom lip.

"Like pulling you into a bush in the backyard and stripping you naked, picnic be damned."

"That wouldn't have been good," Aaliyah said with a laugh. "There were too many kids in attendance playing in and out of those bushes, and there was no way I wanted all those parents angry at us. Plus, the little divas were following us around during most of the party, so they would have caught us."

"I told you the little divas are something else," Bry-

ant said. "When we were all singing with Grandpa tonight, one of them tugged my shirt and told me that I
was being a bad boyfriend for watching you from a distance and not standing next to you."

"That's because they are too young to understand the
art of flirting," Aaliyah said with a sly smile. "Sometimes, flirting from across the room is the best kind
of foreplay."

Bryant's eyes darkened. "There's some other type of
foreplay that I think would be much more enjoyable."

"Oh really?" Aaliyah moved over on the bed to strad-
dle Bryant. "Care to show me what you mean?"

Bryant lifted her tank over her head. "With pleasure." And boy, did he deliver pleasure over and over
and over…

Chapter 15

"This place is amazing," Aaliyah said as they made it to the popular rooftop lounge. Autumn and her husband, Ajay, were the owners of a chain of bars and lounges, with the rooftop bar being their newest addition to one of their Chicago nightclubs.

"All of Ajay and Autumn's places are amazing," Bryant said. "But this place definitely takes the cake."

That morning, Aaliyah had gotten a call from Autumn, who'd invited them to a photo shoot that she and Winter had decided to have for Bare Sophistication at the rooftop lounge. So tonight, the rooftop was closed to the public for the shoot, open only to family and friends.

Although they'd hired a photographer earlier, Autumn had asked Aaliyah if she could come to the lounge and take pictures of the party for their website and social media pages.

Originally, Aaliyah and Bryant were supposed to be on the road headed to a couple of meetings Ben and Bryant had in St. Louis, but Ben had told Bryant that he could handle the meetings so that Bryant and Aaliyah could enjoy another night in Chicago.

"Aaliyah, Bryant. So glad you could make it," Autumn said when they arrived.

"Thanks for telling me about it," Aaliyah said. "You know I'm happy to do anything for my Bare Sophistication ladies." And she was always happy to be behind her camera. She'd already gotten some amazing photos on this trip, and felt inspired to take more.

"And you know we love you for it," Autumn said. "Winter is around here somewhere, but people are starting to trickle in, so go ahead and start working your magic. But we don't want you taking photos all night, so find time to enjoy yourself."

"Okay, I will." When some of Bryant's cousins and their husbands arrived, Aaliyah got to work. She took a healthy amount of photos, but even before she'd gone through some of her shots, she knew she'd taken entirely too many of Bryant.

She really tried to focus on some of the others, but she couldn't. The camera loved him. Like now, he was talking to Kendrick, standing close to the rail that offered unrestricted views of the Chicago skyline. He was wearing a dark blue suit and holding a glass of wine like he had been all night, but he just looked damn good.

"That's it," she said, surfing through some of the latest shots she'd taken of Bryant and others. Although she'd been enjoying her time with Bryant, she hadn't forgotten that she had only five days to turn in her portfolio for the Jacques Simian internship.

"Yes, this is perfect." Thanks to the road trip, Aaliyah had a lot of different shots of wine bottles, wineglasses, liquor bottles, beer glasses and beer bottles. "They want the portfolio to be of food or product," Aaliyah said aloud. "But what if I did something different and kept wine, liquor or beer as the main focal point, but used people as props to the product."

It was a bit unconventional, but it may just be the edge she needed to set her apart from the other nine finalists. They'd seen enough of her other work, so it was time to wow them with something different.

"Do you always talk to yourself, beautiful?" Bryant's smooth, deep voice washed over her skin and caused her to shiver.

"I was working out the details of my portfolio," she said. "I just figured out what types of photos I'm submitting."

"That's good to hear." He brought his lips to her ear. "How much longer do you have to take photos because I must say, seeing you walk around the party in this tight black dress and black heels snapping pictures is giving me all types of wicked ideas."

"Behave," Aaliyah said. "People are watching."

"I don't care," Bryant said. "Everyone saw me kiss you at the party yesterday, and all night they've been watching me watch you."

Aaliyah let out a soft moan when he placed a kiss on the side of her neck. "It's insane that I want you inside me when we just had sex this morning."

"Are you ready to go?" he asked.

"Yep." Aaliyah's answer was immediate. "Let me just tell Autumn and Winter that I'm leaving."

They made quick work at saying their goodbyes, and Aaliyah didn't miss the knowing look that passed between Nicole and Kendrick. When they reached the elevator, a few of Autumn and Ajay's friends were leaving and the elevator was taking a while.

"Stairs," Aaliyah suggested.

Bryant nodded. "Stairs." They were barely through the door that led to the stairs, before Bryant was pulling her into a passionate embrace and kissing her senseless. By now, they knew how each other liked to kiss. Knew what licks and sucks made the other moan. Knew which lust-filled buttons to push to make the other person beg them for more.

"We got to get off these stairs," Bryant said. They took two flights before he pulled open a door to what they thought was the second floor of the club, but was actually a floor that appeared to be under construction.

Words weren't needed as they resumed kissing, using one of the steel beams and the wall for support. Aaliyah groaned in frustration when Bryant broke the kiss, until she felt him pulling down her panties and placing soft kisses on her thighs. When he lifted one of her legs and placed it over his shoulder, she let him, until he reached to lift her other leg.

"I don't want you to hurt yourself," Aaliyah said. "I don't need any foreplay."

"But I do," Bryant said, ignoring her plea. Suddenly, both her feet were off the ground and Bryant was gripping her thighs as he dived his tongue into her sweet center.

She should be used to this move by now, but she wasn't. Every moment with Bryant felt better than the last, and the only thought on her mind, when she released an orgasm so strong she was sure her voice shook the room, was that there was no way he was stopping her from returning the favor.

* * *

Bryant let Aaliyah back down, but her feet were barely on the floor before she dropped into a squatting position and undid his pants. Within seconds, she'd sprung him free and was already sliding him in between her sexy lips.

"Shit." Bryant gripped the beam and the wall, the sight of Aaliyah squatting and sucking him at the same time bringing another fantasy to life that he hadn't known he'd had.

"Aaliyah, it's time," he said as a warning, but she didn't move. He'd said those words before, so she knew they meant that he had to get inside her, or else he was going to come from the motions of her mouth. However, one look at the sly smile on her face before she brought him even farther into her mouth and he knew she was purposely not listening to him.

Minutes later, his orgasm hit him so hard that he hadn't been prepared for the strength of it. He thought that Aaliyah was going to release him from her mouth, but instead, she swallowed every drop, the suction of her mouth easily going down as the most amazing thing he'd ever felt—apart from being inside her.

The moment she stood up, they shared a passionate kiss that went on for minutes, only breaking apart for Bryant to quickly protect them before lifting her so she could wrap her legs around his waist. From there, he entered her in one clean stroke causing them both to moan in pleasure at the perfect fit.

Bryant's strokes were slow and long, completely opposite what they had been this morning. Even though they weren't in the most comfortable of circumstances, he wanted to take his time with Aaliyah tonight. He wanted to build that passion to a point where they couldn't stand it anymore.

So much had happened since they'd arrived in Chicago, but the one thing that had been consistent was the way Aaliyah had supported him and his family. There weren't too many women like Aaliyah, and he knew the value of having someone like her by his side.

"I'm coming," she said, voicing those magic words he loved to hear. Two minutes later, Aaliyah's passionate cries filled the room, her legs squeezing him even tighter.

Bryant followed soon after, his groans sounding a lot less poetic than Aaliyah's, but relaying the same sentiment. They didn't move until their breathing evened out.

"That was… You know what. I don't have words for what that was," Aaliyah said.

"I know the feeling." Bryant gave her a kiss. "As badly as I want to go for round two, we should probably pick things back up at the hotel."

"Good idea." Aaliyah bent down to grab her panties and stuck them in her purse, while Bryant adjusted his suit.

"Stairs or elevator?" he asked.

"Elevator," she said. "My legs feel like Jell-O."

They were still laughing and adjusting their clothes when the elevator stopped on their floor. One look at the people in the elevator, and Bryant wished they'd just taken the stairs.

"Y'all just had sex, didn't you?" Nicole asked.

"They had to," Kendrick said. "Their clothes are disheveled."

"I guess I know why my security manager called

me," Ajay said. He took out his walkie-talkie. "False alarm. Couple on the third floor has been detained."

"I told Ajay it was the two of you," Nicole said with a laugh.

"Give them a break," Autumn said. "Ajay and I have had our fair share of public sex." She looked to Ajay and winked. The look he shot back to his wife was so heated, Bryant looked away to give them privacy.

"Oh crap," Aaliyah said. "Does that mean there were cameras on this floor?"

Ajay laughed. "Yeah, but don't worry. They couldn't make out what you were doing, but had a guess. I'll erase the footage myself. The only reason I decided to check it out instead of a member of my team was because Nicole insisted that it was probably the two of you."

"You can thank me later," Nicole said.

Bryant knew he should feel guiltier about getting caught, but at the moment, the only thing on his mind was getting Aaliyah back to their hotel room so they could finish what they'd started.

Chapter 16

"We're almost there," Bryant said as they began driving up the side of a mountain toward a large wooden resort building. What started off as one extra night in Chicago had turned into two when Bryant's grandfather had asked them to stop over for a last-minute brunch some of his kids had decided to plan for him.

Bryant had asked Aaliyah if it was okay for them to stay an extra day, and she'd agreed. Deep down, she'd hoped that Bryant had realized that she was already growing attached to his family, and she wouldn't have had it any other way.

Since they'd stayed an extra night in Chicago and missed the meetings in St. Louis, Bryant and Aaliyah had decided to return their rental and fly into Denver, Colorado, instead.

Now, they were in another rental two hours shy of

the time Ben and Bryant had to meet with one of their partners in a small town right outside Aspen.

"You're awfully quiet," Bryant said. "Is everything okay? Was the weekend too heavy for you?"

"Not at all," Aaliyah said. "I absolutely loved hanging out with your family, and meeting your grandpa was the best part."

Bryant smiled. "He means everything to me. In case you didn't realize it, our family is female heavy, so there are more women than men. Kendrick and I are only two of four grandsons. The other eight grandkids are female. Some of our family isn't as close as the people you were around at the picnic, including the other two grandsons. Out of all the grandkids, I'm the most like my grandfather."

"He said the same thing," Aaliyah said with a smile. "He said you process things the way he does, and you're also hard to read. He said you take things much deeper than you let on, and sometimes, you're a man of a few words, but your family sees a different side of you."

Bryant smiled. "I'm glad you got a chance to talk to him." He briefly took his eyes off the road to look at her. "My grandmother would have loved you. So would my mom."

"My mom would have loved you too," Aaliyah said. "Aunt Sarah surely does."

Bryant's smile slightly faltered. "Sarah is a really great woman. I'm glad she was there for my dad this weekend."

It was at the tip of her tongue to ask Bryant why it seemed to pain him when he had to pay her aunt a compliment. She'd broached this topic before but gotten vague answers, so she'd decided it was off-limits.

For now, at least. She also didn't want to distract him too much before his meeting.

"Here we are," Bryant said, pulling up to the lodge.

"It's beautiful," she said, stepping out the car. "You said your client owns this place?"

"Yes, he does." Bryant helped the bellboy get their bags, and handed the keys to the valet. "He owns five resorts in Colorado, and at each resort, our wine is the only one he carries. Jack is also one of the first clients I landed when my dad named me vice president, so our relationship with him is newer than some of the others the business has cultivated. But I'm really proud of this partnership."

"Are you going to talk him into doing a trial run with your beers like you had Seth do in Virginia?"

Bryant shrugged. "I would love to, but after my dad just got that news about my grandfather, I don't want to rock the boat too much."

"I understand," Aaliyah said. "I'd probably feel the same way. I'm not saying you should catch him off guard, but maybe right after we check in, you should pull him aside to talk to him before your meeting."

"Okay," he said. "I'll do that."

As luck would have it, though, Bryant wasn't able to make contact with his father before the meeting, so there was no chance to speak to Ben about the beer trial.

"Thank you for meeting with us," Bryant said, taking a seat next to Jack in a comfortable conference room on the lodge's first floor. Ben sat on Bryant's other side, and Jack's business partner and cousin, Sam, was present as well.

"It's great to meet with Burrstone Winery and Distillery," Jack said. "Your wine is doing wonderfully at our locations."

"Better than we ever could have imagined," Sam said. "We are opening up our first two Nevada locations next year, and we were hoping that we could continue our partnership with Burrstone's at those locations, as well."

"We'd love that," Bryant said. "You're a valued client of ours, and our aim is to help and support you as you grow your business. So, anything we can do to assist with the opening, please let us know. We could even be present for the grand opening of the Nevada stores."

Jack smiled. "This is why we love Burrstone's. Always willing to lend a helping hand."

"We value family business," Bryant said. He clutched his father's shoulder. "My father wouldn't have gotten where he is today if it weren't for great partnerships similar to this one, so anything we can do for the cause, we will."

Bryant glanced at his dad, noting a newfound look of appreciation and pride that he hadn't seen in his father's eyes in a long time. The feeling overwhelmed him more than he thought it would.

"When you're ready for us to draw up an additional contract, please reach back out to me," Bryant said.

"We will," Jack said. Over the next thirty minutes, they discussed other orders of business, and eventually, the conversation grew close to an end.

"I almost forgot," Jack said, when they were all standing to leave. "Rumor has it that Burrstone's introduced some custom beer flavors when you were at the wine and cheese festival in Virginia, and everyone was talking about it at a two-day wine convention I was at this weekend."

Bryant's eyes widened. "Really? Industry professionals were talking about beer?"

"So they weren't lying," Jack said. "Burrstone really is diving into the beer business? How can we get a hold of a few cases to test it out in our lodges?"

Bryant looked to Ben, who was wearing an unreadable expression on his face. Thinking quick on his feet, Bryant focused solely on Jack.

"I'll be happy to supply you with some cases and sample bottles when I get back to the office in a couple days," Bryant said. "The rumors were true. Burrstone's is diving into the brewery business, but we're taking things slow since it's a new market for us."

"We'll support you any way we can," Jack said. As they left the room, the only person who didn't seem happy about the direction the conversation had taken was Ben. Bryant knew when his father wore a certain look of disappointment, it was best to leave him alone for a while and revisit the topic later.

"Great meeting," Ben said before he walked toward the elevators.

"Thanks," Bryant said to Ben's retreating back. And just like that, the progress they'd made seemed nonexistent. There was only one person who could make Bryant feel better. Only one person he wanted to see.

"Do you want to talk about it?" Aaliyah asked as they continued to hike up the narrow path on the mountain beside the lodge. Bryant didn't respond. "I thought you didn't like hiking?"

"I don't mind it," Bryant said. They'd been hiking

for almost a half hour, and had finally reached a scenic overlook that opened to a breathtaking view of the valley below.

"Wow," Aaliyah said, taking a seat on the wooden bench positioned in the perfect spot to get an uninhibited view of the scenery. "Care to join me?"

Bryant looked from her to the bench as if he didn't want to sit down, but he did anyway. "I'm sorry I'm in such a bad mood," he said. "I just don't understand my dad sometimes."

"How did the meeting go?" she asked. He'd not said much, and she hadn't pressed him.

"Fine. My dad was even impressed by how well I was handling the meeting, until the client brought up the fact that he'd heard that Burrstone's was dabbling into the brewery business when he went to a wine convention over the weekend. Some folks in the industry must have attended the event in Virginia. Then he asked if he could test out some of the beers in their lodges."

"That's awesome," Aaliyah said. "Your beers did so well in Virginia that I'm not surprised people were already talking about them."

"All of it was great to hear," Bryant said. "But my dad looked so disappointed when I agreed."

"I know you said your dad tried to make the brewery idea work in the past and it failed, but he doesn't strike me as the type of man who'd be upset if his son accomplished what he couldn't."

"He isn't that type," Bryant said. "Quite the opposite. My dad loves seeing my sister and me succeed where he couldn't. That's why this issue is really bothering me. I don't understand why he's so hard on me when it comes to this business. I've already proved to him that I can handle it."

"Maybe I should have Aunt Sarah talk to him," Aaliyah said. "Your grandfather told me that he talks to Aunt Sarah when he needs to get through to Ben. Maybe you could talk to my aunt about your dad."

Bryant frowned. "Yeah, maybe."

Aaliyah tried to ignore it, but couldn't. "What is your issue with my aunt?" Aaliyah said. "I asked you before and you said that you liked her, but that she started dating your dad during a time when yours and Ben's relationship was strained. I got the sense you weren't telling me the whole story, and since you frown when I mention them sometimes, I know I'm right."

Bryant sighed. "I really do like Sarah as a person," he said. "And I know that the main issue I have with their relationship is on my dad's part."

"Anyone can tell they're in love," Aaliyah said. "Don't you want him to be happy?"

"Of course I do," Bryant said. "I guess I just can't get over how I first met Sarah. I thought I could get over it, but I guess I haven't."

"They've been together for a little over two years already," Aaliyah said. "I would think you would have accepted their relationship by now." She was trying not to get upset, but she was very protective of her aunt. She was so wrapped up in her own frustration that she almost missed what Bryant had said.

"Can you repeat that?" she asked.

Bryant held her gaze. "They've been together for more than two years," Bryant said. "They've been together for five years."

Aaliyah did the math. "No, they haven't. We'd just

opened the Bare Sophistication location in LA when Aunt Sarah told me that she and Ben and been dating for a few months. My aunt hasn't even lived in LA for that long."

"She used to come to LA a lot," Bryant said. "Didn't Sarah come there for treatment years ago?"

"Yeah, she did." Aaliyah thought back to Aunt Sarah's battle with breast cancer.

"Sarah was one of the counselors for an LA support group for families who had loved ones battling cancer," Bryant said. "Our family was assigned to her."

"I remember her telling me about the support group," Aaliyah said. "I guess I forgot how many times she went to LA because, for a while, she didn't tell our family where she was going because she felt like we were being too protective over her. She'd been through hell and back, so we didn't want her flying all over the place."

"She was one of the best family counselors we'd had," Bryant said. "Kylie and I had gotten close to her, and we appreciated her point of view since she was a survivor. In my heart, I knew my mom wouldn't survive her last battle because the cancer came back with a vengeance after being dormant for eight years, but I still loved talking to Sarah. She was an outlet for my sister and me."

Bryant ran his fingers down his face. "Unbeknownst to us, my dad had gotten even closer to Sarah than we had. He began going to sessions with her by himself, and he didn't even tell us about it until I'd gone to the support group early one day and saw them kissing in Sarah's office."

Her heart sank as she imagined how that must have made Bryant feel. He'd been hurting, along with his mother, and then to see his father in a situation where he appeared to have already moved on… She shook her head. "Oh no," Aaliyah said. "That's not like Aunt Sarah at all."

"It was definitely my dad and Sarah," Bryant said. "I didn't make my presence known that day, but I followed my dad for the next two weeks, and noticed that every weekend he was seeing Sarah."

"There was a year or two when Aunt Sarah missed our Sunday dinners," Aaliyah said. "She'd told me she was doing some traveling, but she didn't tell me where. In all honesty, I had loved seeing her so happy and care-free. I'd assumed it was the travel that was making her feel that way, but even if I had suspected anything else, I wouldn't have said a word."

"It was a rough time for me," Bryant said. "I didn't tell Kylie. Hell, I didn't tell anyone until now. I remember seeing Sarah at my mom's funeral, and she was crying when she went to view the body. I was filled with so much anger that day. Angry that she had the nerve to show up to my mom's funeral. Angry at my dad for being so distant with my mom and me before she'd passed. Pissed off at the world for taking my mom from me after making me believe for eight years that she would be around for a while."

"That's understandable," Aaliyah said, taking his hand in hers. She wanted to comfort him, but she was also still processing what he'd told her, still shocked at its implications. "I would have felt the same way."

"At the repast, I approached him," Bryant said. "My dad was hugging Sarah, and the moment she walked away, I pulled my father aside and demanded that he tell me what was going on between the two of them.

He denied it of course, and we argued for a while as I let all my anger and feelings loose, not caring if I was hurting his feelings. He may have lost his wife, but I'd lost my mother, and in my mind, it seemed like my dad felt that my mom was no longer a burden, so he could be with Sarah."

Aaliyah swallowed, torn between wanting to defend her aunt, but also wanting to be sensitive to Bryant's feelings. "I can't speak for my aunt, but I know she would never cheat with a married man. She's gone through too much. Survived too much. Lived too much life to do something like that."

"I only knew her through counseling sessions, but it didn't seem like something she would do to me either. But I know what I saw. My dad and I didn't speak for a week, and then one day he walked into my office and told me it was over. That's all he said. Just that it was over and he closed the door. After that, we fell into the weird relationship that you see us in now. We never talked about Sarah, until one day, my sister is visiting and my dad introduces us to his girlfriend at dinner. Kylie remembered Sarah and was elated because she wanted dad to be happy. I love seeing him happy too, but it's harder for me to accept them being together."

"That's a difficult way for her to reenter your life," Aaliyah said. "I'm not sure how I would have reacted either." She leaned her head against his shoulder. "But what I do know is that my aunt and Ben are both great people, and she would never do anything to break up a family. I'm not choosing sides, but I have a feeling you've kept yourself from really getting to know my aunt, so I feel a need to tell you how wonderful and loyal she is. I've never met a woman as amazing as Aunt

Sarah." Aaliyah lifted her head so that she was looking Bryant in the eyes. "All three of you need to talk this out. The secrets have lasted five years too long, so it's time for you to work on rebuilding your relationship with your father."

Bryant frowned, but she noticed the exact moment he began to realize she was right, a softening of his features, a relaxation of his brow. "I'd like for you to do this."

"If that's what you want, I will."

"It's what I want."

The hike back down the side of the mountain was a little less tense than the one up, but Aaliyah and Bryant were silent the entire way. There were so many questions swarming around Aaliyah's mind that she didn't know where to start. Unlike Ben and Bryant, her relationship with her aunt wasn't strained, and she trusted Aunt Sarah. She believed what Bryant had told her, but she also knew that there had to be an explanation for why things had unfolded the way they did.

Chapter 17

Bryant's heart was beating out of his chest when he and Aaliyah reached his dad and Sarah's hotel suite. Aaliyah wasted no time knocking, and Bryant was glad she did because he probably would have stood standing at the closed door for a while.

Sarah answered on the second set of knocks. "Hey, guys, what's up?"

Aaliyah hugged her aunt before taking a quick glance at Bryant. "Aunt Sarah, can we talk to the both of you about something really important?"

Aunt Sarah studied their faces, her eyes growing wide. "Absolutely. Come on in." His dad was already sitting in the living room area reading the newspaper.

"To what do we owe the pleasure?" he asked, putting down the paper. Sarah took a seat in the chair beside Ben, so Aaliyah and Bryant took seats on the couch.

Aaliyah squeezed Bryant's hand for encouragement. "I know this may seem like we sprung this on you," Bryant said. "But I was talking to Aaliyah, and she convinced me that I needed to clear the air and tell you both how I feel because it isn't fair for us to have gone this many years without talking."

"Spit it out, son," Ben said. "What is it?"

Bryant took a deep breath. "Before Mom passed away, I walked in on you and Sarah kissing in her office before one of our counseling sessions."

Sarah's hands flew to her mouth as she turned to Ben before her eyes began filling with tears. Bryant wasn't sure what reaction he'd expected from her, but that wasn't it.

"You don't understand what you saw," Ben said.

"You both were definitely kissing. I followed you for two weeks, and noticed that you made special trips to see Sarah every weekend."

"You followed me?" Ben asked, incredulous.

"We got really close before your mom passed," Sarah said. "But I didn't know you'd seen that kiss. Had you told us, we would have explained."

"He sort of told me," Ben said. "After Sherry passed away, Bryant pulled me aside at the repast and told me that he knew we were fooling around."

"But we weren't," Sarah said, turning to Ben, looking confused and hurt. "Why didn't you tell me Bryant approached you?"

"Because I was a mess that day," Ben said. "I was barely able to dress myself for the funeral because it felt like I'd lost my entire world. Looking back, I realize I was just selfish. I wasn't thinking about my kids or you.

I was grieving and regretting so many things that I'd wished I'd done differently in my marriage to Sherry."

Ben turned to Bryant. "Son, we should have had this conversation a long time ago, and for that, I truly am sorry." Ben looked to Sarah. "Sarah, Sherry and I all went to college together. Sarah was only there for a year before transferring, but she and your mom were roommates when I met them."

"Oh my gosh," Aaliyah said. "Is Sherry the one who you always called Sher? Your roommate from that brief time you went to school on the West Coast?"

"Yes, that's the same Sherry," Sarah said, wiping a tear that had fallen on her cheek. "When I was assigned to Ben and Sherry's family, I called Sherry immediately and told her that I was going to give them to another counselor because I was too close to the situation. But Sherry insisted. We had kept in contact over the years, but due to her illness or mine, time was never on our side. She wanted me to use the time I had to help her family."

"When I saw that the counselor was Sarah, I broke down," Ben said.

"I remember that," Bryant said. "I thought you were grieving over Mom at the time and everything came to a head during that first session."

"It had, but your mom was so tired the day we had that session that she hadn't been able to tell me that I should expect to see Sarah. I'd known that Sarah had gone through her own battle with breast cancer, and for some reason I couldn't hold in my tears any longer."

"Sherry and I weren't just close to your father that year in college," Sarah said to Bryant. "We were close to a couple of your aunts and uncles who'd visited Ben in school."

"Sarah met Mom and Dad after they'd visited me in college one day," Ben said.

"That's why Ed feels so close to you, right?" Aaliyah asked.

Sarah smiled. "Yes, it probably has something to do with it."

"Sarah dated one of my friends that year, and I'd fallen head over heels in love with Sherry."

"We had a good group of friends back then," Sarah said. "But I was never the type to stay stagnant in one place for a long time, so I left college and decided to tour the world. I did some teaching overseas, and then, eventually, I got my sociology degree. But I've always been a wandering soul." Sarah's face grew sadder. "Until the illness knocked me off my feet for a while."

"Sherry kept me up-to-date on Sarah's condition," Ben said. "And when Sarah became our counselor years later, your mom decided to create her own agenda."

Sarah looked at Ben, who nodded at her to continue. "Back in the day, Ben and I had always had a close friendship, but your mom was the apple of his eye. I never told your mom that I secretly had a crush on Ben because I've never been the type to jeopardize my friendship over a man. But Sherry was always so intuitive, so she knew anyway even if I hadn't told her."

Bryant's mind was reeling with this information. "I'd had no idea you all went to college together," he said.

"Our family had so much going on that telling you and your sister things like that didn't seem important," Ben said. "I remember being by your mom's side every day until finally, she started telling me to take Sarah out to dinner or show her around town. I didn't want to do it, but she reminded me that Sarah was our friend."

"I didn't want to go anywhere with Ben either," Sarah said. "It felt too strange since Sherry wasn't there."

"When we went out, it was just like old times," Ben said. "But it felt like we were missing a piece."

"Sherry," Sarah said. "We were missing Sherry. So I went to your dad's house and started spending time with her, sharing stories and reminiscing. After a couple weeks, she asked me if I would do her a favor and if I would check off the items on her bucket list. I told her that I would because there wasn't anything I wouldn't do for Sherry. Except, she had one condition. She wanted me to finish her bucket list with Ben."

Bryant smiled. "Sounds just like Mom."

"Your mom was an amazing woman," Sarah said. "And through the course of fulfilling her list, your dad and I grew closer. Neither of us would ever let anything happen, though. But Sherry wasn't having it. She encouraged us to spend more time together, and then one night she gave me a letter and told me that she wanted to make sure that I helped Ben find love. She felt like he had so much love to give that she didn't want it to end with her." Sarah teared up again. "When I read the letter, I realized she was talking to me. Your mom was giving me her blessing to fall in love with your father."

"Sherry gave me a similar letter," Ben said. "And I couldn't handle it. It had nothing to do with Sherry or Sarah, but I was angry and pissed at the hand that I'd been dealt. I could barely handle the guilt."

"Guilt from what?" Aaliyah asked.

Ben shook his head, as if he were reliving the moment all over again. "Here Sherry was. My wife. The love of my life. The mother of my kids. Dying. And there was nothing I could do about it. She'd asked me to fulfill her bucket list with things she'd never gotten to accomplish, and all I could think of was how much time I wasted in the early years of our marriage trying to start a brewery company when all she wanted to do was live her life with me by her side." Ben wiped his eyes.

And there it is. There was the real reason his dad hated the idea of Burrstone's branching out into the brewery business. He associated it with time lost with his wife.

"I'd been so selfish, and because I'd been chasing a pipe dream, my wife wasn't able to live her dreams," Ben said. "And instead of her asking me to spend her last days by her side, my son had to be there for her because she wanted me to continue to build a relationship with one of her close friends. A woman who I was beginning to like more than I should."

Sympathy welled in Bryant's chest as he began to understand. "Dad, obviously Mom didn't see it that way. She wanted you to live her last days the way that you were."

"I know that, son," Ben said. "But the guilt I felt was slowly consuming me."

"So was mine," Sarah said. "When you walked in on that kiss, it was the kiss of two friends who were saying goodbye to one another. I couldn't handle falling for one of my friend's husbands even with her blessing. It was all too much."

"But after that night, your mom's health took a turn for the worse," Ben said. "Sarah and I promised Sherry to finish her bucket list, and we did. It was hard to do, but we did it."

"And after the repast," Sarah said, "I said goodbye to your father and I thanked him for letting me reconnect with Sherry before she'd passed."

Bryant shook his head. "I'm so sorry that I thought the worst about you both." He'd dealt with his sorrow by turning it into anger.

"Your mom and I should have talked to you and your sister," Ben said. "I can never apologize enough for not being there for you, but I guess a part of me was jealous that your mom needed you around during her final days more than she needed me. I loved the relationship you had with your mother, but my guilt was eating away at me back then. In some ways, it still is."

"So you both didn't talk for three years?" Aaliyah asked.

"Not really," Sarah said. "I stopped the LA counseling sessions, and I tried my best to get my mind off Ben."

"I wasn't any better," Ben said. "Besides that goodbye kiss, nothing physical happened between us while Sherry was still alive, but Sarah and I had definitely developed a beautiful friendship. And although she hadn't known at the time, I was often checking her Facebook page. Then one day, she wrote that she'd landed in LA for a breast cancer walk."

"Ben reached out to me and asked if we could meet before the walk," Sarah said. "We started back talking a couple times a week until finally, he asked me to be his girlfriend and I decided to make the move to LA."

"Just like that?" Aaliyah asked. "You barely gave us any notice that you were moving."

"Sweet cheeks, I'm old, so time is not a luxury I can afford. Plus," she said looking at Ben, "my feelings never dimmed over those three years, so I knew I had to take a chance in life. I'd never lived in one place before, but I was willing to call LA home."

It was still a lot of information to digest, but Bryant was glad that he'd finally spoken with his dad and Sarah.

"How about we talk to Kylie when she gets home?" Ben asked. "I think it's time for our family to stop keeping secrets from each other."

Bryant smiled. "Sounds good to me, Dad. Sounds good to me."

Chapter 18

"Come on. Come on." Aaliyah refreshed the website she'd pulled up on her phone for the tenth time in the past five minutes.

"Whatever it is, don't take it out on the phone," Aunt Sarah said as the shuttle arrived at the downtown area of the small Colorado town the lodge was located in. Aaliyah and her aunt had heard that there was a sidewalk sale for all the shops in the downtown area, and if there was one thing Aunt Sarah and Aaliyah never passed up, it was a sale of any sort.

"I keep refreshing my phone because a couple days ago, Jacques announced that he had a focus group that was going to give preliminary scores for the latest portfolios that the finalists had to turn in a couple days ago. I turned in my wine-inspired portfolio with only an hour to spare."

"Ah, I see," Aunt Sarah said. "Maybe a little shopping will take your mind off it. I think I heard that there is a great jewelry spot a couple blocks away."

"Okay." Aaliyah refreshed her phone one more time before she placed it back in her purse. Her aunt was probably right. She'd find out soon enough if her portfolio was strong enough to move forward. In the meantime, she should enjoy the here and now.

"I'm sorry I never told you about Ben," Aunt Sarah said.

Aaliyah waved off her apology. "You don't have to apologize to me, Aunt Sarah. I'm elated that you've found love, and although you and Ben were brought together by a tragic experience, your story is beautiful. I wish I could have met Sherry."

"She would have loved you," Aunt Sarah said with a smile. "Especially because I remember a conversation she and I had in which she expressed her worry that Bryant would never open his heart up to love because the loss he was going to experience with her was going to eat away at him."

"My heart goes out to Ben and Bryant," Aaliyah said. "To think just one conversation could have saved them from years of heartache breaks my heart."

"It's easy to say that when you're looking at the situation from the outside," Aunt Sarah said. "Sometimes, it's that one conversation that's the hardest to have. For example, have you told Bryant that you want to continue a relationship with him after this road trip ends?"

Aaliyah shrugged. "No, I haven't. We haven't really had the time to talk about what this all means for us."

"It's one conversation," Aunt Sarah said. "But it's not an easy one, and if I know you as well as I think

I do, you're afraid to tell Bryant how you feel and get rejected."

Aaliyah was quiet as she let Aunt Sarah's words sink in. "I've never set myself up for rejection before."

"You haven't," Aunt Sarah said. "Part of that is because you feel the need to control situations where pain might be involved. It comes from a good place, but don't let fear rule you. You were the one who found your mom on your kitchen floor, and instead of freaking out like most kids would have done, you took control of the situation, even deciding to wait to call your dad and sister so that they wouldn't see her the way you had to."

"I've often wondered if that was the right decision," Aaliyah said.

"It was the right one for you," Aunt Sarah said. "I've also played a hand in you wanting to control a situation. Just when you, your dad and your sister got your life back on track after your mom passed, I got sick. Suddenly, you didn't have control again."

"I never thought of it that way," Aaliyah said. "Since there were things in my life that I couldn't control, I decided to control the things I could. That included any relationships I had. The relationship began and ended on my terms."

"You weren't like normal kids," Aunt Sarah said. "Even at a young age, you handled death really well and you always kept your positive demeanor. You dad said you got that from me, but your mom was like that too. Always being the backbone for everyone she knew." Aunt Sarah stopped walking and reached out to grab Aaliyah's face.

"Sweetie, you've faced more death in your thirty-two years than many people your age have. I am so proud of the woman you've become, but I also know that your mom's death, my sickness, the fact that your dad and your sister needed you meant that you put your dreams on hold." Aunt Sarah began rubbing Aaliyah's right cheek. "Have you thought about what it means with you and Bryant if you get the photography internship?"

Aaliyah sighed. "I haven't allowed myself to think about it. He knows about the internship, but he doesn't know it's in Paris and he doesn't know it's for twelve months."

"I want you to live your life," Aunt Sarah said. "But I also want you to find true love, and if Bryant is your future, then you owe it to yourself and him to figure out where you stand."

"Twelve months is a long time to ask him to wait for me," Aaliyah said.

"Not if he's the right one," Aunt Sarah said.

Aaliyah felt herself getting emotional. "Long distance relationships never work."

Aunt Sarah smiled. "Unless both parties are willing to put in the work."

"My feelings for him are so strong that it scares me." Aaliyah blinked back her tears.

"The best things in life worth having are sometimes scary," Aunt Sarah said. "I support whatever you decide to do. But promise me that you will give this a lot of thought."

Aaliyah sniffled. "I promise." She heard her phone ding in her purse, indicating that she had an email. She pulled out her phone.

"They must have posted the scores on the website because I just got an email notifying me."

"Check your scores," Aunt Sarah encouraged her.

Aaliyah tried to stop her hands from shaking as she refreshed her screen to see her score.

"Oh my gosh," she said. "I got the second highest score." Aaliyah smiled. "That puts me in the top three for the competition."

Aunt Sarah pulled her in for a hug. "I'm so proud of you, sweetie." Aaliyah was proud of herself too, but this meant that she had a real chance of winning that internship. *I definitely have some thinking to do.*

"The scenery on this last leg of our road trip has been beautiful," Aaliyah said.

Bryant looked outside at the California mountains. "It really has been. I haven't driven from Colorado to LA in a while."

Bryant's dad and Sarah had decided to fly back early that morning, but Bryant had asked Aaliyah if she was okay with taking the thirteen-hour drive with him back to California. He was enjoying his time with her and wasn't ready to end their road trip just yet.

"Where are we going again?" Bryant asked.

Aaliyah looked at her GPS on her phone. "We're almost there. We're headed to Elmer's Bottle Tree Ranch."

When they'd stopped at a gas station an hour ago, Aaliyah had started talking to a nice couple who was also from the LA area who were headed to Vegas and making stops along the way. One of the stops had caught Aaliyah's attention, so she had Bryant going on a slight detour so they could check out this destination. He didn't mind altering their trip back home. Any excuse to see her face light up.

"We're here," she said, pointing to her left. Bryant

pulled over their rental and parked it near a couple other cars.

They got out and headed into the ranch. "I've never seen anything like this," Bryant said, observing all the metal poles with glass bottles hanging from them.

"I did a little research in the car, and Elmer Long is the man behind this creation," Aaliyah said. "He loves glass bottles, and he created this place to share his passion with others. He had no idea that it would attract thousands of tourists every year."

They walked over to a huge tub filled with glass bottles so that Aaliyah could snap some photos. "He also collects different objects and things that some would consider trash, but he turns it into art. He started building the collection over sixteen years ago, and it's grown over the years."

"Even longer than that," a man said as he approached Bryant. He had a long white beard and a friendly smile. "Hi, I'm Elmer."

"I'm Aaliyah," she said, walking over to shake his hand.

"I'm Bryant. This is quite a collection you have here."

Elmer looked around with pride. "I started collecting some of these pieces when I was just a boy."

"That's amazing," Bryant said. "Proof that you never know where your passions may take you."

Elmer nodded his head. "Exactly." Bryant and Aaliyah talked to the man for a few more minutes before they snapped some photos with him and got back in the car to head to LA.

Once they were in the car, Aaliyah grew quiet. For the first forty minutes, he decided to let her be, but he noticed that she hadn't been as talkative as she normally was throughout the entire last leg of the trip. "Is everything okay?" he asked.

"I'm fine," Aaliyah said. Her smile seemed forced.

"You don't seem fine," he said. "Tell me what's on your mind."

She looked at him. "I guess I'm just trying to figure out where do you and I go from here."

Bryant had been thinking the same thing, but didn't know how to bring it up. He was glad that she'd chosen to bring it up instead. "I like you, Aaliyah."

"I like you too," she said.

"And I know that you live in Miami and only come to LA occasionally," he said, "but I'd like for us to try and date if you think that's something you may be interested in."

She smiled. "I'd like that very much."

As they entered LA hours later when evening approached, Bryant felt a weight lift off his shoulders. He didn't want to push her, but he could tell she still had more on her mind.

"Are you ready for the ceremony for the Jacques Simian internship?"

"I'm ready. A little nervous, but I'm ready."

"You're going to kill the competition," he said. "Your work is great."

"Thanks," she said. "I had the second highest score for the preliminary scoring given by a Jacques Simian focus group for the competition."

"That's amazing." He reached over to squeeze her hand when he stopped at a stoplight. "You're amazing."

Instead of responding, she reached over and planted a quick kiss in the corner of his mouth.

"Where are you staying while you're here?" he asked.

"Kyra has a spare bedroom, so I'll be with her." She wiggled her eyebrows. "Unless you have a better idea."

"Stay with me," he said. He lived outside the city and closer to Southern Cali wine country, but he really wanted Aaliyah to be with him.

"Okay," she said, and he exhaled.

Thirty minutes later, they arrived at his home.

"I always knew you had your own place," she said, "but for some reason I always saw you living on the grounds of the winery."

"I lived in the guesthouse for a while," Bryant said. "But I fell in love with this house that overlooked wine country, so I had to get it."

The moment he opened the door, Aaliyah gasped. "This place is amazing," she said.

"Thanks," Bryant said, locking the front door. "I got it because I loved the clean, modern look and the fact that this community sits on a hill. But the backyard is what really sold it for me."

Bryant bypassed his living room and kitchen to take Aaliyah straight to his outdoor living space. He opened his folding patio doors. "Before I switch on the lights, you have to see this view."

He gently held her elbow as he walked her to the left. "On this side, there's a view of the mountains. Since it's dark, you can only see the outline, but in the morning, the view is breathtaking. And on this side—" he walked to the other side of the space "—you can see the beautiful city lights."

"I love it," Aaliyah said. "I could stay out here all day."

Bryant went to the wall and switched on lights to illuminate the rest of the outdoor living area and swimming pool.

"Okay, I'm never going home," Aaliyah said as she dipped her hand in the pool. "How do you ever leave this place?"

I probably wouldn't if you lived here with me. The thought shouldn't have surprised him, but it did. Instead, he said, "It's hard, but I manage to leave because I know I'll be back." It wasn't a complete lie, but it also wasn't the complete truth.

Aaliyah slipped off her sandals and sat on the edge of the pool, pulling up her red dress to her thighs so that it wouldn't get wet. All Bryant wanted to do was walk over there and join her, but he took a moment to watch her instead, loving how carefree she looked as the night wind blew across her face.

"Are you going to join me?" Aaliyah asked, looking over her shoulder. "Or keep staring at me from a distance."

Bryant didn't need to be asked twice. He switched off the main outdoor lights, leaving on only the twinkly lights he'd had installed. After making his way to her, he slipped off his shoes and sat down beside her.

Aaliyah leaned her head on his shoulder the moment he was situated. "Question time," she said. "On a scale of one to ten, how happy are you that I'm here with you tonight, with ten being 'her being here made my night' and one being 'I should have dropped her off at Kyra's place.'"

Bryant laughed. "That's easy," he said before placing a kiss on her forehead. "A ten."

"Good answer. Your turn."

It didn't take long for Bryant to think of a question.

"On a scale of one to ten, how mad would you be if I pushed you into the pool right now?"

Aaliyah's eyes widened. "You wouldn't dare."

"Oh, but I would." Bryant pretended to shove her in, and Aaliyah got so nervous that she fell in all on her own.

"Bryant!" she yelled. "You pushed me in!"

He laughed. "No, I didn't. I pretended, but you fell in by yourself." She looked so adorable in her wet, clingy dress with the pissed off expression on her face.

"I love pissing you off," Bryant said. He took his cell phone and wallet out, stowed them poolside, jumped in fully clothed and pulled her to him. "We've been getting along so well that I haven't seen that fiery sunshine that shoots from your eyes when you're annoyed by me."

Her facial features softened. "You make me sick," she said.

"I know," he said, right before he pulled her face in for a kiss.

"The lights aren't too bright, but can any of your neighbors see us?" she asked in between kisses.

"Not sure," he said. "How much do you care?"

She leaned back to look at him. "Not much." To prove what she'd said, she lifted her dress over her head and tossed it on the concrete, leaving her in her black lace bra and panties. *Damn.* A dry Aaliyah was sexy as hell, but a wet Aaliyah was downright appetizing.

Bryant let her remove his shirt before he took off his shorts and boxers, followed by her bra and panties. The moment they were completely naked, their lips were back on each other.

I don't think I'll ever get tired of kissing her sweet lips. When Aaliyah kissed him, he felt it in his whole body. Everything about being with her felt right, but he wasn't trying to scare her by coming on so strong so quickly.

How was he supposed to explain how the guy she'd given the nickname Grumpy McGrumperson to had fallen in love with her in a short two weeks? *Love.* Bryant was man enough to admit that he wasn't just falling for Aaliyah anymore. He *had fallen* and it had happened so fast, he hadn't seen it coming.

He pulled her to the corner of the pool so that he could get a better angle, and in one smooth thrust, he entered her.

"That feels so good," she said when he began moving his hips in slow, circular movements.

"You feel so good," he whispered in her ear before placing kisses along her collarbone. A few moments later all talking ceased, and the only sounds that mingled with the outside noises were their passionate moans as they climaxed underneath the night sky.

You have to talk to her, Bryant thought after he began to come down from his lustful high. *After her internship ceremony tomorrow, you have to talk to her about the possibility of her moving to LA.* It wasn't lost on Bryant that asking Aaliyah to move to LA was a huge commitment and one that she was free to reject. But he was taking over Burrstone's and it was headquartered in California.

Or maybe you could open an office in Miami and work there six months out of the year. Bryant was agreeable to that option as well because he wanted to do whatever he could to build his relationship with Aaliyah. Even if that meant leaving the state he called home.

Chapter 19

"Don't be nervous."

"You got this."

"Based off those preliminary scores, they loved you."

Aaliyah tried to block out all the noise and focus on Jacques Simian and his wife, Rachel, who were taking the stage to discuss their photography foundation and the internship.

All ten finalists had been offered tables of eight so that they could invite their loved ones to the dinner. Only one finalist was winning the internship, but each of them had been given a recognition award during the first half of the dinner, and pieces from each of their portfolio had been put together in a beautiful video presentation that the finalists would receive as a gift.

Aaliyah had chosen to invite Aunt Sarah, Ben, Bryant, Nicole, Kendrick, his mom, Felicia, and Kyra. But right now, the only person who was calming her nerves was Bryant.

"Just breathe," he said, taking her hand and rubbing smoothing circles in her palm. Aaliyah smiled as she continued to listen to the speech.

"This year, the talent was amazing," Rachel said into the microphone. "It was difficult for our team to choose a winner for the internship because each finalist brought something different to the table."

"This year, we were looking for someone who had an edge," Jacques said. "A quality that couldn't be taught in a classroom. A uniqueness to the way they were able to take a basic product, object, or piece of food and add personality to it in a way the average eye may never imagine it."

"So without further ado, the winner of the twelve-month internship working directly with Jacques is…" Rachel paused for added suspense. "Johnathan Lansing from Charlotte, North Carolina."

I didn't win. Aaliyah released the breath she'd been holding.

"Fuck them," Kyra whispered to her. Aaliyah laughed. Leave it to Kyra to say something to crack her up.

"Are you okay?" Bryant asked.

She shrugged. "Sort of, but I will be. Johnathan was a few points ahead of me during every round, and his work is great. I'm happy for him, just a little disappointed."

Now, on to the next thing. This internship was just one milestone on her list, but she knew there would be other opportunities. She'd get over her disappointment and start working on new challenges, new projects. She was blessed to have a good family and friends, and now Bryant to support her.

"Before we let you all continue with the rest of your night," Rachel said, "this year, we also decided to place an additional internship on the table that the finalists didn't know about."

Jacques nodded his head. "With this internship, the winner will get a chance to work with Johnathan and me for six months, but will also have the rare opportunity to travel with my wife and learn the business side of being a photographer."

Wow! That almost sounds better than the first internship.

"Connie got high rankings, as well," she whispered to Bryant as she pointed to the table where that finalist sat. "She probably got the second internship."

Rachel smiled to the audience. "And the winner of the second internship is…Aaliyah Bai from Miami, Florida."

Aaliyah's mouth dropped. *Did I seriously win? Am I dreaming this? Did I really hear my name called?*

"Chick, you won," Kyra said. "Get up there."

"I'm so proud of you, sweetie," Aunt Sarah said.

"You won," Bryant whispered in her ear, clapping along with the rest of her table. "Go up there and claim your prize, gorgeous."

Her feet seemed to float to the stage as she walked up to get her award. "Thank you so much," she said, shaking Jacques's and Rachel's hands.

"We were so impressed with your work," Rachel said.

"I'm looking forward to working with you," Jacques said. "My assistant will be reaching out to you in a couple days to schedule our first official meeting before we make plans for Paris."

"Sounds great." It took all her energy not to run back to her seat. She couldn't believe she'd won. It all felt so surreal. She was almost afraid someone would tell her she'd just been pranked.

When she'd nearly reached her table, she slowed down her stride as her eyes made their way to Bryant's. As happy as she was, the reality was that she still hadn't talked to Bryant yet. She may not be gone to Paris for twelve months, but she was going to be gone for six months, still a long time. Especially for a new relationship.

Is that what this is? A relationship? As much as Aaliyah wanted to spend tonight with Bryant and her friends celebrating, she knew she was out of time. She had to talk to Bryant tonight.

"I'm so proud of you," Bryant said when they walked into his home.

"You said that already," Aaliyah said with a laugh. "But I love hearing it, so thank you."

"You're welcome." Although Aaliyah didn't win the internship she'd originally wanted, to him, what she won sounded even better.

Aaliyah walked to the living room and took a seat on the couch while Bryant poured them some champagne.

"What's on your mind?" Bryant asked when he returned with the champagne. "You just won a great internship, yet you don't look happy."

"I am happy," she said. However, her smile didn't quite reach her eyes. Tonight, Bryant had planned on talking to her about their relationship and broach the topic of one of them relocating to see how she felt about it, but she seemed like she had a million things going on in her mind. He wanted to help ease her stress first. His talk could wait.

Bryant placed both their champagne glasses on the table and stood up. "Lean back against the couch," he told her. Once she looked comfortable, he started massaging her shoulders.

"Your hands feel amazing," she said, rolling her neck into his fingers. "This is exactly what I needed."

Bryant smiled. He wished he could see her face, but relieving her stress was more important. "I could tell. You seemed way too tense to have had such a successful night."

"There's a lot on my mind," Aaliyah said. "A lot that I know we need to discuss tonight, but I don't want to ruin our night."

"I wanted to talk about us too," he said. "So you don't have to worry about the discussion ruining our night."

"You may disagree after I tell you this," she said.

"Just tell me," Bryant said. "Telling me is better than trying to figure out when you will tell me for the rest of the night."

"You're right," she said. "But you said you wanted to talk about us too, so how about you go first?"

Bryant laughed. "Okay. I guess the main thing I wanted to know was if you've ever given any thought to moving to LA?"

Aaliyah turned to face him. "You want me to move to LA?"

"I know it sounds crazy since we didn't even discuss officially dating," Bryant said. "But I've never been the type of man to beat around the bush." He sat back down beside her so that they were facing each other. "I understand that this means uprooting your life, so I'm willing to work out of Miami half of the year if it helps."

Aaliyah grabbed his hands in hers. "Bryant, I would have no problem moving for a man if I knew we could have a future together, and when I think about us, I see a future together."

She sighed. "The internship I won will be in Paris for six months. I don't have all the details yet, but they said the winner should be prepared to leave for Paris one month after the awards dinner."

"I see," Bryant said. "So you'd be leaving the country for six months."

"Yes." Aaliyah bit her bottom lip.

Bryant couldn't hide the fact that he was disappointed that Aaliyah would be gone for six months, starting in one month, even as he celebrated her win. It seemed unfair that they connected the way that they had on the road trip, only to learn that they'd be living in different countries for half a year. It seemed as soon as he was on to something good, it was snatched away from him.

"I know what you're thinking," Aaliyah said. "You're thinking that we've barely had time to date, and now I'll be going to Paris for six months." She scooted closer to him. "But I really think we could make it work. I'm willing to try if you are."

Bryant lifted his hand to her cheek. He wasn't about to let her go, to let this happiness drift away. "I'm more than willing to try," Bryant said. "It almost feels like I waited my entire life to find a woman like you, so if that means the next few months of our relationship will include a lot of FaceTime videos and quick visits, then so be it." He placed a soft kiss on her lips. "Just because you're going to Paris doesn't mean you can get rid of me."

"Me neither," she said with a laugh. "I like you too much."

"And I love you too much," he said, loving the way her eyes lit up in surprise. "I passed the falling stage a while ago."

She smiled. "I love you too."

Bryant wasted no time capturing her lips with his. There were still a lot of things they had to discuss, but in his heart, he knew they had time. They may not be in the same city. Or even the same country. However, he was confident that he and Aaliyah would work it out.

"I have one more question," Aaliyah said, breaking their kiss.

"What is it?"

She studied his eyes. "Are we officially in a relationship?"

Bryant laughed. "Are you asking if we're Facebook official?"

"Something like that," she said.

Bryant held her gaze. "Yes, we're in an official relationship," he said. "I'm not dumb enough to let you go."

Aaliyah smiled as she pulled his face back down to hers. Within seconds, Bryant could tell that the kiss was different. There was no uncertainty in it. No matter what the future held for them, they'd always have this moment...this time together. Bryant knew the importance of cherishing the time you had with someone and, thankfully, he'd found a woman who felt the exact same way.

Chapter 20

Three months later...

"How are you feeling?" Bryant asked his grandfather.

"As good as I can be," Ed said. "It's been nice seeing all my family and friends these past few months, but it's also been exhausting."

"I know," Bryant said, walking over to his grandfather's bed. "But you can't help it, Grandpa. Everyone loves you and wanted to talk to you one last night."

Spending the last two months dating Aaliyah long distance while she worked her Paris internship was tough, but watching his grandfather deteriorate over the past few weeks was even more difficult.

When he'd gotten the call from his cousin Imani that Ed had taken a turn for the worse, Bryant hadn't wasted any time flying to Chicago. He'd been here for three weeks straight, only flying back to LA to handle business on the weekends and to relieve his dad so that he could spend the weekends with Ed.

"Is Aaliyah on her way?" his grandfather asked.

"She just landed. Nicole and Aunt Sarah are picking her up from the airport."

Aaliyah was constantly FaceTiming with his grandfather, and the fact that she cared about him so much after only meeting him once truly touched Bryant's heart.

Today, the entire family was gathered at Ed's home for an early holiday celebration. It wasn't lost on the family that Ed didn't have much longer, so everyone had changed their schedules so that they could be together as a family before the holidays.

Once Bryant had heard that everyone would be in attendance, he'd run an idea by his grandfather that involved Aaliyah.

"Are you ready to see her?" Ed asked.

"Ready," Bryant said. "I'm so ready that I have too much built-up nervous energy. Why do you think I'm in your bedroom hiding with you? I needed to avoid all the curious glances."

Ed laughed until his laugh became a cough.

"Slow down, old man. You have to take it easy."

"Then don't make me laugh," Ed said.

"I wasn't trying to," Bryant said. "I already told you I'm nervous."

"She's going to say yes," Ed said. "So there's nothing to be worried about."

All night, his family members had been telling him not to be nervous, but he was a wreck. The past three months with Aaliyah had been amazing, and leading up to her trip to Paris, he'd spent two weeks with her in Miami and she'd spent two weeks with him in LA.

He'd even flown to Paris four times to see her, but she was finally coming home for her holiday break and he couldn't be happier.

"It's great to see you so happy," Ed said. "I knew the moment I met that young woman that you weren't going to waste any time asking her to marry you."

"Do you think it's too soon?" Bryant asked. "Couples typically date a year before getting engaged."

"When you make up your mind, that's it. You've been that way since you were a little boy, and if I know you, when you met Aaliyah over two years ago, you already knew she was it for you."

Bryant laughed. She hated his guts back then, but it's true. He'd known even back then that he would do everything he could to make her his, even if he'd had no clue on how he would go about winning her heart.

"There's my son," Ben said, walking into the bedroom. "Something told me that you'd be in here hiding with your grandfather. I found someone in the hallway who wanted to say hi."

Bryant's heart was beating out of his chest because he thought Aaliyah had landed early, but the face that popped through the door belonged to his sister, Kylie.

"Hey, big brother," she said, running up to give him a hug. "Should I assume that based off that look of panic you're wearing on your face that you thought I was Aaliyah getting here early?"

"Yes," he said with a laugh. "But I'm glad to see you! I heard you got in town a few hours ago, but the house is so packed that I didn't see you."

"You wouldn't have been able to find me because the little divas hijacked me and dragged me into the play-room Grandpa had set up for them. I got interrogated for over two hours, and they talked me out of fifty bucks."

"Consider yourself lucky," Bryant said. "They usually talk me out of one hundred."

Bryant and Kylie talked a bit more while Ben and Ed had a separate conversation.

"Well, I'm going to find me a good seat for the show," Kylie said. "It's not every day your big brother asks someone to marry him." Bryant was still shaking his head when she left the room.

"I'm proud of you, son," Ben said when it was only the three of them. "And it takes guts to propose to a woman in front of all your family."

"Aaliyah always says that she wants to be part of a large family," Bryant said. "She got her introduction to the clan at the picnic, but once she accepts my marriage proposal this will be her family too."

"When are you going to pop the question?" Ed asked.

"Before dinner," Bryant said. "Everyone knows I'm going to propose, so I don't want them spilling the beans early."

"Good call," Ben said. "You can't give this bunch too much rope. They aren't good at keeping secrets, and if you wait too long, one of your cousins will probably do the proposal for you."

Bryant laughed as he ignored that tiny voice in the back of his head that worried that there was a chance Aaliyah would say no. He didn't think she would, but he wasn't sure there was ever a man who wasn't nervous minutes before he was about to propose.

* * *

"Sis, I have to go," Aaliyah said. "I see Nicole and Aunt Sarah."

"Tell them I said hi," Aaliyah's sister, Monique, said. "Dad, Terrance and the girls send their love too."

"I send mine too. I'll see you guys in a couple days." Aaliyah blew kisses over the phone before she hung up.

"I love Paris, but I'm so excited to be back in the States," Aaliyah said to Nicole and Aunt Sarah. When she'd gotten a text from Nicole that she and Aunt Sarah were at the airport, she'd briefly been disappointed that Bryant hadn't come to get her until they told her that he was spending time with Ed.

"You're happy to be in the States?" Nicole asked. "Or are you happy to be reunited with Bryant?"

"Both," Aaliyah said with a smile. "We've seen a lot more of each other than I thought we would have dating long distance, but I couldn't wait for this break so we could spend some quality time together."

As cheesy as it was, the best part about Aaliyah's days in Paris—besides working with Jacques—were the FaceTime calls she had with Bryant. She lived for them, and even with the time difference, they'd managed to make it work.

Every time she talked to Bryant, she fell more and more in love with him. They had so much in common, and the fact that they were so different, yet so similar, was something that Aaliyah had never thought she'd be lucky enough to find in a partner. But she'd found that in Bryant. She found her equal and the person who understood her when no one else did.

"You have that dreamy look again," Nicole teased.

"I love seeing that look," Aunt Sarah said. "The look of love and elatedness."

When they pulled onto Ed's block, Aaliyah's heart started beating fast. Bryant had told her that all the family would be present for an early holiday celebration, but the person she wanted to see most was Bryant.

Kendrick met them at the car when they got to the house and took Aaliyah's bag.

"Glad you were able to make it back for the celebration," Kendrick said, giving her a quick hug. "If you hadn't, I'm sure my cousin would have been on the next flight to Paris."

Aaliyah laughed. "I missed all of you too much to stay in Paris for this. And I especially wanted to see Ed." He'd quickly become like a grandfather to her and she spoke to him at least once a week. Time was limited, so she was going to talk to him as much as she could.

As soon as they entered the house, the first thing Aaliyah noticed was that all eyes were on her. Conversation and chatter around them seemed to cease the farther they walked into the home.

She hadn't seen some of the family members in a few months, but Bryant had been right. It seemed that everyone was in attendance.

"Where's Bryant?" she asked Kendrick when she didn't see him among the family gathered in the dining-room area. The estate was huge, and Aaliyah didn't want to waste any time going from room to room looking for him.

"He's in the family room in the west wing," Kendrick said. "We set Grandpa up there for the holiday, and Bryant is with him."

Aaliyah smiled as she made her way there. She could

hear a bunch of chatter behind her, indicating that a lot of the family was following her, but she didn't care. All she wanted to do was see Bryant.

When she made it to the west wing, she immediately spotted Ed. "Hey, Ed," she said, walking over to his motorized bed.

"Hey, sunshine," he said with a smile. "It's great to see you."

She leaned over and hugged Ed, careful not to put any of her weight on his frail figure. Although she knew they didn't have much longer with him, he was in good spirits and he looked happy despite the circumstances and pain she knew he was in.

"My grandson has been anxious all day waiting for you to get here."

Aaliyah laughed. "I've been the same way. My flight couldn't land soon enough."

At the airport, she'd changed out of her yoga pants and tee and replaced them with a pair of jeans and a black sweater. Then, she'd tossed on a little makeup and fluffed out her curls that had gotten flat on the flight over.

Even though she knew Bryant couldn't care less about how she looked, she wanted to look her best.

"How do you feel?" she asked Ed.

"Oh, you know," he said with a shrug. "Good days and bad days. But today is a good day." Ed reached out to grab Aaliyah's hand. "A very good day."

Aaliyah smiled. She wanted to spend more time with Ed and talk to him some more, but she was ready to see Bryant. Not wanting to be rude, she didn't even look around the room to see where he may be until she heard someone clearing his throat at the base of the stairs to her right.

She looked up and her eyes landed on Bryant's immediately. *There he is.* He looked so sexy in his jeans and sweater. She wasn't even surprised that they were wearing similar outfits, but it still made her laugh.

"Hey, beautiful," he said, walking up to her.

"Hey, yourself." When he opened his arms, she ran into them, the force of her body almost knocking him off balance. He had her. She always felt like he had her.

"I've been waiting for you to get here," he said. "It's crazy how long it seemed to take."

"I know," she said as they broke their embrace. "My flight was already long, but today it felt like we would never land."

"My grandson has been beside himself," Ed said. "I told him that being in love would do that to you. Then I told him to make sure he didn't do something stupid and misplace the most important object for today."

Aaliyah turned back to look at Ed. "What do you mean?"

"I think I know," Bryant said. Aaliyah felt like her head turned back around in slow motion as her eyes connected with a kneeling Bryant.

"What are you doing?" she asked.

He looked down at his kneeling position. "I'd think it was obvious," he said with a laugh. "But in case you need better clarification, I'm proposing to you, beautiful."

Aaliyah's free hand flew to her mouth, while Bryant grabbed her left one. "Aaliyah Bai, when we first met, I know that I was the last person on Earth you wanted to be around." The room laughed, the only indicator

Aaliyah had that others were in attendance because her eyes hadn't left Bryant's since he'd arrived in the room.

"Needless to say, for me, it was the complete opposite. I knew the moment I met you that you were it for me. Now, that didn't mean I wasn't going to fight those feelings, but I had to be realistic and realize that I was fighting a losing battle because to know you is to love you. And I love you fiercely, Aaliyah Bai."

Aaliyah felt wetness on her cheeks as her tears began to fall despite her best efforts to hold them in. It was no use. She couldn't control her emotions in this moment any more than she could control her love for Bryant.

"Before I met you, I was a shell of a man, living in grief instead of just living. Being with you has taught me that it's not about the moments we lose, but rather, we must cherish the moments we have."

Bryant pulled a black velvet ring box from his pocket and opened it. The gorgeous diamond had Aaliyah gasping again, and she didn't miss the oohs and ahhs from others in the room.

"Aaliyah Bai, will you make me the happiest man on Earth by being my wife?"

"Yes," she said, squealing in happiness as he placed the rock on her finger. She was in his arms before he'd even fully stood up, her lips on his in a passionate kiss.

"There are kids in the room," someone yelled. "Save it for the bedroom."

Normally, Aaliyah would have ignored the voice, but it sounded familiar to her. "Dad!" Aaliyah glanced around the room and spotted her dad standing next to Aunt Sarah, Ben, her sister, Monique, her brother-in-law, Terrance and her nieces.

"What are you all doing here?" she asked in surprise.

Monique laughed. "Isn't it obvious, sis?" She pointed to Bryant.

Aaliyah turned back to Bryant. "It's so sweet of you to have the family come down for the proposal."

"Not exactly." Bryant gave her a sheepish smile. "Is now a good time to ask you if we can speed up the wedding?"

She looked at him curiously. "Sure. When are you thinking?" She didn't want a long engagement either, so the sooner, the better.

Bryant looked around the room at all their family and friends before his eyes landed on Ed. Aaliyah followed his line of vision and smiled.

"Is three days too soon?" Bryant asked. "Our families are already in town."

Aaliyah laughed. "If it means that all our loved ones will be there, three days is fine." She knew the situation, and if there was a chance that they could have Ed at their wedding, she was taking it.

Chapter 21

The next day, Aaliyah and Bryant went to get their marriage license and contacted anyone from their wedding party who wasn't already in town.

Summer and Danni were both bridesmaids, so Summer, Aiden and their son, Anthony, were flying in with Danni, Jaleen and their three-month-old daughter, Layla.

Bryant had contacted his friend Seth to be a groomsman, and he and his wife were flying down too.

Everything was going perfectly, considering they had only a couple days to plan it all, with friends and family gathered around.

"Are you ready?" Aunt Sarah asked Aaliyah on the evening of the event itself. Aaliyah looked at her aunt's reflection in the mirror. "I'm more than ready."

"Mom would have loved this," Monique said. "I'm sure she's shining down on you right now, sis."

Aaliyah squeezed her sister's hand, which was on her shoulder. Her sister and Aunt Sarah were also bridesmaids, along with Nicole and Kyra.

"You look beautiful, sweetheart," Aaliyah's dad said as he walked into the bedroom, his eyes rimmed in tears.

"Thanks, Dad." Aaliyah stood to hug her father, so grateful that her entire family had been here for the engagement and her special day.

"And everything looks beautiful outside," Summer said. "You're going to love it."

They'd chosen to get married at Ed's estate so that he could be there for the wedding. It had been Ed's idea to have a large heated tent placed outside to fit all the guests, and Elite Events Incorporated was handling the entire wedding. Aaliyah had only gotten a peek into the tent, but Bryant's cousins Imani, Cyd and Lex, along with their friend Mya, had done amazing work pulling together everything so last minute. She shouldn't have been surprised since the ladies of Elite Events knew how to plan a party, but she was still taken aback by how seamlessly all the planning had gone. They'd even helped her find a beautiful last-minute dress from a local designer who happened to have her size.

A knock on the door got everyone's their attention. "It's almost time," Bryant's cousin Imani said. "And you look gorgeous, Aaliyah."

"Thank you," she said with a smile. "I can't thank Elite Events enough for everything you've done."

"Don't mention it," Imani said with a smile. "We're family, and there is nothing we wouldn't do for family."

The next ten minutes seemed to move in slow motion for Aaliyah. It was hard to believe that this time last year, she couldn't even have pictured herself married, yet now, she was so anxious to wed Bryant, she was hoping that the seconds ticked by faster.

"Be patient, baby girl," her dad said as they waited for the cue that it was time for her to walk down the aisle.

Aaliyah heard the swell of murmurs and laughter from the family and guests, and could only assume that the little divas were putting on a performance.

"I can't believe I'm getting married," Aaliyah said with a smile. She wasn't even cold standing outside in the fall weather, awaiting her entrance.

Aaliyah's dad teared up. "I can't believe my baby girl is getting married either. But Bryant is a good man and more importantly, he sees your worth. I'm so happy for you." He kissed the top of her forehead, and they shared a quick hug before Cyd and Lex, who were standing on either side of the curtain that led to the inside of the tent, gave their cue and the doors opened.

Aaliyah didn't have time to take in the beautiful white lilies that filled the space or the warm lighting that gave their nighttime wedding a dreamy affect. Her eyes saw only Bryant looking devastatingly handsome in his black tuxedo, and wearing a dimpled smile that almost turned her into a pile of mush as she walked down the aisle toward him.

She's breathtaking, Bryant thought as Aaliyah made her way down the aisle wearing a smile that he was sure matched his. The past three days had been a bit hectic, but he hadn't cared if they had only three days or three hours to plan a wedding. It was all worth it to marry Aaliyah.

And Grandpa is still here. They had made sure that there was a special place in the tent for his grandfather's bed so he could watch the ceremony. The only time Bryant took his eyes off Aaliyah was to give his grandfather a wink that he quickly returned.

You're going to have the rest of your life to spend with this woman. It almost seemed surreal that he was lucky enough to spend his time with a woman as amazing as Aaliyah. He considered himself a decent person, but he'd had a rough time over the past few years. Aaliyah ignited a light within him that he'd thought had been dimmed forever.

When she made her way to him and her father placed her hand in Bryant's, it took all his effort to listen to what the reverend was saying because his attention was solely on Aaliyah.

She squeezed his hand as the minister spoke, and on instinct, Bryant leaned toward Aaliyah.

"Not yet," the reverend said, halting his kiss. "I haven't gotten to that part yet, son."

"Sorry," Bryant said as the family and guests laughed. He couldn't help himself. He'd found his soul mate, and he was too happy to hold in his excitement. Too emotional to stand there and not want to sweep her into his arms.

Bryant wasn't sure when it had happened, but Aaliyah wiped a tear from his eye that he hadn't known had fallen, and on the side of the room, he heard his grandfather say he'd won some sort of bet since Bryant had shed some tears during the ceremony.

When it was finally time for them to say their vows and for him to kiss his bride, Bryant's lips were on Aaliyah's before the officiant had even finished the words. The kiss was perfect. Their ceremony was perfect. Aaliyah was perfect.

* * *

"Can you believe we're married?" Bryant asked.

"Yes," she said with a smile. "And everything went better than it could have if we would have had three months instead of three days to plan."

The reception was in full swing, and although everyone was dancing on the dance floor, Aaliyah was content to sit back with Bryant and watch the festivities.

"Did you mean what you said?" she asked. "Are you really coming back to Paris with me?"

"Yes," he said. "My dad has been enjoying his retirement and he and Sarah plan to do some traveling, but he said he'd come out of retirement for the next four months until your internship is over."

She curled underneath his arm. "I can't wait for you to be in Paris with me. It's going to be so great having you there."

"I'm looking forward to it too," Bryant said. "Plus, one of the breweries near where you work has agreed to let me come on and learn about the business. Since Burrstone's will be debuting our brewery next year, I need to be as prepared as possible."

Aaliyah was so glad when Bryant told her that he and Ben had had a real heart-to-heart conversation after they'd all talked in Colorado. Ben had finally given Bryant the reins to run the business as he saw fit, and that included diving into the beer business.

They sat in silence for a while as they watched their family and friends enjoy themselves. "Do you think our moms are looking down at us right now?" Aaliyah asked.

"I sure hope so," Bryant said. "I'd like to think that

they were watching our entire love story unfold while we were on the road trip."

"Or maybe even before that," Aaliyah said.

Bryant looked at her. "I thought you said you hated me when we first met."

"I did," Aaliyah said. "But if I'm being completely honest, I'll admit that I may have had a little crush on you even if you did have resting grumpy face."

Bryant laughed. "You're telling me I could have gotten it without getting rid of my grumpy face."

She slapped him on the arm. "That's not what I'm saying and you know it." Aaliyah held his gaze. "All I'm saying is that although I love seeing you laugh and smile, the old Bryant wasn't as bad as I'd made him out to be. It's possible that I slightly exaggerated my dislike for you because I was so attracted to you, but couldn't believe you were such a grumpy jerk."

Bryant shrugged. "I can't blame you. I wasn't the easiest man to be around." He pulled her closer to him. "But you changed all that, baby. Because of you, my family got to see the man I once was. My grandfather got his grandson back, and my dad and I have a better relationship now than we've ever had." He leaned down so that their foreheads were touching. "I can't wait to spend the rest of my life proving to you that because of your love, because of your faith in me, because of your unwillingness to let me give up on myself and my dreams, I'm a better man. A happy man. A man who will never take life or the time we have together for granted."

Aaliyah wiped a fallen tear. "Why do you always say such sweet things that make me cry?"

Bryant kissed the rest of her tears away. "If you

didn't feel the emotion behind my words, then I would be doing something wrong."

Bryant captured her lips in his, and Aaliyah's toes curled at the delicious kiss she'd received from her husband. *My husband.* It was crazy to think that Bryant was now hers, but she was happier than she'd ever been.

As she sat there kissing her husband, her life partner, her road-trip buddy and the reason she now liked beer, she couldn't help but think that her mom and his had been playing matchmaker in heaven to bring them together. She'd found her forever in Bryant, and she didn't even want to think what may have happened had they not taken that road trip and embarked on their journey to love.

* * * * *

"It's beautiful," she whispered.

"Have you ever seen it at night before?"

"I've driven by, but never really paid much attention." She turned to face him. "I'll never see it the same again."

"Neither will I." He leaned down and touched his mouth to hers.

The kiss lasted a mere second, but warmed Desiree to her toes. He tightened his arm around her and rested his head against hers. As the driver continued toward the river, the sounds of traffic became more distant and the clip-clop of the horse's hooves magnified in the silence. A gentle breeze kicked up, blowing like a whisper across Desiree's face. She closed her eyes and inhaled deeply, wishing the night could last forever. Too soon, they'd returned to the starting point and their idyllic ride ended. They thanked the driver and he bade them good-night. Desiree and Lorenzo strolled hand in hand back to her shop.

"It's getting late and you probably have to get up early tomorrow," Lorenzo said.

"Actually, the store is closed tomorrow, but I have a few things to take care of. I'm sure you have a long day ahead of you, too."

"I do. Where are you parked?" She pointed. He walked her over and waited while she unlocked the door. Turning her to face him, he rested his hands on her waist. "Thank you for your company tonight, Desiree."

"Thank you for inviting me. I had an amazing time."

"Can we do it again sometime?"

Everything in her shouted for her to decline. Instead, she said, "I'd like that."

Sheryl Lister is a multi-award-winning author and has enjoyed reading and writing for as long as she can remember. She is a former pediatric occupational therapist with over twenty years of experience and resides in California. Sheryl is a wife, mother of three daughters and a son-in-love, and grandmother to two special little boys. When she's not writing, Sheryl can be found on a date with her husband or in the kitchen creating appetizers. For more information, visit her website at www.sheryllister.com.

Books by Sheryl Lister

Harlequin Kimani Romance

Just to Be with You
All of Me
It's Only You
Tender Kisses
Places in My Heart
Giving My All to You
A Touch of Love
Still Loving You
His Los Angeles Surprise
A Love of My Own

Visit the Author Page
at Harlequin.com for more titles.

A LOVE OF MY OWN

Sheryl Lister

For all those still fighting Alzheimer's.
We won't give up hope.

Acknowledgments

My Heavenly Father, thank You for my life.
You never cease to amaze me with Your blessings!

To my husband, Lance, you continue to show me
why you'll always be my number one hero!

To my children, family and friends, thank you for
your continued support. I appreciate and love you!

They always say to find your tribe and I've found mine.
They know who they are. I love y'all and can't imagine
being on this journey without you.

A special thank-you to the readers, authors and
book clubs (Building Relationships Around Books,
Cilla's Book Maniacs, Brenda Jackson Book Club,
EyeCU Reading & Chatting and Austin Alumnae Book
Club, to name a few) who continue to enrich my life.

A very special thank-you to my agent, Sarah E. Younger.
I can't tell you how much I appreciate having you
in my corner.

Dear Reader,

I'm excited to introduce the Hunters of Sacramento to you. If you've kept up with the Grays of Los Angeles series, you met all four in Malcolm Gray's story, *Still Loving You*. First up is Lorenzo Hunter and Desiree Scott. Both are more than a little commitmentphobic, but throw in a dose of sizzling chemistry and some warming massage oil (yes, I do have the recipe) and you just might get happily-ever-after. As with many of my stories, I touch on some life issues and this one is no different. If you've ever witnessed a loved one going through the stages of Alzheimer's disease, it is one of the most heartbreaking things ever. I know. Having a strong support system is a must and Desiree will find hers in Lorenzo. You can find more information at www.alz.org.

As always, I so appreciate all your love and support. Without you, I couldn't do this.

Much love,

Sheryl

www.SherylLister.com

sheryllister@gmail.com

www.Facebook.com/SherylListerAuthor

www.Twitter.com/1Slynne

Instagram: @SherylLister

Chapter 1

"You have a few minutes, Lorenzo?"

Lorenzo Hunter paused as he passed his father's office. "I'm on my way to the mini-mall site with Cedric. What's up?" Lorenzo and his cousin Cedric held project executive positions at the construction company founded by their fathers, who were twin brothers.

"Reuben and I need to talk to you two before you leave." His father glanced down at his watch. "It should only take about ten minutes. Let Cedric know and meet me in my office."

Lorenzo studied his father. Something in his expression gave Lorenzo pause. "Okay." He stood there a moment, trying to guess why his father seemed so serious before continuing down the hall to Cedric's office. He stuck his head in the door. "Hey."

Cedric stood and rolled up the blueprints on his drafting table. "You ready?"

"Not exactly. Dad just stopped me in the hall. He and your dad want to talk to us."

His brows knit together. "About what? I hope there isn't another problem with that new park project. They've changed things about ten times."

"I have no idea, but we can talk about that later." Lorenzo and Cedric started back down the hall and entered his father's office. They spoke to his assistant, Laurie, who told them to go on in.

Lorenzo's uncle Reuben gestured for them to sit at a small conference table where he sat with Lorenzo's father. "Good. This shouldn't take long."

"What's going on, Dad?" Cedric asked, taking a seat. Lorenzo slid into the chair next to Cedric.

"In a nutshell, Russell and I have decided to retire."

Lorenzo chuckled. "You and Dad have been saying that since Uncle Nolan retired two years ago." More than two decades ago Nolan Gray, along with his best friend, had started an in-home safety company that designed and manufactured everything from bath rails and specialized mattresses to in-home alert systems for the disabled.

"Effective immediately," Lorenzo's father said.

"What?" Lorenzo and Cedric shouted at the same time.

"You can't just up and retire like that," Cedric said, snapping his fingers and jumping up from his chair. He paced the room.

"Of course we can, son."

Lorenzo just sat, stunned, unable utter a word. He knew this day would come—he and Cedric had been groomed to take over—but he never expected it to happen without warning. And not *now,* when they had two new projects and the potential for another. He finally found his voice. "Dad, how are we supposed to handle all the projects and the day-to-day office operations?" As a civil engineer, he oversaw the planning, budgeting and scheduling and made sure the sidewalks, parking lots and other roadways associated with each project were intact. Cedric, with his construction engineering degree, took care of staffing on the sites, materials and making sure the actual building went up on time. No way could they do both.

His father clasped his hands together and braced them on the table. "You'll have to hire someone to take over your current positions. Reuben and I will be available to help you transition, but we're confident you're more than ready to take this company into the future."

"Uncle Russell, I appreciate your confidence and all, but we need more time. I mean there's staffing, operations, a mountain of paperwork…" Cedric stopped pacing and threw up his hands.

Uncle Reuben folded his arms. "Well, son, you have a week to get up to speed. Russell and I are taking your mother and LaVerne on a two-week cruise the last week in June."

"Dad, that's like *three* weeks from now." Cedric started pacing again.

Lorenzo leaned back in his chair and scrubbed an agitated hand down his face. "Why did you wait until now to tell us? We could have already started the transition process. I'm sure you had the cruise planned before now."

"Yes, we planned the cruise, but didn't decide until yesterday to use that to jump-start our retirement."

Lorenzo stared at his father in disbelief. Granted, he

and Cedric could probably handle everything and he'd known his father and uncle would be retiring at some point, but he'd envisioned this change to be far different.

The two older men stood and his uncle said, "I know you guys are on your way to a job site, so we'll let you get to it and meet next week. I've checked with your assistants and had them clear your schedules for Monday morning."

Lorenzo slowly came to his feet. He glanced over at his cousin, whose shocked expression mirrored his own. "Okay, then." He and Cedric gathered what they needed and left the office. He was grateful that Cedric would be driving because he needed a moment to process.

Before they could pull out of the parking lot, Cedric shifted in his seat to face Lorenzo. "What the hell just happened? I can't even—" He shook his head and blew out a long breath. "We have too much to do for this. I can't be stuck in an office all day, every day, and I don't know if I want to trust anyone to oversee the construction progress. The whole time they were talking I tried to think of someone and not one person came to mind." He pulled out onto the road.

"I hear you, man." He considered himself a perfectionist when it came to the job, but Cedric took it to an entirely new level. Everyone in Cedric's crew abided by his exacting standards or found him or herself looking for other employment. "On my end, I think I'm going to have to hire another technician."

"Joey? I thought he was working out fine. How long has he been on the job?"

"A year. He started out doing well, but over the past two months, when I've popped up at a site, I've found him goofing off with the foreman instead of surveying, like he's supposed to be doing. I've talked to him twice and that's one more time than I should have." He'd hired the twenty-three-year-old young man to help inspect project sites and evaluate the contractor's work in order to detect any problems with a design to take the load off Lorenzo.

"Clearly he didn't understand that you meant business."

"Clearly. He doesn't know I'm coming today. If he's anywhere other than walking the building with that tablet, he's gone. Especially now."

"I still can't believe they just decided to retire like that. There goes my social life. I had a date tonight with a fine sister...curves for days." Cedric had always said he never planned to marry, not because he didn't believe in the institution, he just didn't think it was for everyone. He liked to keep his dating life fluid to minimize issues.

Lorenzo chuckled. "I bet." He didn't have a social life to speak of and hadn't had a date in months. The drama associated with his last relationship had been enough to take him out of the dating game completely. With this new development his work hours would be increasing dramatically and he wouldn't have time to date anyway. That suited him just fine.

Friday evening, Desiree Scott stood and stretched while waiting for the printer to finish. She had several new orders and business was good. When she opened the doors of her business three years ago, she'd only hoped to survive. But her bath and body store, Scentillating Touch in Old Sacramento, was thriving and she couldn't be happier. Once the printer stopped, she stacked everything on her desk then went out front to join the other two women working. She spoke to customers as she made her way to the register.

"Did you find everything you needed?" she asked a woman waiting in line.

"Everything I needed and a few things I didn't. I love your soaps and was torn between the oatmeal, citrus basil and stress relief, so I decided to get one of each."

"I'm glad you like them." The three soaps were her bestsellers, especially the citrus basil, also a big hit with men. Desiree placed the items in a bag then had her sign the credit slip. "Thank you, and please come again."

"I definitely will. My daughter's bridal shower is in six weeks and these would make lovely favors. Do you take special orders?"

"Certainly. If you'd like to make an appointment for sometime next week, we can sit down and put together a nice gift."

The woman beamed. "I'd love to."

Desiree scheduled the appointment and thanked the woman. Inside, she turned cartwheels at the potential of increasing her business and already had some creative ideas forming in her mind. She turned her attention to the next person in line. For the next hour, business stayed steady and she spent time encouraging the customers to try out the lotions, creams, shower gels, scrubs and soaps. She'd had a sink installed specifically for that purpose. People were more apt to buy if they could try the products. Brenda Howard, the store's manager and her best friend, looked over and smiled as four more women left the store with large bags.

Desiree's cell rang and she smiled upon seeing her mother's number. Then she frowned, hoping it wasn't one of her sisters. Both moved in and out of her parents' home like revolving doors. Glad that there were only a couple of people in the store, she took a deep breath, moved to a corner and connected.

"Hello."

"Hey, Desiree."

She relaxed. "Hi, Mom. How are you?"

"Oh, fine. I baked some chicken and wanted to know if yours bleeds when you stick a fork in it."

She went still. "You mean raw chicken?"

"No. I cooked it. I don't remember it bleeding when I cooked it last time."

Desiree stifled a gasp and her heart rate kicked up, but she tried to keep the panic out of her voice. "Usually, when the chicken is cooked, it shouldn't bleed," she said slowly. "What temperature is your oven on?"

"Let me look." Her mother paused. "It's on three fifty."

"Okay. How long did you cook the chicken?"

"Um, I don't know."

Desiree rubbed a hand across her forehead.

Brenda mouthed, "Are you okay?"

Desiree pointed toward the back and started in that direction. After closing the office door, she went back to her conversation. "Mom, did you cook anything else?"

"Yes. I put on some rice right after I put the chicken in the oven." She fell silent for a moment. "Hmm. This rice isn't soft, either."

Still striving to maintain her composure, she said, "Mom, I want you to turn the oven up to four fifty, cover the chicken back up with foil and put it in the oven a little longer, okay?"

"Okay." Pans rattled in the background. "It's in."

"Now, I want you to put a cup of water in the rice, place the top on and turn the fire all the way down low."

"Alright."

"Are Patrice and Melanie there?"

"They haven't been here all day."

She cursed under her breath. For a few months, Desiree had been telling her sisters that something was going on with their mother. "I'll call you back in a little while, Mom."

"You don't have to do that, baby. I know you're at the shop."

"We'll be closing soon, so it's okay. I'll talk to you in a few." She disconnected, tossed the phone on the desk, dropped into the chair and tried to calm herself.

Picking up the phone again, she dialed her sisters. Neither one picked up, which didn't surprise her, since both only bothered to call when they wanted something. Her oldest sister, Patrice, at thirty-four, hadn't always been that way. But after finding her fiancé with another woman, she had become mean and bitter. At thirty, Melanie was one year younger than Desiree and had made it her life's mission to try to take everything Desiree had. If Desiree had it, Melanie wanted it, including boyfriends. After one too many destroyed relationships and broken hearts, Desiree had decided to focus solely on her business. Life was much simpler that way.

As soon as the last customer left, she locked the doors then called her mother back. Satisfied that both the chicken and rice were fully cooked, she told her mother she'd talk with her later.

"What's going on?" Brenda asked, entering the office and propping a hip on the desk.

Desiree recounted the story. "I think something is

really wrong. When I went home a few months ago, she kept repeating herself and I thought maybe it was just her getting older. But, she's been forgetting a few things and that has me concerned."

"What are your siblings saying?"

She rolled her eyes. "Keith said she was acting fine when he went over, but he only stopped by for a short visit." Her brother, Keith, was the oldest at thirty-six and relatively even tempered. "Melanie and Patrice keep denying anything is wrong and accusing me of trying to cause trouble."

Brenda shook her head. "They're a piece of work. I see why you stay far away from home. If I had to deal with them on a regular basis, somebody would end up with a black eye."

She gave a mirthless chuckle. "Yeah. Believe me, the thought has crossed my mind." Desiree had moved to California from Chicago to attend UC Berkeley and liked Northern California so much she ended up staying and had settled in Sacramento soon after graduating.

After they finished closing, Desiree cleaned up everything, collected the orders from her desk and headed home. She decided to wait and try her sisters again tomorrow.

Later, in bed, she still couldn't get rid of the nagging feeling that something was terribly wrong. The earlier conversation with her mother played over in her mind and added to her growing worry.

Desiree tossed and turned all night and when she woke up the next morning, felt no more rested than when she went to bed. She dreaded having to call her sisters, but knew it couldn't be avoided since she had no way of immediately getting to her mother.

She dressed and drove to the park near her home and walked along the path. The store wouldn't open for another two hours, so she had plenty of time. She inhaled deeply, trying not to worry about her mother. Their conversation the previous night still bothered her. Not even the beautiful surroundings—flowers in various colors, lush, green grass, tall shade trees and warm late spring temperatures—could pull her out of her troubled thoughts. At the end of the path, she spotted an empty bench and sat. Gearing up for battle, she took out her cell and tried her sisters again. She got Patrice's voice mail, hung up and called Melanie.

"Hey, Melanie," she said when her sister answered. "Why were you blowing up my phone last night?"

"I'm fine, and how are you?" she said sarcastically. Melanie snorted. "What do you want?"

Desiree slowly counted to ten, then told her what happened with their mother the previous night. "I think something is really wrong. Can you guys take her to the doctor?"

"There's nothing wrong with Mom. You're always trying to start problems. If you're that concerned, then come up here and take her your damn self!"

"You know I can't pick up and leave."

"You think you're all that since you got that *shop*," she sneered. "Little Miss High and Mighty, always trying to tell people what to do."

"Melanie, I'm not trying to tell anyone what to do," Desiree said wearily. "I'm only concerned about Mom."

"There's *nothing* wrong with Mom, so stop calling me."

Desiree should have been used to her sister hanging up on her by now, but it still hurt. Why did it have to be like this all the time? She wouldn't bother calling Patrice because Melanie had probably called and given her version of the conversation before the dial tone was complete. Times like this made her miss her father even more. When he died of cancer three years ago, she'd lost her only ally. Her brother intervened occasionally, but most often steered clear of the disagreements and told them to work it out. A tear slid down her cheek. She was tired of fighting alone.

Chapter 2

Lorenzo Hunter increased his pace, the *slip slap* of his running shoes hitting the pavement with a steady rhythm. The run felt good after working long hours all week. Although he loved the engineering job at his family's company, sometimes having to oversee so many projects left him drained with little time to do much else besides sleep. Now, with his father and uncle's sudden retirement announcement yesterday, he felt his nice, organized life about to spiral out of control. He and Cedric had stayed at the office until almost ten last night trying to decide how to shift some of their workload to the lower level supervisors. He smiled inwardly thinking about Cedric trying to explain to his lady friend that he had to cancel their date. The woman hadn't seemed too pleased and Lorenzo couldn't have been happier that he didn't have to worry about some woman waiting on him. He did miss his niece and nephew, though. Because of his hectic schedule, he hadn't seen them in over three weeks. But, he planned to rectify that later today.

Nearing a curve, he spotted a woman sitting on a bench up ahead. Even from that distance, he could see her beautiful face. As he got closer, she turned her head in his direction and he sucked in a sharp breath. She was even more gorgeous than he first thought. Then he frowned. Her face held such sadness and he briefly wondered about it, but had no intentions of stopping to find out. The last damsel in distress he rescued, he'd ended up dating—a disaster of gigantic proportions— and he promised himself he would never make the same mistake twice. Lorenzo heard her sniff and noticed the tears on her cheeks as he passed. *Son, you never pass by someone in need. God put us on this earth to take care of one another.* His father's voice rang clearly in his head. He cursed his upbringing. He slowed, then stopped running, turned and walked back.

"I'm only checking to see if she's alright. That is all," he muttered under his breath. She sat with her head bowed and her hands clasped tightly in her lap. "Excuse me, miss. Are you okay?" His gut clenched when she looked up at him with tearstained eyes, catching him off guard, and he thought about getting as far away from her as possible, as quickly as he could.

"I'm… I…" Her voice cracked and the tears came faster.

He felt his eyes widen and his heart thumped in his chest. Had he made it worse by asking? Before he could stop himself, he dropped down on the bench beside her and reached up to touch her shoulder. She surprised him by leaning against him and burying her face in his chest while sobbing. "Ah, I was running and…um… I'm probably…ah…a little sweaty." She didn't seem to hear him or care. Not knowing what else to do, he draped his arm around her shoulder and whispered that everything would be okay until she stopped crying.

"Miss, is everything alright?" he asked again. She stiffened and gasped sharply before jumping away from him so fast she almost fell off the bench. He quickly placed his arm around her waist to steady her. "Whoa. Not so fast."

She regained her balance and swiped at her face, but wouldn't look at him. "I'm sorry," she said hastily. "Oh my. I'm so embarrassed."

"No harm done. You seem really upset. Are you going to be okay?" When she looked up at him, a strange sensation started somewhere in the center of his chest. Suddenly, he had an overwhelming need to touch her rich, brown skin to see if it was as soft as it looked. The sunlight hit her hazel eyes in such a way that the brown and green flecks shimmered like jewels.

She squared her shoulders and said, resolutely, "I have to be. I don't have a choice."

Lorenzo stared intently at her. Her softly spoken declaration made him speculate on what life tragedies she had suffered. "Are you sure? Do you need me to call someone for you?"

She gave him a small smile. "I'll be fine. Thank you. I'm sorry for, you know…crying all over you."

She stood and he slowly came to his feet, towering over her by more than half a foot. He waved her off and chuckled. "Don't worry about it. Happens all the time."

She laughed a little. "I can imagine. I don't usually make a habit of crying on strangers, just so you know."

He stuck out his hand. "Lorenzo." When she placed her small hand in his large one, something akin to electricity surged through his body. He glanced down at their hands then back at her face.

Her eyes widened. "Desiree." She quickly withdrew her hand.

"Now we're not strangers."

"Does that mean I'm free to cry on you anytime?" she teased.

He shrugged. "Next time you might want to wait until I'm a little better-smelling." A smile bloomed on her face, her eyes sparkled and her soft, husky laugh stirred something deep inside him. Lorenzo couldn't remember ever reacting to a woman so strongly.

"I'll try to remember that. If you need something to help with your *scent*, I can help you out."

His eyebrows shot up. "Excuse me?" She dug into her purse, pulled out a card and handed it to him. He read it and laughed. "Oh, okay. I see—Scentillating Touch Bath and Body Products. Hmm, sounds interesting."

"I'm certain you'll find something you like and, if I don't have it, I'll create it."

He was even more intrigued now. "You make the stuff yourself?"

"I do. Everything is made from natural ingredients. Maybe when you have a free moment, you can come by and browse. The store hours are on the card. I'll be happy to help you find something for yourself or your significant other."

Significant other? He chuckled inwardly. If she only knew he hadn't been on a date in over nine months. "I might just do that."

"Great. I have to go. Thank you, again, for your shoulder and I'm really sorry about interrupting your run."

"I'll see you around." She blessed him with another beautiful smile before turning away. He watched as she hurried back up the path, her curvy bottom swaying with each step. Several minutes later, he still stood there wondering what happened—why his heart beat in his chest harder than when he had been running at full speed. To say he was mildly curious would be an understatement, but then he reminded himself what transpired the last time his curiosity got the best of him. "Shake it off, man." Since his body had cooled significantly, he saw no use in continuing the run. At least he'd gotten in a good mile and a half. Unclipping the phone from his waist, he dialed his sister to make sure she would be home. He glanced down at the card in his hand once more, then headed back to his car.

Desiree hurried to the parking lot, trying to put as much distance between her and that man as she could. Her hands shook so bad, she dropped her keys twice before being able to press the remote. She settled on the seat, started the car, then turned the air conditioner on full blast. Leaning her head back, she closed her eyes and recalled everything about the stranger who'd held her so tenderly as she cried. Never had she done something like that before.

The first thing she remembered was the sound of his voice—deep, soothing and sexy. But then, the same thing could be said about the man himself—definitely sexy. Smooth nut-brown skin, super fine face with those killer dimples, dark chocolate eyes, and that body. *Goodness!* She'd felt his strength when his arms were wrapped around her and when he kept her from falling off the bench. His shoulders were wide enough to block out the sun. The hard ridges of his chest and abdomen were clearly outlined in the sleeveless Under Armour shirt that clung enticingly to his upper body. She seriously considered sending the company a thank-you note for creating that piece of clothing. That, along with the rest of his impressive build and towering height made her wonder if he might be a professional athlete.

Desiree had never cared for men with locs and pierced ears, but Lorenzo's neatly done shoulder-length style and diamond studs made him even sexier, causing her to question that stance. Her reaction to him surprised her. When they shook hands, sparks shot up her arm and she saw the knowing look on his face. She shrugged and backed out of the lot. It didn't matter because there was no way she'd ever be able to keep a man like that. None of the men in her past had looked like that or exuded such potent masculinity and she couldn't keep their attention for more than a month or two—they always left her for someone else. So she knew she had no chance in holding the attention of a man like Lorenzo. Besides, he probably wasn't single, especially since he didn't deny it when she mentioned him maybe purchasing some of her products for a significant other. She heaved a deep sigh. Right now she had more important things to worry about than fawning over a man, no matter how fine he looked.

When Desiree arrived at her shop, her assistant, Sandra, stood at one of the long tables in the room they used for crafting and removing blocks of soaps from their molds.

"Hey, Sandra. Let me put this stuff in my office and I'll help you cut those."

"Hi, Desiree. I think these batches are going to be great. They're so smooth—no cracks anywhere. I can't wait to get a bar of this ylang-ylang and vanilla mix. It smells so good."

She dropped off the papers, locked her purse in the drawer and came back to the soap making area. Desiree picked up one of the bars and sniffed. "Mmm. I think you're right. This smells heavenly." The slightly floral scent of the ylang-ylang mixed with the sensual warm vanilla and cocoa butter produced a decadent soap designed to keep the body soft and hydrated.

They cut all ten blocks into bars and placed them on racks to cure, a process that would take four to six weeks, then Desiree went out to the front to make sure there was enough inventory. She had difficulty concentrating and had to keep recounting products because her mind kept wandering back Lorenzo.

"Morning," Brenda said, poking her head through the door several minutes later.

"Hey, girl."

"Did you ever talk to your sisters?"

Desiree sighed. "Yeah, Melanie. It was the usual conversation. She basically told me that nothing was wrong with my mother and if I think there is, that I should come to Chicago and take her to the doctor myself. Of course, she added some other nasty comments."

Brenda shook her head. "I'm sorry. What are you going to do?"

"Well, I'm going to try and talk to my brother first, then see what happens. I'm hoping he'll be able to handle it."

"Let me know if you need me to do anything. I'm going to do payroll. Any orders?"

"Yes. The list is on your desk. Thanks."

She continued to make notations then restocked items. Desiree made sure all the testers were filled and paper towels had been placed at the sink, before going over to unlock the door and turn on the Open sign.

They had a steady flow of customers for the first few hours so when her mother called, she let it go to voice mail. When there was finally a break, she left Brenda out front and went into the office to return her mother's call. After speaking for a few minutes, she hung up with a promise to send her mother more of her favorite lavender vanilla lotion.

She held the phone against her heart. Today her mother sounded like her old self, but somewhere in the back of Desiree's mind, she knew things were only going to get worse. She made a mental note to call her brother tonight and hoped he'd be more receptive than her sister, and then went back out front until closing.

Desiree went to the back and finished packing orders, including her mother's. Then, remembered to call her brother.

"Hey, baby girl," Keith answered.

"Hey, Keith. How are you?"

"Not too bad. What's up?"

She told him what happened the night before with their mother and asked if he could make an appointment to take her to the doctor. "I know she seems like herself a lot of the time, but I'm really worried that she's going to forget something serious like turning off the stove or adjusting the temperature on her bathwater before getting in. Please, can you do this for me?"

"What about Patrice and Melanie?"

Desiree blew out a long breath and told him about her earlier conversation with Melanie. "I'm not trying to start any trouble. I just want to make sure Mom is okay." Her voice cracked.

"Melanie is a drama queen. Don't cry, Desiree. I'll make the appointment and let you know what happens, alright?"

"Thank you."

"Are you still at the shop?"

"Yes, but I'm leaving after I hang up with you. Do you need something?"

"Well, now that you mention it, I could use some more of the citrus basil soap and aftershave. Women love that stuff on me." He laughed. "I have to beat 'em back with a stick."

She chuckled. "Yeah, right. Whatever. I'll send it out on Monday."

"Thanks. I'll talk to you later."

"Okay." Desiree hung up feeling much better and hoping the doctors wouldn't find anything serious. She turned to where Brenda sat waiting. "Ready?"

Brenda stood. "Yep, and I'm starving."

She and Brenda locked up and walked to a nearby restaurant.

"How's your mom today?" Brenda asked as they ate a late dinner.

Desiree finished chewing the bacon-wrapped shrimp before answering. "She sounded like her old self, but I *know* something isn't right. I did talk to my brother, though. He's going to take her to the doctor and let me know what happens."

"At least he didn't blow you off."

She nodded. "I hope it's not what I'm thinking."

Brenda took a sip of her tea. "What do you think it could be?"

"Some form of dementia or the onset of Alzheimer's. That's what scares me the most."

Her best friend set her glass down and shuddered. "I've read about what that disease does and it's terrible."

"Yeah." They continued to eat and talk and Desiree noticed a couple of guys staring. "There are two guys over to the left of the bar that keep staring over here."

Brenda turned and one saluted her with his drink. "They're not bad-looking, but I think they're a little too young for my tastes."

"I know what you mean." She chuckled and reached for her drink. When she glanced up, she saw a man standing at the bar who reminded her of Lorenzo. He stood halfway facing the bar, so she couldn't see his features clearly. She froze with the glass halfway to her mouth.

"Who are you looking at like that?"

Desiree took a hasty sip of her lemonade. "Um, nobody. I thought I saw someone familiar."

Brenda smiled. "Which one?"

"The guy wearing the blue shirt and jeans."

She scanned the area where Desiree indicated and turned back. "Are you talking about the guy with the dreadlocks? You always said you didn't care for that look on a man."

"I know. But I met a guy this morning—"

"What? When? Why didn't you tell me? Is that him?" Brenda craned her neck, trying to get a better view.

"No. It's not him." She told Brenda what happened at the park. "Girl, I was so embarrassed. The man is drop-dead fine and, not only does he wear his hair in locs, his ears are pierced—sexy."

What's his name?"

"Lorenzo."

"Hmm. Sexy name, too. Did you notice him wearing a wedding ring?"

"No, but that doesn't mean anything. Besides, with his good looks, I can't imagine him being single."

"Well, you should find out. It's about time for you to find someone."

"Yeah, right. Like I have time for a man. I'm busy with the shop and now this mess with my mom. I've had enough drama where men are concerned and I don't even want to go down that road again." Memories of her many broken hearts surfaced. No, she never wanted to feel that kind of pain again.

Chapter 3

Lorenzo lay on his sister's couch with his three-year-old niece, Lia, sitting on his chest. She tried to tell him something about going to school and he understood only about half of what she was saying.

"I go to school."

"You went to school?" She nodded vigorously. "What did you do?"

"Play toys and read books."

"Wow. Sounds like fun. What did you read about?"

"A-mi-nals."

He chuckled. "You mean a-*ni*-mals?"

"Uh-huh."

His sister, Alisha, came into the family room. "Okay, Lia, it's time for bed. Tell your uncle good-night."

"*Nooo!* I wanna stay Unca Wenzo." She leaned down and wrapped her small arms around his neck tightly.

Alisha smiled. "You can't stay with Uncle Lorenzo."

He sat up, cradling Lia in his arms. "I'll put her to bed, sis." Standing, he told his niece, "Give your mommy a kiss and say good-night."

Lia kissed her mom and giggled. "'Night, Mama."

"Good night, baby." She laughed and told Lorenzo, "You might as well get ready to tuck Corey in, too. He's putting away his toys."

"No problem. I got my little man covered." After putting the children to bed, he went in search of his sister and found her in the kitchen washing the few dishes in the sink. He grabbed a towel and helped dry.

"Everybody all tucked in?" she asked.

"Yeah. Although, Lia was trying sweet-talk her way out of going to bed and Corey had to tell me every little detail all about the end-of-the-year activities in kindergarten."

Alisha laughed. "He's been so excited. I can't believe that my little baby is going to be a first grader in a couple of months." She paused a moment before continuing. "So, I talked to Mom earlier and she told me about Dad and Uncle Reuben retiring. How are you and Ced feeling about it?"

"I'd be lying if I said it's all good. It would probably be fine if they planned to stick around for more than a week to help get things settled. To tell the truth, I'm still in shock. It seems so sudden. I mean, no warning, no next month we're going to be leaving. Just *bam*, we're out."

She paused in washing dishes and faced Lorenzo. "I see where you're coming from, but you guys have worked for the company since you were teenagers and know it as well as Dad and Uncle Reuben, if not better."

A smile played around the corner of Alisha's mouth. "I do agree that it would've been nice to give you a longer transition window, though. Talk about baptism by fire," she added with a chuckle, and resumed her task.

"Tell me about it," Lorenzo mumbled. "Are you working tomorrow?"

Alisha sighed. "Yep, bright and early at seven. There are a couple of emergency surgeries scheduled." She worked as a surgical nurse.

"Do you need me to keep the kids for you?"

"No, but thanks. Wayne's mother is going to babysit."

Lorenzo grunted and placed a plate in the cabinet.

She came, stood next to him and hugged him. "They'll be fine. You're the best big brother a girl could have. I don't know what I would do without you, Mom and Dad."

"Has Wayne tried to see Corey and Lia?" His sister's ex-husband decided one day he no longer wanted to be a husband and father and left Alisha eight months pregnant with a three-year-old son.

"No," she answered softly. "But his mother tries to see them as often as she can. Even she's angry with Wayne."

"So am I." He dropped a kiss on her hair. "Do you need anything? Money?"

"No, Lorenzo." Alicia shook her head. "You always ask me that and I keep telling you I'm good. Even without the child support, I can take care of everything."

"I know. I guess I've looked out for you so long, it's habit." Five years older than his sister, Lorenzo had been taking care of Alisha his entire life. He dried and put away the rest of the dishes, then leaned against the counter.

She gave him a sly smile. "What you need is your own woman to worry about."

A quick image of Desiree popped into his mind and he wondered if she was okay.

Alisha paused in washing the cup in her hand. "What kind of look is that?"

"What are you talking about? I didn't have any *look*."

"Yes, you did. Wait. Did you meet someone?" Her eyes lit up with excitement. "Don't even try lying."

Lorenzo let out a deep breath and ran a hand over his locs. He'd forgotten that she could read every expression that crossed his face like a neon sign. "I met someone, but it's not like you think." He recounted the incident in the park. "I saw her crying and just wanted to make sure she was okay."

"Well, what does she look like?" she asked while wiping off the table.

"Absolutely beautiful."

"You should go for it. I haven't seen you with anyone in a long time."

He snorted. "With good reason. You remember what happened the last time I tried to be a Good Samaritan?" Just the thought made his stomach turn.

Alisha rolled her eyes. "I do. But, I also remember telling you I suspected something was up with Veronica."

Lorenzo shook his head. "Too bad I didn't listen." He'd stopped to help Veronica Watson when her car broke down. She had been charming and insisted on taking him out to repay him for helping her. Within three weeks they'd started dating exclusively. Though he had never experienced all the emotional fireworks, they got along reasonably well and, nine months later, he had thoughts of moving toward something long-term. But that was before he found a bag hidden in his laundry room filled with enough drugs to get his engineering license revoked and put him in prison for at least a decade. That same day he'd gone to the store and found all the money mysteriously missing from his wallet. When he confronted her, she'd had the audacity to be upset and asked, "What's the big deal?" Since that time, he'd been leery of women, especially those in trouble.

Alisha shrugged. "She played the game well. But, the signs were there—lying about where she worked and never wanting you to pick her up from the job or home. Forget her," she said, waving her hand and coming to stand next to Lorenzo. "Tell me about this new woman."

"Her name is Desiree and she owns a bath and body shop in Old Sac called Scentillating Touch. You ever heard of it?"

"I have. A couple of the nurses have been raving about the products, but I haven't had a chance to get down there. See, she's already ahead of the game. Obviously she has no problems telling you where she works. And you said yourself she's beautiful."

"True. But, I'm not sure I want to deal with someone who seems to have a lot of issues again. Besides, she could already have a man."

"How will you know if you don't ask? I know that look—you're interested." Alicia bumped him playfully. "At least find out before you cut her off the list."

Lorenzo chuckled. "Look who's talking? I don't see you out there dating."

"Hey, I have two children to think about. I'm not bringing any men around them unless it becomes serious. And, I have had a couple of dates. Just because things didn't work out the first time doesn't mean it won't with someone else."

He nodded. "Wise words." He reached over and tugged on her ponytail. "I thought I was supposed to be the older sibling—the wise one."

She laughed and winked. "You are. I learned everything I know from you."

He joined in her laughter. "Okay. I'll go with that. I'd better get going so you can get some sleep." They walked to the front door.

"Thanks for helping with dinner and the dishes."

They embraced. "No problem. See you later."

As he drove home, Lorenzo thought more about the conversation with his sister. Maybe he should think about jumping back into the dating game. Then again, with his new ramped-up work schedule, maybe not. Even if he did decide to take the plunge, he couldn't be sure Desiree would be the right woman. The more he thought about it, the more he convinced himself she was another disaster waiting to happen. That being the case, he had no intentions of getting involved with her. He liked his drama-free life just fine.

Despite the many conversations he'd had with himself over the past week about not wanting to get involved with a woman who seemed to have lots of baggage, Lorenzo found himself walking through the doors of Scentillating Touch Sunday afternoon. Immediately, women stopped and stared, making him wonder, until he realized he was the only man in the store. A couple of them openly flirted and he chuckled to himself. He nodded politely and meandered around the store. She had everything attractively displayed and, despite its small size, the store's layout made the space feel larger. He was pleasantly surprised to find an area with products for men—everything from soap and shower gels to shaving creams and aftershave. Lorenzo picked up one of the aftershave bottles labeled Tester and sniffed. He nodded and picked up another one. Both were manly enough for his tastes. Then he smelled a bar of citrus basil soap.

"Nice," he said under his breath.

"Hello. May I help you find something?"

He turned to see a tall, young blond-haired woman with a wide smile. Returning her smile, he told her, "I'm just looking around."

"Is this your first time here?"

"Yes. Actually, I was looking for Desiree Scott. Is she here?"

"She's in the back right now, but I'm sure I can help you find whatever you need."

The woman, whose name tag read Casey, took a step closer, leaving little room between them. He arched a brow but, before he could respond, a curvy brown-skinned sister walked over.

"Is everything okay, Casey?" she asked.

"Just fine, Brenda. It seems as though this gentleman is looking for Desiree."

The woman stared at him for a long moment, then smiled. "I'll get her for you."

"Thank you."

While waiting, he continued to wander around. He saw several crates filled with objects in various shapes called bath bombs. "I wonder what these do," he mumbled, picking up a blue one shaped like a robot, turning it one way, then another before putting it back. Desiree came from the back as he turned and he saw surprise cross her features.

He slowly walked to where she stood and smiled. "Hi." Today, she wore a pair of black pants, a light blue short-sleeved shirt and a black apron bearing the store's logo. Even with her hair pulled into a ponytail and her face clear of any makeup, he still thought she was one of the most beautiful women he'd ever encountered. She had a sweet aura about her that drew him in ways he didn't understand.

"Lorenzo. Hi. What are you doing here?" she whispered.

"Don't you remember you gave me your card last week and told me to come by?"

"That's not what I meant. I mean…" She sighed deeply.

He chuckled softly at her flustered state. "I know what you meant." He gestured around. "This is a nice place you have."

She smiled shyly. "Thanks. Did you see anything you like?"

"Actually, I did. I think I want to try some of that citrus basil stuff. It smells good."

Her eyes lit up and her smile widened. "It does, and it's one of my bestsellers."

Just like before, her smile did something to him. "I do have a question, though."

"What?"

He walked back over to the crates. "What are these for?"

"They're bath bombs. You put them in your bathwater and they fizz while they dissolve, making the bathwater soft while giving off a relaxing scent. Some of them color the water, as well. You want to try one?"

"Maybe next time."

She laughed. "Oh, I see. You're not the bath type, huh?"

"Not really." He looked down at his watch. "So, what are you doing after you close up in twenty minutes?"

"I don't have anything planned. Usually I stay around for a while. Why?"

"I was hoping we could go out and maybe grab a bite to eat."

She opened her mouth to answer and the woman named Brenda beckoned her.

"Could you excuse us for a minute? I'll bring her right back," she said latching on to Desiree's arm.

He nodded. "Sure." The way the woman hustled Desiree off made him wonder if he had missed something. However, he hadn't missed his own racing heart reaction to Desiree the moment he saw her, only he didn't know whether it was a good thing or not.

"What's going on, Brenda?" Desiree asked, concerned.

"I heard him ask you out and I *know* you were about to give some lame excuse as to why you can't go," she whispered pointedly. "You don't have one, so get your butt back over there and accept that invitation."

"But, I was going to…" She trailed off when Brenda folded her arms and scowled.

"Girl, why are you acting like the man has three eyes, Bugs Bunny teeth, bad breath and looks like the bottom of an old shoe? The brother is *F-I-N-E*! You'd better believe if it was me he asked out, I'd already have my purse and be dragging him out the door."

Desiree rubbed a hand across her forehead. "I know, I know. It's just that I can't even remember the last time I went out on a date, and I've never gone out with someone like him. Besides, I don't think this is a good time to get involved with anyone. I'm really busy here with the shop and now there's the stuff going on with my mom." She glanced back over to where he stood. "He does seem like a nice guy, though." Brenda waited. "Oh, okay." One date couldn't hurt.

"Good. Go tell him you'll go. Casey and I will lock up and you can leave now."

"Yes, *Mother*," she said sarcastically.

Brenda grinned. "You can thank me at your wedding."

Desiree's mouth gaped and she shook her head. "I doubt things will get that far." She would never be lucky enough to have that happen. She walked back to where he stood waiting.

"Lorenzo?" she called. "I'd love to go out with you."

His dark eyes sparkled and he gave her his full dimpled smile, making her heart skip a beat. "Great. I can wait for you. I saw a bench at the end of the block."

"That's not necessary. Brenda and Casey will close, so we can leave now. I just need to get my purse."

"Sounds good."

She went to the office, then came back and waited for him to make his purchase. Turning to Brenda, she said, "I'll see you later." Brenda mouthed for her to call and she nodded. She looked up at Lorenzo. "I'm ready."

He opened the door for her to precede him. "Do you want to go anywhere in particular? I haven't been down here in a while and looks like there are a lot of new places."

"Well, there are quite a few choices. Is there anything you don't eat?"

"As long as the food is cooked, I'll eat it."

She slanted him an amused glance. "I guess sushi is out, huh? How about we walk around and see what catches your eye?"

"That'll work. Lead the way."

He placed his hand on the small of her back and heat flooded her body. Whenever she was near him, her body reacted in ways she'd never experienced. Several times while walking, he pulled her close to let other people pass, causing her to tremble and she didn't know how much more of his closeness she could take.

Chapter 4

Desiree and Lorenzo continued down the street. She tried to put some space between them to regain her equilibrium, but the number of people milling around made it nearly impossible. She gave up trying and decided to go with the flow. This would most likely be their only date, so she could handle him for the next hour or two. They stopped at a couple of places and she waited while he read the menus. He shook his head and they kept walking.

Taking her hand, he led her across the cobblestoned street. "Have you ever eaten at Joe's Crab Shack?" he asked, pointing to the restaurant across the train tracks.

"Once. The food is not too bad, but the wait is usually really long and it's pretty loud inside."

"I'd rather go someplace quieter, if you don't mind." He stopped and looked down at her. "This is our first date. I want to give you my undivided attention."

Oh. He's smooth. "Alright."

They continued to walk and settled on Fat City Bar and Café, where they only had to wait about half an hour. Once seated and presented with menus, Desiree realized she knew nothing about this man, except his first name. Where did he work? Did he even have a job? Did he have a wife at home? He'd called this a date, so surely he was single, right? She took a discreet glance at his left ring finger. No ring or tan line, but that didn't mean anything these days. She perused the different menu items and prices—although not super expensive, they weren't cheap, either. Letting out a deep breath, she lowered the menu. His eyes were waiting.

"Is something wrong?" he asked in that deep, velvet voice, studying her.

"Not really. Well, actually, yes. I don't know anything about you except your first name."

He raised an eyebrow. "Are you concerned that I might not be able to afford dinner?"

Warmth crept over Desiree's face and she lowered her head.

Lorenzo reached across the table and covered her hand. "I promise you I can pay for our meal. And you won't have to order salad and water."

Her face flushed even deeper. "I didn't mean—"

"I know. I'm messing with you." He grinned. "What do you want to know?" He placed his elbow on the table and leaned forward. "Let's see. My name is Lorenzo Alexander Hunter. I'm thirty-four, never been married and I'm not seeing anyone currently. I'm six feet two and a half inches tall and weigh one hundred and ninety pounds. I work as an engineer, am in perfect health and, oh yeah, the teeth…" White teeth sparkled against his mahogany face. "They're mine. Better now?"

She giggled. "Much." He smiled and shook his head and she laughed harder. "I'm sorry. Some of the men I've encountered were not always what they presented."

"I understand. I've run into the same thing. So, what looks good?" He gestured to the menu.

"I'm torn between the tequila lime steak and the shrimp and vegetable stir-fry. What about you?"

"I want to try the tequila lime steak."

"Then I'm getting the stir-fry."

A waiter appeared, took their orders and came back minutes later with the drinks.

He leaned back in his chair. "So, tell me, how did you get into the soap business?"

She took a sip of her drink before answering. "Actually, it was by accident. I initially wanted to be a pharmacist and had enrolled in the pharmacy program in college. I also worked part-time as a pharmacy clerk. A friend of mine asked me to go with her to one of those one-day classes put on by the Parks and Recreation. They were teaching how to make soaps, lotions and bath salts. I was totally hooked by the end of class. I went home, researched recipes on the internet and started making all kinds of stuff. My friends and family loved it and I started selling it to them. Brenda convinced me to pursue it, so I got a degree in chemistry instead.

"She and I spent a Saturday here when we were going to school at UC Berkeley and I fell in love with the quaint shops located in Old Sacramento. From that time on, I dreamed of owning my own little shop. The opportunity presented itself and I opened up the store three years ago." While she was grateful for the money her father left her, she wished he were still alive to see her accomplishment.

"That's really inspiring. Not too many people are able to pursue what they love as a career. Since you know all my vital statistics, I'm going to throw the same questions back to you."

"Alright. I'm thirty-one years old, never been married, not seeing anyone and you've seen where I work. I'm five-six and, like you, am in perfect health. What type of engineer are you?"

"You skipped a couple of questions," he said with a twinkle in his eyes.

"What do you mean?"

"Your teeth—are they yours or...?" He shrugged.

"Of course they're mine," Desiree said with mock outrage.

"And the other question?"

She narrowed her eyes and cocked her head to the side. "I know you aren't asking me how much I weigh."

"Nah. I know how you women are."

"Whatever." She rolled her eyes, but couldn't hide her smile. She never would have thought him to be a teaser or so down to earth. "You didn't answer my question."

"I'm a civil engineer. The company I work for does everything from residential and commercial buildings to roads and bridges. It's something I'd wanted to do since I was a kid."

Remembering how he looked in the park and thinking that he might be an athlete, Desiree wouldn't have guessed that as his line of work. "It must be amazing to be able to create something from nothing."

"It is. Something we have in common—creativity."

"Yeah," she said quietly.

The waiter returned with their food and her stomach growled softly. After blessing the food, they both dug in. Silence reigned for the next several minutes.

"How's the steak?" she asked.

Instead of answering, he cut a piece and put it on her plate. "You tell me."

"Mmm. This is good." She put some of her food on his plate.

He forked it up and nodded. "This is good, too."

They continued to eat and every time she looked up, he was watching her. "What?"

"I'm enjoying watching you eat. I love a woman with a good appetite."

"I have no problems putting away a good meal. Besides," she said with a wicked grin, "I don't want you to waste your money."

Lorenzo threw his head back and laughed. "I appreciate that." Still chuckling, he went back to his meal.

"Is that all you enjoy?" *Where in the world had that come from?* Desiree wanted to crawl under the table. No way had she meant to ask the question out loud.

He studied her a long moment before answering. "Actually, there are a few more things I enjoy. Maybe I'll have a chance to show some of them to you."

Desiree brought another portion of food to her mouth, thinking that she might be in over her head.

"Would you like dessert?" Lorenzo asked when they finished eating.

"No, thank you." Desiree pushed her empty plate aside. "I'm thinking about walking over to the Chocolate Factory. There's a caramel apple with peanuts calling my name."

He sat trying to figure out something else they could do because he didn't want the evening to end just yet. "Are you in a rush to get home?"

"No. Why?"

"I was thinking we could walk around for a little while after you get your apple."

"That would be nice."

He settled the bill and escorted her back out into the evening. Although nearing dusk, the temperature was still warm with almost no wind.

"I think we're going to be in for a hot summer," he said, peering up at the cloudless sky with its orange, red and purple colors exploding on the horizon.

Desiree glanced up. "I think so, too. Summer is still almost two weeks away and it's already in the nineties."

As they started down the street, Lorenzo reached down and entwined their hands. He felt the same spark he'd felt yesterday. He had yet to figure out why this woman made him react this way. The shy smile she'd given him when agreeing to their walk stirred something deep in his gut. It was a total contrast to the confident one that bloomed on her face when she talked about her business, making him wonder about her experience with men.

They crossed the cobblestoned street and stepped onto the wooden sidewalk. Laughter and music spilled out of buildings, and people passed them eating ice-cream cones, candy and other gooey confections.

"So, is everything okay with you?" he asked.

"What do you mean?"

"Yesterday." She didn't answer immediately and he

instantly regretted asking the question, thinking it may have conjured up the troubling memories again.

Finally, Desiree said, "Oh. I'm worried about my mother. She seems to be forgetting things and I'm afraid that something serious may happen. It's frustrating because I can't see for myself what's going on and my sisters don't think there's anything wrong."

He frowned. "She doesn't live nearby? What about your dad?"

"She lives in Chicago and my dad died three years ago."

"I'm sorry." He squeezed her hand. "Maybe you could pay your mother a visit. I'm sure she would enjoy it and you could see for yourself how she's doing."

Desiree smiled up at him. "I may just do that. My brother is going to take her to the doctor and I think I'll wait to see what he finds out before making any plans."

"How many siblings do you have?"

"Three—two sisters and one brother. My brother is the oldest and I have one older and one younger sister. What about you?"

"I have one sister, who's five years younger. She has two children. My nephew, Corey, is almost six and my niece, Lia, is three."

"You sound like a proud uncle."

Lorenzo smiled. "Yep, I am." He gestured across the street. "There's your store. We can get your apple now, if you want."

"Sounds good."

He led her over to the store and the smell of chocolate immediately engulfed him. While she stood in line, he checked out the display cases, noting they had chocolate-covered everything—pretzels, graham crackers, marshmallows, gummy worms and Oreos.

"Do you see anything you'd like to have, Lorenzo?" Desiree called over to him.

"Yeah. Plenty. I wasn't planning to get anything, but I'm going to have to get a couple of those chocolate-covered Oreos and a caramel peanut bear."

Desiree placed their order, paid and, smiling, handed him a bag. "My treat." She laid a hand on his arm. "Thank you so much for dinner."

Her touch sent warmth flowing through his blood. "My pleasure. Are you ready?"

She nodded.

He draped an arm around her shoulder and steered her back out into the night. He spotted several horse-drawn carriages farther down the street and headed in that direction.

"Where are we going now?"

"You'll see," Lorenzo answered with a sly smile. Her face mirrored confusion, but he pulled her along until they reached the end of the block. Stopping, he inclined his head. "Might I interest milady in a carriage ride?"

Desiree's eyes lit up with excitement. "Yes! I've always wanted to do that."

"Good. Let's do it." He didn't stop to analyze the measure of satisfaction he felt at her delight. He spoke to the driver and selected a tour that would take them by the Capitol and along the Sacramento River.

Lorenzo assisted Desiree into the carriage, climbed up and pulled her close. He glanced down at the look of pleasure on her face and felt a tug in his chest. As the driver started off, he tried to remember the last time he'd enjoyed spending time with a woman so much.

* * *

The driver made his way through the crowded streets of Old Sacramento and took them on a slow journey through downtown, exchanging the lively sounds of laughter for that of car and motorcycle engines. Desiree snuggled against Lorenzo's body, relishing a closeness and contentment she'd never felt with any other man. The Capitol, flanked by large trees on either side rising like shadows in the darkness, stood lit against the clear, night-blue sky, making for a picture-perfect postcard.

"It's beautiful," she whispered.

"Have you ever seen it at night before?"

"I've driven by, but never really paid much attention." She turned to face him. "I'll never see it the same again."

"Neither will I." He leaned down and touched his mouth to hers.

The kiss lasted a mere second, but warmed Desiree to her toes. He tightened his arm around her and rested his head against hers. As the driver continued toward the river, the sounds of traffic became more distant and the clip-clop of the horse's hooves magnified in the silence. A gentle breeze kicked up, blowing like a whisper across Desiree's face. She closed her eyes and inhaled deeply, wishing the night could last forever. Too soon, they'd returned to the starting point and their idyllic ride ended. They thanked the driver and he bid them good-night. Desiree and Lorenzo strolled hand in hand back to her shop.

"It's getting late and you probably have to get up early tomorrow," Lorenzo said.

"Actually, the store is closed tomorrow, but I have

a few things to take care of. I'm sure you have a long day ahead of you, too."

"I do. Where are you parked?" She pointed. He walked her over and waited while she unlocked the door. Turning her to face him, he rested his hands on her waist. "Thank you for your company tonight, Desiree."

"Thank you for inviting me. I had an amazing time."

"Can we do it again sometime?"

Everything in her shouted for her to decline. Instead, she said, "I'd like that."

They exchanged phone numbers, and she added her address at his request. He helped her into the car, leaned down and kissed her softly. "Good night. Drive safe."

It took a minute for Desiree to recover from the sweet kiss that momentarily rendered her mindless before she could reply. "You, too." He closed the door and she started the car, waving as she drove off. She caught a glimpse of Lorenzo in her rearview mirror and wondered how she would keep herself from succumbing to his charms.

Chapter 5

Desiree arrived at the shop Wednesday morning earlier than her usual time. With summer right around the corner, she would have an increased number of customers and wanted to be prepared. During the winter months, she only opened Thursday through Sunday, unless the area had some special event that drew a crowd. In the summer, she added Wednesday to her operating hours. She gathered the ingredients for lotion and added them to the double boiler. It would take a few minutes for the shea butter and beeswax to melt in the sweet almond oil. Then she would add fragrance and whip it to make it light and creamy.

"It's been three days and you still have that smile plastered on your face."

Desiree jerked up from the lotion she was stirring and smiled over at Brenda leaning against the door. "Hey, girl."

"So, have you talked to Lorenzo since your date?" Brenda asked, coming farther into the room.

Desiree turned her attention back to the pot. "Last night. He's on a job site in the Bay Area and had to be there this morning at six, so we only talked for a few minutes."

"You seem really happy."

She shrugged. "He's a nice guy. I'm going to enjoy our time until it ends."

Brenda frowned and angled her head. "Who says it has to end?"

She released a deep sigh. "Come on, Bren. A guy who looks like that? He could have any woman he wants. I'm sure he'll be moving on as soon as someone more exciting comes along."

Brenda shook her head. "Des, I don't know why you don't see yourself as beautiful. You are. You're also smart, independent and have a heart of gold. Why wouldn't he want to be with you?"

Desiree shrugged. "That may be true, but it's never happened before." None of those positive traits had kept her ex-boyfriends from walking away. "You, of all people, know my track record. Men only stay around until the next pretty young thing comes along."

"Not all men. There are a lot of good men out there."

"I'm sure there are." She removed the lotion from the heat and started funneling it into bottles. "I'm just not lucky enough to find one."

Brenda patted her on the shoulder. "Maybe your luck is changing. I'll be in the office."

Yeah, right. Although her date with Lorenzo had been like something out of a fairy tale, she wasn't holding out hope for a happily-ever-after with him. Men like him didn't settle for women like her. Yes, she was intelligent and tried to be a nice person, but that didn't mean much these days. Scrubbing a hand across her forehead, she expelled a long breath. The short time she'd spent with Lorenzo had been unlike any other date she'd had and, if she were honest with herself, she'd admit to liking him. Then again, she would be better off keeping those growing feelings on lockdown. She couldn't handle another broken heart.

Desiree cleaned up and got ready for her meeting with Mrs. Daily. The woman would be coming to discuss wedding shower favors for her daughter. She set up the small folding table kept for this purpose in a corner of the shop, covered it with a white tablecloth and placed a variety of fragrances, samples and molds on top. She lifted her head when Mrs. Daily rapped on the window. Desiree assumed the young woman with her must be her daughter and the bride.

"Good morning, Mrs. Daily," Desiree said as she opened the door.

"Good morning, Ms. Scott. This is my daughter, Laura."

"Call me Desiree. Hello, Laura. It's nice to meet you. Won't you ladies come in, have a seat and we'll get started."

"Thank you," Laura replied. She walked through the store, stopping at various tables and bins, before coming over to the table Desiree had set up. "This place is fabulous. I love the soaps my mother bought."

Desiree smiled. "Thank you. Do you have any ideas about what you'd like to include in your favors?"

"Not really. At first, I thought about a bar of soap but, now that I'm here, I see so many other things that would be nice." Laura walked over to another area.

Desiree watched as Laura moved around the shop again, stopping to sniff bottles and rubbing on lotion. She waited for Laura to come back to the table before beginning.

Mrs. Daily smiled and patted her daughter's hand. "I'm sure Desiree will be able to help us find something nice, Laura."

Desiree went through several gift choices. "Laura, you mentioned having a bar of soap. I'd suggest going with a sample-sized gift box. That way you can include more than one item." She showed her the different sizes. After a lengthy discussion, Laura decided on a gift box that included mini sizes of shower gel, lotion, soap and a bath bomb. Desiree thanked them and gave both women samples to take home.

Once the ladies were gone, she cleaned up and checked her inventory to ensure she had everything to complete the order. Thankfully, she had just done a batch of the lavender vanilla soap two weeks ago. Desiree removed one of the loaves, cut it into guest-sized bars and placed them on a rack to dry. She put the mold back in its place and hurried across the room to catch her ringing phone. Her brother had taken their mother to the doctor today and had promised to call afterward. Seeing his name on the display, she quickly connected.

"Hey, Keith. How did it go?"

"Hey, sis. Well, I didn't get much information outside of the fact that Mom has lost nine pounds since her last visit three months ago."

"That's a lot, considering she's not on a diet or anything." Desiree's thoughts automatically centered on whether her mother had been forgetting to eat. She made a mental note to do some extra cooking while in

Chicago. If she prepped some meals, her mother would be able to just heat and go. It would also provide Desiree with a little peace of mind knowing she didn't have to worry about the food being fully cooked. The conversation with her mother about the half-done chicken still made her shudder.

"I agree. The doctor was out with an emergency and they scheduled her with another doctor who suggested we wait to talk to Dr. Jamison when he gets back, since he's more familiar with her case. I wasn't too happy about it, but I scheduled another appointment for next Monday."

"I think I'm going to fly up and go with you. How did Mom seem today?"

"She's pretty good, but I don't like that big weight drop. I really hope there's nothing serious going on."

"So do I. Thanks for taking her."

"You don't have to thank me. She's my mother, too. I'm going to do better about checking in with her."

"Did you talk to Melanie and Patrice yet?"

"No. But Melanie did call me the other day, complaining about her conversation with you."

"I'm not surprised," Desiree murmured. "And she, no doubt, left out the part about her hanging up on me."

Keith chuckled. "She skipped that part." He paused. "You know, I didn't want to believe something might be wrong with Mom, but she does seem to be repeating herself a lot more than usual."

"That's what I'm afraid of." First, her father, and now her mother. She didn't think she could handle it if the results turned out like she feared.

"Anyway, Des, I need to run. Text me your flight information and I'll pick you up."

"Okay. Talk to you later. Tell Mom I said hi."

"I will. Love you, girl."

"Love you, too." Desiree leaned against the counter and closed her eyes. *Please don't let it be Alzheimer's or dementia.*

She stood there a few seconds longer, then went to spoon the lotion into containers. She reserved a portion and put them into the one-ounce sample jars for Laura's gift box. Earlier, Laura had chatted excitedly about her upcoming wedding and spoken about her fiancé in glowing terms. Desiree found herself experiencing a little envy. None of her relationships had ever lasted long enough to speak of a man that way and not one of those men had ever done anything memorable for her. Until Lorenzo. Their one date had been better than all her dates combined and she found herself longing for the type of relationship Laura and her fiancé seemed to have or one like her parents had—a deep, abiding love that weathered the storms of life.

She dismissed the foolish notion, stood and began cleaning off the table, but her thoughts remained on Lorenzo and when she would see him again.

Thursday morning, Lorenzo walked around the partially completed San Francisco high-rise making notations on his iPad and checking on the progress of the landscaping and road construction that would surround the building. He stopped to speak to one of the workers briefly, then continued toward the front. Barring any unforeseen obstacles, the building should be completed within eighteen months. Lorenzo joined Cedric and the foreman as they pored over the blueprints.

"We can start adding here," Cedric said to the foreman, pointing at an area on the sheet. "I want to get as much done as possible before the weekend."

"No problem." The foreman turned to Lorenzo. "Hey, Zo. When is the back part of the lot going to be finished?"

"The concrete is being poured today, so it'll be ready for your guys to start the parking structure on Monday."

"Thanks. See you later."

Lorenzo waited until the man left, then scanned Cedric's face. "Rough night?"

Cedric slanted him an amused glance. "Depends on your definition of rough. I'm tired as hell, but it was worth it. Of course, I needed a double shot of caffeine to get going this morning," he added with a wry chuckle. "You should try it sometimes. It works wonders for releasing stress and we've had a lot this past week."

Lorenzo smiled. "I bet." A vision of Desiree flashed in his mind. She seemed a bit reserved and he wondered if she'd be the same in bed. He immediately dismissed the thought, but it came right back.

"Didn't you tell me you met some woman?" Cedric made a notation on the blueprint.

"Yeah. Her name is Desiree and she owns a bath and body shop in Old Sac. She's nice, but has a lot of baggage—family drama—and I don't know if I want to be bothered with all that." It had been almost two weeks since their impromptu date, yet, he hadn't been able to stop thinking about her or wanting her. Those few kisses they shared had only made him want more, but he still hadn't figured out how he wanted to proceed.

"I hear you, man. That's exactly why I keep my liaisons moving—a month or two at the most. That leaves no time to get involved with drama or other issues."

"We've only gone out once, so I haven't decided one

way or another what'll happen next. Anyway, we never got around to talking about how to deal with the new changes the McBrides want to add to the building," he said, changing the subject. After the design was approved and the groundbreaking had started, the land developers wanted to make a significant change to the building design that would add at least three weeks to the completion date, not to mention increasing the cost, but still expected them to finish on time and foot the bill.

"What did you have in mind? You know I got an email from their office yesterday hinting that they might want another change."

Lorenzo shook his head. "In addition to the new design fee and materials cost, we're going to add a surcharge for any structural changes after a design has been approved. Also, each major change will add four to six weeks delay in the completion time." In their contracts, Hunter Construction allowed for a thirty-day window for changes, and Lorenzo always built a small cushion in the budget for unexpected related costs. Every so often, a client did make a few modifications after the allotted time period, but only minimal ones that didn't require any structural changes.

Cedric angled his head thoughtfully. "I like it. I wonder why our fathers never added that stipulation."

"Probably because they never ran into this kind of situation. I actually did a little research on some of the McBride's previous buildings and it seems as though they have a reputation for trying to change in the middle of a project."

"Well, let me know how it goes."

"I will. I'm headed back to the office. What time do you think you'll be back?"

Cedric checked his watch. "It's eleven now and I don't plan to be out here more than a couple more hours. If the traffic's not too bad, I should get there around three or three-thirty."

"Okay. I'll see you then. I have a couple of interviews this afternoon for another technician." Lorenzo had ended up firing Joey. Not only had the young man not done his job, but Lorenzo also found out that he had left the site early three days in a row. The first two candidates he had interviewed hadn't impressed him, but with any luck, today's meetings would go better.

"Do they look promising?"

"On paper," he said with a smile. "Later." He walked to where he'd parked the company truck he'd driven, tossed his hard hat on the seat and got in. He contemplated whether to stop and get something to eat now or wait until he made it back to Sacramento. In the end, he chose to wait. The traffic should be fine, but one never knew when it came to the Bay Area.

The drive went smoothly and Lorenzo spent much of it thinking about Desiree. When he crossed the overpass in West Sac where he had a clear view of downtown, it took everything in him not to veer left at the Highway 80 split and head to her shop. At the last moment, he went right toward Reno and his Roseville office. Once there, he sought out his father and uncle to get their input on the new surcharge he planned to implement. Both were in agreement. "I'll try to have the fee schedule finished by tomorrow. I have a couple of interviews to do today." His parents, aunt and uncle would be leaving next week for their cruise and he wanted to have everything in place before then.

"Sounds good. We knew you were ready to take over," his uncle said.

His father nodded. "Just bring it by when you're done. If you don't finish it tomorrow, we can talk about it at the house on Saturday."

"Okay." Lorenzo stood and walked to the door. "I'm going to get something to eat. You guys want me to bring you something back?"

"No thanks," they chorused.

He left and walked to the deli located in a nearby shopping plaza. Back in his office fifteen minutes later, he ate while drawing up the figures for the new policy.

"Lorenzo."

Lorenzo's head came up when he heard his assistant's voice. "Hey, Tanya."

"Your three o'clock is here."

He took a glimpse at his watch. She was ten minutes early—a good sign. "Thanks. I'll be right out."

Tanya smiled and nodded.

He disposed of his food wrappers, straightened his desk and went to greet his first interviewee.

Two hours later, Lorenzo had all but decided on the first candidate. Joann Adams had impressed him the moment she walked through the door with her knowledge base and work history. And she'd been on time, unlike the young man who'd come after her. He went out to ask Tanya to type up an offer letter, and then walked down the hall to see if Cedric had returned. Cedric's assistant indicated that he had and told Lorenzo to go in.

Cedric glanced up from the pad he'd been scribbling on and set his pencil down. "How did it go?"

"I just had Tanya type up an offer letter for the new hire. Her name is Joann Adams and I think she'll work out well. She reminds me of how we were when we first started."

"Passionate, ready to take on the world…?"

"Bingo."

"And now that the world is here, are we still passionate?" Cedric asked with a laugh.

Lorenzo grinned. "Something like that." They did a fist bump. "Let's take it."

"How long are you planning to be here tonight?"

"Another two or three hours, why?"

"I wanted to get your opinion on something."

He propped his hip on the corner of the desk and folded his arms. "What's up?"

Cedric rotated his laptop so Lorenzo could see the screen.

"A house?" He studied the rendering of a two-story home. "I didn't know you'd taken on a new project."

"This one is personal. Jeremy went to Lake Tahoe a couple of months ago and loved it so much he wants to build a vacation property there." Jeremy was Cedric's younger brother and a robotics engineer.

Lorenzo picked up the laptop and clicked on the various rooms. It had three bedrooms, each with a private balcony, and three and a half baths. "Nice. I should do the same thing. It would be great to have somewhere to go when I want to get out of Dodge that doesn't require a flight."

"My thoughts exactly. I checked out some areas slated for building and found a few that might work. All of them have a partial view of the lake, which is only a short walk away."

"And perfect for all your *dates*."

"Oh hell no! The only women allowed would be our

mothers, aunts, Alisha, Siobhan and Morgan." Siobhan and Morgan were their cousins in Los Angeles and daughters of their fathers' sister. "I don't bring women to my house. I don't want them invading my space and getting any ideas. You start doing that and the next thing you know, they'll be asking for a key." He frowned and took the laptop. "That will *not* be happening."

Lorenzo laughed. "Relax, Ced."

"I don't see you talking about taking Desiree or some other woman to your house."

"I just met Desiree. Besides, I tried that before, remember?" He wasn't eager to bring another woman to his home after the last one. Just thinking about all the trouble he could have been in still pissed him off.

"Hmm, I wonder what Veronica is doing now."

"I could care less, as long as she stays the hell away from me. I'm going back to my office. Let me know about the Tahoe land. I might start working on one for me, too."

"Okay." Cedric turned his attention back the computer.

Seated behind his desk a minute later, Lorenzo spun his chair around and stared out the window. He'd thought he had gotten over Veronica's betrayal—he hadn't thought about her in over a year—but the mention of her name had conjured up the same bitterness that had plagued him for weeks after he had sent her packing. Now there was Desiree. Somehow, he couldn't see her doing something so deceitful. However, it didn't change the fact that he didn't want to get too close. *Then why are you still thinking about her?* He didn't have an answer.

Chapter 6

Lorenzo reached for his cell and, before he could stop himself, called Desiree.

"Hello."

The sound of her sexy voice had him contemplating making the drive clear across town just to see her. "Hey, Desiree. Did I catch you at a bad time?" He'd forgotten that her shop didn't close until six. She had another hour to go.

"Hi, Lorenzo. Not really. It's a little slow right now, so I have a minute. How's your project coming?"

"Not bad, but the client has decided he wants to implement some major changes."

"Didn't you tell me you'd already broken ground? I hope you're going to charge him a pretty penny for the extra time and money that'll cost."

Lorenzo chuckled hearing her sound all fired up.

"I'm working on a cost estimate as we speak. How's your day been?"

"We had a steady flow of traffic for a good portion of the day. Brenda and I have been working on getting the online store fully up and running and, once that's done, I'm hoping it'll increase business."

"Sounds like it might be a lot more work for you."

"I'm sure it will be, but I don't mind investing in my dream."

He and Cedric shared the same philosophy and it was one more thing that drew him to her. "Have you talked to your mother?"

She sighed. "Briefly, yesterday. My brother took her to the doctor, but he was out with an emergency and he had to reschedule. I'm going to fly up this weekend and go with him on Monday."

Though her going out of town gave him the distance he said he needed, he felt a measure of disappointment that he wouldn't be able to see her. "When are you leaving?"

"Saturday morning."

"I hope everything goes well."

"So do I."

They fell silent for a moment. "Well, I don't want to hold you. Maybe we can get together when you get back." He'd had to cancel their date last week.

"That would be great. I'll talk to you then."

"Have a safe trip."

"Thanks."

They said their goodbyes and Lorenzo disconnected. He tried to concentrate on his work, but thoughts of Desiree kept messing with his focus. After another few minutes, he spun around in his chair and stared out the window, unable to get her off his mind. Lorenzo turned back to his desk and his cell rang before he could write one word. He picked it up and saw his sister's name on the display.

"Hey, Alisha," he said after connecting.

"Hey, Lorenzo. I need a big favor. Surgery ran longer than expected and I won't get out of here for another hour. Can you pick up the kids from day care? I tried to call Mom, but she wasn't home."

"Of course. You want to get them from my house or I can bring them home?"

"I'll come get them. Thanks. I really appreciate this, big brother."

"No thanks needed. You know I'm always here. See you in a while."

"Okay. Gotta run."

Lorenzo shut down his laptop, shoved it in the bag, along with the files he'd been working on. He walked down the hall to Cedric's office and stuck his head in the door. "I need to go pick up Corey and Lia for Alisha, so I'm taking off."

"Okay. Give them a hug and tell Lisha I said hi. I have to get over there to see them. It's been a while."

"I will. Later." Outside, he took a moment to put the car seats in the backseat of his SUV. He'd bought them so his sister wouldn't have to worry about having to leave them at the day care just in case she needed one of them to pick up the kids. His parents had done the same. Lorenzo drove the twenty minutes to the Roseville day care center next door to the school that Corey attended. He stopped at the front to sign them out.

"I need to see your ID, sir," the young woman seated behind the desk said.

Lorenzo handed it over and waited for her to check for his name on the approved list. When she did, she smiled and waved him inside. He stepped over a few toys and scanned the room for his niece.

"Unca Wenzo!"

He turned and was nearly bowled over by Lia when she ran full speed and wrapped her arms around his legs. "Hey, baby girl," he said with a smile, lifting her off the floor and kissing her cheek. "How are you?"

"I'm good."

One of the teachers brought Lia's backpack over and handed it to Lorenzo. He thanked her and went to the other room where the older children were to find his nephew. He spotted Corey and threw up a wave.

Corey stood, gathered his belongings and crossed the room. "Hey, Uncle Lorenzo. Where's Mom?" he asked as they walked out to the car.

"She had to work late, so you guys are going to hang out with me for a little while. She shouldn't be too late."

"Okay."

Lorenzo strapped them into their seats and drove home. Once there, he put in one of the Disney videos they loved and went to cook dinner. Thankfully, he'd taken out a couple of chicken breasts to thaw. He added pasta with a lemon butter sauce and steamed broccoli and fixed their plates. He still marveled at the fact that Corey and Lia actually liked broccoli. He remembered trying everything he could to get out of eating the vegetable as a youngster. It had taken him over ten years to try it again. The children were halfway through the meal when Alisha arrived.

"You look tired," he said, placing a kiss on her temple.

Alisha sighed heavily. "I am. All I want to do is fall out and sleep."

"I made dinner, so that's one less thing you'll have to do when you get home."

"You are the best big brother *ever*."

Lorenzo laughed. "Yeah, I know." He winked and gestured her to the kitchen.

"Hey, babies." She bent to kiss each of them. They returned her greeting around mouthfuls of food.

"Sit and I'll fix you a plate." He grabbed two plates, filled them and came to the table.

"This smells so good." Alisha recited a quick blessing and dug in. "Mmm. Maybe I need to work late more often. It's nice to have a meal waiting after work. I always wondered how it would feel," she added wistfully.

Lorenzo opened his mouth to comment about her no-good ex, but remembered the children. Instead, he forked up a portion of the pasta.

"Uncle Lorenzo, can we finish the movie now?" Corey wiped his hands on a napkin.

He glanced over at Corey's empty plate. "Yes." He stood, cleaned up Lia, who had finished her food as well, and settled them in the family room where he had paused the movie. Lorenzo came back to the table and resumed eating. "Do you have a long day tomorrow?"

"No. As long as there are no emergency surgeries." Alisha went to get a glass of lemonade, then reclaimed her seat. "How're you and Ced doing?"

"Okay. We still haven't filled our old positions, so it's been hectic." They had considered promoting a couple of the lower level supervisors, but hadn't yet because they were hesitant to turn over the reins.

"You both are pretty anal when it comes to your jobs,

so I know that's a factor. But you're going to have to let go sooner or later."

"Probably."

"Are you still seeing the woman who owns the bath and body store?"

"Yeah, why?"

Alisha smiled. "Just asking. It's been a couple of weeks and you're still interested, so I'm guessing this relationship is going somewhere."

"I have no idea. We've only gone out once. I had to cancel last week and she's going out of town this weekend, so we'll see." He shrugged.

"But you like her, I can tell."

"She's nice."

"And she has a good job," she said, pointing her fork for emphasis. "I'm going to have to get over there soon. Maybe introduce myself and check her out."

Lorenzo groaned and leaned back in his chair. "That's not necessary." No telling what his sister would say to Desiree.

She finished her food, picked up hers and the children's plates and took them to the sink. "If she's a potential sister-in-law, I need to see what she's like." She folded her arms and leaned against the counter.

"Wait. Potential what? Hold up, girl. Nobody said anything about that. As I told you, we've only gone out once, so you're getting *way* ahead of yourself."

Alisha shrugged. "Maybe, maybe not. Even though you're not saying so, I know you're feeling this woman. Your whole expression changes when you mention her name and I have never seen you react that way when it comes to a woman. Not even the last one, who shall remain nameless." She straightened. "I'd better head home."

He came to his feet and followed her to the family room, still trying to figure out what she meant by his expression changing and what reaction she had seen.

"Time to go home."

"Aw, the movie's not over yet," Corey said.

"We have the same movie at home, so you can finish it tomorrow. Put your shoes on." She got Lia's shoes and put them on the little girl.

Lorenzo got their backpacks and walked her out. He rubbed his nephew's head. "Later, Corey."

"Bye." Corey climbed into the car and buckled himself in.

He went around to the other side of the car, leaned in and kissed Lia's cheek. "See you later, baby girl." He tickled her.

Lia giggled, blew him a kiss and waved.

He hugged his sister. "Text me when you get home."

"Okay. Thanks again for picking up the kids and for dinner. Night."

He stood in the driveway until her car disappeared around the corner before going back inside. While he rinsed and put the dishes in the dishwasher, he thought about his sister's comments. Potential sister-in-law? He didn't see himself taking that trip in the near future. Then why couldn't he stop thinking about her or the way her mouth fit against his? In the kisses they had shared, he'd tasted a sweetness that he hadn't been able to forget. And he wanted more.

Lorenzo glanced at the clock on the wall. Not stopping to analyze his decision, he started the dishwasher and drove to Desiree's condo.

He parked in a visitor spot and sat in the car for a good five minutes wondering what the heck he was doing. He had never driven to a woman's house for the sole purpose of kissing her. "This is crazy," he muttered. After another minute, Lorenzo finally got out, walked to her unit and rang the doorbell. His heart started pounding when she opened the door.

Desiree's eyes widened. "Lorenzo! Hey. What are you doing here?"

"May I come in?"

"Um…sure." She moved back for him to enter.

Lorenzo closed the door behind him and gathered her into his arms at the same time his mouth descended on hers. Too ravenous to be gentle, he devoured her mouth with an intensity that stunned him. But he couldn't stop. Her hands burned a path across his chest and wound around his neck. She gripped the back of his head and held him in place. Each stroke of her tongue against his brought him closer and closer to the brink of losing control. And he never lost control. Ever. He eased back and rested his forehead against hers. "I needed that."

She didn't say anything, but her labored breathing and the desire still glittering in her eyes told him she needed it, too. Desiree nodded, confirming it. "Me, too."

Her admission made him smile. Lorenzo captured her mouth again, this time swirling his tongue around hers slowly, absorbing her luscious taste into his very being. His hands slid down her spine. He caressed her hips and drew her flush against the solid bulge at his midsection so she could feel just what she did to him. At length, he lifted his head. He continued to gift her with fleeting kisses along the softly scented column of her neck. Her breathless sighs made him even harder.

"Lorenzo," Desiree whispered.

The sound of her calling his name tempted him to carry her to her bedroom and take his time acquainting himself with every inch of her sexy body. But he needed to slow down. And he needed to leave. Now. "I'm gonna go."

Her brows knit in confusion.

"I know you feel how much I'm attracted to you, but I don't think either of us is ready to take this further. But if I stay one minute longer…"

Desiree smiled. "I understand, and you're right. We need to slow things down and I'm not sure I'm looking for anything serious right now."

"I feel the same, but I do enjoy being with you."

"I like being with you, too. Can we keep it light, no ties?"

"Absolutely." A light affair worked perfectly for him.

She came up on tiptoe and kissed his cheek. "I did enjoy your kisses."

Lorenzo chuckled. "I enjoyed yours, too. We'll have to get a few more in when you come back."

"Deal."

He reached behind him and opened the door, but his feet refused to move. Kissing her once more, he stepped out and closed the door behind him away from temptation. *So much for trying to stay away from her.*

Chapter 7

Sunday afternoon, after grocery shopping, Desiree started cooking while her mother rested. She had noticed her mother moved much slower. Her typical brisk pace had been replaced with measured, almost-unsure steps. And what normally would have taken less than thirty minutes ended up taking double that time.

While going about the task, her mind drifted to Lorenzo. From the moment he left her house on Thursday evening, she had been thinking about the way he had kissed her. She had only known him a couple of weeks, but being with him felt different than with any other guy she had dated. Desiree couldn't believe he had driven to her house for the sole purpose of *kissing*. He'd had every molecule in her body on fire and she was glad one of them had the good sense to stop, otherwise they would have ended up in her bed. Never had a man made her feel so out of control and ready to throw caution to the wind. Putting him out of her mind, she refocused on the food. Two hours later, they sat down to dinner.

"Goodness, I've missed these enchiladas," her mother said after the first bite.

Desiree smiled. "Good thing I made enough for leftovers then, huh?" She'd gotten the recipe from a friend and loved them so much, Desiree now never made the dish any other way. She opened her mouth to say something and heard the front door open. Her sister, Patrice, appeared in the kitchen a minute later.

"Hi, Mom." Patrice bent to kiss their mother's cheek. "Hey, Desiree. Melanie said you were here."

"Hey, Patrice."

Patrice surveyed the pots and baking dishes on the stove. "Wow, Mom. You threw down today. Can I take some of this home?"

"I made the food and all of it is for Mom so she won't have to cook this week," Desiree said pointedly.

Patrice made a face. "All of it?"

"*All* of it. I made just enough for her to have two servings, so there really isn't extra."

Patrice glared at Desiree. "Mom, can I take some home?"

Her mother gave Patrice a sidelong glance. "Only if you're planning to come by this week and make some more. Desiree is giving me the week off from cooking and I plan to enjoy it."

Desiree wanted to cheer. She smiled over at her sister, who looked like she wanted to explode, then resumed eating. Obviously, Patrice hadn't been too happy about not getting food and, thankfully, left after a few minutes.

When they were done, Desiree stored all the food and cleaned up the kitchen. She hadn't cooked this much since her last visit at Christmas. By the time she finished, it was well after ten and *tired* didn't begin to describe how she felt. Her mother had already gone to bed, and Desiree showered and did the same. Although exhausted, her mind still raced with thoughts of what the doctor would say. Her cell buzzed and startled her.

Desiree picked it up and saw a text message from Lorenzo: Just wanted to make sure you arrived safely.

She smiled and replied: I did, thank you.

Lorenzo: What time do you get in tomorrow night?

Desiree: Ten. Why?

Lorenzo: I'll pick you up. I'd like to see you.

Her pulse skipped. She had planned to take an Uber home. Her thumbs hovered over the keyboard briefly. She typed: Okay. I'll send you my flight information in the morning.

Lorenzo: Great. Hope all goes well with your mother. Good night.

Desiree: Good night.

Desiree plugged the phone into the charger. Lorenzo's thoughtfulness made it hard for her to resist him. Memories of all her failed relationships rose and she sighed. She needed to proceed with caution. Besides, she had more pressing matters to deal with. She turned over and tried to get comfortable, but had a hard time going to sleep.

When she woke up Monday morning, she felt as if she hadn't slept more than ten minutes. Knowing her brother would be there in less than two hours to pick them up, Desiree left the bed and got dressed. Her mother had always been an early riser and Desiree found her sitting at the kitchen table reading one of her daily devotionals.

"Good morning, Mom." She kissed her cheek.

"Morning, baby."

"Have you—" Desiree went still upon seeing her sister Melanie shuffle into the kitchen. By her attire, Melanie must have spent the night. Desiree hadn't heard her come in.

Her mother glanced up from her booklet. "When did you get in, Melanie?"

"Late. You were asleep." Melanie turned Desiree's way briefly, but didn't speak.

Desiree sighed inwardly. "Mom, have you had breakfast?"

"Not yet."

"What would you like? I'll fix it."

Her mother looked up at her with a blank stare.

Desiree came back to where she sat and touched her shoulder. "Is there anything special you'd like to eat for breakfast?"

Her brows knit in confusion. "I... I don't know." She sounded as if she didn't understand the question.

Melanie brushed past Desiree, went to the refrigerator and poured a glass of orange juice. "I don't know why you're asking. Just fix her something and put it in front of her. She'll eat it." She went to the connecting family room and turned on the television.

She spun around, hoping her mother hadn't heard and stalked across the floor. "Is that what you've been doing? She is not some animal," she whispered harshly. "She's our *mother*, and as long as she can choose, I'm going to let her." Taking a deep, calming breath, she turned back to her mom. "Mom, would you like some oatmeal or eggs and toast?" She'd chosen two of the things she knew her mother ate regularly.

"I think I'd like to have the oatmeal." She started to stand. "But I can make it."

"I got it. You just finish reading and it'll be done in a few minutes." Desiree glared at her sister, then made breakfast. She dearly hoped Melanie didn't plan to go with them to the doctor. "What time do you have to be at work, Melanie?" she asked, placing the bowl of oatmeal, sugar and milk in front of her mother.

Melanie divided her gaze between Desiree and her mother, who looked up. The uncomfortable look on Melanie's face made Desiree suspect she didn't have a job. Again. Melanie changed jobs like people changed clothes. "None of your business."

She shook her head, sat at the table and fixed her own bowl of oatmeal. Keith arrived just as they finished eating.

Keith kissed their mother. "Hey, Mom." Then repeated the same gesture with Desiree and Melanie. "You going with us to the doctor, Mel?"

Melanie snorted. "No. I have other stuff to do."

"Desiree, is that Dr. Jamison on the TV?" her mother asked. "I've been wondering why I can't get ahold of him."

Desiree and Keith whipped their heads around to the

television. An old episode of the show *Charmed* was on the screen. Desiree said, "Um, no. That's an actor."

"I know that's him." She stood and pointed at the screen. "Wait until I call his supervisor. He's messing around on TV when he needs to be seeing patients."

"Mom, we're going to see Dr. Jamison this morning," Keith said. "Why don't you go get ready?"

She viewed him skeptically. "Are you sure that's not him?"

"Positive. You'll see him yourself when we get there."

"Alright." She still didn't sound convinced, but walked out and came back with her purse a few moments later so they could leave.

During the drive, Desiree continued to be bothered by what her mother had said. She pulled a notepad out of her purse and wrote down a few questions she wanted to ask the doctor. When they arrived, Keith let them out at the front and went to park the car. Desiree checked her mother in and took a seat next to her.

They waited fifteen minutes before being called back, and then five more in the examination room.

Dr. Jamison came in. "Good morning, Helen." He extended his hand to her mother.

"Good morning, Doctor," her mother responded. She made no mention of the earlier television incident.

Desiree stuck her hand out. "I'm Desiree, her daughter, and this is my brother, Keith." When the doctor shook her hand, she passed him the piece of paper with her questions and concerns.

"Nice to meet you both." He pulled the computer over, stepped behind it and discreetly read the note. He nodded Desiree's way. "How've you been feeling, Helen?"

"I've been a little tired lately, but okay."

"I see from last week's visit that you've lost some weight over the past three months."

"I have?"

"Yes." He sat on a stool in front of her. "I'm going to ask you a few questions, okay?"

"Okay."

Dr. Jamison asked her mother a series of questions, including the day, month, year and current president. Then he gave her lists of three to five words and asked her to repeat them back.

She did fine with three, but had increasing difficulty with the others.

He handed her mother a pen and pad. "Helen, now I want you to draw a clock and show the time to be eleven o'clock."

"Okay."

Desiree watched her mother make a circle then start putting in the numbers. She felt her eyes widen when her mother kept adding numbers past twelve. She got to fifteen and handed the paper back to the doctor.

"That's all that will fit."

"Did you draw the hands to make it say eleven o'clock?" the doctor asked gently.

Her mother looked at the paper again, then nodded. "Yes."

"Okay. Can you write your name on the paper for me? Then we'll be done."

Desiree's heart broke watching her mother struggle to form the letters in her name. Her usual flawless writing now resembled that of someone just learning to write in cursive. Desiree's emotions rose so sharply she had to look away to hide the tears. She glanced over at Keith.

"I know," Keith mouthed, his expression pained.

"I need to step out for a minute, Mom," Desiree said. "I'll be right back." She quickly exited. Outside the room, she drew in a shaky breath.

Dr. Jamison stepped out and closed the door. "Are you okay?"

"I don't know. What's going on with my mother?"

"All of those questions were part of a mental test and indicate she may be developing some dementia or early-onset Alzheimer's disease. I'd like to refer her to the geriatric clinic, where they can do more testing and give you an idea of what you might be looking at." He answered the questions Desiree had written down. "If you have any more questions, you can email me anytime."

"Thanks." He went back inside and she let the wall take her weight. She'd lost her father. She couldn't lose her mother, too.

"I'm sorry the news about your mom wasn't great. How are you doing?" Lorenzo asked. He sat behind his desk scrolling through his emails.

Desiree's sigh came through the line. "I'm devastated and I don't know what I'm going to do, especially since I live so far away."

He understood her dilemma and couldn't imagine how he'd feel if it were one of his parents. "Hang in there, sweetheart." The sadness in her voice made him want to wrap her in his arms and let her know he'd be there for her through this ordeal. Lorenzo brought his thoughts to a screeching halt. *What am I saying?* Being there meant long-term. He wasn't looking for long-term.

He spun in his chair and saw his father standing in the doorway with a raised eyebrow. Apparently, he'd heard the endearment that Lorenzo hadn't intended to say. Lorenzo groaned inwardly.

"Thanks," she said. "I have to go. We're boarding now."

"Have a safe trip and I'll see you later." He pressed the end call button and tossed the cell on his desk. "Hey, Dad. What are you doing here? I figured you'd be finishing up your packing for tomorrow's trip."

"I'm already packed. I just wanted to make sure you were okay with things before I left." He sat in one of the chairs across from Lorenzo's desk. "I may not say it often, but I'm proud of you, son. I know you have some apprehension about the way Reuben and I did things, but you're ready. So is Cedric. You boys have far exceeded our every expectation and we're more than comfortable giving you two full control."

"Full control?"

"Yes. This is your company now, and every decision will be up to you and Cedric."

Lorenzo stared. He figured his father and uncle would still play a part in determining the direction of the business.

His father laughed softly. "Don't look so shocked, Lorenzo. You've worked here in some capacity for almost twenty years and know the business inside and out."

"Thanks, Dad. That means a lot coming from you."

He smiled. "So, who's the young lady you were on the phone with? I didn't know you were dating someone."

"I… We're not dating exactly. I just met her recently."

"Then what *exactly* are you doing? I may be getting older, but calling someone *sweetheart* usually means a little more is going on." He stood. "What's her name?"

"Desiree, but—"

"You should bring her by when we get back from the cruise. Your mother and I would love to meet her."

Bring her by? Meet her? That would be akin to making a statement about their relationship. One Lorenzo had no intentions of making. His dad looked at him expectantly. "We'll see. Be sure to text me when you guys get to Miami tomorrow."

"Okay."

He came around the desk and the two shared a rough embrace. "Have a good time."

"We will." His father opened the door and paused. "I have one piece of advice. Don't get so busy that you don't take time to live. I did that for the first several years and I found myself starting to burn out. Your mother helped me to see I needed some balance in my life. I know you tend to work long hours, but don't make it a habit. Maybe you need someone to help you see the same," he added with a smile.

"I'll see what I can do." His father knew him well. Lorenzo had had a similar conversation with his cousin, Brandon Gray, who had taken over as CEO of their family's home safety company a couple of years ago. At one year older than Lorenzo, Brandon had bordered on being a workaholic until he got married. *Maybe you need someone to help you see the same.* It dawned on him that his father's last statement referred to a woman. Lorenzo liked his life fine and didn't see the need to settle down. He could find balance on his own.

He stood there a moment longer, and then sat at his

desk and pulled up the notes on the park project. The concrete had been laid in almost all the areas and they would be starting on the landscaping next week. Cedric had sent him an email to let him know that the building supplies for the planned community center would be delivered then, as well. Seeing a new project come to life always filled him with excitement and a sense of pride. He got so caught up that he didn't realize how much time had passed. Desiree's nine o'clock flight would be arriving in thirty minutes. If he left right then, he would get there by the time she landed. Lorenzo shut down his laptop, shoved it in his bag, locked up and rushed out to his car.

Thankfully, he didn't encounter any traffic. He parked and checked the flight status as he walked across the lot. Her plane had gotten in a few minutes early and he quickened his strides. He told himself he was only hurrying so she wouldn't have to wait, but the rapid pace of his heart and the anticipation of knowing he'd see her told an entirely different story. Lorenzo spotted her at the base of the escalator scanning the terminal. Their gazes connected and she gave him a smile that stirred something deep in his belly. He momentarily froze. *What the hell is going on?* He had never experienced these kind of crazy emotions with a woman, particularly one he'd only known a short time.

Seeing Desiree coming toward him, Lorenzo finally got his feet moving and met her halfway.

"Hi," Desiree said. "I can't tell you how much I appreciate you picking me up, especially since I know you worked a long day." She leaned up and brushed her lips across his.

The contact sent a jolt straight to his groin. "I'm glad

I could do it." He eased the bag from her hands. "Do you have any more bags?"

"No. Just the one."

Lorenzo reached for her hand and headed toward the exit. "I'm in the lot. How was your flight?"

"Long," Desiree said with a laugh. "Aside from that, it wasn't too bad."

"And your mom? I know you mentioned the appointment hadn't gone as well as you'd hoped."

She sighed. "The doctor seems to think she might be in the beginning stages of dementia or Alzheimer's."

He gave her hand a sympathetic squeeze. "I'm sorry."

"Me, too," she murmured.

When they got to his car, he opened the door for her, placed the bag on the back seat and got in on the other side. "Is there any place you'd like to stop first or maybe get something to eat?"

"No, thank you. I had a salad in the airport during my layover. I'm just glad the shop isn't open tomorrow so I can sleep in. I have a few things to make, but they'll keep until later in the day."

Lorenzo paid and exited the parking lot. He briefly glanced over at Desiree. She sat with her head against the seat and her eyes closed. He didn't offer any conversation, sensing she still might be trying to process what was happening to her mother. He knew he would have a hard time, too, if he were in her shoes.

Desiree yawned. "Do you have a long day tomorrow?"

He chuckled. "All my days seem long. And a couple of weeks ago, my father and uncle decided to retire on the spot, leaving my cousin and me in charge of running the company."

She sat up. "Are you saying you *own* the construction company?"

He slanted her an amused glance. "Yep, along with my cousin Cedric."

"When I asked you what you did for a living, you made it sound as if you merely worked for the company." Desiree laid a hand on his arm. "Congratulations, Lorenzo. I know you two will bring even more success to your company. By the way, what's the name of it?"

He had been hesitant in sharing the information previously because the last woman he'd dated, who found out he would be taking over the company at some point, had ended up being more interested in his bank account. "Thank you." Lorenzo smiled. Her compliment made him feel like he could do anything. "And it's Hunter Construction."

She laughed. "I don't know why, but I was expecting some catchy name."

"You mean like *Scentillating Touch*?"

She laughed. "Yep. I don't think Scott Bath and Body Products would inspire someone to enter the store." She wrinkled her nose.

He roared with laughter. "Yeah, no." He drove into her complex, parked and went around to help her out of the car, then got her bag. Still chuckling, he draped an arm around her shoulder and started up the path.

"See, with all the laughing you're doing, I know I made the right decision." Desiree smiled and playfully rolled her eyes. She unlocked her door and looked up at him. "Thanks again for picking me up. You really didn't need to walk me to the door."

"A gentleman always walks a lady to her door."

"You are a perfect gentleman," she said softly, holding his gaze.

Lorenzo's plan had been to walk her to the door with a quick good-night and be on his way. She tempted him like no other woman, and without trying. The way she stared at him made it hard to keep the distance he usually craved. "And you are a perfect lady." Unable to resist, he backed her into the house, tilted her chin and captured her mouth in an intoxicating kiss, feeding from the sweetness he always found there. "Would you like to go out to dinner with me tomorrow night?" he asked, in between kisses.

"Mmm, yes. What time?"

"Seven?"

"That works."

Lorenzo's tongue slipped between her parted lips and he, once again, lost himself in her. "You have the softest lips. I can't stop kissing you."

Desiree smiled against his lips. "I use a sugar scrub on them. It has coconut oil, cocoa…"

"Whatever's in it is doing a helluva job. You must use it on your face, too." He lightly ran his lips over the smooth skin of her cheeks.

"Mmm-hmm. A good scrub works wonders for the whole body."

His arousal was instantaneous. The thought of exploring her smooth body sent his own body into overdrive. As much as he wanted to indulge tonight, he had to be on the road at four in the morning. "I've got an early morning tomorrow, so I need to get going."

"Okay. Are you going back to San Francisco?"

"Yes, to meet with a contractor."

Desiree pulled his head down and kissed him. "Be safe."

"I will. I'll see you tomorrow."

"Good night."

"'Night, baby." Lorenzo sauntered back to his car, a smile still on his face. No, he hadn't planned this, but for now, he would just go with the flow and enjoy it.

Chapter 8

Tuesday afternoon, Desiree mixed the ingredients for the lavender bath bombs and pressed them into the molds to dry. She stifled a yawn. After Lorenzo left last night, it had taken her body hours to calm down. The man knew how to use his mouth and hands in a way that caused her to lose all rational thought. And that made him dangerous to her heart. If she had any sense, she'd have that dinner date tonight, then tell him she couldn't see him anymore. Lorenzo moved her in a way unlike any of the previous guys she'd dated and she could easily fall for him. If she were being honest, she'd admit to being halfway there already, even though they'd only known each other a short time. Desiree set the first mold aside, grabbed the next one and repeated the process.

"Girl, that face and lip scrub you asked me to test out

is to die for!" Brenda crossed the room and propped a hip on the counter where Desiree worked. "It smells so good, too." She reached up and patted her face. "I don't think my face has ever been this smooth."

Desiree smiled. "I'm glad you like it. It does feel nice." She had been working on expanding her products to include facial products—cleanser, scrub and moisturizer. She and Brenda usually tested new items out on themselves before putting them up for sale.

"And it keeps my lips moisturized." Brenda puckered her lips. "Now I need a man to try them out on."

The memory of Lorenzo's comment about her lips flashed in Desiree's mind, along with the sensual kisses that followed, sending heat straight to her core.

"Speaking of dating, how are things going with you and Lorenzo?"

"He picked me up from the airport last night and we're supposed to go out to dinner tonight."

"I hear a *but* in your voice."

"He's a really nice guy, but I don't know if I want to put myself out there to get hurt again."

"Who says you'll get hurt? Don't let your fears from the past keep you from the right guy."

She stopped pressing the mixture and shifted to face Brenda. "I can't help it. The last guy who claimed to love me one day decided the next that we needed to see other people. The two men before that blatantly cheated. I'm tired of putting myself out there, only to come away with my heart being ripped to shreds. I think it's best if I stop this thing with Lorenzo before it gets too deep. Besides, I have a feeling I'm going to be really busy with my mom. The doctor thinks she may be in the beginning stages of dementia or Alzheimer's."

"Oh no," Brenda said. "I'm so sorry, Des."

Desiree told her about the doctor's visit and mental test. "It broke my heart to see her trying to draw that clock and putting in all those numbers. She thought she'd done exactly as he'd asked. I'm not sure how it's going to go, so I don't think this is the time to start a new relationship."

"Actually, I think it's the perfect time. You'll need something or someone to help take your mind off your mother and a hot guy who seems to be into you is just the ticket."

"I don't know." What her friend said made sense and Lorenzo's concern had touched her, but how long would it last? "We'll see. Now that he's taken over his family's construction company, I can see things changing rather quickly."

"He *owns* a construction company?"

"Along with his cousin. Apparently, their fathers came in, said they were retiring and left it to them."

"How cool is that?" Brenda whipped out her cell. "What's the name of the company?"

"Hunter Construction."

She typed for a moment, the held out the phone. "Their fathers are good-looking men."

Desiree leaned over to see. "I agree. They must be twins." The men looked almost identical. Lorenzo favored both of them and she couldn't figure out which one might be his father.

"Ooh, this guy is fine. Cedric Hunter…hmm…sexy name," Brenda said, scrolling down the page and pointing at a younger man. "Is this Lorenzo's brother? They look alike."

"It must be the cousin he mentioned who would be

running the company with him. Lorenzo told me he has a younger sister." Cedric looked just as good as Lorenzo and stood the same height, but his chocolate-colored skin was a shade lighter than Lorenzo's and Cedric had a little more bulk on his muscular frame.

"I wonder if he's single." Brenda continued to search the website.

Desiree smiled. "I have no idea, but I can ask if you like."

"You do that. I guess all that hammering and whatnot does a body good."

She laughed. "It does a body *really* good." She remembered the feel of Lorenzo's hard body pressed against hers, the touch of his strong hands traveling over her spine, hips and…

"Did you hear me, Desiree?"

Desiree frowned. "What?"

Brenda shook her head. "I asked if you're done."

She glanced down and realized that she'd been standing there with the mold in midair. "Oh yes." Desiree placed the last mold on a shelf and cleaned up.

"Are you going to do anything else today?" Brenda asked. "I'm almost finished setting up the online store, so I think I'll stay a little longer."

"Probably not. It's already after four and I want to have time to get ready for my dinner date. If I start something else, I won't get out of here for another couple of hours." She had no idea what to wear and hadn't thought to ask where they were going. Maybe she'd send him a text to find out whether she should be dressy or casual. They left the crafting room and headed to the office.

"Well, have a good time and I'll see you tomorrow. What time are you coming in?"

"Around eleven. This is the last week before we're open on Wednesdays, so I'm going to take advantage." The store would open at ten just in time for the Fourth of July holiday, and she typically arrived at least an hour before. Desiree got her purse out of her locked drawer. "Are you doing anything next week for the Fourth?"

"After we leave here, going home and praying those fools out there don't lose their minds with all those illegal fireworks. What about you?"

"Same. See you later." The weekends were crowded enough, but add in a holiday, and it made for a mess trying to get out of the area.

Leaving the shop close to five put her right in the middle of rush hour traffic and it took nearly an hour for her to make it to her Roseville condo. She undressed and went to take a bath.

Desiree sank down in the tub, rested her head against the pillow she kept there and closed her eyes. Her mind drifted to her mother. She'd mentioned that she had always wanted to visit San Francisco and Desiree, not knowing how things would progress, had booked her a flight for two weeks from now. Because they didn't want her to fly alone, her mother had asked Melanie to come with her. Desiree would have preferred her brother accompany her. She'd even rather deal with Patrice—Desiree knew Melanie would make this trip a living hell and she wasn't looking forward to it. Hopefully during the visit, her mother would be her old self and keep Melanie in line.

She got so preoccupied in her thoughts that she lost track of the time. She glanced over at the small clock she'd kept on the counter and sat up straight, splashing water over the side of the tub. She had only had twenty minutes to wash up and get dressed. Desiree quickly finished her bath, wrapped a towel around her and flipped through the clothes in her closet. She should have sent that text. Lorenzo would more than likely be on his way, so she nixed the idea and settled on a black-and-white sleeveless sheath dress and a pair of black low-heeled wedge sandals.

As the minutes ticked off, Desiree sat waiting and realized she had gotten dressed for nothing. It was seven forty-five and Lorenzo had yet to show or return the message she'd left a short while ago. She would have never pegged him for the type to stand a woman up, but obviously she had been wrong. At least it happened before she'd invested too much of her time and emotions. Deciding that she'd waited long enough, Desiree stood and went to her bedroom to take off the dress. She had just reached for the zipper when the doorbell rang. She went to answer it and found Lorenzo standing there wearing a black T-shirt and jeans that were covered in mud, his locs held back in a wide band.

"Hey, I'm so sorry I'm late."

"Hey." Desiree backed up so he could enter, but shifted out of his reach when he bent to kiss her.

Lorenzo studied her a moment. "You thought I stood you up."

"The thought did cross my mind, since it's after eight."

He placed his hands on her shoulders. "Baby, I would never do something like that. We had an emergency at the site and I ended up leaving later than planned from San Francisco. You know how the traffic can be. My phone is in my cousin's truck and I didn't realize it until I was halfway here. Rather than stop at my house and be even later, I came straight here."

"Oh." She felt bad for lumping him in with all the other men she'd dealt with.

The corner of his mouth kicked up in a smile. "So, do you think I can get my kiss now?"

Desiree tried to hide her own smile. "Yes." He covered her mouth in a gentle kiss, but kept his body from touching hers. As always, warmth flooded her.

"I know it's a little late, but we can still go if you want. I need to stop by my house and shower first, though."

She took in his hopeful gaze and gave the only answer she could. "I still want to go." She was also curious about where he lived. She reached behind him for her purse and wrap. "I'm ready."

As they walked out to the parking lot, Lorenzo said, "I'm apologizing up front. I have the company truck right now."

Desiree laughed. "As long as my seat is clean it's no problem."

He slanted her a glance. "That's just wrong." He held the door open to the newer model Ford truck and lifted her onto the seat. "Clean enough?"

She made a show of looking around. "It'll do."

Lorenzo shook his head, closed the door and got in on the other side.

"I saw on the door it says your office is in Roseville. Is it close to here?" She lived on the north side of the city and to get to the freeway without going backward, she had to cut through Antelope.

"It's off Sunrise Boulevard."

She noticed that he was heading farther into Roseville. "Do you live in Roseville, too?"

"Granite Bay."

Their company must be doing *really* well for him to be able to afford a place in that area and it made her even more curious. She expected a modern high-priced condominium or something similar, not the two-story family home with a three-car garage on a cul-de-sac where he stopped. "This is very nice."

Lorenzo chuckled. "Not what you were expecting, I bet."

He'd read her mind. "How did you guess?"

"The look on your face gave you away." He got out and came around to her side.

"What look?"

He placed his hands on her waist and lifted her out of the truck, but didn't immediately put her down. "Shock." He set her down carefully and they started toward the front door. "I like my space and my father told me it was good investment. He typically gives me good advice, so I had no problem taking it."

"I see. And I'll admit I was a little shocked. I figured you lived in one of those high-priced bachelor pads."

Lorenzo smiled. He unlocked the door and gestured her inside. "Welcome to my high-priced bachelor pad."

Desiree laughed. She froze two steps into the entryway. "This is so not a bachelor pad." Highly polished wood floors opened into a large expensively decorated living room on one side and partially closed-off formal dining room on the other. "It's gorgeous. How long have you lived here?"

"Thanks. Almost two years." He led her to the family room. "But I can't take credit for the decor. I had several projects going and didn't have time to furnish anything except my bedroom and this room. My mother volunteered to help and she went way beyond what I had planned."

She had wondered about the difference in furnishing styles. The family room had a decidedly male touch with black leather seating, large wall-mounted television and fireplace. "She has great taste."

"Yeah, if you like those pimped-out houses in magazines."

She smiled. "I take it you have simpler tastes." She wandered over to French doors and saw a deck, outdoor kitchen and beautifully landscaped yard in the fading light.

"Yep, and that's why the two upstairs bedrooms don't have furniture yet. She started moving my things around and talking about canopied beds and lace curtains, and I had to rein her in. I love my mama, but she gets out of control when it comes to decorating."

Desiree giggled. "How many bedrooms do you have?"

"Five. I turned the two down here into an office and gym. Feel free to look around. You want to watch TV or listen to music?"

She glanced over at him. "The music is fine." He picked up a remote and pushed a button. Music flowed from speakers placed around the room. "Somehow, I didn't expect jazz."

He grinned. "Blame it on my parents. My tastes are pretty eclectic. I listen to jazz, R & B, hip-hop and rap, and even a little classical sometimes. I find that the jazz relaxes me after a long day. I'll be back in a few."

"Okay."

Before he took a step, the doorbell rang. "Seriously?" Lorenzo groaned. "Excuse me."

He came back with a handsome man who favored him enough to be his brother, the one she remembered seeing on the website and knew it had to be his cousin.

"Desiree, this is my cousin Cedric. Ced, Desiree."

Cedric smiled. "It's nice to meet you, Desiree."

"Same here." The photo she'd seen on the website didn't fully capture his handsome face or the dimples that she knew probably had women swooning everywhere he went. Even so, she didn't feel the same pull she did with Lorenzo.

"I see why my cousin was in such a hurry to leave and forgot his phone." His gaze traveled up and down her body. "I can't blame him, though."

Desiree felt her cheeks warm.

Lorenzo shook his head. "Give me my phone and go home."

Cedric chuckled and handed it over. "Later, cuz." To Desiree, he said, "I hope to see you again. Enjoy your evening."

She didn't know how to respond to the first part of his statement, so just said, "Thank you."

"I can find my way out." He divided his gaze between Lorenzo and Desiree as if he knew something, smiled and strode out.

"Family. Gotta love 'em."

Desiree chuckled. "Is he married?"

Lorenzo let out a short bark of laughter. "Cedric? Hardly." He pressed a kiss to her forehead. "I'll be quick."

Desiree nodded and watched as he disappeared around the corner and reappeared at the top of the stairs a moment later. She sauntered through the first level and saw an office filled with enough books to start a library and a state-of-the-art home gym. She wondered what his bedroom looked like, but didn't dare climb those stairs to find out. She went back and took a seat in the family room to wait.

Desiree could hear the water running upstairs and it took everything in her to stay seated. She tried to focus on the music—a saxophonist she didn't recognize. Her jazz was limited to what she occasionally heard on the satellite radio station she listened to, but she found herself drawn in to the sensuality of the music. She briefly fantasized how it would feel to run her hands all over Lorenzo's rock-hard body as the water cascaded over him. Heat pooled between her legs and she squeezed them together to quell the insistent throbbing. Desiree thought it best to turn her mind elsewhere.

"Okay, I'm ready."

Desiree stood at the sound of Lorenzo's voice. He had on a pair of black slacks and a short-sleeved button-down gray silk shirt. He'd left his hair loose and, with the diamond studs twinkling in his ears, gave off an air of masculinity that made the faint drumming at her center start up again. "You clean up nicely."

Lorenzo closed the distance between them and slid an arm around her waist. "Thanks. And if I failed to mention it earlier, you look beautiful."

"Thank you." For several seconds, neither of them moved. With him so close, she recognized the scent of the citrus basil soap he'd purchased at her shop. She had always liked the fragrance for its clean notes, but on him, it was more like an aphrodisiac. To distract herself from the rising temperatures, she said. "I really like this music. Who is it?"

He eased her close and started a slow sway in time with the rhythm. "Boney James." He lowered his head and, without missing a beat, planted kisses along her cheek, neck and shoulder. "You smell good. Something you created?"

Desiree trembled. "Yes," she answered on a breathless sigh. The combination of his lips trailing across her skin and his body moving sensually against hers, along with the captivating wail of the saxophone, almost made her melt in a heap. "Um…what's the name of the song?"

"'Seduction.'"

Figures. "Is that what this is?"

Lorenzo lifted his head and stared into her eyes. "It's not something I planned. No." They continued dancing. Then he said, "Would you like to be?"

"Be what?"

"Seduced."

She almost fainted. Still holding his gaze, she said, "I don't know. If you were to seduce me, what would you do?" *Where did that come from?* Desiree was supposed to be thinking about telling him they couldn't see each other, *not* asking him to seduce her.

A wolfish grin curved his lips. "I'd start by kissing you…*everywhere*. Like this."

His tongue teased the corners of her mouth before slipping inside. He took his time tasting and swirling his tongue around hers, then he transferred his kisses to her throat and the tops of her breasts visible above her dress. Desiree stood on shaky legs, her breath coming in short gasps. She felt the slide of her zipper, then

Lorenzo pulling the dress and her bra straps off her shoulders. He latched on to one nipple and she cried out.

"Then I have to touch you. I'm going to caress every inch of your soft skin."

He lightly trailed his hands over the spots that he'd kissed, lingering on her lips and breasts. He reached down and caressed her thighs, sliding her dress higher and higher until he reached her center. He moved her panties to the side and slipped a finger inside her, sending shock waves of pleasure through her.

"So, do you want to be seduced, Desiree?" Lorenzo asked, adding another finger and speeding up his movements.

"Yes," she screamed as an orgasm ripped through her. She didn't care about dinner or that speech about not seeing him anymore. The only thing she wanted was more of him. *All* of him.

Chapter 9

Lorenzo swept Desiree into his arms, strode up to his bedroom and placed her in the center of his bed. He hadn't planned for them to sleep together so soon, but he had no intention of turning her down. He would have never guessed that she'd say yes to his question, but if she wanted to be seduced, he'd do his damnedest to fulfill her request. He took in the sensual picture she made lying on his bed with her dress half on and her hair spread out on his pillow and felt himself growing harder by the moment. Lorenzo kicked off his shoes, removed his shirt and placed it on a chair, then sat on the edge of the bed. "Ease up, baby." When she lifted her hips, he pulled the dress down and off, leaving her clad in a black bra and matching panties. He laid it over the chair, climbed back on the bed and gently turned her onto her stomach. "Now, shall we continue?" Lorenzo traced a path down her spine with his tongue. Her sounds of pleasure further stoked his passions. He massaged and kissed his way down her body and up again, alternating between light and deep pressure.

"Lorenzo!" Desiree let out a loud moan.

Lorenzo turned her over, captured her mouth in a long, drugging kiss and caressed her breasts. He bent to suckle, first one hardened nipple, then the other. His hand traveled down the front of her body to her wet center and he slid two fingers inside, determined to seduce her in a way he'd never done with any other woman. He didn't understand it and, for now, didn't try.

Desiree ran her hand over his abs, chest and arms, and called his name again. "I...ohh... What are you doing to me?"

"You said you wanted to be seduced. I want to give you everything you've asked for." It was his turn to groan when she reached down and cupped him through his slacks. Electricity shot from his groin to his feet. He crushed his mouth to hers, mimicking the movements of his fingers.

She tore her mouth away and screamed.

He stood, rid himself of his pants and underwear and donned a condom. He slid his body along hers and reveled in the feel of her bare skin against his. "Your skin is so soft. Are you ready for the next part of this seduction?"

She pulled his head down and kissed him with a passion that made him shudder. "Does that answer your question?"

Holding her gaze, Lorenzo eased his shaft inside. He watched the play of emotions on her face, the darkening of her eyes and experienced a funny feeling in his belly. Dismissing it, he concentrated on taking them on a trip to ecstasy that neither would forget. Lorenzo moved in and out at a leisurely pace, going deeper with each thrust. "I'm going to make love to you slowly, thoroughly," he whispered against her ear, "and give you all the pleasure you can handle."

"Then give it to me." Desiree swiveled her hips and locked her legs around his back.

She drew him deeper, her tight walls clenching him. Lorenzo lifted her legs onto his shoulders, gripped her hips and kept up the intense rhythm. He felt her contracting around him and knew she was about to come. He wanted them to come together. He thrust harder, grinding his body into hers. An orgasm seemed to hit her at the same time as one hit him, sending a flurry of sensations whipping through him. Lorenzo buried his head in her neck and groaned her name. Their bodies trembled for what seemed like forever and their harsh breathing filled the room. He lowered her legs and rolled to his back, taking her with him.

"I think I like being seduced," Desiree murmured, laying her head on his shoulder.

He chuckled and placed a tender kiss on her lips. "Glad to hear it." Gathering her in his embrace, he pulled the sheet over them and drifted off to sleep.

When Lorenzo woke up, almost an hour had passed. He glanced down at Desiree cuddled in his arms. What he was beginning to feel for her went beyond physical attraction and he couldn't explain how she managed to slip beneath the barrier he'd erected around his heart in such a short time. He had no plans to tell her, however. She was the first woman he had brought to this house. He'd told her he purchased the house as an investment.

That had been only partly true. He hadn't revealed that after the fiasco with Veronica, he'd felt that she'd violated his previous home—his sacred space. He'd *had* to move. Lorenzo's stomach growled, reminding him that they had never made it to dinner. He hadn't eaten since before noon and needed to find some food.

Desiree stirred, then her eyes fluttered open. "What time is it?"

"Ten-thirty."

"I guess it's too late for dinner."

He shifted to face her. "There are a couple of nearby places that stay open late. You can check out the menus of each and see which one you prefer. We'll get that real dinner in another time. I promise."

"Sounds good." She sat up and the sheet slipped down, exposing her breasts. She snatched it up.

"Don't cover up on my account. Besides," he said, reaching under the sheet and caressing her breasts, "I've already seen your beautiful body and like every inch of it." She averted her eyes and seemed embarrassed. Not wanting to make her uncomfortable, he said, "How about we get cleaned up and find something to eat?"

"Okay. I'm starving."

Lorenzo scooped her up, rose from bed and headed for the bathroom. "You can shower in here." He placed her on her feet and pointed. "Towels are in that cabinet."

"Thank you. I won't be long." Desiree came up on tiptoe and kissed him. She winked and gave him a saucy smile.

He knew right then he was in trouble. Big trouble.

Thursday afternoon, Desiree sat in her office printing out the online orders. The flow of traffic in the store had slowed and she wanted to get a jump start before it picked up again. Brenda had finished uploading all the products Tuesday after Desiree left and the orders had been pouring in ever since. It meant a lot more work, but the income from those sales gave them a lot more financial breathing room. She grabbed the sheets from the printer and headed to the back room to package and ready them for shipping. Desiree worked at a steady pace, placing items in the gift boxes with her logo, then in the larger box to mail. She glanced up at the clock and realized it was closing time. Obviously Casey and Brenda didn't need the extra help out front, which would give her time to finish the last few before leaving.

"We have more orders?"

Desiree turned at the sound of Brenda's voice. "Twenty-two more than the ones you left on my desk."

"Are you *serious*? I didn't think placing those ads would pay off this fast." Brenda had done ads on all the social media platforms and left postcards in several places.

Casey stuck her head in the door. "I'm headed out, unless you need me to stay and help."

Desiree turned. "No, we're good. If the orders keep increasing, I may be taking you up on your offer."

She grinned. "Just let me know. See you guys in the morning."

"Bye," Desiree and Brenda chorused.

Desiree pointed to a line on one of the order forms, continuing their previous conversation. "It was probably that ten percent off your first online order offer that did the trick increasing the orders. This was a genius move."

"I agree. People like the convenience of being able

to buy online, but with this upsurge, we may have to hire someone part-time to help out."

"True. Otherwise, we would be here all night, every night trying to package and ship this stuff."

Brenda laughed. "Hey, it's not like I have anything else to do these days. You on the other hand…" They fell into a rhythm, packing and labeling boxes. After a few minutes, she asked, "Oh, yeah, how did your conversation with Lorenzo go? I was so busy yesterday with all the promo I forgot to ask. Did you decide to break up with him?" She picked up an order sheet and began filling a box.

Their sensual night together came back in a rush. Breaking up had been the last thing on Desiree's mind after the first kiss. And she still couldn't believe she'd basically asked him to seduce her. "Not exactly."

She paused. "What does that mean?"

Desiree placed the gift box inside of a mailer and taped it. "He was almost an hour late for dinner." She added the address label, set it aside and started on the next one.

Brenda whipped her head around. "*An hour?* I hope he had a good excuse because, if not, I would've tossed his butt out the door."

"He had an emergency at a work site in San Francisco and came straight from there, muddy clothes and all. We went back to his house so he could shower and change."

"Where does he live? Just from looking at him, I'd guess some high-priced condo that screams 'bachelor pad.'"

Desiree laughed. "He lives in Granite Bay and his

home is far from a condo. More like an estate that would house a family of six comfortably."

Brenda stared. "Really? Sounds like he's ready to settle down."

"He said he'd bought the house because it was a good investment." Lorenzo hadn't said anything about settling down and from his statement about liking his space, she didn't think that would be at the top of his list. "I only saw the downstairs area, but it's very nice." Not exactly the truth. She'd seen his bedroom—sort of. He'd turned on a lamp that cast a low light over the room, but he'd had her body so on fire, the only thing she could say for sure was he had a big bed. "Oh, and I met his cousin Cedric. Lorenzo left his phone in Cedric's truck, which is why he couldn't call on the way home."

Brenda's eyes lit up. "Did you find out if he's single or not?"

Desiree laughed. "Yes, he is. But the way Lorenzo answered when I asked makes me think Cedric is nowhere near ready for a steady relationship. He's a serious flirt and has killer dimples, even deeper than Lorenzo's. I don't mean those cute little boy ones, either. Girl, he has a smile that would make a sane woman willingly cross over into sin."

"Sounds like he'd show a woman a good time. So where did you and Lorenzo end up for dinner?"

"A little bar and grill not too far from his place," Desiree said, steeling herself for the questions she knew Brenda would ask.

Brenda stopped packing a box, came to where Desiree stood and folded her arms. "You mean to tell me you got all dressed up and he took you to some little grill. I expected him to do better than that." She studied Desiree.

Desiree didn't comment. She had no idea how to explain that she'd slept with a man she'd known less than a month.

"Well?"

She shrugged. "By the time he'd showered and changed clothes, it was a little late." Not a complete lie. "So, we just chose something easy. The food tasted pretty good."

"Ah, most restaurants don't close until about ten. Unless he takes two hours to shower, you should have had no problems finding—"

Desiree hazarded a glance Brenda's way.

Brenda's eyes widened and she brought her hand to her mouth. "Oh my goodness. Did y'all do the wild thing?"

She felt her cheeks warm.

A sly grin curved Brenda's mouth. "I guess this little relationship is moving pretty quickly."

Desiree scrubbed a hand over her forehead. "Faster than I ever imagined. One minute we were dancing and the next we were upstairs in his bedroom." A vision of Lorenzo trailing his tongue and hands all over her body came back in a rush and a soft throbbing started between her thighs.

Brenda chuckled. "And by that look, it was well worth the delay."

"I can't deny that, but it only complicates things further. I'm supposed to be backing off, remember?"

She folded her arms and leaned against the counter. "If you couldn't remember your little breakup speech before you slept with him, I highly doubt you will now."

Desiree couldn't argue that point, either. However, she didn't want to run the risk of putting herself out there, only to end up with another broken heart. She and Lorenzo had never defined their relationship and she needed to know where they were headed. She braced her hands on the counter. "I don't know what to do."

"I do," Brenda said. "Enjoy it, sis. He just may be Mr. Right."

"We'll see. Anyway, my mom is coming for a visit next weekend. She wants to go to San Francisco and I want to make sure she does before—" Desiree couldn't finish the sentence. "I'm thinking of taking her on Saturday."

Brenda waved a hand. "You know Casey and I will take care of the shop. Sandra is scheduled to work, too. Speaking of the shop, I'm thinking we should go ahead and look for some part-time help. I'll run the numbers and see how many hours we can afford."

Desiree glanced at the stack of boxes they'd filled and the remaining orders that needed to be finished. "That might be a good idea." Her phone rang and she walked over to the desk where she'd left it, hoping something hadn't happened to her mother. She saw Lorenzo's name on the display and her pulse skipped. "Hey, Lorenzo."

"What's up, beautiful? How did your day go?"

"Busy for the most part and it's not over yet," she answered with a little laugh.

"I thought you closed at six. It's almost eight."

"Our online store is open and we've received a ton of orders, so I'm filling those."

Lorenzo chuckled. "That's good for business, but I don't know if I like you being there so late. The doors are locked, right?"

His concern touched her. "Yes, and I'm not here alone." Desiree glanced over her shoulder and saw Brenda standing there, leaning against the counter with her arms folded and a smile on her face.

Brenda said softly, "Look at you all smiling."

She rolled her eyes and refocused on what Lorenzo was saying.

"I'm glad to hear it because I was seriously considering driving over."

"I appreciate that Lorenzo, but that's a long way to come. Besides, I'd probably be gone by the time you got here. Are you at home?"

"Nope. Still at the office."

"And you're talking about me. Maybe *I* should be making sure you get home at a decent hour." Desiree wanted to snatch the words back as soon as they were off her tongue.

The soft rumble of his laughter came through the line. "I know the perfect way to get me out of my office. Are you up for another round of seduction?"

Heat pooled in her center. She was more than up for it. "What are we doing here, Lorenzo?"

There was a brief pause on the line. "What do you mean?"

"This…this relationship."

"I thought it was two people enjoying each other's company. I never put a name to it. Are you looking for a specific definition?"

"No, but things have gone far beyond just hanging out casually."

"Yes, and like I told you that night, it wasn't something I'd planned. Desiree, I enjoy being with you."

"Same here, but we've never really defined where this is going or if we're…"

"I'm not seeing anyone else, if that's what you're wondering. I'm far too old for those kind of games. But if we're not on the same page, I'd like to know."

"I guess I'm just not sure what page that is."

"Then how about we keep figuring it out and see where we end up?"

He'd given her the perfect chance to give him her maybe-this-isn't-a-good-idea speech, but Desiree couldn't get the words out. Despite all the turmoil swirling around in her life, she liked this man and enjoyed being with him, too. "Sounds like a plan."

"We can talk more the next time we get together."

"Okay."

"Well, you and I both need to finish up and go home. Call me when you get there, so I know you're safe."

"I will. Good night."

"'Night, baby."

Desiree ended the call and smiled.

"Mmm-hmm, so much for that speech."

She whirled around. She'd totally forgotten about Brenda. "Don't you know it's rude to eavesdrop on people's conversation?"

Brenda laughed. "Ha! If you wanted privacy, you should've left the room."

"Oh hush and let's finish up." Desiree tried to hide her smile as she snatched an order from Brenda's hand and grabbed a box. Maybe being with Lorenzo wouldn't be a bad thing.

Chapter 10

Friday afternoon, a week later, Lorenzo and Cedric sat in the office's conference room discussing the new policy they'd put in place with the McBride brothers. Neither man looked happy.

"You can't just implement these fees in the middle. We have a contract," Jerry McBride said, jabbing his finger on the table. As the oldest of the two, he most often acted as the spokesperson. They came from old money, were in their late fifties and had thinning blond hair slowly being taken over by the gray.

"Actually, we can," Cedric countered mildly. "Maybe you missed it, but if you turn to page nine of the original contract, it clearly states below the cost estimate that those numbers are subject to increase depending on structural modifications or additions."

Lorenzo couldn't have been happier when he spotted that line. He and Cedric had missed it before. Obviously, his father and uncle had the foresight to include the clause and it made him speculate on whether they had run into a similar situation. He leaned forward and clasped his hands together. "With that in mind, if you direct your attention to the fee schedule, we can go over the new building costs." He outlined what each change would cost and provided a new completion timeline. "If you're in agreement, please sign the amendment sheet where indicated. You also have the option of continuing with the current blueprints, which will keep the costs and completion schedule the same."

Cedric handed the men pens.

Jerry started to balk, but his brother impatiently said, "Just sign the damn papers, Jerry. You can't win." He snatched up a pen and signed his name.

Still grumbling, Jerry did the same. Five minutes later, with all their signatures affixed and copies made, the McBrides left.

"Well?" Lorenzo asked Cedric after seeing the men out and returning to the conference room.

A slow grin made its way over Cedric's face. "I think I'm going to like being the boss. I wonder what our pops will say. Even though they said we're in charge, they're going to ask."

He chuckled and propped a hip on the table. "We've scaled our first hurdle and I hope it sends a message that just because our fathers are no longer in charge that nothing has changed." Their parents would be back in a few days and he hoped they enjoyed the long-awaited vacation. When he'd visited before they left, his mother had been ecstatic.

"Exactly. It's interesting that the McBrides only mentioned the changes *after* the retirement was announced. They must have believed they could put one over on us, but I'm glad we proved them wrong. So, how did your dinner at Ruth's Chris go with Desiree the other night? She's a beautiful woman and those eyes... I've always had a thing for women with different-colored eyes. Watching them change while you're—"

Lorenzo held up a hand. "I get it." He knew exactly what Cedric meant. Desiree's eyes had sucked him in the moment they'd connected in the park. Since then, his attraction to her had been steadily growing and, somehow, had taken on a life of its own. Hence, how they ended up in his bed for a night of pleasure he hadn't been able to stop thinking about. "We ended up at Yard House."

Cedric frowned. "So you make plans to go out to a nice restaurant and end up... I mean, not that it's a bad place, but that's like two steps down. Did you forget to make reservations or something?"

"No. I made them." He didn't make a practice of kissing and telling, even to Cedric, and they were close as brothers. But Cedric's questioning gaze never wavered and Lorenzo knew he'd have to answer. "We sort of got caught up in the moment and missed the reservation."

"That must have been some moment."

The memories of her hushed request to be seduced came back with vivid clarity and his groin stirred. "Yeah, it was." And he couldn't put his finger on why the encounter seemed different.

Tanya poked her head in the door. "Excuse me. I don't mean to interrupt."

Lorenzo shifted his gaze toward his assistant. "You're not interrupting. What's going on?"

"There are three men here to see you and Cedric."

His brows knit together. "I don't have any appointments this afternoon. Do you, Ced?"

"No. Did they say what they wanted, Tanya?" Cedric asked.

"No." She walked farther into the room and whispered, "I recognize a couple of them, though. One is a Cobras football player and the other I remember as a model some years ago."

Lorenzo and Cedric shared a look, smiled and stood, having no doubt about the identities of their visitors. Before they took a step, the three men pushed through the door. In usual fashion, Brandon, the oldest of the Gray brothers, spoke first.

"So this is how you two do business around here, keeping folks waiting?"

He shook his head at his cousins. Brandon headed up the Gray family's in-home safety company, Khalil was a former model and now owned two fitness centers and Malcolm started as the star running back for the LA Cobras professional football team. They all lived in Los Angeles. After a round of greeting and rough hugs, Lorenzo asked, "Your wives gave you permission to leave the city?"

Malcolm snorted. "Whatever, Zo. We don't need permission."

Lorenzo caught Tanya's confused gaze. "Tanya, these are our cousins from Los Angeles, Brandon, Khalil and Malcolm Gray."

Tanya whipped her head around and her mouth dropped.

"Nice to meet you," they all chorused.

"Nice to meet you all, too," she said, shaking each

man's extended hand. To Malcolm, she said, "I'm a big Cobras fan. Oh, and I remember you, Khalil, from your modeling days."

Brandon chuckled. "Sorry, I'm not famous."

"Nah, he's not famous," Cedric said. "He only heads up one of the largest in-home safety companies in the country."

Tanya angled her head, as if thinking, "Wait. You're *those* Grays?" They nodded. A smile blossomed on her face. "Do you think I can get a picture with you all?"

"Sure," Khalil said.

"My husband is going to be so jealous." She rushed from the room and was back in a flash with her cell phone.

Cedric, standing closest, eased the phone from Tanya's hand. "I'll take them." He snapped one of Tanya with each of them, then a group shot.

"Thank you, guys. Can I get you something to drink?"

They all declined.

"If you need anything, I'll be out front." She departed with a smile.

Lorenzo gestured the men to sit. "What are you doing in our neck of the woods?"

"Dad mentioned that Uncle Russell and Uncle Reuben retired, so we thought we'd come congratulate you two in person," Khalil answered. "Sounds like it was kind of sudden."

Cedric nodded. "They called us into the office, said they were retiring effective immediately, and that was it. No transition, nothing. And now they're gone on a cruise."

Malcolm chuckled. "Damn, that's cold."

"Do you guys need help with anything?" Brandon asked. As the oldest male cousin, he always made time to help or be a sounding board if any of them needed one.

Lorenzo leaned back in his chair. "Not right now, but thanks for the offer. How long are you going to be here?"

"Just for the evening. We were thinking we'd grab some dinner and drinks. We're taking the last flight back to LA tonight. We probably should have called first to make sure you didn't have any plans."

Cedric shot an amused glance at Lorenzo. "My schedule is free, but Lorenzo's might not be."

Lorenzo's LA cousins stared at him curiously. He glared at Cedric. "Ced doesn't know what the hell he's talking about."

Cedric let out a short bark of laughter. "No? Zo may be the next one taking that trip down the aisle. Desiree is fine as hell and had a brother so caught up, they missed their dinner reservations."

Laughter broke out around the table. Finally, Malcolm stood. "It four-thirty and I know you don't have any other appointments. We definitely need to hear all about this new woman over dinner. And you do remember all the teasing you did when I was fighting my feelings for Lauren, right?" He smiled. "Yep, this visit is going to be much better than I anticipated."

Still chuckling, Brandon came to his feet and clapped Lorenzo on the shoulder. The other men followed suit. "Let's go, cuz. Falling in love is a good thing."

"Indeed it is," Khalil said.

Lorenzo didn't comment. And who said anything about falling in love? He, admittedly, enjoyed being with Desiree, but that didn't mean he was ready to walk down any aisle. Or even commit to some kind of long-term relationship. Yet, he couldn't explain the strange emotions that always plagued him every time he kissed her. He glanced up to find four pairs of eyes focused on him expectantly. He had planned to stay at the office until heading over to Desiree's later. Sighing, he stood and strode out of the office with the others following. Lorenzo stopped to tell Tanya they were leaving and that he would have his cell if anything came up.

After much discussion, they decided to go to Claim Jumper, a short ten-minute drive away. While everyone else piled into the SUV that Brandon had rented, Lorenzo opted to drive his own car. They arrived before happy hour got into full swing and only had to wait fifteen minutes to be seated. They took advantage of the snack and drink specials, in addition to their full meals.

After the server brought back beers for them all and took their orders, Lorenzo asked, "How are Faith, Lexia, Lauren and the babies?"

Brandon took a swig of his drink. "Faith is doing great. Her website business is growing and she's started teaching entrepreneurship classes to teens. Zola is almost a year old and is a daddy's girl," he added proudly.

"I bet she has you wrapped around her little finger," Cedric said with a grin. "How are you liking fatherhood, Khalil?"

"I'm enjoying my baby boy." Khalil and his wife, Lexia, had welcomed Khalil Jr. two weeks after Zola's birth last year. "I expanded the day care at the gym, so he goes to work with me. I love being at home with Lexia and KJ, which is why this visit is going to be cut short."

Lorenzo shook his head. "Y'all got it bad." He shifted his gaze to Malcolm. "Well, Mal, when are you and Lauren going to add to the growing number of babies in your family?"

"In about six months."

All eyes turned his way. Brandon and Khalil shot rapid-fire questions about why he hadn't told them, due dates and whether their parents knew.

"Morgan is the only one I told." Malcolm had always confided in his twin sister.

"Of course," Brandon said.

"Lauren and I are going over to Mom and Dad's tomorrow to tell them about the babies."

Khalil choked on his drink. "*Babies?* As in more than one?"

A wide grin covered Malcolm's face. "Yep. Twins."

Lorenzo chuckled. "Aunt Dee is going to be beside herself. Congrats."

"Yeah, and *our* mothers are going to be all over *us* even more to settle down," Cedric groused.

Brandon, Khalil and Malcolm laughed.

The server returned with their meals. After he departed, they ate in silence for a few minutes, then Brandon asked, "Speaking of settling down, how long have you and Desiree been dating, Lorenzo? And what does she do?"

Lorenzo added ketchup to his burger. "A few weeks. She owns a bath and body shop in Old Sacramento and it's nothing serious."

"It's serious enough that you've already slept with her at *your* house." Cedric didn't look up from his plate.

He skewered Cedric with a glare. "I never said I slept with her."

"You didn't have to." Cedric leaned forward and spoke to their cousins. "He made reservations at Ruth's Chris, but they ended up at Yard House."

Khalil burst out laughing. "Man, a sports bar? That's not even close. I mean it's high-end, but still a sports bar."

Cedric saluted Khalil with his bottle. "Exactly. He was supposed to be just stopping there so he could shower, since he left the job site late, but—"

"Things heated up before you could get out of the house, huh, Zo?" Malcolm finished.

Lorenzo wanted to knock the smug smiles right off Cedric's and Malcolm's faces.

Brandon finished chewing his steak and studied Lorenzo. "You think she might be the one you settle down with?"

"I have no idea and I'm not sure I want to get serious with anyone. And she has a lot of baggage."

Malcolm shook his head. "Don't we all? You know I had no intentions of settling down after what Lauren put me through, and I definitely didn't plan on getting back together with her, but I'm glad I took the risk. I couldn't be happier."

"Hey, even Uncle Thad got married again and he'd been divorced for close to thirty years. So you don't have an excuse," Brandon tossed out. Brandon's father-in-law had been separated from his daughter, Faith, for twenty-eight years due to his ex-wife packing her up and moving because she couldn't deal with Thad's PTSD.

"But Lauren and Uncle Thad's ex didn't do anything to potentially get you thrown in jail." He popped a French fry into his mouth. He had confided in them at Malcolm's wedding a year ago.

"Key word is *potentially*. At least you didn't *actually* spend thirty-six hours in a Mexican prison for the same reason," Khalil said quietly.

"What?" Lorenzo and Cedric said at the same time.

By the grim expressions Brandon and Malcolm wore, Lorenzo suspected they already knew the story. They listened as Khalil shared how, during his modeling days, his ex-girlfriend and a few other models used their assignments as drop-off points for drugs. He had been arrested with them and, even though he'd been innocent, was sent to jail. Khalil had been released thanks to his agent and the fact that he'd had airtight alibis for all of the times the trades had occurred. He had only shared the story with his brothers after his wedding.

Khalil pointed his fork Lorenzo's way. "I almost lost Lexia because I couldn't let go of what Michaela had done. Don't make the same mistake if you think Desiree might be the one for you."

Lorenzo didn't know what to say. His experience didn't come close to what his cousin had suffered. "Damn. I'm sorry."

"Me, too. Sorry that I let the hurt and anger rule my life for over eight years." They fell silent. "But, it's all good now."

They finished the meal. Lorenzo glanced at his watch.

"Late for your date?" Brandon teased.

"It's not a date. We're just going to hang out at her place and talk."

"Ha! Let us know how *that* works out."

"Shut up, Brandon." He stood and reached for his wallet.

Brandon waved him off. "I got it. Go enjoy your evening."

They engaged in a round of one-arm hugs. "I'll have to get down there soon to see the babies."

Khalil hugged Lorenzo last and said for his ears only, "Let go of the anger and fear, and if you ever want to talk about it, give me a call."

"Thanks." He threw up a wave and sauntered out. Spending time with them reminded Lorenzo of summers growing up. He, Alisha, Cedric and Cedric's brother, Jeremy, usually went to LA for a week or two to hang out with their cousins. He didn't know how his aunt and uncle handled all nine of them, but those were some of the best times. As a result, they'd all grown up close.

He got into his car and drove off and Khalil's words played in his head. Lorenzo noted the contentment on each of his married cousin's faces, but he didn't know if he could let go. His thoughts shifted to Desiree and his growing feelings. Cedric had been dead-on. Lorenzo *had* been caught up in that moment and every other one since, and he didn't know how to make it stop. Or even if he wanted to.

Chapter 11

As Lorenzo drove to Desiree's condo, he kept reminding himself that he and Desiree shared only a strong physical attraction and nothing more. But by the time he arrived and she opened the door to him wearing a pair of skimpy shorts and a tank top with the smile he'd come to look for, all those thoughts went right out the window. His gaze made a slow tour down her body and back up again. "Hey."

"Hey, yourself. Come on in." Desiree stepped back so he could enter.

He closed the door behind him and pulled her into his arms. "I've been waiting all day to kiss you."

She gave him a sassy smile. "Then what are you waiting for?"

"Permission."

"Granted."

That was all he needed to hear. Lorenzo slanted his mouth over hers and kissed her with an intensity that stunned him. She kissed him back with the same fire and he felt his control slipping but didn't stop immediately. "There is just something about your lips that I can't resist," he murmured before covering her mouth again. He nibbled on the corners, gently sucked on her bottom lip, then plunged inside again. She moaned softly and the sound sent a jolt straight to his groin. Finally, Lorenzo lifted his head. He needed to slow down. He took her hand and led her to the sofa.

Desiree sat and tucked her feet under her. "So, that was some kiss. If I didn't know better, I'd think you missed me or something."

The corner of his mouth tilted in a slight grin as he lowered himself next to her. "Or something."

"Do you want something to drink or eat? I have some chicken enchiladas."

"No, thank you. My cousins from LA showed up this afternoon and we went to dinner."

"That's nice. You all must be close. Has it been a long time since you've seen them?"

"Yes, we are, and I saw them when we all went down for Malcolm's wedding last year. We talk or text often, though." She placed her hand on his thigh and the heat penetrated his jeans as if she'd touched his bare skin.

"You should have said something. We could've gotten together another time."

"It's no problem. They're taking the last flight back tonight."

She stared. "You mean they spent all that money to fly down here just for a few hours?"

Lorenzo chuckled at her expression. Their families were very close and the spontaneous visits weren't uncommon. It helped that they had been financially blessed enough to do it. "Yes. We've done the same on occasion."

"I guess your company is doing pretty well," she murmured.

Had any other woman said it, he would have taken it as a ploy to find out just how much he was worth, but not Desiree. He chuckled inwardly remembering their first date and her concern over him being able to pay for their meals. "We've been very blessed or fortunate—however you want to look at it—to build a solid company and it's afforded us a few luxuries. Like I said, we've always been pretty close, so we try to support each other."

A shadow crossed her face. "It sounds like a great thing."

Belatedly, Lorenzo remembered that her family wasn't as tight-knit as his. Thinking about all the women in his family, he instinctively knew Desiree would fit in perfectly. *Where the hell did that thought come from?* "So, did you get all your online orders sent out?" he asked, changing the subject to keep his mind from heading to places he didn't want it to go.

"Yes, but it took all three of us to get them all done. We're looking into hiring someone part-time and hopefully, it won't take long to happen."

"Will you have time to make your products if you're spending so much time with this?"

"Thankfully, my assistant, Sandra, helps me out. It takes the soap about two months to be ready, so we have to stay on top of inventory. Pretty much everything else can be used the same day."

It still boggled his mind that she created everything he saw in her shop. And he couldn't deny how much he liked the soap he'd bought. It lasted far longer than anything he had purchased in the stores.

"You said we'd talk about where we're going with this relationship."

"Where do you want it to go?"

Desiree angled her head thoughtfully. "I'm not sure exactly. In all honesty, I haven't had much luck when it comes to dating. Things are okay now, but I don't see you sticking around for long."

"Why would you think that?" True, he wasn't planning on anything long-term, but her tone gave him pause. She sounded as if she'd been hurt by a man, and more than once.

She averted her eyes.

"Are you thinking I'll eventually cheat on you?" She didn't answer and he realized she believed exactly that. Having been betrayed in his own relationship, he understood completely. She didn't trust any more than he did. Lorenzo scooted closer to her and tilted her chin. "Sweetheart, I don't know what he did to hurt you, but I would never cheat on you or disrespect you in any way. I have no idea how this thing between us is going to play out, but you don't have to worry about something like that. I've never cheated on a woman and I won't start now. You are an intelligent and beautiful woman. Any man would be lucky to have you by his side." He brushed his lips across hers. The vulnerability he saw in her gorgeous eyes tempted him to promise he'd always walk by her side. Lorenzo brought his thoughts to a screeching halt. He had no idea where the notion had come from and it sent a measure of dread down his spine. Yet, he couldn't stop the surge of emotions swirling in the pit of his stomach. He was falling for this woman and there wasn't a damn thing he could do about it.

"I believe you, Lorenzo. So what do we do now?"

A smile curved his lips. "We enjoy the ride."

Desiree returned his smile and nodded, then leaned up and kissed him.

He wasted no time taking over the kiss. He angled his head and deepened it, tasting, teasing. She met him stroke for stroke. He groaned at the feeling of her hands sliding across his chest. Without breaking the seal of their mouths, Lorenzo shifted her until she straddled his lap. His hands charted a path up her firm thighs, around to her shapely backside and ground her center against his straining erection. "Do you feel what you do to me, how much I want you?"

Desiree gasped softly. "Lorenzo," she whispered on a ragged moan.

The sound sent his desire straight through the roof. If he didn't stop now they would be in her bed in the next minute. As much as he wanted to indulge in another round of *seduction*, he sensed that he needed to be gentle with her, build up her trust. Lorenzo also needed to understand what he was feeling and exactly what he wanted to do about it. Desiree rested her head on his shoulder and he could feel her rapidly beating heart against his. "Did you have a busy day?"

"Yep. With summer starting, we get a lot of foot traffic, especially on the weekends. The shop doesn't open until ten tomorrow, but I plan to be there around eight."

"Why so early?"

"I'm making some lip scrub to include in a gift set

for someone's bridal shower. She's picking it up in the afternoon and I want to have it all packaged and ready. I just decided to add the scrub as an extra for her."

The mention of the scrub brought to remembrance her soft lips and how much he liked kissing them. "That's nice." He had never considered a gift set and briefly wondered if his mother would like something like that. He knew his sister would.

"Do you plan to work once you get home tonight?"

Her voice broke into his thoughts. "Probably. Why?"

Desiree shrugged. "Because you always seem to put in a lot of hours."

She was right. He had always been the first to arrive and, often, the last to leave. His father had cautioned him more than once about burnout and finding balance in his life. Their last conversation filtered through Lorenzo's mind. *Your mother helped me to see I needed some balance in my life. I know you tend to work long hours, but don't make it a habit. Maybe you need someone to help you see the same.* He promptly dismissed it. "I do, but I'm working on balance. Not sure how well it'll work out now that we're heading the company, but we'll see."

Desiree lifted her head. "You need to schedule in some downtime or fun every now and again. I make a point of getting it in because I find it helps clear my mind, then I'm more productive."

Lorenzo studied her. "Hmm, I never thought of it that way." But he'd never had a problem with productivity because he loved every aspect of his job, even though parts of it could be grueling. Yet, he couldn't deny that he'd been exhausted lately. "What kinds of things do you do for fun?"

"I schedule a 'me time' day once a month and get a massage, pedicure, manicure and take myself to lunch. I do the pedicure twice a month. Brenda and I typically spend a couple of days in Lake Tahoe or San Francisco once or twice a year, as well."

Lately, he had only gone to San Francisco for work and had forgotten all the fun he and his cousins used to have when they visited. "You mentioned San Francisco. Would you like to go soon? I know you work on the weekends, but we can figure something out."

"Actually, my mother is coming for a visit next weekend and that's where she wants to go." Desiree smiled. "I hate driving in the city. If you drive, I'll make it worth your while." She kissed him softly. "Totally worth your while."

Meeting her mother took things to a whole new level and he usually steered clear of anything remotely close to family introductions. Desiree kissed him again, using her tongue to take him to the brink of his control, once again. "Yeah, I'll take you." As always, something about her kiss did something to him. He'd agree to take her anywhere she wanted to go, despite the warning bells in his head telling him this was moving way past a *light affair*.

Saturday morning, Desiree divided her time between waiting on customers and filling online orders. She had packaged Laura's gift sets with the free mini container of lip scrub in an ivory box with dividers and a clear lid, and tied a wide, sheer purple ribbon around it to match the bride's color scheme. She had also taken the liberty of creating a special honeymoon gift basket for the bride and groom, filled with a variety of edible and flavored massage oils, warming oils and body paints.

Sandra came to where Desiree stood arranging the items in the basket. "I know they're going to enjoy those oils. There's going to be a lot of massaging and licking going on and my bet is that she'll be pregnant before they return home." She leaned against the counter. "Des, you really should consider selling these."

She angled her head thoughtfully. She had toyed with adding a sensual line to her inventory, but hadn't made a firm decision, as yet. "I'm thinking about it."

"And this chocolate body paint." Sandra picked up the jar. "All I have to say is *hallelujah*! You're making all this decadent stuff—I sure hope you're trying it out, because I sure am."

Desiree laughed, plucked the jar out of Sandra's hand and placed it in the basket. "I'm glad you're having fun." She hadn't tried them out herself because there had not been a man in her life to try them with. An image of Lorenzo's hands and mouth on her body flashed in her mind. She wouldn't mind trying them out on him in her own brand of *seduction*. She closed the cellophane wrap with a twist tie, used a heat gun to shrink wrap it and added a bow.

"Desiree, there's a woman asking for you."

She turned at the sound of Casey's voice. It must be Laura. "I'll be right there."

Casey nodded and disappeared from the door.

Desiree carefully stacked each small box inside a larger one, making room for the basket. She picked it up and carried it out front. She scanned the shop, but didn't see Laura or her mother. She placed the box on the long counter behind the register. "Casey, you said someone was looking for me?"

"Oh yes. She's over there next to the bath bombs." Casey pointed to the woman.

Desiree's brows knit in confusion. She didn't recognize the woman. She crossed the floor to where the woman stood sampling a hand scrub. "Excuse me. Hello, I'm Desiree." The woman stood an inch or so taller than Desiree.

The woman faced Desiree and a smile bloomed on her face. "Yes. I'm Alisha Hunter and I've heard so many good things about your shop."

"That's always nice to hear," she said with a little laugh. "Is there anything in particular you're looking for?"

"Everything. And I wanted to meet the woman my brother is falling in love with."

Desiree stared, stunned. It dawned on her that Alisha said her last name was Hunter. It took her a moment to find her voice. "You're Lorenzo's sister."

"Yes."

"I'm not sure what your brother has told you, but I'm certain love has nothing to do with it. We've only been dating—"

"Yeah, I know…less than two months. No, he hasn't said it—and he probably won't admit it anytime soon—but I know he is." Alisha chuckled. "Trust me. Anyway, what do you recommend for an overworked mother who needs five minutes of relaxation?"

She found it hard to keep up with this woman. Alisha changed the subject on a dime and was now sniffing different scents of body scrubs. "Depends on what types of fragrances you like. For relaxation, I'd suggest something with lavender, vanilla, chamomile, sandalwood, ylang-

ylang." Desiree picked up the vanilla and ylang-ylang scrub and handed it to Alisha. "I have a few blends that might work." She explained the properties of the scrub, then did the same with the lavender sandalwood and lavender vanilla blends. "We use real essential oils."

"Mmm, all of these smell good. I think I'm going to get all three. I'd love to get the bath bombs, but my kids would be banging on the bathroom door before the thing could melt." Alisha shook her head.

She laughed. "I can only imagine. The body scrubs will work well in the shower. You can experience a little calm in a short amount of time. I also have face and lip cleansers and scrubs, as well as moisturizers and body lotions and creams." She had Alisha try out each.

"Okay, I'm sold. My coworkers rave about your products and now I see why." She placed a few more products in her basket and carried it over to the register.

Desiree rang up her purchases.

Alisha inserted her credit card. "I need you and Lorenzo to hurry up and get married, so I can get a family discount. Otherwise, I'll end up spending half my paycheck in here."

She didn't respond to the comment. "I hope you enjoy everything."

"And I hope things work out between you and my brother." She held up the bag. "I'll let you know how it goes." She strode out of the store.

Oo-kay. That was interesting. What had Lorenzo told his sister about them and why did Alisha seem to think Lorenzo was falling in love? The only thing Lorenzo had said was that he liked being with Desiree. That didn't qualify as falling in love, at least not in her book. Desiree shook her head and moved to the next customer. A few minutes later, Laura entered holding the hand of a tall, blond-haired man who Desiree assumed was Laura's fiancé.

Laura smiled at Desiree and started toward the register.

"Hi, Laura."

"Hi, Desiree. I'd like you to meet my fiancé, Jacob."

"It's a pleasure to meet you, Desiree. Laura's been raving about your products," Jacob said.

"It's nice to meet you, as well, Jacob. And thank you, Laura. I have your gifts all ready." Desiree turned, retrieved the box and placed it in front of Laura and Jacob. "I hope your guests will like them. I added a little something extra in the boxes."

Laura took one out. "This is beautiful. Thank you so much. I love them." She held it closer. "A lip scrub?"

She smiled. "Yes."

"These are so pretty. I want to keep one for myself."

"You asked for thirty-five, but I made two extra—one for you and one for your mother. Also, my gift to you and Jacob for your honeymoon." She lifted the gift basket.

"Oh my. This is so wonderful."

Jacob chuckled. "Honeymoon? I think I might want to try that chocolate body paint tonight."

Laura's cheeks reddened. *"Jacob!"*

"What, baby?" He took out his wallet and paid the invoice. Then they departed with a wave.

Jacob stared at Laura with such adoration Desiree had to look away for a moment. What she wouldn't give to have a man gaze at her that way. *Not just any man. Just Lorenzo,* her inner voice chimed. Because despite her best efforts, she was falling for him.

Chapter 12

Desiree rushed around her condo, trying to get ready for the trip to San Francisco. Between worrying about her mother and dealing with her sister's antics, it had taken her a long time to fall asleep last night. She had slept straight through her alarm and now had less than an hour to dress and prepare and eat breakfast before Lorenzo arrived. Lorenzo. She hadn't seen him since that Friday night a week ago. They had only talked a couple of times over the past eight days because of both of their hectic schedules and she was looking forward to seeing him. Desiree only hoped Melanie didn't try her old tactics of flirting, as she typically did whenever Desiree had a boyfriend. Desiree had caught more than one of her teenage crushes in a lip-lock with her sister. However, she didn't think Lorenzo would be that gullible, but she had been wrong before and it added to her growing list of concerns for the day. She also worried how her mother would do on the day-long trip. So far today, she seemed to be her usual upbeat self.

"Desiree, what time are we leaving?"

She glimpsed over her shoulder at her mother. "Lorenzo should be here in about twenty minutes."

Her mother came over to the sink where Desiree stood rinsing off the dishes and placing them into the dishwasher. "Let me do that, baby." She eased the bowl from Desiree's hand.

"Mom, is there anything special you want to do while we're in San Francisco? I know you mentioned wanting to walk around Pier 39 and take a cruise."

"That'll probably be enough," she said with a laugh. "Whatever you have planned will be fine, honey. Don't stress yourself. I'm just glad to be here with you for a couple of days." They shared a smile.

Melanie came into the kitchen and leaned on the bar. "How long does it take to get to San Francisco?"

"About two hours without traffic."

"Ugh! First you have me sleeping on that hard sofa and now you expect me to sit in a car all day?"

Desiree took a deep breath and mentally counted to ten. Her sister had been complaining about one thing or another since Desiree picked them up from the airport last night. "You're more than welcome to stay here." She shifted her gaze and stared at Melanie. "We wouldn't want you to be subjected to a long car ride. And if the accommodations here aren't up to your standards, I'd be happy to drop you off at a hotel."

"Melanie, stop all this fussing," their mother said.

Desiree opened her mouth to say something and her doorbell rang. She glanced over at the microwave clock.

Lorenzo was fifteen minutes early. "I'll be right back." She went to open the door. Lorenzo stood there leaning against the door frame wearing a pair of jeans and a fitted tee that reminded her of the first time she'd seen him in the park. "Hey."

Lorenzo smiled. "Morning, baby." He leaned down and placed a soft kiss on her lips. He scanned her face. "Are you okay?"

"Yeah, fine."

He eyed her skeptically. "You sure?"

Desiree nodded. "Just dealing with my sister. Come on in. We're about ready. Can I get you something?"

"Yeah, but what I want isn't doable right now," he said close to her ear.

She stopped so abruptly that he nearly knocked her over. "What?"

He held her gaze intently. "I thought of a new way to seduce you." He tossed her a bold wink. "Are you game?"

Desiree almost melted on the spot. And, yeah, she was all for him seducing her again. She couldn't think of a suitable comeback, so she didn't reply. "Um…let me introduce you to my mom and sister."

Lorenzo chuckled. "You're not going to answer my question?"

She glanced around to make sure her sister wasn't eavesdropping. "No," she whispered.

"I can make it totally worth your while. *Totally.*"

Desiree couldn't hide her smile. "I bet you could. Now will you behave and come on?"

"For now."

She shook her head. "I don't know what I'm going to do with you."

"Comments like that will get this trip canceled and you naked."

His words sent heat spiraling through her, her body responding with a resounding *let's do it*. She pivoted and started for the kitchen, his laughter trailing. Her mother was standing at the sink putting the last of the dishes into the dishwasher, but turned when they entered. "Mom, I'd like you to meet Lorenzo Hunter."

"Mrs. Scott, it's a pleasure to finally meet you," Lorenzo said.

A wide smile blossomed on her mother's face. "It's so nice to meet you, too, Lorenzo. Thanks so much for agreeing to be our driver. I hope we're not putting you out."

"Not at all. I'm looking forward to it."

Desiree shifted her gaze to her sister, who had a sultry "I'm available" expression on her face and wished she could skip the introduction altogether. "And that's my younger sister, Melanie."

Lorenzo nodded Melanie's way. "Nice to meet you."

"Same here. So, do you work with Desiree or something?"

He smiled at Desiree. "Or something. Are we ready?"

"Yes," Desiree said, trying to stifle her laughter at the stunned look on Melanie's face. "I just need to get my jacket and purse. Mom, I'll bring yours out."

"Thanks, baby."

She was gone and back in a flash and they all piled into Lorenzo's Lexus SUV. Desiree sat in front, while her mother and sister took the second row. "This is nice." She had only seen his work truck and the Audi sedan.

"Thanks," he said, pulling out onto the road. "My

cousin, Siobhan in LA, has one and I drove it on one of my visits and liked it. It's big enough for me to carry a few things for the job, but not bulky or too much of a gas guzzler."

They kept up a steady stream of conversation for the duration of the ride, with her mother asking questions about Sacramento and the Bay Area. Melanie, thankfully, didn't make any snide comments. "I thought we were going to make it all the way without traffic," Desiree said once they got to Emeryville.

"Unless you're coming before the crack of dawn or late at night, there's always traffic here with all the freeway interchanges." The mass of ramps led to several Bay Area cities and it took a good fifteen minutes to go two miles.

The traffic was also backed up at the bridge leading into San Francisco. Desiree handed Lorenzo the toll fare before he could reach for his wallet. He started to argue, but she cut him off. "You drove, so I'll pay the toll."

Lorenzo studied her a long moment, then finally took the money. "This goes against everything I've been taught," he muttered.

She laid a hand on his arm. "I promise to tell your parents, if I ever meet them, that they raised a perfect gentleman. Five dollars doesn't change that." He stared at her with a tender look that had her heart beating faster. "What?"

"Nothing." He kissed her hand and inched up one car length.

Desiree heard her sister snicker from the backseat and mumble something that sounded like, "I hope you don't think that's going to keep him satisfied."

She chose to ignore Melanie and hoped they could get through the day without any drama.

Once there, Lorenzo parked in the garage across from Pier 39. As they walked toward their destination, he said to Desiree, "You mentioned wanting to do one of the Golden Gate cruises. We should probably buy the tickets now, just in case they sell out."

"You're right." Apparently lots of people decided to take advantage of the midseventies temperatures, as the streets were already filling. "Are you okay with that, Mom? It's just a little ways up the street."

"That's fine. I made sure to wear my good walking shoes."

Desiree chuckled and they started up the street. She made sure to keep her pace slow so as not to tire her mother out. Lorenzo reached down and entwined their hands.

"Lorenzo, where do you work?" Desiree's mother asked after a few minutes.

"I work as a civil engineer for my family's construction company."

"That probably keeps you really busy."

He laughed. "Yes, ma'am, it does."

"It must pay well, especially since your family owns it," Melanie said, smiling up at Lorenzo as if he was her favorite treat.

Lorenzo lifted a brow and glanced down at Desiree with a look that asked, "Is she for real?"

Desiree glared at her sister. "That's none of your business, Melanie." She was glad he hadn't mentioned that he now owned it. Her materialistic sister would have propositioned him right then, regardless of the fact that he and Desiree were dating. She'd done it before.

Lorenzo glanced over his shoulder at Melanie. "It pays like any other job."

Desiree mouthed an apology. Lorenzo gave her a sympathetic smile and squeezed her hand. They walked the rest of the way in silence. Several large groups congregated near the ticket booth and she worried that all the sailings for the day would be sold out.

Her mother opened her purse. "Desiree, let me give you some money."

"That's okay, Mom. This is my treat. I just want you to have a good time." Of course, Melanie hadn't even considered offering to pay for her own ticket.

Desiree and Lorenzo went to the window, while her mother and Melanie stood off to the side to wait. Fortunately, there were still spots for the afternoon. "I'd really like to do the sunset cruise, but I think my mom will be too tired to enjoy it." It didn't leave until seven in the evening and Desiree had noticed last night and when she'd gone home that her mother tended to have more difficulties the later it became.

He stared up at the posted schedule. "How about the three forty-five or four-fifteen trip?"

She checked her watch. "It's twelve-thirty now. If we do the four-fifteen, that will give us a good three hours to sightsee and grab something to eat without having to rush." Passengers were required to arrive thirty minutes prior to departure.

"That works," Lorenzo said as they got in line. At the window, he whipped his credit card out.

"Lorenzo, this was my trip. I can't ask you to pay for my mother and sister. That wasn't my intent when I invited you along." It would cost over a hundred dollars for all of them.

"I don't recall you asking me to pay, baby. I'm offering." He signed the slip, took the tickets and handed them to Desiree.

"I totally get that your parents raised you to always be a gentleman, and you are that. But this is different."

He chuckled and draped an arm around her shoulders. "Not in my book. Let's go show your mom a good time. Oh, and you mentioned wanting to do the sunset cruise. We'll make time to come back and do it. Just the two of us, okay?"

"Thank you." Desiree felt the scales in her heart tilting further toward him.

As they walked along the pier, Lorenzo scrutinized Desiree's tight features. While her mother appeared to be enjoying herself, her sister complained about everything. Whenever Desiree made a suggestion, Melanie found some reason as to why it wouldn't be a good idea.

"Oh, I haven't been on a carousel since you guys were kids," Mrs. Scott said as they approached the popular ride.

Melanie let out a snort. "I know you aren't thinking about riding that, Mom. We're not kids anymore and nobody wants to ride that thing."

"Why not? I used to love them." She placed a hand on her hip. "But you don't have to. You can sit right here and wait while we ride. Hopefully, by then, your attitude will have changed." She shook her head. "Lorenzo, where do we buy tickets?"

Lorenzo pointed. "The ticket booth is right over there."

Mrs. Scott smiled. "Good. Let's go get some."

He grinned at her no-nonsense stance. She reminded

him of his own mother. He briefly wondered how the two women would get along. Instinctively, he knew they would bond instantly.

"Now that we're out of earshot of my nosy youngest daughter, how long have you and Desiree been dating?"

Lorenzo should have known he'd been set up. "A couple of months."

"Your intentions and feelings for her?"

"We're still getting to know each other, but I like her a lot," he answered carefully.

She nodded. "How long have you worked for your family's company?"

"Since I was fifteen. My cousin and I have recently taken over the leadership now that our fathers retired." He hadn't offered the information to Melanie earlier because, as Desiree had stated, it was none of her business. However, he wanted to make a good impression on her mother, which didn't make sense, unless he planned for his and Desiree's relationship to become something other than a casual fling. The thought gave him pause and he felt his old fears rising. He got so lost in his musings it took him a moment to realize it was their turn at the window. Lorenzo pulled his wallet from his pocket.

"Young man, you leave that wallet right in your pocket."

"But, Mrs. Scott—"

"Don't *but* me. I'm paying for the tickets. It's the least I can do." She gave him that patented mother's glare that brokered no argument.

He sighed inwardly and replaced his wallet.

She opened her purse, counted out what was owed and handed it to the woman. The woman gave Mrs. Scott the tickets and she handed them to Lorenzo. As they walked away, she smiled up at him. "You're a nice young man and I think you're going to be good for Desiree. My baby has always been the peacekeeper in the family, even more so since her father passed. That's a heavy burden for one person, especially with my brood," she added with a little laugh. "It's good to see her so happy."

Lorenzo didn't know what to say. He could tell all of those things about Desiree by the way she had handled Melanie, and it seemed as if she'd been doing it all her life. Did her mother think he had something to do with Desiree being happy? Parts of him were secretly elated that he could bring her a measure of joy. The other parts of him couldn't be sure if that was a good thing or not.

"I don't know what you did to get him, but if I wanted to, I could take him just like that," Lorenzo heard Melanie say as they approached. Melanie chuckled bitterly. "I've done it before."

His mouth settled in a grim line. He didn't know what he'd do if he had to deal with that kind of behavior from his sister all the time. He saw the pain and anger in Desiree's eyes. Without thinking, Lorenzo placed a soft kiss on her lips, trying to communicate that she was the only woman he wanted. Her responding smile warmed his heart. "The line's not too long, so we should be able to get on next." He shifted his gaze and met Mrs. Scott's smiling face. Melanie wore a frown. They got in line and he handed Desiree and Mrs. Scott their tickets.

"Where's mine?" Melanie asked.

Mrs. Scott whipped her head around and glared at her youngest daughter. "You just said you didn't want to ride and I'm not in the habit of wasting my money. Are you saying you changed your mind? If so, you'd

better hurry and get your ticket before the ride stops."
She shooed Melanie. "And you might have more fun
if you stopped being such a grouch." That said, she
turned back around.

It took everything in Lorenzo not to laugh at the
look of disbelief on Melanie's face. He and Desiree
shared a smile.

Desiree shook her head and muttered, "She is a piece
of work."

Apparently, the setdown her mother had delivered
made Melanie reassess her attitude because she hadn't
uttered one complaint since the carousel ride. They continued the tour of the pier and ended up at Bubba Gump
Shrimp Co. for lunch. Afterward, they walked back to
Pier 43 ½ for the cruise. On board, they chose inside
seating. The temperatures had cooled and the breeze
kicked up. However, Desiree took her mother out on
the deck to take pictures.

Lorenzo watched Desiree's smile and sparkling eyes
as she interacted with her mother, and the sight made
the familiar pounding in his heart start up. When Mrs.
Scott came back inside, he excused himself and went
to where Desiree still stood at the rail.

"Hey, beautiful. How're you doing?"

"Better, now that Melanie has stopped complaining.
I'm enjoying seeing my mom have such a good time."

Lorenzo fit himself behind her and wrapped his arms
around her. "Has your sister always been like this?"

"Pretty much." She angled her head to meet his gaze.
"The crazy thing is she doesn't act the same with our
older sister. Just me." She turned back toward the water.
"I never understood why."

He dropped a kiss on her hair. He didn't, either. Desiree was one of the sweetest women he had met. Not once had she responded to her sister in a harsh way, though it certainly would have been justified. His mind went back to what he'd overheard Melanie say and the boast that she'd done it before. Lorenzo now understood why Desiree was so gun-shy when it came to men. Obviously she'd been hurt more than he had. He tightened his arms around her. "Well, rest assured, no matter what Melanie said, she will never be able to take me away from you."

Desiree turned in his arms. "I appreciate you saying that, but like you heard her say, she's done it before. It's a good thing she doesn't live here. Even if she couldn't lure you away, she'd make our lives a living hell trying to do everything she could to interfere."

"Sweetheart, it wouldn't matter if she lived here and we saw her every day. I wouldn't ever be interested in her because she's not my type. You, on the other hand, are exactly my type—intelligent, beautiful inside and out, ambitious. And you have a heart of gold. That's worth more than anything to me." He had no idea where those words had come from and had never uttered anything like them to a woman before. Hell, he was still trying to understand why this particular woman affected him so.

"Lorenzo," she whispered.

Lorenzo framed her face with his hands. "Yeah, you're exactly my type," he repeated just before capturing her mouth in a deep, sensual kiss that shocked him in its intensity. But he could no more stop himself than he could stop breathing. Despite all the warning bells going off in his head and his fears of letting go, he was falling for Desiree. Completely.

Chapter 13

Sunday afternoon, Desiree walked with her mother and sister through the airport to the tram that would take them to their gate, already missing her mom. She gave her a strong hug. "I'm so glad you came, Mom."

"I am, too. I enjoyed myself. Oh, and Lorenzo is such a sweetheart. He's a cutie, too," she added with a giggle. "I think your dad would've liked him."

She smiled. She thought Lorenzo was pretty special, as well. All the while they were in San Francisco, he'd stayed by her side, giving her a comforting touch just when she needed it most. Not to mention he had paid for everything except the bridge toll and the carousel ride. No amount of pleading had made him budge. "He's a great guy." The tram arrived. "Call me when you get home."

"We will." They shared another quick hug. Her

mother stepped onto the tram and waved. "Love you, baby."

"Love you, too, Mom." Desiree opened her mouth to say goodbye to her sister, but Melanie got on behind their mother without a backward glance. As the tram departed, Desiree watched it speed down the track with tears stinging her eyes. She didn't know what she would do once her mother's condition worsened. More than ever, she wanted to be there for her mother. Desiree had made a good life in California and her shop was doing well. It pained her to think she might have to give it all up to move back to Chicago. The thought of losing her anchor scared Desiree more than she cared to admit. She could move her mother here, but knew that would be a battle of epic proportions with her sisters. Neither of them would think about taking on the responsibility of caring for their mother as the disease progressed, but they wouldn't want Desiree to do it, either, most likely because they couldn't take advantage of their mother anymore. Desiree blew out a long breath and started back to her car.

On the way home, she toyed with going over to the shop, but decided against it. In her present mood, it would be best for her to stay away. Besides, they'd be closing in an hour. When she parked in her spot and got out, Desiree went still upon seeing Lorenzo coming toward her, wearing basketball shorts and a T-shirt.

"Lorenzo. Hey."

Lorenzo gave her that sexy smile. "Hi. Your mom and sister get off okay?"

"Yes. What are you doing here?"

"I figured you might be a little down and missing

your mom, so I came to keep you company for a while, if that's okay."

She smiled, came up on tiptoe and kissed him softly. She was coming to like this man more and more. "Yeah, it's okay. Thank you." Desiree grasped his hand and led him up the walk. Once inside, she placed her purse on an end table, dropped down on the sofa and told him, "Make yourself comfortable."

He sat next to her and pulled her close. "What did you have planned tonight?"

Desiree laid her head on his shoulder. "Playing around with a few recipes."

"It wouldn't be any more of that lip scrub, would it?"

She laughed. Most men would have immediately thought she meant food. "No. I've been trying to decide whether to add a sensual line of products."

Lorenzo sat up and a big grin covered his face. "I'm more than willing to sample them."

She rolled her eyes playfully. "I bet you are."

"I'm serious. What are you making?"

"Body paint, and some flavored massage oils and body butters that will warm up when you blow on them or um…lick them off."

Desire leaped into his eyes. "How long do they take to make?"

"Not too long. Why?"

Lorenzo lifted a brow. "Why do you think?"

Laughter spilled from Desiree's lips. "I can't believe you."

"What?" He lifted her onto his lap. "I'm just trying to help a sistah out."

"Mmm-hmm, more like you're trying to help yourself out."

He grinned. "That, too. And like I told you before, I can totally make it worth your while."

His heated promise from yesterday flashed in her mind and she knew, without a doubt, he could make good on it. Her body tingled just thinking about all the ways he'd made her body come alive. He trailed his tongue across her chest, stopping to nibble and suckle various spots. Her breath stacked up in her throat and her eyes slid closed.

"So what are we making?" he murmured, freeing one breast and latching on to an erect nipple.

"I...*ohh*." Desiree didn't know how he expected her to answer. Pleasure shot straight to her core.

"You didn't answer."

She opened her eyes and Lorenzo lifted his head. "I hadn't decided. Maybe a strawberry body oil or a whipped chocolate body butter."

"I think I'll help. The faster you finish, the faster I can try them out on your sexy body." Lorenzo fixed her clothing and stood with her in his arms. "Where to?"

"The kitchen." Desiree looped her arms around his neck as he carried her through the living room to the kitchen. She had thought about asking him to try out the new products, but not tonight.

He placed her on her feet and leaned against the counter. "What do you need me to do?"

"Nothing, really. The massage oil just requires mixing a few ingredients together. The body butter takes a little longer because I have to melt the oils and blend it."

"I vote for the massage oil."

Shaking her head, she gathered all the ingredients from the cabinet where she stored her crafting materials. "You would. Since you volunteered, I'll let you combine everything." She placed the four ingredients in front of him and had him measure out the amounts of the first three.

"Honey? I think I'm going to enjoy this oil." Lorenzo wiggled his eyebrows.

Once he'd done that, she had him add the strawberry flavored oil. "Okay, just do a quick stir and pour it in here." She gestured to a dark blue glass bottle and handed him a funnel.

"That's it?" he asked, following her directions.

"Yep."

Lorenzo scraped out some of the residue from the spouted cup with his finger and drew a line across her chest above her tank top. "Now for the taste test." He made a slow path over the area with his tongue. "Mmm, sweet."

Desiree sucked in a sharp breath. The heat from his mouth and the warming effects of the oil made her knees buckle and she braced herself against the counter to keep from sliding to the floor. "I think I want a taste, too," she said breathlessly. She dipped some out, pushed his shirt up and branded him the same way. She took her time and slowly and methodically licked off every drop of the oil. He groaned and slanted his mouth over hers in a hungry kiss, making her senses spin.

Lorenzo whipped her shirt over her head, tossed it aside and did the same with his. He lifted her onto the counter and stepped between her legs. "I don't think this little bottle is going to be enough, baby." He unclasped her bra and dragged the straps down and off. Reaching for the bottle, he poured a small amount into his hand and massaged it over her breasts.

He licked his way to her nipple and took the hardened bud into his mouth. Desiree cried out at the exquisite sensations taking over her body. Through the sensual haze, she thought she heard a buzzing sound, but dismissed it. A moment later, she heard it again.

Letting out a low curse, Lorenzo snatched his phone out of his pocket, glanced at the display and connected. "There had better be a damn building on fire," he gritted out.

She watched his face go from irritation to what looked like shock in the blink of an eye. She could only hear his side of the conversation, but she knew it had something to do with one of his job sites.

"I'll be there in a bit." He ended the call and rested his head against hers. "I have to go."

"The San Francisco site?"

"No. A park project here." He grabbed his shirt off the floor and put it on, then picked up Desiree's and helped her down.

Desiree slipped into her tank and followed him to the front door.

Lorenzo gave her a quick kiss. "I'll call you."

"Okay. I hope everything turns out okay."

"So do I," he said grimly, and walked out the door.

She closed it behind him and went back to the kitchen to clean up. The sight of the oil brought back every pleasurable moment and she vowed that they would finish it, one way or another.

Lorenzo gripped the steering wheel tighter as he drove to Cedric's house. He reached down and cranked the air conditioner as high as it would go. Even with the turmoil swirling in his gut from his cousin's call, his erection hadn't gone down and his body remained aroused at a level he had never experienced. He dragged a hand down his face and the scent of strawberries immediately engulfed him, along with the tantalizing memories of tasting Desiree's soft skin. He glanced at the speedometer and realized he had been driving fifteen miles over the limit and eased off the gas. Lorenzo didn't need to add a speeding ticket to his list of concerns tonight.

He turned onto the Rocklin cul-de-sac where Cedric lived, parked in the driveway and hurried up the walk.

Cedric opened the door seconds after Lorenzo rang the bell. "Hey. Come on in."

Lorenzo followed him back to the family room and dropped down in one of the brown leather recliners. "What's going on? What's this about some of our building materials being questionable?"

"I have a friend who works for the local paper and—"

"A woman no doubt."

A grin curved Cedric's mouth. "Hey, don't hate. I can't help it if the women love me."

He shook his head. "Whatever, man. I can't wait for the one woman who's going to have you so turned inside out you won't be able to see straight."

"Please. There isn't one woman who can make me change my single status. You, on the other hand…"

Lorenzo waved a hand. "Anyway, what happened?"

Cedric retrieved his phone, pushed a few buttons and handed it to Lorenzo. "Read for yourself. This is the story that's supposed to run tomorrow. She said since it's not necessarily earth-shattering or breaking news, she might be able to get the article pushed back by a day or two."

As he read, he felt his eyes widen and his heart nearly stopped. "What the hell…?" He jumped up from the chair. "We've never used substandard materials!" The article alleged that the lumber used for the community center building in their park project didn't meet city codes or have a stamp indicating it was fire retardant.

"I know that. We checked and had it tested, and we always use the same lumber company, so I have no idea how this happened."

"I was going to San Francisco tomorrow, but I'll be at the park site first thing in the morning." Lorenzo didn't even want to think about what would happen to the company and their reputations if this got around.

"You and me, both. We've got to nip this in the bud, and fast. Why is it that everything is happening *now*, after our pops' retirement?" Cedric lowered himself onto the sofa and buried his head in his hands. "I feel like somebody's playing a bad joke on us."

He blew out a long breath and reclaimed his chair. "Tell me about it." He checked his watch. "There's still about an hour's worth of daylight."

Cedric didn't hesitate. "Let's go."

Since the project was nearby, it only took them ten minutes to get there. They walked around the property, taking pictures and inspecting some of the lumber. Most of the framing wood that had been used bore the fire-retardant stamp, but they did find a few that didn't.

"I sent out samples of this wood—more than most companies—and I don't understand how these got in the mix."

"Well, we'll be talking to Jim as soon as he's open tomorrow." Jim was the owner of the lumber company they used.

"If I find out he's the one trying to cut corners to save a few dollars, I'm going to be tempted to kick his ass, then he's gone," Cedric tossed out. His cell rang. "This is Tara. Let me see what she found out." He connected. "Hey, Tara."

Lorenzo walked a few feet away, checked some of the piled-up lumber and saw a few more two-by-eights without the stamp. He agreed with Cedric.

His cousin joined him a few minutes later. "Tara is going to bump the article for a couple of days. There were some higher priority stories that came in, thankfully."

"Let's just hope we can get to the bottom of it before all hell breaks loose."

They started back to Lorenzo's car and Cedric asked, "So how was San Francisco with Desiree and her mother?"

"It would've been better if her younger sister hadn't come. She is a piece of work. Complained about everything, harassed Desiree and bragged that she could take me away from Desiree."

He swung his head around and stopped walking. "Desiree's sister *actually* said that to you?"

"No. I overheard her saying it to Desiree. Apparently, she's been doing it since they were teens." Lorenzo opened the driver's side door and got in.

Cedric slid into the passenger seat. "I wish Jeremy would try some crap like that. I'd beat his behind up and down the street. What did Desiree do?"

He started the engine and pulled out onto the road. "Ignored her, for the most part. I talked to her mother and she told me Desiree has always been the peacemaker in the family and that it's not an easy thing." He recalled Desiree's hurt expression and the overwhelming need he'd felt to protect her.

"So you're talking to her mother now. I guess that means things are moving to the next level with you and Desiree."

"I don't know how you got all that from me just helping Desiree out by driving to San Francisco and having a two-minute conversation with her mother."

Cedric chuckled. "Did her mother grill you?"

"Yes," he answered reluctantly. Lorenzo knew that would be all the ammunition Cedric needed.

"Ha! I rest my case. If it was as casual as you're trying to make it out to be, then her mother wouldn't have needed to find out your intentions with her daughter. That is what she asked, right? I'm real curious about your answer."

He slanted his cousin an irritated glare. "Yes, she asked it and I told her Desiree and I are still getting to know each other." He shrugged. "I like her, that's all."

"That's what you're telling yourself, huh? When I called you earlier, you nearly ripped my head off. I know you were at Desiree's place and the way you growled at me says y'all were doing far more than just having a conversation."

Cedric had hit the nail on the head. He had interrupted one of the most erotic encounters he'd had, and Lorenzo was eager to go back and finish it. His feelings for Desiree were steadily intensifying and had taken on a life of their own. He had no idea how to make them stop at this point, or if he even wanted to. And not all of it had to do with physical attraction. He enjoyed talking and laughing with her as much as he did kissing and making love to her.

"Your silence tells me I'm right. You do know this is

how it started with Brandon, Khalil and Malcolm and where they all ended up?"

"Keep talking and you're going to be walking the rest of the way home."

Cedric laughed. "Yeah, you got it bad, man. Can't wait to call the cousins and tell them to dust off their tuxes." He sat back with a smug smile.

Lorenzo said nothing for the remainder of the ride.

"We need to discuss a strategy for tomorrow," Cedric said when Lorenzo stopped in his driveway. "I can throw something on the grill or we can order takeout. With these hundred-degree July temperatures, I'm thinking takeout."

He turned off the engine. "Takeout." Though he knew this was a priority, his body didn't care. It only wanted one thing: more of Desiree.

Chapter 14

Lorenzo and Cedric hit the ground running on Monday morning. They'd put in a call to the subcontractor first thing, then went out to the site to determine just how much lumber needed to be replaced. Cedric also sent out more samples of both the stamped and nonstamped wood for testing. By midday, Lorenzo's stress level had climbed two notches. Somehow, even though the article hadn't been printed, rumblings about their predicament had gotten out to a few of their previous and existing customers. He had left Cedric at the site and gone back to the office to field calls and make assurances. It didn't help that he hadn't received a callback from the owner of the lumber company. The receptionist told Lorenzo the man was out of the office. However, in Lorenzo's mind, with twenty-first-century technology, Jim could call back regardless of his location.

By late afternoon, he snatched up his keys and drove over to JMM Lumber. He introduced himself to the receptionist and told her he was prepared to wait all evening if necessary. Evidently, she remembered his previous calls and noted the irritation on his face because her eyes widened and she made a beeline to the back office and came back with a younger man who resembled Jim.

The man stuck out his hand. "I'm Grant Macklin. Jim is my father."

Lorenzo shook the proffered hand. "Lorenzo Hunter."

"I understand there's a problem. My dad is out until Thursday, but maybe I can help you. Let's talk in my office."

He followed Grant back to a cramped space and sat in the chair across from Grant's desk.

"Now, what can I help you with?" Grant asked, taking a seat and clasping his hands together.

"You can start by telling me how over ten percent of the lumber we purchased from you failed to meet fire retardant city codes." Grant's eyes widened for a split second before he schooled his features. However, it was just enough time to raise the hairs on the back of Lorenzo's neck.

"I don't know what you mean. Are you accusing me of something?"

He lifted a brow at the slight edge in the man's voice. "I'm asking you a question. Is there any reason I should be making an accusation?"

"Of course not," Grant snapped. "Your company has been doing business with ours for years and there've never been any problems."

"You're right. Until now." He scrutinized Grant for a long moment.

"All of our lumber meets code—always has."

"Yet, I have a pile of it that says otherwise. I'm very curious as to how that could've happened. Any thoughts?"

Grant's voice had been steadily rising with each question, further solidifying the fact that the man was lying. Lorenzo hadn't raised his voice once. In fact, he'd been deadly calm, something his family knew meant his anger had reached a boiling point. He leaned forward and pinned Grant with a lethal glare. "Let's cut the bull. You and I both know that lumber came from here. Whether it was a mistake on your part—for your sake, I hope that's the case—or you're cutting corners to increase your profit margin, that lumber has to be replaced in the next week. And we aren't paying a dime more." He provided an estimate of how much they'd need.

Grant jumped to his feet. "You can't just expect me to *give* you more lumber. You haven't even proven we're at fault. There's a surcharge for expedited service. I'll be happy to go over the estimates with you," he added with a smug smile.

It took every ounce of control Lorenzo possessed not to knock the hell out the man. Grant was lying through his teeth. Their company had always dealt with Jim directly, except on this project. It made him speculate on whether Jim knew his son was up to no good. Lorenzo didn't see the old man being party to such foolishness because he'd never had one blemish in the thirty years since founding JMM Lumber. Jim struck Lorenzo as a man with principles. However, he couldn't say the same for Grant. Lorenzo smoothly came to his feet and walked to the door. "One week. The next visit will be from our attorneys."

"Are you threatening me?"

He paused with his hand on the doorknob. "You'll know if I'm threatening you." He left without further comment. Once he reached the truck, he drew in several calming breaths to rein in his temper. For the first time in his professional career, he'd come close to losing it. His hands trembled and his heart raced. When he relaxed some, he started the engine and drove off toward his office. Two minutes in, his cell rang. He engaged the Bluetooth.

"Hello."

"Lorenzo? Are you okay?"

"Hey, baby." The sound of Desiree's voice made his anger dissipate like a puff of smoke. "It's been a rough day."

"It sounds like. Is there anything I can do?"

"No, but thanks." He briefly filled her in on the situation. "I apologize for not calling you last night. Cedric and I were up late last night and hit the ground running early this morning."

"Wow. So, this company sold you wood that didn't meet standard? That doesn't make sense. How long will it take you to replace it?"

"I told the guy he had one week. My parents just got back from their cruise, so I'll call my dad to get the owner's direct number. We've never dealt with his son before now."

"Hmph. He seems a little shady, if you ask me."

"That's exactly why I'll be calling Jim without letting his son know." If Jim didn't know what Grant was up to, he didn't want to tip Grant off by saying anything, which is why he'd hustled himself out of the office. He also wondered if he'd done the same thing to other companies. "I'm sorry our evening got interrupted. I'll make it up to you." He'd awakened in the middle of the night from an erotic dream that had him hard and aching.

"I'm counting on it," Desiree said with a little laugh.

He smiled. "With the way things are going, I have no idea when." Lorenzo sincerely hoped it wouldn't be too long.

"Well, we can play it by ear."

"Did your mom and sister make it back home okay?"

"Yes. I talked to her last night after you left. She said she wanted all my siblings and me to get together soon so she can put something in place, just in case. That means I'll be making another trip to Chicago."

With the way Melanie acted, Lorenzo could just imagine how that visit would go. It bothered him that Desiree might have to battle all her siblings alone. "How do you think it'll go?"

Desiree's sigh came through the line. "Honestly, I'm not looking forward to it. You met Melanie, so you already know what her response will be. My older sister, Patrice, is better, but not by much and my brother, Keith, just tends to steer clear of it all."

"Leaving you as the only person to handle things."

"Pretty much. Anyway, I know you have a lot on your mind right now and I didn't mean to add my concerns. I won't keep you."

"Desiree, you're not adding anything. I'm really sorry about how things are shaping up and praying your mom won't need too much help." He had noticed Mrs. Scott repeating herself and asking the same question several times within a short time. He had marveled at Desiree's patience.

"Please let me know if you need anything or if you want to vent. I'll be here."

The spaces in Lorenzo's heart opened in that moment. No other woman had offered to help shoulder his burdens. "You don't know how much I appreciate that, sweetheart. I just may take you up on it. I have to go, but we'll talk soon."

"Okay. Don't stay at the office too late."

He chuckled. "Can't make any promises, but I'll try. The next couple of days are going to be long ones."

"I realize that. I'll be thinking good thoughts."

"Thanks. Talk to you later." He parked in front of his office and drummed his fingers on the steering wheel. He had no name for the emotions flooding him. No, that wasn't the truth. If he were being honest, he would admit that he was falling in love with Desiree. The admission scared him and he didn't know how to handle it. After another minute, Lorenzo hopped out of the car. Maybe he needed to take Khalil up on his offer. He'd call his cousin as soon as he had a free moment.

"I wondered how long you planned to sit out in this July heat daydreaming."

He spun around at the sound of Cedric's voice. "I didn't see you pull up."

Cedric angled his head thoughtfully. "No, I suspect you didn't."

Lorenzo frowned and started toward the door. "What does that mean?"

"It means that you were thinking about Desiree—you're still seeing her, right? The goofy smile on your face gave you away."

"You must be seeing things."

"I am, very clearly. I hope you are, too."

Had he really been sitting in the truck smiling? "Anyway, Jim wasn't there, but I met his son, Grant. My gut tells me he's up to his neck in this mess. It took all I had sitting across from him not to knock that smug smile off his face."

Cedric stopped in his tracks. "You think Jim is cutting corners now?"

"What I think is Grant is going behind his father's back, which is why I'm going to call Dad and get Jim's number."

He held the door open. "I really hate having to call because I don't want them to think we can't handle things. We're not even two months out of the gate yet."

"I hear you, but the sooner we get on this, the sooner we can get back to business." Lorenzo said the words, but his worries mirrored Cedric's. The last thing he wanted was to disappoint his father, not when the man he regarded as his hero had entrusted Lorenzo with his life's work. Cedric followed Lorenzo to his office and propped a hip on Lorenzo's desk. "Might as well get the call over with."

Lorenzo hit the speakerphone button and dialed his parents' home number."

"Hello."

He smiled upon hearing his mother's soft voice. "Hey, Mom. How was the cruise?"

"Lorenzo. Hi, honey. It was *fabulous*." She paused. "It's after five. Why are you calling from the office?"

Cedric chuckled. "Hey, Aunt LaVerne."

"Cedric, you're there, too? Don't you boys start staying at that office day and night."

Sensing his mother on the verge of one of her tirades about living life to its fullest and not working himself to death, Lorenzo cut her off. "Mom, we need to talk to Dad for a minute."

"Is everything okay?"

"Nothing we can't handle," he lied. He and Cedric shared a look.

"Oh alright. Hold on a moment. Be sure to come by so I can show you the pictures we took. I'll probably have Alisha and the babies over on the weekend for dinner, so plan on it. Cedric, you and Jeremy come, too."

"Call me with the details, Mom, and I'll let Cedric and Jeremy know."

"Okay. Here's your father."

"How are you, son?" Lorenzo's father asked when he picked up the phone.

"Dad, we have a problem. About ten percent of the lumber we purchased from Jim didn't meet the fire retardant city code."

"What? We've never had a problem with Jim's company before."

"I know. Most of it hasn't been used, but we did find some of it on one wall of the building's frame."

"Hey, Uncle Russell," Cedric chimed in. "Jim didn't handle this order, his son did."

"Do you think he's doing something underhanded?"

"It looks that way," Lorenzo answered. Apparently, someone tipped off a reporter. The story hasn't run yet, but a few of our clients got wind of it and I've been fielding calls all day. I wanted to get Jim's direct number from you. He's on vacation and we need to get to the bottom of this before it gets out of hand."

"I can call him and—"

"That's okay, Dad. We'll handle it."

His father fell silent briefly. "You're right. You and Cedric are fully capable. Rueben and I trust you completely."

"Thanks, Uncle Russell. That means a lot."

"Yeah, Dad, it does." Having his father's faith in their ability to resolve this issue lightened his burden slightly. But he wouldn't rest until it was over.

Desiree packaged the last batch of the strawberry massage oil and placed the bottles on the shelf. After her Sunday encounter with Lorenzo, she had decided selling it might be worth a shot. For now, she would test the waters by offering only a few options and expand based on customer response. It had been three days since she'd talked to Lorenzo and four since she had seen him. Every second of their time Sunday evening hovered at the forefront of her mind. She hadn't been able to enter her kitchen without thinking about the way he'd used the oil and the feel of his hands and mouth on her. Desiree's eyes drifted closed as she recalled the way she had slowly licked her way across his muscled chest. If they hadn't been interrupted, they would have ended up in her bed and she wouldn't have protested in the least.

Even with all he was facing, he still showed concern for her. When they'd spoken Monday evening, he once again asked about her mother and made her promise to let him know if she needed to talk or have him come over no matter the time. Desiree had fallen in love with him at that moment. She didn't know how it would all work out, but she couldn't deny her feelings any longer.

"I see you finally took my advice," Sandra said, coming to stand next to Desiree.

She jumped slightly. "You startled me."

"Sorry. You probably should've made more than those few little bottles because, I'm telling you, it's going to fly off the shelves. Has Brenda added it to the online store?"

"Not yet. I think I'll wait a couple of weeks and see how these do first." Along with the strawberry massage oil, she had done honey and passion fruit. She'd also made edible whipped caramel and chocolate body butters that could double as a body paint. "If the response is high, then I'll add a few more choices in the store and on the website."

Sandra reached for a bottle of passion fruit massage oil and one jar each of the caramel and chocolate body butter. "I'll take these off your hands."

Desiree laughed.

"Girl, I spend half my paycheck in here. I should just have you take out an automatic payment each time." She slung her purse on her shoulder. "I know Casey is going to talk trash because I told her I wasn't going to buy anything else until August. We're still two weeks away and I've already caved." Sandra up the bottles. "I'll let you know how they work out."

"As long as it's the G-rated version, fine."

"Ha! We shall see. I'll start the citrus basil soap as soon as I get in tomorrow."

"Thanks, and have a good evening."

"Oh, I will," she said with a wiggle of her eyebrows and a smile.

Desiree shook her head and chuckled. "At least one of us will be putting the oils to good use," she mumbled. Depending on how long it took for Lorenzo to settle his dispute, she might not see him for several more days. She looked forward to seeing him and having their almost-nightly phone calls. Sometimes, they would only talk for a few minutes and, other times, for an hour or two. This week, however, they had only exchanged a couple of quick text messages. He and Cedric had been working until well past nine in the evening and, though she really wanted to call, she hadn't. Desiree didn't want to bother him because she knew he was exhausted.

Her own shop had closed thirty minutes ago and she didn't plan to stay much later. She and Brenda had scheduled two interviews for the morning before opening, so they had agreed on an early night. As if she had been aware of Desiree's thoughts, Brenda came in with her purse and tote.

"You almost ready?"

"Yep. I'm just going to wash up these few containers. I should be done in about five minutes."

"Okay. I'll wait for you." Brenda took a seat on one of the stools. "Have you talked to Lorenzo? I heard something on the news about what's going on."

"Not since Monday. He has his hands full and I don't want to bother him." She had heard a news report, as well, and the reporter intimated that there might be other companies involved, as well. "It does sound like his company won't be held liable if they can find where out where the wood came from, so that's a plus."

"True. Maybe then you two can resume your love connection."

Desiree snorted and rinsed out the dishes she'd washed. She may have slipped up and foolishly fallen in love, but Lorenzo had never said anything past, "I like you." So she planned to keep her sentiments to herself for the time being. She dried and put away the containers, then wiped down the workspace. "I'm ready." On the way out, she retrieved her purse and stuck a few ingredients into her tote, just in case she decided to work on another recipe.

As they walked to where their cars were parked, Brenda said, "I have no idea what I'm cooking for dinner. It's too hot to even be in the kitchen, let alone turning on the stove." The late-July temperatures had topped the one-hundred-degree mark for several days.

"For real. It feels like an oven out here." Desiree's phone buzzed in her pocket before she could comment further. She dug it out and saw a message from Lorenzo:

Another long night, so I'm not sure how late I'll be. Will try to call you.

She typed back: No worries. Just be sure to stop and eat.

Lorenzo: Probably in a couple of hours. Need to finish up paperwork.

Her heart went out to him.

"Lorenzo?" Brenda asked.

"Yes." She stuck the phone back into her pocket. "He's working late again." Parts of her had wondered if all the late nights had really been work-related. But she kept reminding herself that Lorenzo hadn't lied to her, and she found herself trusting him more.

"That has to be hard on him."

"I think it is, but he's not really saying so." They stopped at Brenda's car. "I'll see you in the morning."

"Alright. I hope one of the two interviewees works out."

"So do I." She waved and walked the short distance to her own car. As Desiree drove home, she thought about what Lorenzo had said about taking a break. She knew that he most likely wouldn't. There had been several times when she'd gotten so preoccupied with her recipes that she went hours without eating, resulting in her having a massive headache that always took a day or two to subside. With the amount of stress Lorenzo had been under, she could see that happening to him. An idea popped into her head. A smile curved Desiree's lips. She would take him dinner. And get at least one kiss.

Chapter 15

Desiree tried to remember what restaurants were near Lorenzo's job. She considered pizza, something easy, but realized she didn't know what he liked. She could have called to find out, however, that would ruin the surprise. Since she had driven up Greenback Lane, she figured she could find something at one of the many eating spots near Sunrise Mall. Desiree ended up at Buffalo Wild Wings and ordered wings, potato wedges and salads for both Lorenzo and Cedric, reasoning it would be rude not to include his cousin.

When Desiree got to office, she saw Lorenzo's SUV parked out front. She tried the door and found it locked. She pulled out her phone to call him.

"Desiree, hey," Lorenzo said when he answered. "Is everything okay?"

"Hi, and yes. I don't mean to disturb you, but—"

"You're not."

"I brought you dinner."

"Wait. What? You're *here*?"

"Yep. The front door is locked."

"I'll be right there." Lorenzo appeared a minute later and unlocked the door. He took the bag, brushed a kiss over her lips and locked the door behind her. "We lock it after business hours." Taking her hand, he led Desiree to his office.

Desiree surveyed the spacious room with its large mahogany desk, small conference table and drafting table. The opposite side held a bookcase filled with all sorts of engineering titles. "This is nice."

"Thanks." Lorenzo set the bag on the table and pulled her into his arms. "I appreciate you bringing dinner, but you didn't need to go out of your way to do this. I know you had a long day, too."

She smiled. "Hey, I gotta keep you fed. Can't have you falling out from exhaustion, and you have an interrupted evening to make up for," she added with a wink.

He laughed. "And I definitely don't want to disappoint you."

"No worries on that front." He hadn't disappointed her once and always went out of his way to show her that not all men were the same. "You're so different from other guys I've dated."

Lorenzo shrugged. "I'm just me. No games, no pretense."

"I like *just you*, Lorenzo Hunter."

He stared intently at her. "I more than like you, Desiree Scott."

He captured her mouth in a slow, drugging kiss. Desiree shuddered as his tongue swirled all around hers and his hands roamed over her body. Nobody could kiss like this man. She fell deeper and deeper as the seconds ticked off.

"Hey, Zo. I—"

She startled, jumped away from Lorenzo and stumbled backward. Lorenzo caught her and steadied her. She felt her cheeks warm with embarrassment.

"Oh, I'm sorry. I didn't realize you were occupied." Cedric divided a speculative gaze between Desiree and Lorenzo.

"Cedric, you remember Desiree," Lorenzo said.

A knowing smile spread across his face. "I certainly do. It's good to see you again, Desiree."

"Same here," she said, or at least it might have been had he not busted her and Lorenzo halfway making out in his office. "Um… I just stopped by to drop this off." She pointed to the bag on the table. "I'll get out of your hair so you guys can get out of here at a decent hour."

At Cedric's confused expression, Lorenzo explained, "Desiree brought dinner."

"Really? Thanks, Desiree. I appreciate it."

"You're welcome. I wasn't sure what to get, so I hope you're okay with wings, potato wedges and salad. I opted for the sweet barbecue and teriyaki sauces on the chicken to be on the safe side."

Cedric walked over to the table and peeked into the bag. "It's more than okay. I'll just take mine and eat in my office." He fixed a plate and headed to the door. "She's a keeper, Zo. Thanks again, Desiree." He exited with a smile.

Desiree glanced over at Lorenzo to gauge his reaction to his cousin's comment, but his expression gave away nothing.

Lorenzo gestured Desiree to a chair. "Join me."

"Oh, I hadn't planned to stay."

"Why not? Have you eaten yet?"

"No," tumbled out before she could stop it.

He chuckled and pressed a kiss to her temple. "Good. Join me, baby." Lorenzo pulled out the chair for her, waited for her to sit, then took the chair next to her. He arranged the food on the table and handed Desiree a plate. "Fix yours first."

Desiree added three wings, a few potato wedges and some salad to her plate.

Lorenzo filled his plate, took her hand and recited a short blessing, then dug in. They ate in silence for the first couple of minutes. "This hits the spot. I can't thank you enough for bringing me dinner. What are you going to do when you get home?" He got up and went over to a compact refrigerator that she hadn't noticed. "I have bottled water, iced tea and cranberry apple juice."

"I'll take the cranberry, please. I think I'm going to indulge in a long bubble bath and read for a while. I've been trying to finish a suspense novel for weeks."

He came back to the table with their drinks. "Why are you teasing me? I'm never going to get any work done thinking about you naked in that tub, when all I want to do is be in the tub with you, touching you…" He lightly stroked her arm. "Kissing you…" He leaned over and kissed the sensitive spot at the base of her neck.

Desiree shuddered and moaned softly. Her head fell back and her eyes drifted closed as he continued to touch and kiss her, and describe in hushed tones all the ways he planned to make love to her in the tub.

"We should probably finish dinner before Cedric comes back and finds us doing more than kissing," Lorenzo murmured. He kissed her one last time, and then straightened in his seat.

She had forgotten all about her food. She slowly opened her eyes and met Lorenzo's heated gaze. His labored breathing matched hers and it wouldn't take much to push either of them over the edge. Desiree glanced down at her plate and back at him. The only thing she had a taste for at this moment was *him*.

Lorenzo was two seconds away from locking his office door, laying Desiree on the conference table and burying himself deep inside her. He'd never been so out of control with a woman in his life. Something about the way she kissed him always made Lorenzo lose all rational thought. He took a huge gulp of his iced tea and tried to concentrate on his meal. He still couldn't get over the fact that she'd driven out of her way to bring him dinner. Lorenzo forked up some of the salad and glimpsed at Desiree. Though she kept her eyes on her plate, he sensed her struggle. The sexual tension in the room had risen to a level that had them both on the edge.

At length, Desiree said, "I saw the reports."

"Yeah. We were hoping to get it resolved before word got out." When the story broke yesterday, he and Cedric had been inundated with calls, emails and text messages from their clients. They'd spent countless hours visiting current sites and assuring past clients that this particular batch of lumber had been the only tainted bunch.

"How has this affected your clients?"

"They're concerned, but so far, we've been able to convince them there aren't any problems with their buildings." She licked the barbecue sauce off her finger and the sight spiked his arousal once more.

She wiped her hands on a napkin, then took a sip of her juice. "At least the reporter didn't make it sound like it was all your company's fault. I hope you can get to the bottom of it soon. I can't even imagine the stress this is putting on you guys."

"That's been a positive." Only because Cedric knew the reporter had they been fortunate not to have the story sensationalized. She had given the facts objectively. He finished the last piece of chicken on his plate.

Desiree laid a hand on his arm. "If you need anything and I do mean *anything*, please let me know. I don't know anything about the construction business, but I'll help in any way I can."

Lorenzo brought her hand to his lips and placed a kiss on the back. "Thanks, baby. We'll be okay." He said the words, but didn't know who he was trying to convince more. He had no idea what he'd do if this destroyed his business.

When they finished eating, she cleaned up the remnants of her food and stood. "I should go so you can get back to work."

He came to his feet and put all the empty containers into the bag, and held it out for her to do the same. Then he deposited it all into the trash. As much as he wanted her to stay, he had too much to do tonight. "I'll walk you out." He entwined their fingers and led her outside to her car. Lorenzo wrapped his arms around her. "Call me when you get home."

Desiree smiled up at him. "I will. And don't you stay here all night," she added, poking her finger in his chest.

"I'll try." At her frown, he said, "Hey, that's the best I can do."

She caressed his face. "I know. But you look exhausted, Lorenzo."

"I'm fine."

"Nice try. You're not fooling me. I'm a business owner, too. Remember? So, I know you're burning the candle at both ends, as my mama would say."

She was right. He'd surpassed exhaustion two days ago and now ran on pure adrenaline. He doubted he'd slept more than three hours each night since this mess began. His stress level hadn't been this high since he sat for the Principles and Practice of Engineering exam, the final step in becoming a licensed civil engineer. Lorenzo had studied for months and, with little more than half of the people passing on the first try, had worried he wouldn't be in that number. But he had been. Now he faced a greater threat.

"Promise me you'll shut it down a little earlier, go home and rest, baby. You can't fight if your head isn't clear."

He went still. She had never called him *baby* before. "I promise."

Desiree unlocked the car door by remote and Lorenzo reached around her to open it. "Thanks," she said as she slid in behind the wheel.

"We need to spend some time together soon."

"Yes, we do. I miss hanging out with you and our nightly phone calls."

"So do I." Lorenzo bent and kissed her lightly. He didn't trust himself to do more. "Soon. Don't forget to call me."

"I won't. Good night."

"Night, sweetheart." He stood there until her car was out of sight before going back inside. He went to Cedric's office.

Cedric glanced up from his computer. "Desiree gone?"

"Yeah."

"When did you guys decide to do dinner?"

"I had no idea she was bringing it until she called to tell me she was here."

He spun around in his chair to face Lorenzo. "In my experience, women don't typically go out of their way to do something like this unless they're trying to win brownie points or they really care. Which category does Desiree fall into?"

Lorenzo didn't want to answer because it would only give Cedric more ammunition.

Turning back toward the computer, Cedric chuckled. "Never mind. I already know the answer. The fact that she brought me food, too, says she really cares about you. Are you going to surrender?"

His brows knit in confusion. "Surrender what?"

"To what I know you're feeling for Desiree. She's not Veronica, cuz. Don't punish her by closing off your heart. She just might be the one for you."

"I'm not." Desiree had sneaked into his heart before he realized it and even if he wanted to, he couldn't close the door again. "Not sure how you're dispensing all this advice when you've maintained that you don't ever plan to settle down and marry."

Cedric shrugged. "Because I don't see it for myself doesn't mean I don't believe in love. I know great relationships exist—look at our parents, Uncle Nolan and Aunt Dee and our cousins—I just prefer being single."

Lorenzo grinned. "You know it's going to be so funny when a woman comes along and challenges your stance. And she *is* coming. Mark my words." He glanced down at his watch. "It's almost nine. I'm going to finish up one last thing and call it a night."

Cedric dragged a hand down his face. "I hear you. I'm so tired I can barely think straight. Five years ago, I could stay up for twenty-four hours, grab some coffee and be ready to go. Now…" He shook his head.

"Now, you're old and need your sleep."

Cedric glared. "In case you forgot, we're the same age, so what does that make you?"

"Experienced," Lorenzo said. He pivoted on his heel and strode out, laughing at the string of expletives spilling from his cousin's mouth. He was still chuckling when he got back to his office. As soon as he pulled up a document on his computer, his cell rang. He saw Desiree's name on the display and connected. "You made it home?"

"Yep. I'm here."

"Good. I'll call you tomorrow."

"Okay. I'm going to hop in the tub, light some candles and put on some music."

"You know you're wrong for telling me that."

Desiree's soft laughter came through the line. "Well, you can join me next time. I guarantee you a good time."

"Woman, I'm about two seconds from jumping in my car and coming over there. Lucky for you, it's a weekday and I know you work tomorrow. But the next time you tease me, be prepared." For the past four nights, she had invaded his dreams, each one more sensual than the last. If she said the word, he would be on her doorstep in twenty minutes ready to finish what they'd started on Sunday evening.

"Oh, I will be. Talk to you later."

"Bye, baby." Lorenzo disconnected the call and tapped the phone against his chin. *She's a keeper.* Cedric's words came back to Lorenzo. He began to think his cousin might be right.

Chapter 16

"I don't know why we need to do all this. Just because Mom is forgetting a few things doesn't mean she needs someone else to start making all the decisions for her."

Desiree released a deep sigh and banged her head softly on her office desk. She hadn't planned to start her Saturday morning this way. "Melanie, Mom is the one who wants us to have the power of attorney and medical directives in place."

"I have to agree with Melanie on this one, Desiree," Patrice cut in. "What's the purpose of going through all this trouble? I mean, we're all here and can help Mom with whatever she needs…well, except you."

She recognized the slight dig. Her sisters never let Desiree forget that *she* had left the family to do her own thing, as if she'd abandoned them.

"Alright, let's calm down," Keith said. "I know this

thing has us all on edge, but we have to do what's best for Mom."

"Thanks, Keith." Her brother rarely stepped in and Desiree was glad to hear him do so now. "As the oldest, I think you should be in the first position on both documents and one of us can be the alternate."

Melanie snorted. "I'm not doing it. Y'all aren't going to be accusing me of doing anything wrong for Mama."

Desiree rubbed her temples, feeling the beginnings of a headache. When her mother asked Desiree and her siblings to conference about this, she had known it would be a struggle.

"I'm at home with Mama more than Keith is, so I should be the one making the decisions."

"Then you can be the alternate, Patrice," Desiree suggested.

"I don't *want* to be the alternate. Let Keith be the alternate."

The conversation dissolved into an argument about who should do what and who refused to do something else. After a few minutes, she'd had enough. "Can we not argue, please? Mom needs us to handle this for her."

Her brother's voice broke into the heated discussion. "Patrice and Melanie, calm down. Des is right. Mom trusts us to take care of business, so let's get to it. Melanie, you said you didn't want to do it at all and Patrice, you don't want to be an alternate. That means Desiree and I will handle it."

"Fine by me," Melanie huffed.

"Patrice?" Keith prompted.

"Whatever. I don't care. Just don't come to me when you need help with something."

Good grief. If only Desiree's father was still alive.

There would be no need for all this drama. "Keith, just send me what I need to sign and I'll overnight it back."

"Des, it has to be notarized, and you have to do that in person."

"Okay." Desiree figured she wouldn't have to make that additional trip since her mother asked them to talk by phone. This flying back and forth seriously cut into her finances and her work schedule. "I'll let you know when I can come. I have to go. The shop is opening in an hour and I still have a few things to do."

"Just text me your info. Oh, and I think that you should be the primary and I'll take the alternate position."

"*What?*" Melanie and Patrice yelled at the same time.

"Keith," Desiree started, "I don't think that's a good idea. With me being so far away, it would make more sense for you to be the primary."

"Nah, baby girl. The distance doesn't matter. You've always been the one to take care of things and you do it well."

She could barely hear what Keith said above her sisters' shouting. Her headache intensified and right now she didn't have the strength to argue. She just wanted to end the call. "Fine. I'll talk to you guys later." Desiree tossed the phone on her desk and buried her head in her hands. Maybe if she sat quietly for the next five minutes, the dull throbbing in her head would subside.

She had an hour to make two batches of body cream and more of the massage oils. Just as Sandra had predicted, the twenty two-ounce bottles had sold out in two days. Thankfully, they had hired a woman to help with filling the online orders, so Desiree had one less thing to worry about. Her phone rang again. She groaned. *Please don't let it be one of my siblings.* She'd had enough for the day. She picked it up and breathed a sigh of relief when she saw Lorenzo's name on the display.

"Hey, Lorenzo."

"Morning, beautiful. I wanted to catch you before the shop opened. How's your day going?"

"Don't ask."

"What happened?"

Desiree filled him in on the conversation she'd had with her siblings. "And somehow, like always, I'm going to end up being the one taking on all the responsibility."

"Wow. I'd think your brother would want to do it since he's there."

"Yeah, so did I." She groaned again. "My sisters were arguing and I know at least one of them will call or text later to tell me why I shouldn't even be on the documents and how I'm always trying to take over."

"I'm sorry, Desiree. Is there anything I can do?"

"Not unless you have a secluded island you can whisk me off to for the next twenty years," she answered with a laugh.

"I admit, that island does sound good right about now."

She'd momentarily forgotten about everything going on with his company. "Any headway?"

"A little. We finally spoke to the owner of the lumber company and he promised to check it out. But we still haven't received the replacement lumber, which is putting us behind schedule."

"And your client is probably not happy."

"No, they are not. Neither are we." They fell silent for a moment. "What does your schedule look like for the next couple of days?"

"I don't have anything planned after work tonight.

The shop closes at four-thirty tomorrow and we're closed on Monday. Why?"

"Just thinking that what you said about needing to get away sounds like a good idea. What if we got lost for a day or two to clear our heads? We've both been under a lot of stress. It won't be that island, but I can promise you we'll have a good time."

Desiree leaned back in her chair. "That sounds heavenly. Let me check with Sandra about tomorrow and I'll let you know in a little while. What about you? Can you afford to be off?"

"The office is closed on the weekends and, if we get back midday on Monday, Cedric should be able to handle everything until then. I'll call him as soon as I hang up."

"Okay. Where are we going?"

"I don't know yet, but it'll have to be somewhere in driving distance, in case I need to get back. Just pack enough for two days, maybe bring a dressy outfit since I still owe you dinner, and we'll play the rest by ear."

"Count me in." Normally, she would have insisted on finding out where they were going, but this time, she didn't care. And she trusted Lorenzo.

"Oh, and make sure you bring some of that massage oil."

She laughed. "Most definitely. I'm getting ready to make more right now. Any particular flavor?"

"Strawberry and honey," he answered without hesitation.

"I'll make sure to bring enough."

"You do that because this time there will be no interruptions."

Heat went straight to her core. "I'll be ready."

* * *

Lorenzo rang the doorbell to his parents' home early Saturday evening and his niece and nephew ran toward him with squeals of delight as soon as he crossed the threshold.

"Uncle Lorenzo!" Corey launched himself into Lorenzo's arms.

He swung his nephew up and hugged him. "How are you?"

"I'm good. I went swimming yesterday."

"You did? Did you have fun?"

Corey nodded vigorously. "I wasn't even scared."

"Unca Wenzo."

Lorenzo glanced down at Lia with her insistent smacks against his leg as she bounced up and down. "Hold on, baby girl." He set Corey on his feet, picked her up and kissed her cheek. She returned the favor by placing a wet, sloppy one on his cheek, then wrapping her arms tightly around him.

Alisha shook her head. "You'd think they haven't seen you in months the way they're all over you. I don't even get that kind of greeting and I'm the one feeding and clothing them."

He leaned over and kissed his sister's forehead. "Don't hate. Hey, Mom." He kissed her smooth, brown cheek.

"Hey, honey. Alisha, you and Lorenzo used to do the same thing when your father came home. I did all the work and he got all the affection. I barely got a hello."

"That's not true, Mom," Alisha said with a surprised laugh.

"Yes, it is." She turned and walked out, leaving them to follow.

In the family room, Lorenzo's father sat watching a baseball game. "Hey, Dad."

His father rose to his feet and the two men shared a quick embrace. "How're you doing? You look tired."

"I am, but I'm okay." His dad scrutinized him a long moment. "Really, Dad. I'm fine." Lorenzo would be even better in a couple of hours when he and Desiree were on their way to Napa. "So where are the pictures?"

His mother came over with her iPad and handed it to him. "You and Alisha should really take a cruise. We had a blast."

Alisha sat next to Lorenzo on the sofa. "Mom, you know I'd love to take a cruise, or go anywhere, but remember these two here?" She pointed to Corey and Lia.

"Girl, you know I'd be happy to keep my babies."

"Mmm-hmm, you say that now. But you put it out there and I plan to take you up on the offer as soon as I can."

Lorenzo chuckled as he swiped through the photos. His parents, uncle and aunt looked liked they had a great time. "So I guess you enjoyed the beach." More than half the pictures had been taken at one beach or another.

"Who wouldn't?" his father said. "Had I known how relaxing it would be, I'd have convinced Rueben to retire years ago. We should've made time to do more of those things." He glanced at Lorenzo over his glasses. "Don't wait until retirement to enjoy life. You, too, Alisha. Just because it didn't work out with Wayne, doesn't mean all men are that way," he added pointedly.

"I know." Alisha nudged Lorenzo. "What about you, big brother?"

"What?"

"When are you going to settle down with a nice young lady?"

Lorenzo skewered her with a look. "It's perfectly

acceptable to enjoy a cruise alone. People do it all the time." He continued scrolling. Though going alone had never entered his mind from the first picture.

She smiled and whispered, "True, but I think you'd have way more fun if you took Desiree. I like her."

His head came up. "How did you—you went to the shop." Alisha had always been outgoing and straightforward and he could imagine what she'd said. Yet, Desiree had never mentioned it.

"Yep. I'll be going back, too. The body scrub is to die for. You two need to hurry up and get—"

"Dinner," their mother called.

"Thank goodness," Lorenzo muttered, jumping to his feet.

Cedric and Jeremy arrived as everyone settled at the table. After a round of greetings, they sat and Lorenzo's father recited a blessing.

"I saw some of Mom's pictures from the cruise," Jeremy said, filling his plate with fried red snapper, shrimp, potato salad, macaroni and cheese, mixed green salad and rolls. "Looks like a great time. I need to take one soon."

"You should," Lorenzo's mother said. While everyone ate, she continued chatting about the various ports they had visited.

As the meal concluded, Lorenzo peeked at his watch. He planned to pick Desiree up at eight and he was anxious for their weekend to start. "Thanks for dinner, Mom. That hit the spot." He didn't eat everybody's potato salad, but he'd had two helpings of his mother's. No one could make it like she did.

"I'm glad you enjoyed it. I made peach cobbler for dessert."

Another one of his favorites. "Can I take it to go?"

"You're leaving?"

"I'm meeting a friend." Lorenzo met the knowing grins on his sister's and cousin's faces. He leveled a glare their way that dared them to say anything.

"Sure, honey. Let me get you a container." She stood and started toward the kitchen.

He followed her.

"Tell Desiree I said hello," Cedric called out nonchalantly.

Lorenzo froze. So did his mother.

"Oh my." His mother clasped her hands together. "You're dating someone? Is she a nice girl?"

"Yes, she is."

"And this is the same woman I overheard you call 'sweetheart,' right?" his father asked.

He nodded.

"That's wonderful. I hope we get to meet her soon." His mother looked at Lorenzo expectantly.

"We'll see." Lorenzo wanted to strangle Cedric.

"Well, let me get your cobbler. I'll send enough for Desiree."

While his mother cut some of the dessert, he said his goodbyes and hugged everyone at the table. When he came to Cedric, he whispered through clenched teeth, "I'm gonna kick your ass when I get back."

Cedric merely laughed. "Have a good time."

LaVerne Hunter came back still wearing a huge smile and handed him a bag. "I put it in a couple of those plastic containers, so you don't have to worry about returning it. There are forks and napkins in there, too. It's a shame you won't have some of the homemade ice cream to go with it."

"Thanks." Lorenzo hugged her and took the bag with the still-warm cobbler. "I'll see you later."

The drive to Desiree's would take about thirty minutes. He had planned a weekend he wanted them to remember for a long time. The closer he got to her place, the more excited he became and all the emotions that had been steadily growing surfaced. He engaged the Bluetooth. "Dial Khalil."

"Hey, Zo. What's up?" Khalil said when he answered.

"You have a minute?"

"Just about that. Lexia and I are going on a movie outing with her friend, Elyse. She runs a school for the hearing impaired."

"Are you okay?" Lorenzo hadn't noticed anything with Khalil's hearing when they'd visited. Khalil had temporarily lost his hearing in an accident, and although he regained it in one ear, he still wore a hearing aid for the other.

"Yeah, man. When I was struggling with the hearing loss, Lexia took me to the school to talk to Elyse and there was a kid there who'd recently lost his, too, and was having a hard time. I've been keeping a check on Anthony ever since. His dad brings him to the gym and I try to hang out with him when I can. He's doing well now. So, what's on your mind?"

"You said to call you if I needed to talk."

"Desiree?"

"Yes."

"You realize you're falling in love with her and want to run like hell, I take it?"

"One minute, yeah, then in the other I don't ever want to let her go."

"Have you told her how you feel?"

"No. We've only been dating a couple of months and I don't recall any of these out-of-control feelings with my ex."

Khalil chuckled. "Those are the kind that hit you like a ton of bricks and there isn't a thing you can do about it."

"Exactly." He had tried to suppress the feelings, but they refused to stay buried.

"Since you called me, I'm going to tell you what my mother told me. Don't let your ex steal another moment of your life, cuz. If you think Desiree is worth it, take the risk. Trust me, it's worth it."

Lorenzo quieted for a moment. "How do I know she won't do the same thing?"

"You don't. There will be some hiccups along the way, but you have to decide if you're going to be in the relationship for the long haul."

He tried to process his cousin's words. Thoughts of his last betrayal surfaced, but he forced them down and reminded himself that Desiree wasn't Veronica. "Thanks."

"Anytime. Are you planning to see Desiree soon?"

"I just pulled up to her place. We're going to spend a couple of days in Napa Valley."

"Then it'll be the perfect time for you to tell her how you feel. I have to go, but let me know how it turns out."

"Okay. Tell Lexia I said hello." Lorenzo sat in the car a moment longer thinking about his cousin's advice. He had to decide whether he was ready to put his heart on the line.

Chapter 17

Desiree opened the door for Lorenzo and smiled. "Hey. Come in." She leaned up and kissed him. "I just need to grab my jacket."

"Hey. Where's your bag?"

"Right there." She pointed to a small rolling suitcase and tote on the sofa, then got a jacket from a closet near the front door. She turned off all the lights except a small table lamp.

Lorenzo picked up both bags. "You ready to get this party started?"

"Yes, I am." They shared a smile and he led her out to his car. She was a little nervous because the last time she had gone on a weekend trip with a man, it turned out to be the worst mistake of her life. Not only had the guy flirted right in front of her, he had expected her to chip in and pay for the hotel suite *he* had booked. When he decided to go down to the club at the hotel that first night without her, she'd gathered her belongings, called for a rental car and drove the two hours back to Sacramento from Reno, Nevada. Desiree couldn't see Lorenzo being so callous, however, she sensed that this would be a turning point in their relationship. As Lorenzo merged onto I-80 West, she guessed they would be going back to San Francisco like he'd promised. She settled into the seat, leaned her head back and made herself comfortable.

"Long day?" Lorenzo asked.

"A little. I had a headache for the first few hours and trying to keep a smile on my face when every move made the throbbing worse turned out to be a real challenge. But I'm fine now." Desiree rolled her head in his direction. "Did you get some rest?"

"I got about five hours of sleep last night, which is two more than I've gotten each night all week. I did some work from home, then went to my parents' for dinner. My mom sent dessert."

She sat up straight. "You told her about us?"

"Not exactly. When I was leaving, Cedric said to tell you hello. It just snowballed from there."

Desiree wondered what he had told his family about her, and if Alisha had mentioned that she'd come to the store. "What did they say?"

Lorenzo slanted her a glance. "My mother asked if you were a nice girl and I said yes. She wants to meet you."

"And how do you feel about that?"

He reached for her hand. "I'd love for her to meet you. And it's only fair, since I've met your mother."

"Um…okay." True, he had met her mother, but that was different. Or was it? She stared out the passenger window. A man did not introduce you to his mother unless he planned to take the relationship to another level. Desiree closed her eyes and a smile curved her lips. She intended to enjoy each second of these next two days. Lorenzo hadn't let go of her hand. He idly stroked the back and her stress level started to drop. She relaxed, inhaled deeply and let the breath out slowly. The last thing she remembered was Beyoncé singing about the way she felt.

Desiree jumped slightly when she felt the warmth against her cheek.

"Wake up, sleepyhead." Lorenzo's deep voice filtered through the fog clouding her brain.

Her eyes fluttered open, and she sat up and stretched. "Hey. We're here?" She glanced around the unfamiliar surroundings, confused. "This isn't San Francisco."

Lorenzo chuckled and placed a kiss on her temple. "No. Napa Valley. What made you think we were going to Frisco?"

"You mentioned us going back."

"And we will. But this time, I wanted us to be someplace a little quieter. Come on, baby. Let's get checked in." He got out and came around to her side to help her. After grabbing their bags from the trunk, they headed for the resort lobby.

Desiree surveyed the area. The lighted grounds illuminated the meticulously manicured lawn with its lush, green grass, towering trees and beautiful flowers. They entered a colonial mansion-type building that was equally impressive. It took only a moment to check in and she couldn't mask her surprise when he escorted her down to a secluded structure in a gated community on the far side of the property. "This is gorgeous! How did you find it?" She had expected a nice hotel room, not this elegantly furnished, beautiful one-bedroom cottage.

Lorenzo set the bags on the sofa. "Google search."

She placed her purse and tote next to the bags. "Well, I love it." She walked over to the full kitchen and peered into cabinets and the refrigerator, then went around to a sliding glass door leading to a private patio. The space held two loungers with a small table between them. She couldn't wait to relax out there in the morning.

Lorenzo came and stood behind her and slid his arms around her waist. "That's why I chose this place. I did plan a couple of things for the weekend, but if you'd rather stay here and chill, we can do that instead."

Desiree turned in his arms and rested her cheek on his chest. She could hear the strong, rhythmic sound of his heart beating beneath her ear. "What did you have in mind?"

"I booked a wine train tour through the hotel for to-morrow. Check-in is at ten-thirty for the eleven-thirty trip. It's about three hours and it includes lunch."

"That sounds like fun. It still leaves plenty of time to relax."

"Among other things," Lorenzo said, nuzzling her neck.

"Mmm."

"How about we get comfortable, have some dessert and then…have a little more dessert?"

The sensual proposal sent a sweet ache flowing through her. "I'd like that. So, who's showering first?"

"If we do it together we can save time."

He slanted his mouth over hers in an explosive kiss that stole her breath and weakened her knees. She moaned and tore her mouth away, her breathing ragged. "Or not."

Staring into her eyes, he said, "Yeah. Not." Lorenzo swept her into his arms and strode into the bedroom. "The shower can wait. I can't." He laid her on the bed and stretched his hard body over hers. "Do you know how much I want you? How many nights I've dreamed of you lying beneath me like this?"

He'd starred in her nightly dreams, as well as invaded her waking hours. "Show me how much."

Before she could take her next breath, he locked his mouth on hers. His tongue curled around hers and delved in and out with a slow finesse that made her tremble. He ground his lower body against hers in blatant imitation of what she knew would come next. Desiree gripped his shoulders and arched into him to feel the solid ridge of his erection more snugly at her center.

Without breaking the seal of their mouths, Lorenzo pushed her sundress up to her waist, hooked his thumb in the waistband of her panties and pulled them down and off. He slid two fingers inside her. "Do you remember what I promised…? All the ways I'm going to make love to you?"

She cried out and spread her legs wider to give him better access. She recalled every detail of his erotic oath. He sped up his movements and the pressure built, starting low in her belly and flaring out to her body. Desiree exploded into a thousand pieces, calling his name on a low moan.

He withdrew his fingers and had her naked in the blink of an eye. He whipped his shirt over his head, tossed it aside and trailed kisses from the shell of her ear and the expanse of her neck to her breasts. "The oil. Did you bring it?"

He had her so on fire, it took Desiree a moment to understand what he meant. "Yes," she breathed. "In my tote."

Lorenzo slid off the bed, left the room and came back with the tote. "I didn't want to go in your bag."

Though she appreciated him not wanting to invade her privacy, tonight it only served as a delay. She reached blindly into the bag and found the four-ounce bottle of strawberry massage oil. He'd said previously that the two-ounce wouldn't be enough and she wanted to make sure they had plenty.

Lorenzo set the tote on the chair, removed the rest of his clothes and donned a condom. He climbed back on the bed and took the bottle. "Now, to pick up where we left off on Sunday." He squirted some in his hand and massaged it into her chest and breasts.

Immediately, Desiree felt the warmth of the oil. He cupped her breasts and pushed them together and lowered his mouth to her nipples. He blew lightly on them, making the liquid even warmer on her skin, then sucked them into his mouth. Spasms of pleasure shot straight to her core. He made a path with the oil down the front of her body and followed with his tongue, and she wondered just how much more she could handle.

"Damn, baby. You taste so sweet. But I think I want something a little sweeter." He stood and pulled her to the edge of the bed. Dropping to his knees, he trailed the oil up her inner thighs and sucked, kissed and licked his way to her center.

She screamed. The slow, hot licks of his tongue against her clit felt so incredible that she gripped the sheets to keep from flying apart. She didn't last a minute before another orgasm ripped through her and she screamed again. *"Lorenzo!"* she chanted over and over. Desiree didn't have time to recover before he turned her onto her stomach and entered her with one long thrust.

He set a driving rhythm that rocked the entire bed. Lorenzo whispered a mixture of tender endearments and erotic promises as he stroked deeper and deeper, reaching a part of her no man had ever touched. Her whole body began shaking and she came again with a force so strong, she thought she would pass out.

Moments later, Lorenzo went rigid against her and shouted her name as he climaxed. His body shuddered above hers for what seemed like forever, and then he collapsed on top of her, being careful not to place his full weight on her. They were both panting. Finally, he moved her to the center of the bed, slid in behind her and draped an arm across her middle.

Desiree didn't think her heart would ever return to a normal pace. Her body still tingled and hummed with pleasure.

"I think I'm going to buy stock in that oil. I need a bottle of every flavor you've got."

She chuckled tiredly. "I was thinking the same thing." She would never forget this night. And when she got home, she planned to make a *gallon* of that oil.

Monday morning, Lorenzo stood at the patio door staring out at the predawn sky. It seemed as though he and Desiree had just arrived in Napa and now, in a few hours, they would be heading back home. After the wine train tour, they had sat on the patio talking and laughing about anything and everything for hours, then taken a walk and watched the sunset. Instead of going out to dinner, they had opted to purchase groceries from a nearby market and cook together. Lorenzo had enjoyed the relaxed domesticity and could see spending more evenings together doing just that. Later, she had turned the tables on him and treated him to a sensual encounter unlike anything he had ever experienced. If he had any prior doubts about his feelings, this weekend had solidified that he had fallen completely in love with her. The lovemaking was off the charts and he knew he would *never* forget that massage oil. But that wasn't what had captured him. As he'd told her before, she was exactly his type and her heart had won him over.

"I'm ready."

He turned at the sound of Desiree's voice. "I've put everything in the car, so we'll be able to get on the road as soon as we get back."

Desiree's brows knit in confusion. "Get back from where? I thought we were leaving early to beat the traffic and so you'd have time to work today."

"We have one more thing to do before we leave."

"At four-thirty in the morning?" she asked incredulously. "Exactly where are we going?"

Lorenzo shook his head. "Can't tell you. It's a surprise."

She gave him a sultry smile. "If you tell me where, I'll make you more massage oil when I get home."

Lorenzo grinned. "Nope, I'm not biting. I told you, it's a surprise." He took a quick peek at his watch. "We have to get going so we don't miss the shuttle."

Desiree rolled her eyes playfully. "Okay, but this surprise better be good. I don't get up this early for anybody."

He laughed. "It will be. I promise." They took the shuttle to a spot a few miles away and joined the small knot of people already waiting.

She stopped walking and her eyes widened. "Wait, is that a hot air balloon? *That's* what we're doing?"

He nodded. Three balloons lay on the grassy field in various stages of inflation. She let out an excited squeal and jumped into his arms, almost knocking him down. "Whoa, sweetheart," he said with a laugh. "So, does this count as being a good surprise?"

"Beyond good! I've always wanted to do this. Thank you."

"This is why I had you pack long pants and a jacket." The happiness reflected in her face and her sparkling eyes had his heart beating double time in his chest. Her mother's words came back to him: *You're a nice young man and I think you're going to be good for Desiree... It's good to see her so happy.* Lorenzo liked making her happy, he realized, and she turned out to be just as good for him. After the fiasco with his ex, he didn't think he would ever be able to open up his heart again, but Desiree possessed a sweet and gentle spirit that he was helpless to resist. He placed a soft kiss on her lips. "This will be my first time going up, too." At the predawn check-in, the company had provided coffee, an assortment of teas and juices, pastries and fruit. He and Desiree chatted with a few people as they indulged in the snack. When they finished, the pilot conducted a brief orientation and then led them to the launch site. Lorenzo asked Desiree, "Do you have your sunglasses?" The sun would be rising shortly.

Desiree got them out of her purse and slid them on. "Is it crazy that I'm scared to death and super excited, all at the same time?"

"Not at all." He'd wondered himself a time or two since booking about the safety of the ride, or what if one of them fell out of the basket. Lorenzo glimpsed over his shoulder to see a couple of people holding one balloon open while a high-powered fan forced air into it, and another one already upright with a group climbing into the large basket.

"Shouldn't we get in line to board?"

"We aren't going with the group. We're taking a private flight."

She lifted a brow. "I know that costs significantly more. You didn't need to do that, Lorenzo." She wrapped her arms around him. "You are so wonderful."

Lorenzo caressed her cheek. "And so are you. I wanted this to be special…for both of us. It's my first time, too."

Desiree stared up at him. "Just being with you is enough for me."

In that moment, she'd captured his heart totally.

A few minutes later, Lorenzo helped Desiree into their basket, and then climbed in. He placed his arm around her and prepared for takeoff. It happened so smoothly, he hadn't realized they had lifted off the ground until they were a few feet in the air. As they ascended, he watched the play of emotions on Desiree's face and knew that the trip had been worth every penny he'd spent.

"I can't even describe how amazing this is," she said. "It's breathtaking, exhilarating, beautiful and so serene."

He agreed. "I don't think I'll ever see the sky the same." Seeing Desiree's gorgeous face as the sun broke through the horizon in an explosion of pink, blue and yellow behind her had to be the most beautiful sight he had ever seen. He turned her face toward his. "I love you, Desiree."

"You…what?"

Lorenzo smiled. "I said I love you. I don't know

when or how, just that I do." She stared at him as if in disbelief.

Desiree didn't say anything for a few moments. Then, "I love you, too, Lorenzo."

He relaxed and released a long breath. He eased her close and, being mindful of the pilot standing there, gave her a short, sweet kiss. They shared a smile and resumed watching the passing landscape. The pilot took the balloon up to about fifteen hundred feet, where they had a panoramic view of rows and rows of grapes, the mountains and valley. At points, he dipped low enough to skim the trees where they could reach out and touch the tops. Neither of them felt the slightest breeze because the balloon flew with the wind, as the pilot explained. The man pointed out various landmarks and answered the few questions Desiree asked. A short hour later, the pilot started the descent. Lorenzo braced himself and Desiree in anticipation of a bumpy landing, but it turned out to be smooth as silk. Only when it settled, was there a slight jostling. Afterward, the shuttle took them to a nearby winery for a champagne breakfast.

Over the meal, Desiree said, "I can't get over that view, or how calm and peaceful I felt being up there. I wish we could've stayed up there forever, far away from all the drama in our lives." She grasped his hand. "I don't know how I'll ever thank you. This was the best weekend I've ever had and I will never forget it."

Lorenzo brought her hand to his lips. "Neither will I." He could see them taking trips like this for the rest of their lives. And for the first time, he wanted what his parents had, what his cousins had. A love of his own.

Chapter 18

Desiree spent all of Tuesday making soap. Between her and Sandra, they'd done twenty loaves of her most popular fragrances. While Sandra finished the last two batches, Desiree started on the massage oil. She couldn't keep it in stock and many of the people buying were repeat customers. As she added the ingredients, she thought about her weekend with Lorenzo. They had used the entire bottle over the course of the two nights and she had been tempted to make more when they returned home yesterday. But she knew he needed to get to his office, and hopefully, the problems with the lumber company had been resolved or were close to it. Desiree's mind drifted to how much fun she'd had with him. From the wine train tour and relaxing on the patio to the incredible hot air balloon ride, she couldn't have asked for a better getaway. It had been just what she needed to prepare her for the battle with her sisters she knew was coming next week.

Lorenzo's confession of love still resonated within Desiree and her head remained in the clouds. She hadn't expected him to say it, and she couldn't have been happier to know he returned her feelings. But her old insecurities hovered in the back of her mind. Would he change his mind and walk away like all the others? The last man who claimed to love her had conveniently left out that he "loved" three other women, too. But this relationship felt different. Lorenzo was different and that gave her hope.

"Des, I've stored all the loaves and washed up the pots. Do you need anything else before I take off?" Sandra asked. "Since I'll be off for the next four days, I went ahead and did the whipped body cream, as well." Sandra didn't work on Sundays and had every other Monday off.

"No, and thank you. Enjoy your sister's wedding."

"I will. And thank you for the gift basket. She's definitely going to enjoy her wedding night."

Desiree smiled. "I'm sure she will."

"See you on Monday. Oh, wait, you'll be gone to Chicago, right?"

"Yep. I'll be back on Wednesday."

"Have a safe trip."

"Thanks." After Sandra left, Desiree funneled the oil into bottles, cleaned up and went to her office. She answered emails from customers and suppliers and printed out orders from the website. She got so engrossed in the task it took her a minute to recognize the insistent buzzing from her cell phone. Desiree snatched it up from the desk. "Hey, love," she said to Lorenzo when she answered.

"Hey, sweetheart. Are you still at the shop?"

"I am. I'll be packing up in about half an hour. What about you?" It was already after six.

"I'll be leaving around that time, too. I wish we were still in Napa, though."

"Mmm, same here. Any progress on the lumber issue?"

"Yeah. The owner found out his son was purchasing some of the lumber from one of his friends who sent substandard materials and they were both lining their pockets. The new lumber should arrive tomorrow."

"I'm so glad everything turned out well for you and Cedric. I bet the owner of the lumber company was pissed."

"Yeah. Jim is good people and he's been in business for over thirty years. He fired his son and reported the other guy. Apparently, he threatened his son with criminal charges unless he paid back every cent he stole."

"Wow. At least now you guys can get back on track. We need to celebrate your good news, but it'll have to wait until I get back from Chicago, since my assistant will be out the rest of the week. I'm really not looking forward to going this time."

"I do want to celebrate with you but I can wait. Have you talked to your mom?"

"No, but my sisters have been calling and telling me that I don't have the right to be anywhere on the power of attorney documents since I don't live there."

"I'm so sorry, baby. What about your brother?"

"Keith hasn't said much after being the one to suggest I have the power of attorney. My mother typically keeps Mel and Patrice in line, but I have no idea how she'll be once I get there."

"I wish there was something I could do."

"You wouldn't by chance have another one of those hot air balloons stashed somewhere that can whisk me away?"

Lorenzo laughed softly. "No, but I have a better idea."

"What?"

"How about I go with you? That way you won't have to deal with them alone."

Desiree stilled. As much as she would love to have him with her, she couldn't ask him to take two days off from work. Then there was Melanie and her boast that she could easy shift Lorenzo's attention. *No. He said he loved you.* "I can't ask you to be off again."

"You didn't. I'm offering. I don't like the thought of you having to deal with them without having anyone in your corner. I love you and I will protect you from anything and anyone, including family."

Her heart melted and tears filled her eyes. "Thank you. I love you and I would like it if you were there. Besides, my mom really likes you and asks about you every time we talk. She thinks you're cute."

"Hey, what can I say?"

She laughed. "Yeah, yeah, don't get a big head."

"I don't know what you mean," he said innocently. "Text me your flight info and I'll try to get on the same flight."

"I'll do it right after we hang up."

"Okay. And call me when you get home."

"I will." They spoke a minute longer, then said their goodbyes. After she texted the flight information, Desiree leaned back and held the phone against her heart. Each sweet gesture from Lorenzo made her fall deeper in love.

"Uh-oh, you must be thinking about Lorenzo, sitting here staring into space." Brenda came in and dropped down in the chair across from Desiree's desk.

Desiree couldn't stop her smile. "I can't help it. He keeps doing things that amaze me. He just offered to go with me to Chicago, so I don't have to deal with my siblings alone."

"Girl, I told you that man is a keeper."

She hadn't shared much about her Napa weekend with Brenda outside of the wine train tour and hot air balloon ride. "He told me loved me this weekend."

Brenda's eyes widened and her mouth fell open. "Are you *serious*? Obviously, way more stuff happened in Napa than just a train and balloon ride. This wasn't one of those after-sex confessions, was it?"

"No, when we were in the hot air balloon. It was the most romantic thing. I still can't believe it."

"I hope you told him you loved him, too. I know you do."

Desiree nodded. "Yes, but—"

"But what?"

She leaned back in the chair and rubbed her temples. "What if he walks away like all the others? I don't think I could take it."

"Any man who goes through all the trouble to set up a romantic weekend and offer to fly across the country with you isn't going to just change his mind like that." Brenda snapped her fingers.

"I know, I know. It's just that—"

"That you're afraid. I get that and you have good reason to be, but Lorenzo doesn't strike me as a man who doesn't know what he wants or one who plays games with a woman's heart."

"No, he doesn't." Her heart agreed, but her mind told her she needed to be careful.

From the time they boarded the plane Sunday afternoon until they landed that evening, Desiree seemed on edge. Now, as they parked in front of her mother's house, Lorenzo could feel the tension rolling off her in waves. Lorenzo held her hand as he helped her out of the car. "Stop worrying. Everything is going to be okay."

Desiree gave him a small smile. "I'm trying. I really appreciate you being here with me. It helps more than you know." She glanced around. "That's my brother's car. He's probably here to see why I didn't need him to pick me up, like I usually do. I'm going to apologize up front for any drama."

He chuckled and dropped a kiss on her forehead. "I can handle any drama thrown my way, and you don't need to apologize." He grabbed their bags and followed her to the front door.

She unlocked the door and stepped inside. "My mom is most likely in bed, since it's almost nine."

Lorenzo followed her through an immaculate living room and kitchen to the family room at the back of the house. Three pairs of eyes turned their way—Mrs. Scott's lit with delight, Melanie's with disdain, and a man, whom Lorenzo assumed to be her brother, with challenge.

Desiree's mother was up in a flash and engulfed Desiree in a crushing hug. "Oh, I'm so glad to see you, baby."

"I'm glad to see you, too, Mom."

Mrs. Scott turned to Lorenzo and lavished the same attention on him. "It's so good to see you again, Lorenzo. I've got your room all fixed up."

He smiled. "It's nice to see you, too, Mrs. Scott. And you didn't have to go through any trouble."

She waved him off. "Nonsense. You're a guest…for now," she added with a giggle. "Are you two hungry? I can fix you something."

Desiree shook her head.

"No, thank you," Lorenzo said. Out of his periphery, he could see Desiree's brother sizing him up. He stuck out his hand. "Lorenzo Hunter."

"Keith Scott." The man grudgingly shook Lorenzo's hand.

He turned to Melanie. "Hey, Melanie."

"Hey." Melanie divided her gaze between Lorenzo and Desiree. "I bet she had to do a lot of begging to get you to come here."

"Not at all. I volunteered and wouldn't take no for an answer." Lorenzo slung his arm around Desiree's shoulder and gave her a reassuring squeeze. He laughed inwardly at Melanie's stunned expression. Clearly, that wasn't the answer she wanted to hear.

She snatched up her purse. "I'm leaving."

Mrs. Scott folded a throw blanket and laid it over the arm of the sofa. "Well, if you guys aren't hungry, I'll show Lorenzo to his room and then I'm going to bed."

"I can do that, Mom," Desiree cut in. "We'll see you in the morning."

"Okay, then. Lorenzo can sleep in Keith's old room. Good night." She hugged Keith and patted his cheek. "Be careful driving home. You, too, Melanie." She hugged her daughter.

Keith smiled for the first time. "I will, Mom. Good night."

They all watched as Mrs. Scott shuffled down the hallway.

"I'll be here tomorrow," Melanie said. "And don't try to sign any of those papers until Patrice and I get here."

Desiree let out an impatient sigh. "Melanie, don't start."

"I'm sure your mother would like to have you all here, Melanie." Lorenzo hoped to head off any confrontations before they got started.

"Fine." Melanie stormed out.

"I'm going to check on Mom," Desiree said. "I'll be right back."

Lorenzo nodded.

As soon as Desiree was out of earshot, Keith said, "You two seem pretty cozy."

"Yeah, we are."

"Well, she's my sister, so you'd better watch your step."

He stood a good two inches taller than Keith and probably outweighed him by twenty pounds of pure muscle. "And that means exactly what? If you're concerned about me hurting her, you can stand down. I love her, and make no mistake about it, she's mine and I will protect her from anyone and everything, including family." Lorenzo stared Keith down until the man looked away.

A ghost of a smile appeared on Keith's face. "Good to know. Tell Desiree I'll see her tomorrow."

"Will do." Keith left and Lorenzo dropped down on the sofa. *It's going to be a long two days.*

"Where's Keith?" Desiree said when she returned.

"Gone home. He said he'll see you tomorrow." He eased her down onto his lap. "How're you doing, sweetheart?"

"I'm fine. I fully expect that this won't go smoothly." She shrugged. "I'll just deal with it like always."

"Well, tonight you can just relax. Is your mom all settled in?"

"Yes. She was halfway asleep before I left the room. She did say she planned to fix you a big breakfast in the morning. She figures it's the least she can do since you came all this way."

"I like your mom."

"Apparently, she likes you, too," she said, rolling her eyes playfully.

"Don't be jealous."

"Whatever." They sat in companionable silence for a long while. "We should probably get some sleep. Tomorrow's going to be a long day."

"You're right." Because he would be gone for two days, Lorenzo had gotten up early and worked at home for five hours before the flight. He stood with her in his arms, then set her on her feet. "Which way?" He picked up the bags.

Desiree pointed down the hall and they stopped at the second door. "You're in here. The bathroom is across the hall here and the towels are in the cabinet."

"Where's your room?" Lorenzo placed his bag on the floor.

"Next door."

He carried her bag to her room and placed it inside the door. As much as he wanted to hold her throughout the night, he would never disrespect her mother's house that way. "Get some sleep." He placed a tender kiss on her lips. "See you in the morning."

"Good night." She backed into the room and closed the door softly.

Lorenzo stood there a moment longer, then went to his own room. Fifteen minutes later and freshly showered, he laid his weary body down in bed. He tried to sleep, but his mind continued to race about the job, Desiree and what would happen tomorrow. He hated seeing the look of sadness and stress on Desiree's face and wished he could do something to prevent it. He closed his eyes and willed his mind blank.

It seemed as if he had just closed his eyes when the soft beeping of his phone alarm sounded. Lorenzo blindly reached over to the nightstand where he'd put it and shut it off. He sat up and thought he heard voices. Leaving the bed, he dressed and prepared his mind for the coming conflict. Surely, it couldn't be as bad as Desiree anticipated.

Lorenzo was wrong. Dead wrong. As soon as breakfast ended, both Patrice and Melanie weighed in. It seemed almost as if the two had gotten together beforehand to strategize. He sat listening to them arguing for almost two hours about all the reasons Desiree shouldn't be considered as a designee on the power of attorney forms. It took all his control not to tell them to shut the hell up. Desiree tried to remain diplomatic, while Keith basically checked out of the conversation. Even Mrs. Scott became frustrated. If he and his sister were faced with having to do this for one or both of their parents, he sincerely hoped they would go about it in a more civilized manner. He couldn't see Alisha behaving this way for any reason.

After another thirty minutes of heated discussion, Mrs. Scott finally settled the matter based on Keith's recommendation as the oldest. Desiree would be the primary designee and Keith the alternate. Mrs. Scott also decided to add Keith to her bank accounts, just in case she needed someone to have access. That decision started another firestorm. Thankfully, the notary arrived and, with Patrice and Melanie glaring, Desiree and Keith signed their names on all the documents.

Once Mrs. Scott saw the notary to the door, she came back and said, "I'm glad that's done. I can have some peace of mind. Keith, we may as well go to the bank now. And I need to stop at the store on the way home. I want to fix dinner for Desiree and Lorenzo since they're leaving tomorrow. It'll be nice for us all to eat together."

The look on Desiree's face said she disagreed and Lorenzo couldn't blame her.

Keith stood and grabbed his keys off the table. "Ready when you are."

When they left, Lorenzo took Desiree's hand and led her to the bedroom he was using. "Are you okay?"

"*Okay* might not be the right word," Desiree said laughingly. "I feel a lot of things. I'm angry with my sisters for all the nonsense, my brother because he never speaks up like he should, and I'm sad because of what this means. I don't want to lose my mom." Her voice cracked.

"Come here." He pulled her into his arms. He didn't know what to say, so he just held her. There would be no words that could console him if he were in her shoes. At length, he eased back and tilted her chin. The tears standing in her eyes made his heart ache. "Is there anything I can do?"

"You're already doing it." She swiped at her eyes and backed out of his arms. "I'll be back in a minute." She leaned up and kissed him. Desiree turned back when she got to the door. "Thank you."

"Anytime." Lorenzo sat on the bed and scrubbed a hand down his face. He hated the helpless feeling he had.

"Well now."

He glanced over and saw Melanie leaning in the doorway.

"I think you'd have far more fun with me than with Desiree."

He did not need this right now. "Melanie, whatever game you're playing, I'm not interested. I love your sister."

Melanie snickered and sauntered toward him. "I've heard that before."

Before he could reply, she pushed him backward on the bed and climbed on top of him. "What the hell?" Lorenzo pushed her off, none too gently and jumped up. His angry gaze collided with Desiree's hurt one. He cursed under his breath. "Desiree, this is not what you think."

Melanie slowly rolled off the bed. She smoothed down the short dress she wore and strolled across the room like she didn't have a care in the world. She stopped in front of Desiree. "Yes, it's exactly what you think." With a chuckle, she exited.

"Baby—"

Desiree held up a hand. "I can't do this right now, Lorenzo."

He closed the distance between them. "Please tell

me you don't believe I would cheat on you with your *sister*," he said through clenched teeth.

"I'm not saying that, and I know how Melanie operates."

"But…"

"I don't know. Something like this happens every time and I don't want to always wonder whether you're going to find someone else."

Lorenzo couldn't believe his ears. "Have I ever given you any reason to doubt me?"

"No. And I know this is going to sound cliché, but it's not you, it's me. I've been burned so many times that I'm always waiting for the next shoe to drop. I don't want to put either of us through that."

He placed his hands on her shoulders. "I love you, Desiree, and you'll never have to wonder about me."

"I believe you, Lorenzo. And I love you, too."

"But you're willing to throw what we have away for…what?"

"I'm not saying that. I just need a little time."

"Time? And while you're deciding, what am I supposed to do?"

Desiree stared up at him briefly, then averted her eyes.

Lorenzo tried to understand where she was coming from—he'd been hurt before, too—but he had put his heart out there and now she wanted to throw it back at him. Instead of saying something he would regret later, he gathered up all his belongings and walked out. She could have all the time she needed. He wasn't going to wait around for her to stomp on his heart a second time.

Chapter 19

The moment Lorenzo walked out of her mother's house, citing a work emergency, Desiree felt her heart shatter. But what did she expect? She had all but told him she didn't trust him. Though the blame for the fiasco rested totally with her, he didn't say so. He had even kissed her, as if everything was okay between them. Only she knew the difference. Felt the finality in the kiss. It didn't help that Melanie wore a triumphant smile every time their gazes met.

Desiree struggled to get through the family dinner and tried to put on a good face, but all she wanted to do was curl up in a ball and cry. She excused herself and went to her room. After a few minutes, she grabbed up her cell. "Hey, Brenda."

"Hey, girl. How's it going?"

"Oh my goodness, I messed up with Lorenzo." All

the events leading up to him leaving tumbled out in a jumble.

"Oh, honey. I'm so sorry. And I can't believe Melanie. That damn girl needs her butt kicked."

"The thing is I know Lorenzo didn't do anything to lead her on or reciprocate her advances. It's just when I saw them, every relationship in my past flashed in my mind, and I didn't want this one to end the same way. I told him I needed time to think, but I'm just scared."

"I totally get that, Des, and I'm sure Lorenzo understands."

"I hurt him, Bren. He left this morning right after and won't answer my calls."

"Give him a little time," Brenda said. "You said he loved you and if that's true, he's not going to be able to just turn it off."

"I hope you're right." Desiree didn't know what she would do if she had pushed him away for good.

"I am. And if he doesn't respond to your calls, go to him. Show up in something guaranteed to make his eyes pop out and take some of that edible massage oil. He won't know what hit him."

She laughed. "I'm so glad you're my friend. Thanks, Bren."

"Anytime. Don't let all the crap that happened in the past keep you from having the love you deserve. Oh, and if Melanie says one more thing, knock her into the middle of next week. You've been the good guy for far too long."

"I'll do my best." Desiree had always tried to do the right thing, but maybe the time had come for her to put all that to the side and let them all know she was done with being the one who took the high road. She and Brenda spoke for a moment longer and ended the call.

Later, Keith helped Desiree clean up the kitchen.

"Lorenzo is a cool guy."

She slanted him a glance. "He is, but how do you know that?"

"We sort of talked last night when you were helping Mom."

Desiree paused in wiping down the counter. "You mean you tried to interrogate him."

He shrugged. "Hey, that's what big brothers are supposed to do." He hung the towel he had used to dry the dishes on the rack under the sink and folded his arms. "But the brother stared me down, told me he loved you and would protect you from everyone, including us."

Great. She felt worse.

"He didn't have an emergency at work, did he?"

Desiree shook her head. "It was me. I don't want to talk about it right now."

Keith hugged her. "If you want to talk, let me know. This isn't usually something a big brother says, but I hope it works out."

"Thanks." They left the kitchen and walked in on the tail end of Patrice and Melanie's conversation.

"I told her I could get Lorenzo," Melanie boasted. "All it took was one little push."

Patrice giggled. "As fine as he is, I don't know what he sees in her anyway."

Apparently, their mother heard it, too. "Melanie! Patrice! Apologize to your sister right now. I don't know what's gotten into you two."

"Sorry," they mumbled.

"Yes, you both are *sorry* and I'm not accepting your

apology this time." Desiree had had enough. "All my life, I've given you a pass for everything you've done or said just to keep the peace, but I'm done." She leaned down close to Melanie. "Melanie, you have one more time to get in my face or try to make a play for a guy I'm dating and I'm going to knock the hell out of you." She turned to her mother. "Sorry, Mom. And Patrice, I am sorry for what Ellis did to you. No one deserves to be left standing at the altar. But I'm not the one who left you there and you will not take out your anger on me ever again. Keith, I need you to be my big brother and stop standing off to the side." Desiree hunkered down in front of her mother and grasped her mother's hands. "Mom, I know I promised to do everything I could to keep the peace in this family, to make sure that if something happened to you, I would see to it that the four of us remained close, but I can't do this." Tears filled her eyes and spilled down her cheeks. "I love you, but I just can't do it." She had sacrificed so much of her life for them and had gotten nothing in return. And she'd let a good man walk out of her life, all because she let her insecurities get the best of her.

Her mother wiped away Desiree's tears and sighed heavily. "You're right, baby. I should have never put that on you. That burden is too heavy for one person. We all need to do our parts for this family to thrive. Starting now."

Desiree laid her head in her mother's lap and sobbed. Her heart was breaking because she doubted that she and her sisters would ever bridge the gap that had widened steadily over the past decade, because she knew that someday her mother would, more than likely, forget Desiree's name, and because she had messed up the best thing in her life. She cried until she had no more tears left. She hugged her mother and, without a word, went to her bedroom.

She retrieved her phone from her purse. Her finger hovered over the call button on Lorenzo's name for a full minute before she pushed it. She had no idea what she would say if he answered, but she had to try. It went straight to voice mail and she swallowed her disappointment. She left him a message apologizing and asking him to call her.

Desiree stayed in her room until her siblings left. A knock sounded on the door. "Come in." She had expected to see her mother, not her brother. "I thought you were gone."

Keith stepped inside the door. "I did leave, but I came back because I wanted to apologize." He came and sat next to her on the bed. "You were right, sis. I checked out. I don't have an excuse except that it was easier than getting involved in the drama. I didn't realize that by not taking your side, I was hurting you."

"Keith, I never asked you to take my side, just that if you knew what Patrice and Melanie were doing or saying was wrong, to step up and say something other than 'you guys work it out,' leaving me to do it all. Especially when Daddy died. You were MIA."

"I know. Dad was my hero and when he got sick, it shook me."

"It shook us all. I don't want a repeat of the same thing if something happens to Mom," Desiree added quietly.

"It won't be. I promise."

She leaned her head on his shoulder. "Thanks."

"You need a ride to the airport tomorrow?"

"Yes, but I'll Uber. I don't want you to have to take off from work again." Since Lorenzo had reserved the car, he'd taken it when he left.

"I've been working at the electric company for almost fifteen years and I never take vacations. I have enough leave time to take six months off, if I want. What time does your plane leave?"

"Ten-thirty in the morning." She had originally planned to leave on a later flight, but changed it after Lorenzo left. She wanted to go home.

"See, works perfectly. I'll go in after I drop you off."

"Thanks."

"Love you, sis." Keith kissed her cheek. "I'll see you in the morning."

"Love you, too." Desiree smiled. At least things would be better with one of her siblings. Now she had to straighten out the other parts of her life, and prayed it wouldn't be too late.

Lorenzo stripped and stepped into the shower. He let the warm stream of water run over his head and body for a good five minutes. For the past three days since returning from Chicago, he'd been working on-site alongside the construction workers, hoping it would distract him from thinking about Desiree. It hadn't. The only thing he had managed to do was work his muscles to failure.

He picked up the soap and cursed. Because she knew he liked the soap he had purchased from her shop, she had given him several more bars. The scent sent his mind to the one place he tried to stay away from: wanting Desiree. Images of their Napa weekend flooded his mind, from cuddling while watching the sunset and the most passionate lovemaking he had ever experienced, to the sweet kisses and declarations of love they'd shared in the hot air balloon. Lorenzo cursed and slammed his hand against the granite wall. He quickly washed up and shut off the water.

After drying off, he padded naked into his bedroom and grabbed a pair of shorts out of the drawer to put on. Lorenzo noticed the blue light flashing on his phone and saw he had three voice mail messages. He hit the playback: *Hey, big brother. Congrats on getting the lumber mess straightened out. Also, Mom and Dad's anniversary is next month and I wanted to talk to you about a party.*

Lorenzo went to the next one. *Zo, we got a call from one of the contractors on the mini mall site after you left. They need you to come out and inspect some of the electrical work.* He had planned to be in San Francisco all day, but would call in the morning and adjust his schedule.

The last message started and he froze. *Lorenzo, I know you're angry with me and I don't blame you. I'm so sorry I hurt you. I hope we can talk soon. Despite what you think, I do love you.*

He dropped down on the side of the bed and ran his hand over his head. That was the third one Desiree had left. She'd texted twice, as well, and he had deleted all of them without reading or listening to the messages. Lorenzo tried not to be moved by the sadness he heard in her voice. She sounded as miserable as he felt. For a brief moment, he contemplated calling her, but changed his mind. He only gave a person one chance to hurt him and Desiree had used hers up.

Later, lying in bed, Lorenzo couldn't stop replaying

Desiree's message in his head. Parts of him still wanted to call her back. She said she loved him, but love didn't walk away so easily. *Then why did you walk away?* his inner voice questioned. He turned over to get comfortable, but it took a long time for him to fall asleep.

When he woke up the next morning, he felt as tired as he did the night before and doubted if he had gotten more than two hours of sleep. It would take a double shot of caffeine to get him going and he needed to be alert, especially with the long drive to Frisco. Lorenzo lay there a few minutes longer and mentally went over his schedule. He had a presentation for a community meeting next week on a proposed subdivision project. He would have to spend time reviewing the regulations and preparing PowerPoint slides for the two environmental impact statements he'd be presenting.

Just as he'd thought, it took two cups of strong black coffee to clear his head. He inspected the electrical work to make sure it was up to code and made a few suggestions about potential improvements to the current design. He arrived in the Bay Area around noon and met with his engineering technician. Hiring Joann had been the best decision he had made. The young woman would make a hell of an engineer in the coming years and he planned to make sure she stayed with their company. Afterward, he conferred with the architect and foreman, then hit the road again.

Lorenzo had just sat down at his desk with the late lunch he had brought back when Cedric appeared in the doorway.

"Everything okay at the sites?"

"Fine." He unwrapped his chicken burrito and took a bite.

Cedric sat across from him. "And Desiree?"

"What about her?"

"When are you going to talk to her? You came back a day earlier than planned from Chicago. You haven't worked on a building in almost seven years, yet you were out there this week from the time the workers started until the day ended." He leaned forward. "Something happened."

He set his food down and released a deep sigh. He told Cedric about the blowup Desiree had with her family over assigning a power of attorney for her mother, the conversation he'd had with her brother and how he'd felt bad for Desiree. "After all that, her sister, Melanie, came on to me and Desiree walked in on it. The crazy thing is Desiree believed that nothing happened, but she said she couldn't put me through her always wondering when I would walk away."

Cedric frowned. "Why would she think that? Has she seen you flirting with another woman or something?"

"No." Lorenzo told him what Desiree had shared about her past relationships and how her sister always interfered.

"So let me get this straight. Desiree's sister tries to make a play for the guys Desiree dates and has been doing it from day one."

"Pretty much. Apparently, Melanie has been successful on more than one occasion. When we went to Frisco, I overheard her bragging about it and telling Desiree that she could do the same with me. I love Desiree and tried to assure her I'm not the same but she doesn't even want to try. She said she needed time." All the hurt came back in a rush.

"Wait. Sounds like she just needs to think through some things. I thought she ended the relationship."

"It's the same thing in my book."

"Zo, come on, man. Try to see it from her side. With all the stuff she's had to go through with men *and* having a messy sister, I can see why she'd be insecure. And I know you. She's probably called all week and you've ignored her."

"I'm giving her the time and space she wants."

"No, you're acting like an ass and punishing her because she hurt you." Cedric shook his head. "If you love her like you say you do, don't push her out of your life. You know how you are when it comes to grudges."

Yeah, he knew. Lorenzo tended to be pretty easygoing, but once a person crossed him that was it. His family always said he had one big flaw: he could hold a grudge *forever*.

"I believe Desiree is the woman for you and I know she loves you, too. Talk to her. I'm tired of seeing you miserable. And according to a few of my workers, you've been kind of grouchy, and that's not like you."

He opened his mouth to deny it, but couldn't. There had been a couple of instances where he had been short-tempered about something that usually wouldn't cause a blip on his radar. "She's probably calling just to break it off." He wasn't sure he wanted to give her another chance to break his heart further.

Cedric stood. "You don't believe that crap any more than I do. She's probably just as miserable. I can't believe you just left her there, knowing how they are."

A pang of guilt hit him. Lorenzo had told Keith that he would protect Desiree, but Lorenzo hadn't. Instead, he'd walked away to protect his heart, living up to her expectation that she couldn't count on a man. "I'll call her this weekend." His intercom buzzed and he hit the button. "Hey, Tanya."

. "Cedric has a call."

"Can you put it through in here?" Cedric asked.

"Sure."

It rang a moment later and Cedric picked up. "This is Cedric." He listened for a moment. "I'm not sure how long we'll be here tonight, but I'm sure we could accommodate your schedule." He looked to Lorenzo and mouthed "Seven-thirty okay?"

"Yeah, but I'm leaving at seven-thirty," Lorenzo said quietly. His mind just wasn't on the job tonight.

"We should be here until seven-thirty, so you can go ahead and send the information." He hung up.

"Who was that?"

"A potential client. They promised to have their info here before we leave. I'll bring it over when it arrives." Cedric walked to the door. "See you later."

"Okay." He picked up his food and resumed eating.

After he finished, Lorenzo worked steadily. When he looked up, two hours had passed. He hadn't heard anything from Cedric about the potential client and it was already past seven. He shut down his computer and packed up. He did not plan to spend his Friday evening at the office. Lorenzo needed to do something to clear his head. He thought about driving over to Alisha's so he could hang out with Corey and Lia, but nixed the idea. He wasn't ready to explain what happened between him and Desiree and Alisha would know something had happened. Ideally, a run would be the thing to clear his head. However, the temperatures still read in the nineties. He started to go find Cedric just as his cousin entered the office. "I was just about to call you. Did you get the information? If not, I'm leaving and we can deal with it on Monday."

"I have it." Cedric reached back and opened the door wider. "There's someone here to see you."

Lorenzo felt his eyes widen. His heart stopped and started up again. Desiree stood there wearing one of those dresses with the shoulder opening that molded to every sensuous curve and stopped midthigh. His gaze traveled down her long bare legs to a pair of black strappy sandals. He hardened immediately.

Chapter 20

Cedric chuckled. He sidled up next to Lorenzo and said quietly, "I do believe Desiree just declared war. I suggest you go ahead and wave the white flag, my brother, because you will not win this one." Louder he said, "I'll lock up on my way out. Ah, enjoy your evening."

Lorenzo and Desiree stared at each other for what seemed like hours.

Finally, Desiree said, "Hi."

"Hey. What are you doing here?"

"Since you didn't return my calls, I decided to come in person."

"How did you know I'd be here?"

"Cedric."

It dawned on him. She was the potential client.

"I figured you wouldn't answer if I called, so..." She shrugged. "Can we talk?"

He pulled out a chair and gestured her to the table. Desiree closed the door and walked over to where he stood. The sweet warm scent of vanilla wafted into his nose as she passed him and sat. The dress slid higher up her thighs and he sucked in a sharp breath. She had indeed come dressed for battle.

Lorenzo took the chair next to her and waited.

"I'm sorry. The last thing I wanted to do was hurt you. I thought I would be okay without you. I'm not. I don't want to give you up, Lorenzo. I *can't* give you up."

"This time. How do I know you won't do the same thing again?"

"Because I love you."

"You said you loved me before and in the same breath asked for space," he gritted out. He didn't plan to make this easy for her.

Desiree lowered her head. "I was wrong. For so long, I've lived with the expectancy that every relationship I had with a guy would ultimately fail. Then you came along and challenged that in every way. And I thought I had finally moved past those fears." She lifted her head and locked her gaze with his. "When I saw Melanie up to her old tricks again, those fears came back, even though I knew you'd done nothing. I figured it would be easier to get out now, before I fell too deeply in love, but it's too late. I'm already there. And the one thing I wanted—your love—you gave and I walked away. I'm so sorry. I want you. I want *us*, and I pray it's not too late."

The tears standing in her eyes were Lorenzo's undoing.

She stood and straddled his lap. "Tell me it's not too late."

With her body pressed against his and her dress hiked up, he didn't stand a chance. "No. It's not too late." He crushed his mouth against hers. He'd missed kissing her. *Missed* it more than he realized. He could never resist those kisses. Her tongue tangled with his as she moved closer, forcing a low groan from his throat.

Desiree tore her mouth away and rested her head on his forehead, her breath coming in short gasps. She reached behind her, picked up her phone and pushed a few buttons.

Lorenzo recognized the familiar sound of Boney James's "Seduction." He lifted a brow.

She trailed kisses along his jaw. "I thought this would be an appropriate song."

"For?"

A sultry smile curved her lips. "Seduction. Is it working?"

"Hell, yeah. Can't you feel it?" He grasped her hips and brought her flush against his erection.

"I feel it. And I feel you. You understand what I like, anticipate my every need." Desiree caressed his face. "You soothe my soul and I love you with everything I am."

"Baby, I love you." This time when they kissed, something burst free inside him. Lorenzo deepened the kiss and tried to communicate just how much he loved her, wanted her and needed her in his life. His hands roamed down her back and hips to her bare thighs. He slid his hands under the dress and caressed his way up. He went still when his hands came in contact with the bare flesh of her backside. "Desiree, where are your panties?"

She chuckled. "I was coming to seduce you and I figured they'd just be in the way. Was I right?"

Instead of answering her, he stood and placed her on the table. He dropped his pants and underwear, donned a condom and entered her with one driving thrust. They both moaned. "Does this answer your question?"

"I brought more oil...caramel," she said breathlessly.

He felt himself grow harder inside her. "I hope you brought enough because I'm going to use the whole damn bottle."

Desiree smoothed down the sleeveless purple dress. "Do you think this is okay? It's not too short? I don't want to meet Lorenzo's parents dressed any kind of way."

Brenda folded her arms and shook her head. "Girl, relax. You look great. And the dress is not too short. It's almost touching your knees."

"If you say so." She continued to critically examine herself in the mirror hanging behind her office door. Lorenzo would be picking her up from the shop in twenty minutes for dinner at his parents' house. After their Friday night makeup in his office, he'd spent the night at her place. His mother had called Saturday evening and when she found out they were out together, invited Desiree to Sunday dinner.

"Go ahead and admit it. Aren't you glad you took my advice?"

Desiree couldn't stop the wide grin spreading across her face. "I am. I've never made up quite like that before." True to Lorenzo's word, they had used every drop of that caramel oil.

"I'm jealous," Brenda said with a chuckle. "I need to find me a guy like him so I can get my freak on."

"You are a nut." She peeked inside the large gift bag to make sure she had everything.

"What's in there?"

"I made little gift packs for Lorenzo's parents, sister and her two kids."

"Aw, that's so sweet. I hope you included a couple bottles of that massage oil and body paint for his parents."

Desiree whipped her head around and stared at Brenda like she had lost her mind. "Of course not!"

"Honey, mark my words, they're probably getting busy just like you and Lorenzo. Besides, if you include that, I guarantee you'd have their blessing before y'all left the dinner table."

She and Brenda burst out laughing.

Casey stuck her head in the door. "Lorenzo's here, Desiree."

"Thanks, Casey. I'll be right out." Desiree took one more glance in the mirror and picked up the bag. "Wish me luck."

Brenda waved her off. "You don't need luck. Just be who you are. They're going to love you."

"I hope so." The one time a guy had introduced her to his parents hadn't gone well. She hadn't been dressed right, didn't sit a certain way and wouldn't sign him on as a partner in her newly started business. Out front, she spotted Lorenzo right away. He had on a pair of black linen shorts, silk pullover and black leather sandals. He looked good enough to eat. Again. When he turned and smiled at her, Desiree's heart started pounding and the love she felt for him rose up and nearly overwhelmed her.

Lorenzo closed the distance between them and brushed his lips across hers. "Hey, sweetheart. You look gorgeous."

"Thank you. You look pretty good, yourself." The store still had a few customers who stared on with smiles.

"Ready?"

"As ready as I'll ever be."

"They're going to love you as much as I do." He smiled, entwined their fingers and led her to where he had parked. "I couldn't believe I found parking so close to the store." As he helped Desiree in the car, he asked, "What's in the bag?"

"Some stuff for your family."

Lorenzo closed the door, went around and got in on the other side. "You weren't supposed to bring anything."

"And you didn't need to drive all the way down here to pick me up when I could've just met you there." Desiree rolled her eyes and shook her head. "You were already close to their house."

As he pulled off, he said, "You can roll your eyes all you want, but you were *not* going to meet me at my parents' house. A man does not have his woman meet him when he's going to introduce her to his parents."

She laughed at him mumbling under his breath about independent women, chivalry and a man not being allowed be a gentleman. "I love you, too."

"Yeah, yeah." He slanted her an amused glance.

They rode in companionable silence interspersed with soft conversation. The closer they came to his parents' house, the more nervous she became. By the time he parked in front of the huge two-story structure, the butterflies in her belly were doing an all-out samba. After getting out of the car, Desiree took a deep breath and let Lorenzo lead her up the walkway.

The front door opened before they reached the porch and a beautiful middle-aged woman stepped onto the porch and greeted them with a wide smile. She met them halfway down the four steps and reached for Desiree's free hand. "You must be Desiree. I'm LaVerne Hunter. It's so wonderful to finally meet you."

"It's very nice to meet you, too."

"Hey, Mom." Lorenzo placed a kiss against his mother's smooth, brown cheek.

"Hi, baby. Come on in. Alisha and the kids are already here."

They led Desiree through an expensively decorated, but comfortable-looking living room to a sunken family room near the back of the house. "Your home is beautiful, Mrs. Hunter."

"Thank you, dear."

An older man with features reminiscent of Lorenzo's stood at their entrance.

Lorenzo made introductions. "Dad, this is Desiree. Desiree, my father, Russell Hunter."

"It's a pleasure to meet you, Mr. Hunter," Desiree said.

"The pleasure is all mine, Desiree. Please, have a seat and get comfortable."

She perched on the edge of the sofa and Lorenzo sat next to her. She shifted her gaze to his sister. "Good to see you again, Alisha."

"Same here, Desiree." Alisha had a knowing smile. "These are my babies, Corey and Lia."

Desiree spoke to the children, who smiled and waved.

"By the way, that body scrub is heavenly." Alisha pretended to swoon. "I'm going to need more real soon."

"I'm glad you liked it."

"Oh, that's right," Mrs. Hunter said. "Desiree, Lorenzo told us you have your own bath and body shop in Old Sac. I've got to get down there and check it out."

"Actually, I brought something for you all."

"That's what I'm talking about," Alisha said.

Lorenzo shook his head.

Desiree passed out all of the gift sets she had put together. She had included a strawberry bubble bath for Lia and a clear glycerin soap bar with a dinosaur inside for Corey. In order to get to the toy, he would have to use the soap until it was almost gone.

Corey's eyes lit up. "I love dinosaurs! Thank you."

"You're welcome."

Alisha chuckled. "Lately, I've been having trouble getting him to wash up well. He's always in a hurry. Maybe this will get him clean."

Everyone laughed.

"Alisha, when you mentioned that you didn't have time for a long bath, but liked the bath bombs, it got me to thinking and I came up with something similar that you can put on the floor of the shower. It'll dissolve and you still get the fragrance and feeling of a spa treatment."

"Thank you, thank you! I'm so glad my brother and you are dating." She hugged Desiree.

The gesture took Desiree by surprise. "Um, you're

welcome." She had done a lavender vanilla gift set with soap, shower gel, bath bomb and lotion for his mother, and the citrus basil for his father.

Mrs. Hunter sniffed. "This is so nice. Thank you, Desiree. Isn't she a doll, Russell?"

"Yes, she is." He glanced at Lorenzo over his glasses. "Son, I hope you plan to hold on to her."

Desiree felt her cheeks warm.

Lorenzo took Desiree's hand. "Actually, Dad, I plan to do more than hold on to her." He slid off the sofa and onto one knee.

His mother and sister gasped.

Desiree's heart skipped and she forgot how to breathe.

"Desiree, the day I saw you sitting on that park bench, I knew you would change my life. When I'm with you, everything is right in my world. You will never have to wonder about my love and no one will cherish you more than me. From now until eternity you will never walk alone." He placed her hand on his heart. "Let my heart be your shelter, and my arms, your strength. I know you are the only woman for me and I vow to protect this love that is our own for the rest of my life."

He opened the small black velvet box in his hands to reveal a heart-shaped diamond solitaire that had to be at least two carats, with bead-set diamonds lining either side of the band. She brought her hands to her mouth as tears filled her eyes.

"Will you marry me?"

Desiree could only stare. Emotion clogged her throat.

Lia climbed up on Lorenzo and reached for the ring. "Ooh, pretty."

Alisha rushed over and plucked the toddler from

his back. "Sorry. Oh, and Desiree, you might want to hurry up and answer. He's almost thirty-five and that knee isn't going to hold up much longer."

They all laughed.

Lorenzo skewered his sister with a look.

Smiling around her tears, Desiree said, "Yes." He slid the ring onto her finger and she launched herself into his arms.

"I love you, baby." He placed a tender kiss on her lips.

"I love you, Lorenzo Hunter. For always."

Epilogue

One month later.

Lorenzo paced the small holding room at the church and checked his watch for the tenth time. Only two minutes had passed.

Cedric placed his hands on his cousin's shoulders. "Nervous?"

"No. Just anxious to do this. It's been a long four weeks."

He chuckled. "I don't think *long* is the appropriate word to describe a wedding taking place a month after the engagement. My mother told me last night after the rehearsal I'd better not give her this short time frame when it's my turn."

Lorenzo smiled. "The original plan was for Christmas, but we have no idea how long Desiree's mother will be well enough to attend and there's no way I would cheat my baby out of having her mother here." So far Mrs. Scott's health had held up well and she'd only had a few episodes of memory loss. When he and Desiree had called to tell her the news, she had cried and told them she was buying her ticket to their Labor Day weekend wedding as soon as they hung up.

"I'm glad she's well enough to be here. I hope Desiree's sisters don't try anything to ruin the day. You know we do not play when it comes to family." They did a fist bump.

"I doubt it. Apparently, after I left Chicago, Desiree put them all in their places."

"Good." Cedric glanced down at his watch. "It's about that time."

"Finally." Lorenzo and Cedric met the minister in the hallway and the three men entered the church. Moments later, the music started. Jeremy escorted Lorenzo's mother to her seat and Brandon escorted Mrs. Scott. He smiled upon seeing the entire Gray clan seated in the sanctuary. He wouldn't trade his family for the world. Brenda entered next and took her place as Maid Of Honor, and his nephew and niece served as ring bearer and flower girl.

When the music changed and everyone stood, Lorenzo's heart kicked up and it was all he could do to stand still. Desiree entered on her brother's arm wearing an ivory, strapless, formfitting creation that made him want to skip the ceremony and go straight to the honeymoon.

Keith relinquished Desiree to Lorenzo and kissed her cheek. "Be happy, sis."

Desiree smiled up at Lorenzo and his heart beat even faster. "You are exquisite."

"You, my love, look good enough to eat," Desiree whispered. "And I plan to sample *all* the goodies later." She winked and turned her attention to the minister.

He sucked in a breath and tried to focus on repeating his vows and not how fast he could get her out of that dress. The ceremony lasted less than thirty minutes and, after an hour of photos at the church and in the gardens at Capitol Park in downtown Sacramento, the limousine drove them to the hotel where the reception would be held.

"Do you think we could sneak upstairs for a quickie?" Lorenzo asked as they made their way toward the ballroom.

Desiree's eyes widened. "What? No. Behave."

He trailed kisses behind her ear. "Believe me, I'm trying. But I don't know how much longer I'm gonna last."

She giggled. "We can't just disappear. People will notice we're gone."

"Not if we don't go into the ballroom now. We can go upstairs to our suite and be back in twenty minutes. They'll think the pictures took longer."

Desiree glanced up at him, seemingly giving his proposal some thought. "Twenty minutes?"

A wolfish grin played around the corners of his mouth. He nodded. "I can totally make it worth your while."

"Okay."

The words were barely off her tongue when Lorenzo changed directions and nearly dragged her to the bank of elevators on the opposite side of the lobby. They got into the just-arriving car and rode up to their floor. He swept Desiree into his arms and strode down the hallway, stopping at a room halfway down the hall. Inside, he placed her on her feet. His mouth was on hers before the door closed. He backed her into the room, carefully pushed her dress up over her hips and placed her on the closest piece of furniture, which happened to be an end table. He slid the barely there scrap of her panties down and off.

"Don't mess up my hair," Desiree said breathlessly. She had it up in some elaborately done twist.

"I won't." He undid his pants, stepped between her legs and buried himself to the hilt. "You're my everything." Lorenzo had taken the risk and won. He had his *one* and a love he could call his own.

* * * * *

**Soulful and sensual romance featuring
multicultural characters.**

Look for brand-new Kimani stories
in special 2-in-1 volumes starting March 2019.

Available July 2, 2019

Love in New York & Cherish My Heart ✓
by Shirley Hailstock and Janice Sims

Sweet Love & Because of You ✓
by Sheryl Lister and Elle Wright

What the Heart Wants & Sealed with a Kiss ✓
by Donna Hill and Nikki Night

Southern Seduction & Pleasure in His Arms ✓
by Carolyn Hector and Pamela Yaye

Get 4 FREE REWARDS!

We'll send you 2 FREE Books plus 2 FREE Mystery Gifts.

Harlequin® Desire books feature heroes who have it all: wealth, status, incredible good looks... everything but the right woman.

FREE Value Over $20

YES! Please send me 2 FREE Harlequin® Desire novels and my 2 FREE gifts (gifts are worth about $10 retail). After receiving them, if I don't wish to receive any more books, I can return the shipping statement marked "cancel." If I don't cancel, I will receive 6 brand-new novels every month and be billed just $4.55 per book in the U.S. or $5.24 per book in Canada. That's a savings of at least 13% off the cover price! It's quite a bargain! Shipping and handling is just 50¢ per book in the U.S. and 75¢ per book in Canada.* I understand that accepting the 2 free books and gifts places me under no obligation to buy anything. I can always return a shipment and cancel at any time. The free books and gifts are mine to keep no matter what I decide.

225/326 HDN GMYU

Name (please print)

Address   Apt. #

City   State/Province   Zip/Postal Code

Mail to the **Reader Service:**
IN U.S.A.: P.O. Box 1341, Buffalo, NY 14240-8531
IN CANADA: P.O. Box 603, Fort Erie, Ontario L2A 5X3

Want to try 2 free books from another series! Call 1-800-873-8635 or visit www.ReaderService.com.

*Terms and prices subject to change without notice. Prices do not include sales taxes, which will be charged (if applicable) based on your state or country of residence. Canadian residents will be charged applicable taxes. Offer not valid in Quebec. This offer is limited to one order per household. Books received may not be as shown. Not valid for current subscribers to Harlequin Desire books. All orders subject to approval. Credit or debit balances in a customer's account(s) may be offset by any other outstanding balance owed by or to the customer. Please allow 4 to 6 weeks for delivery. Offer available while quantities last.

Your Privacy—The Reader Service is committed to protecting your privacy. Our Privacy Policy is available online at www.ReaderService.com or upon request from the Reader Service. We make a portion of our mailing list available to reputable third parties that offer products we believe may interest you. If you prefer that we not exchange your name with third parties, or if you wish to clarify or modify your communication preferences, please visit us at www.ReaderService.com/consumerschoice or write to us at Reader Service Preference Service, P.O. Box 9062, Buffalo, NY 14240-9062. Include your complete name and address.

HD19R2

SPECIAL EXCERPT FROM

*Completely captivated by his new employee, André Thorn
is about to break his "never mix business with pleasure"
rule. But amateur photographer Susan Dewhurst is
concealing her true identity. Although she's falling for the
House of Thorn scion, she can't reveal the secret that could
jeopardize far more than her job at the flagship New York
store. Amid André's growing suspicions and an imminent
media scandal, does love stand a chance?*

Read on for a sneak peek at
Love in New York,
*the next exciting installment in the
House of Thorn series by Shirley Hailstock!*

As she turned to find her way through the crowd, she came up short
against the white-shirted chest of another man.

"Excuse me," she said, looking up. André Thorn stood in front of
her.

"Well," he said. "This time there isn't a waiter carrying a tray of
champagne."

"I apologized for that," she said, anger coming to her aid. She was
already angry with Fred and had been expecting this sword to drop
all day. Unprepared to have it fall when she thought she was safe,
her sarcasm was stronger than she'd expected it to be. "Please excuse
me."

She moved to go around him, but he stepped sideways, blocking
her escape.

"Let me buy you a drink?"

Susan's sanity came back to her. This was the president of the
company for which she worked. Susan forgot that she could leave and

get another job. She knew what it was to be an employee and to be the owner of a business.

"I think I've had enough to drink," she said. "I'm ready to go home."

"So you're going to escape my presence the way you did at the wedding?"

Her head came up to stare at him. Instead of seeing a reprimand in his eyes, she was greeted with a smile.

A devastating smile.

It churned her insides, not the way Fred had, but with need and the fact that it had been a long time since she'd met a man with as much sexual magnetism as André Thorn. No wonder he fit the bill as a playboy.

"I guess I am," Susan finally said. From the corner of her eye, she saw Fred sliding out of the booth. He should know who André Thorn was, but if he planned to put his arm around her in front of another man, he would be making a mistake. "Excuse me," she said and hurried away.

Susan stood in front of the bathroom mirrors. She freshened makeup that didn't need to be, stalling for time. Why had she reacted to André Thorn that way? Embarrassment, she rationalized. She'd run into him at her friend Ryder's wedding. Judging from where he'd sat in the church, he must know Ryder's bride, Melanie. He would. Frowning at her reflection, she chided herself for the unbidden thought. It was a total accident that she'd slipped and tipped the waiter's tray filled with champagne glasses. André had reached for her, and the comedy of flying glasses and fumbling hands and feet would have made her laugh if it happened in a movie. But it had happened to her—to them. And there was nothing funny about it.

Too embarrassed to do anything but apologize and leave, Susan had rushed away to try to remove the splashes that had hit her dress and shoes. She hadn't returned.

She'd never expected to see the man again, so their eyes connecting across the orientation room had been a total surprise, but the recognition was instant. And now she had to return to the bar where he was. Snapping her purse closed, she went back to her group.

Don't miss Love in New York
by Shirley Hailstock, available July 2019
wherever Harlequin® Kimani Romance™
books and ebooks are sold.

Copyright © 2019 Shirley Hailstock

KPEXP0519

Want to give in to temptation with
steamy tales of irresistible desire?

Check out **Harlequin® Presents®,
Harlequin® Desire** and
Harlequin® Kimani™ Romance books!

New books available every month!

CONNECT WITH US AT:

Facebook.com/groups/HarlequinConnection

 Facebook.com/HarlequinBooks

 Twitter.com/HarlequinBooks

 Instagram.com/HarlequinBooks

 Pinterest.com/HarlequinBooks

ReaderService.com

**ROMANCE WHEN
YOU NEED IT**

PGENRE2018

Love Harlequin romance?

DISCOVER.

Be the first to find out about promotions, news and exclusive content!

Facebook.com/HarlequinBooks

Twitter.com/HarlequinBooks

Instagram.com/HarlequinBooks

Pinterest.com/HarlequinBooks

ReaderService.com

EXPLORE.

Sign up for the Harlequin e-newsletter and download a free book from any series at **TryHarlequin.com**.

CONNECT.

Join our Harlequin community to share your thoughts and connect with other romance readers!
Facebook.com/groups/HarlequinConnection

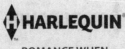

HARLEQUIN®

ROMANCE WHEN
YOU NEED IT

HSOCIAL201R

Need an adrenaline rush from nail-biting tales
(and irresistible males)?

Check out **Harlequin Intrigue**®,
Harlequin® **Romantic Suspense** and
Love Inspired® **Suspense** books!

  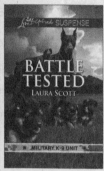

New books available every month!

CONNECT WITH US AT:

Facebook.com/groups/HarlequinConnection

Facebook.com/HarlequinBooks

Twitter.com/HarlequinBooks

Instagram.com/HarlequinBooks

Pinterest.com/HarlequinBooks

ReaderService.com

**ROMANCE WHEN
YOU NEED IT**

SGENRE2018R